CANAL BOAT SERVICE

BRAVE PURSUIT

Books by Marguerite Allis

WATER OVER THE DAM

LAW OF THE LAND

THE BRIDGE

The Field Family Saga

NOW WE ARE FREE

TO KEEP US FREE

BRAVE PURSUIT

Brave Pursuit

A NOVEL BY

MARGUERITE ALLIS

PEOPLES BOOK CLUB

CHICAGO

This is a special edition published exclusively for the
members of the Peoples Book Club, P. O. Box 6570A,
Chicago 80, Illinois. It was originally published by
G. P. Putnam's Sons.

Library of Congress Catalog Card Number: 54-5475

MANUFACTURED IN THE UNITED STATES OF AMERICA

To
my kinswoman and lifelong friend
EMILY DAIN SEYMOUR
this book is affectionately dedicated.

Foreword

PREJUDICE DIES HARD, and that against female education proved no exception. Well into the nineteenth century men who drove reluctant sons to school with a horsewhip and made great personal sacrifices to send ambitious boys to college, doomed their daughters to ignorance of books. Even early female seminaries, to which an occasional well-to-do and broad-minded man sent his girls, offered courses only in reading, writing, needlework, music, drawing and —of all things—French. Woman's place was, definitely, in the home. There mothers taught daughters to bake, brew, spin, weave and cut and sew the fruit of their looms into clothing, including breeches which few females aspired to wear.

It was not that men loved daughters less than sons. Frequently the girls were closer to their father's hearts, as was the case in this story. The stand Ashbel Field took seems harsh and arbitrary today. Then, however, there was a widespread belief that "book larnin'" deprived females of their natural functions, and although Ashbel Field did not share this superstition, he knew no man wanted a barren woman, and he was appalled at the thought of leaving his rowan—this child of his middle age—defenseless at his death. There was no place in society for a spinster. If she had an inheritance, it made her fair game for avaricious men since by law a woman's property passed to her husband on marriage. And if she were left penniless, there was as yet no means by which a woman could earn an honest living.

All through the long dark ages when no woman was free to plan and live her own life, there were rebels who secretly resented such complete bondage in a land where men fought, and died, for liberty and the pursuit of happiness. Here and there among the pages of recorded history one catches a glimpse, or a whisper, of discontent. From such glimpses and whispers the author of this novel has epitomized these rare and courageous rebels in Constitution Field. While this novel is the third in the saga of the Field family, it is also a story complete in itself.

BRAVE PURSUIT

Chapter 1

S HE was over tall for fourteen, over slender, and almost over-powered by a long thick black braid that dragged back her head, lifting her chin and accentuating a proud look often mistaken for arrogance. As she stood in the doorway of the family home gazing toward the public square, it was not admiration for the Cuyahoga County Courthouse—the only frame building in Cleveland—that lighted the girl's dark eyes like lamps between the curving curtains of her lashes. Nor was it the town pump and watering trough which also stood amid the rotting stumps on the public square, faced by two taverns and one general store. It was none of these aides to the comfort of man and beast the girl re-garded so eagerly. It was a new little log cabin on which several men were nailing the roof shingles. In this, Cleveland's first school-house, the Field rowan—the last late crop—saw her dream about to materialize.

Her name commemorated the culmination of one of her father's dreams. She had been born at the time of the convention of 1802 which drew up the legal code for the new state of Ohio, and so was christened Constitution. Ashbel Field set great store by education. Himself a Yale graduate, he had made considerable sacrifice to send his eldest son east to that college. And now, a leading lawyer and owner of much local land, Ash had subscribed generously to the school fund. Small wonder then that his only daughter felt sure of being among the first pupils to enter that dedicated door.

Already she could read, write and cipher, thanks to her eldest brother, Malachi, who resembled their mother's people in looks (all the Marvins had pale thin hair, pale skin and pale myopic eyes), but he had inherited his father's brains. And when he came home from Yale it was with a diploma *cum laude* and horn-rimmed spectacles.

Need for those aids to vision kept Mal from joining the other Fields in defense of the Canadian border during the War of 1812, but he did his best to keep the home-fires burning. He chopped and carried wood to the camp where the militia mustered, and to the hospital to which the wounded were brought back. He shared nursing duties with womenfolk, and with grandsirs shared day or night patrol of the frontier settlement. In his father's log law office on the other side of Superior Street from the family blockhouse, Mal gathered a group of small boys and taught them as a labor of love and a patriotic duty to keep alight the feeble flame of learning.

As her patriotic duty, Connie split kindling and weeded the kitchen garden to the drone of the multiplication table from across the way. It was tantalizing that she could not catch the words, and one day she threw down the hatchet and went over to the office. Mal promptly ordered her out, not because he considered the female mind inferior, but because the presence of his young sister demoralized the boys. When class was dismissed, however, he called Connie in and questioned her. Mal was amazed at her keen intelligence and eagerness for knowledge. Thereafter, he loaned her textbooks and heard her recite from them each evening after supper until curfew sent him out on night patrol.

In those days, before any church steeple pierced the sky and with very few clocks in Cleveland homes, settlers were warned of bedtime by nine slow strokes of a crowbar on the iron wagon tire suspended between two posts on the public square. From curfew to cockcrow folks slept, unless roused by the fire alarm beaten wildly on that same wagon tire, or by a commotion in barn or byre. For the town, with less than six hundred inhabitants, was still surrounded by dense primeval forest filled with all kinds of wild beasts. Every chimney breast sprouted antlers on which firearms were racked and ready in peacetime. But even had there been any gun left in the blockhouse, Mal could not have hit the broad side of the barn, much less a marauder making off through the dark with a pig or a lamb. By the time Captain Field came home, wounded, the family flock was badly depleted.

Ash had left his youngest son at Fort Meigs in a hero's grave. But the other two soldier sons returned intact at the close of the war, only to leave home again shortly, Jedediah to seek his fortune on

4

the Ohio River, and Ezekiel on Zane's Trace. Then, as soon as Ash's arm healed enough to push a pen, Malachi too left home with his books and his bride to join the faculty in the reopened Ohio University at Athens.

Connie missed Mal sadly, missed him more and more as time passed and their father made no move to carry on her lessons. She told herself that Pa couldn't spare the time, that he was too busy reclaiming the law practice he had left to save the nation. For in his absence several younger attorneys had hung out shingles in the county seat. Her father's interest in the new schoolhouse, however, revived the girl's hope that her education would soon be resumed. Yet weeks went by after a master "deemed suitable" had been installed and classes opened, and still Connie waited in vain for word to join them. When she could bear the suspense no longer, she went over to the office.

Ashbel Field at fifty-eight was a tall gaunt man with a thick dark thatch bleached at the temples. But there was not one thread of white in the bushy black eyebrows drawn together in a frown while he looked over his ledgers. The frown deepened at the sound of footsteps, and he looked up prepared to be short with any time-waster, he-gossip, land-sharper, or pleader of poverty who wished to escape payment of bills rendered and long overdue. When he saw his daughter, the frown vanished and his cavernous dark eyes softened. Ash was proud of his first-born, but his last-born—his rowan—he loved more than he had ever dared admit to himself, much less to her. Cocking one eyebrow, he inquired kindly, "Well, what can I do for you, my girl?"

"You can send me to school," she replied quickly.

The frown returned and his eyes hardened. "I'll do nothing of the kind," he said curtly. "Your mother is capable of teaching you everything any female need know. The only reason she hasn't already instructed you in certain household skills is because when we moved here from Marietta there was no room in the wagon for her wheels and loom. It was my intention to go back for them, but there was so much to do here, and before I got round to it, we had word the house had burned and everything in it. And then the war came——" Ash paused and passed a nervous hand through his graying hair. Then, shaking his head as though to rid himself of war

5

memories, he said, "But about those wheels. They shall be replaced just as soon as I can get round to it." With that promise, his thoughts went back to business.

Connie knew she was dismissed. Nevertheless, she stood her ground. "But, Pa," she expostulated, "there's no wheelwright hereabouts. To send east for a spinning wheel will takes months. Can't I go to school in the meantime?"

Astounded at such persistence, Ash glanced up again and glared. In that silent clash of wills the resemblance between father and daughter was startling. From beneath black brows more delicately etched than his she gave him stare for stare, black, brilliant and steady. And her young jaw was set in the same determined line as the jaw from which the stubble had been shaved that morning. Ash would have gloried in such a show of spirit in a son; in a female it was distasteful, disturbing. During his absence the girl had grown out-of-hand as well as out of her petticoats. Soon she would reach marriageable age. Men wanted biddable wives, capable of bearing and rearing large families to share the labor of homesteading. Although he took no stock in the superstition that book learning made females barren, Ash knew that the kind of mate to whom he would give his girl would never ask for a strong-minded female. What was to become of her if she did not marry? A man's world offered single women no means of self-support. Ash hoped to leave all his family well-provided, but nothing was certain except death and taxes. His widow would never want for a home among their sons, but he felt he had no right to burden them with an old-maid sister. It was his duty to rid his rowan of such dangerous notions without loss of time. He did not, however, feel duty-bound to explain his reasons for denying her what he believed to be a mere passing whim.

Father and daughter continued to stare at one another in silence. Finally, Ash said, "Let me hear no more of this nonsense. Now go home and help your mother get supper."

Faith Field was ten years younger than her husband. She had never been a beauty. What had attracted Ash on first sight was the grace of her body and spirit. For beneath the plain exterior he sensed an inner quality more enduring than any pretty face and

6

golden curls. Years of toil, hardship and sorrow had proved Faith's staying power and deepened her husband's love. To Ashbel Field the mother of his children was the perfect pattern for all womanhood.

Connie was too young, too inexperienced, too different in temperament for any real appreciation of Faith's character. Ma was just ma—a pious good woman with no thought above her own hearthstone. As Connie entered the kitchen, she saw her mother's straight back bent over the kettle on the crane. Mindful of her father's orders, she exclaimed, "Give me that spoon, Ma. I can stir a hasty pudding even if I can't make johnnycake fit to eat."

Faith turned, tilting her head back to look at the girl. The firelight shadowed the thin faded hair, the faded blue eyes and touched only the chin, and a large generous mouth parted in a smile of great sweetness.

There was sweetness in the tired husky voice too as she said, "Now your pa's able to chop kindling and do all the barn chores, you'll have time to larn how to make biscuits light as feathers and pies that'll melt in a man's mouth. There's nothing like prime victuals to win a man's heart, I always say."

Here was food for thought. It occurred to Connie for the first time that books might not hold all the world's wisdom, that a woman with a husband and four grown sons might be wise in the ways of men. There was no stir of the mating instinct in the girl; what she longed for was her father's approval. If she could set before him a meal prepared entirely with her own hands, perhaps he would relent about school.

Ash, who considered the matter closed, permanently, made no reference to it at supper. He talked about business. Times were hard. Bills long overdue, sent through the post, were ignored. When he rode about the country pressing for payment, more often than not, all he could collect was a side of salt pork, a bushel of root crops or a bag of beans.

"There's nothing tastier or more filling than a mess of beans baked with a nice piece of fat pork and a little molasses," remarked his wife.

"True," Ash agreed. "But I can't pay taxes with beans."

7

Faith said, "No, I suppose not." Then she brightened, suggesting, "But you can sell a parcel of land to one of these new folks for cash money, I presume to say."

"Like enough," he replied. "But I won't—not at today's prices. Someday Cleveland is bound to become the metropolis of the West. That may never be in our time, and if our children don't live to see it either, their children will. This land is their heritage." His gaze turned toward the hearth as though he saw in the glowing coals a vision of teeming streets and shining towers.

The revelation that her father too was a dreamer of dreams stirred Connie deeply. And the revelation that he was land-poor gave her further food for thought. It was one thing for a man to confess a shortage of ready cash in the bosom of his family, and quite a different thing for him to make public that shortage and claim free schooling for his child. The more she thought about it, the more certain Connie grew that Pa's real motive for denying her petition was inability to pay the master.

As she washed the supper dishes in the dry sink, Connie considered ways and means of earning. Able-bodied housewives did their own washing, ironing, scoured their own pots and pans. Females too old to work lived with married children or, if they had none, went to the poorhouse. There was no rich widow living alone in Cleveland, and even if there were, Ashbel Field would never allow his only daughter to hire out as a servant. That night, and many nights thereafter, as Connie tossed sleepless in her feather bed, she turned over in her mind one wild scheme after another, only to discard them all as utterly impractical.

Then one night when the harvest moon was at the full, the great idea came to her—came with sounds of commotion in the barnyard. There was no mistaking those cries of fear and agony; another wolf had invaded the village. While hunters were away with the militia, the wolf-pack had increased in size and boldness. That very day Connie had seen a notice pegged to the post on the Public Square—notice that the sheriff would pay three dollars bounty for each scalp of a full-grown wolf and half that sum for scalps of cubs under six months old.

Connie slid out of bed, slipped into moccasins and made for the stairs with intent to snatch the butcher knife on her way out the back door. The commotion had also awakened Ash in the ground floor chamber, and he ran for the rifle which was kept loaded on the antlers above the hearth for just such emergencies. Before the girl was halfway down the stairs a shot rang out, then the death howl. Connie went back to bed wondering whether she could have done it, anyway. While the wolf tore at the throat of its victim, could she have slipped into the sheepfold and slit the wild beast's throat? She had to admit it was doubtful, but she knew she would have made the attempt even at risk of her life.

At dawn she threw on her clothes and hurried out to see just how much damage the killer had done before it died. There was damage enough to bring tears to any female's eyes. One ewe was bleating pitifully over the mutilated body of its lamb. Another lamb hungrily nuzzled its cold dead mother. Behind the barn Connie found her father digging a grave for his victim. It was a she-wolf, evidently with sucklings.

The tenderhearted girl cried, "Oh, the poor cubs! Now they'll starve to death! How dreadful!"

Ash remarked, dryly, "Not nearly so dreadful as having them grow up to kill more sheep and lambs."

It was true, Connie was forced to agree. But she begged her father to be merciful—to search the forest for the she-wolf's lair and kill the motherless cubs rather than leave them to slow starvation.

Ash shook his head. "That would be like looking for the proverbial needle in the haystack," he said. "I can't spare the time."

Connie had time, but she knew she would never be allowed to spend it in any such pursuit as a wolf-hunt. Slowly a plan took shape in her mind. She was by nature honest, forthright, scornful of weasel ways and beating about bushes, but eagerness for an education drove her to subterfuge. When food was scarce in wartime, the village children had helped out by gathering all the nuts in the immediate neighborhood. Nuts were still a welcome addition to any winter larder, and now that she was older and the forest safer by daylight, surely she would be allowed to go nutting—alone!

To this Ash readily agreed, never suspecting the girl of any other purpose. Plans for her real purpose kept Connie awake late that night. She must have a weapon. Pa had scalped the she-wolf

9

before burying the carcass, but what had he done with the butcher knife afterward? It was not in its usual place, Connie knew, for she had looked before coming to bed. She had not so much as glanced at the lethal weapon returned to its place on the chimney breast, aware that, even if she could get away with the rifle, it was much too heavy for any female hand. An axe she could wield as well as her brothers, but what excuse could she give for taking an axe on a nutting expedition? None. Connie finally fell asleep with the problem still unsolved.

In the gray dawn she woke, dressed and went down to find her mother cutting bread beside an open jampot.

"I've already put an apple in the basket," Faith said. "Here, fix your own snack whilst I turn the pancakes for breakfast."

Connie spread jam on one slice of bread, covered it with another, and wrapped both in a scrap of clean old linen before stowing the parcel in the basket. Then she glanced around, saw her mother's back bent over the frying pan, and slipped the bread knife under the lunch. It was nowhere near so stout a blade as the missing butcher knife, but it would have to do.

The day, typical of early November, was uncertain, an "open-and-shut" day likely to clear off and just as likely to rain. Over the pancakes Ash suggested that the nutting expedition had better be postponed. Connie's heart fell so hard, it seemed to her that Pa must hear the thud. She had screwed herself up to find those cubs, and if it was not done today, she was not sure she could muster the courage again.

"Pa," she pleaded, "let me go. Once it starts to rain, it's liable to keep on for days, and by the time it clears off, the squirrels will have got all the nuts."

The argument was good. In the absence of hunters squirrels had multiplied even faster than wolves; the forest teemed with bushy-tailed rodents all busy at this season in preparing for winter.

Ash agreed to let Connie go today, provided she took along the family umbrella. "But take care you don't leave it lying around; some squirrel might take that ivory knob for a new kind of nut and make off with it," he concluded, with a chuckle.

Connie laughed outright. Pa wasn't often in a joking mood; if it lasted until her return—with the booty—all would be well.

Among the oaks, beeches and buckeyes the forest contained, there were many butternuts, hickories and black walnuts, but the girl did not stop to gather any of their fruits, for she had a long way to go. If she came back with an empty basket, she would fill it with nuts. If she brought back what she hoped to bring, there would be no room in the basket for anything else, nor any further need for excuses or subterfuge. The place she had in mind was a rocky glen some miles in the hills to the east. By the time she reached this objective a reluctant sun had reached the meridian, and she sank down on a boulder to rest, munch her snack, and free the basket. Then she trudged on deeper into the glen.

Perhaps it was some sixth sense of the wilderness-born which led her to a cave where three furry young creatures played together like overgrown kittens. It was a pretty sight and Connie's heart misgave her. After all, how could she kill anything so young and helpless? Then one of the cubs caught the human scent, opened a toothless red maw, and spat spitefully. The other two cubs followed suit, glaring with red eyes so balefully that her heart hardened. She poked the litter apart with the point of the umbrella, seized one cub by the scruff and bore it off at arm's length, with the animal clawing and snarling. Then, taking a fresh hold on the middle of the furled umbrella, she stunned the little beast with one blow of the ivory knob. Swiftly then, and neatly—for she had helped prepare many a pig for the brine barrel—Constitution Field cut off the wolf-cub's scalp with both ears attached, as required by law. Twice she re-entered the cave; twice more used the bread knife to good purpose. Only when the bloody business was done and the booty in the basket, did it occur to the girl that these might not be the killer's cubs, but those of some other mother away on the prowl for food.

Connie lost no time then in putting as much distance as possible between herself and the cave. She had not gone very far, however, when she had a sense of being followed. Was it just imagination? Or was there actually something on her trail? Her instinct was to run, for she was fleet of foot and in her brother's breeches capable of outdistancing anything on four legs. But, hampered by petticoats as she was, Connie knew flight would be fatal. It was the nature of canines to chase fleeing prey, and although wild beasts rarely attacked human beings by daylight unless provoked, what stronger provocation for a she-wolf was there than the scent of her own brood's blood?

For a moment Connie was tempted to abandon the basket, but that would mean the abandonment of her whole project. There must be some other way, if only she could think quickly enough. As though in answer to her need, Connie seemed to hear her father's voice telling her brother, "Attack is the best defense."

In one motion she dropped the basket, turned and opened the umbrella squarely in the face of the beast at her heels. The wolf, caught off guard, sat back on its haunches, and snarling teeth bared. Furling the umbrella, the girl struck—struck with such force that something cracked like a pistol shot. Connie did not wait to discover whether it was the wolf's skull she had broken or the knob of the umbrella. She ran and ran until she could run no longer. Then, panting, heart pounding, she glanced fearfully over a shoulder. The trail was empty. A glance at the improvised weapon showed it to be undamaged. But had she actually killed the wolf, or merely stunned it? Would it be safe to go back and collect the larger, more valuable scalp? Temptation was great. Common sense warned against trying good luck too far. Connie wavered. Then, picking up the basket, she took the trail for home.

The brief autumn afternoon was far spent when the girl emerged from the forest. A candle gleamed behind one of the courthouse windows, and Connie hurried toward the light before it should be snuffed out and the office closed.

When "the Field gal" set the basket on the table before him, the sheriff showed no surprise. Only the day before Captain Field had brought in the scalp of a she-wolf, and it was natural to conclude that he had gone after the cubs and sent his daughter to collect the bounty.

"Thank you, sir," Connie managed to gasp as she thrust four silver dollars and a fifty-cent piece into her petticoat pocket. Then she fled before the officer should start asking embarrassing questions.

As the weary girl trudged across the square, she realized that she faced questions at home—questions as to why she returned so late and with an empty basket. The white lies already told lay heavy on her conscience and she shrank from further fabrications. But if she told the truth, what would Pa say? What would he do? Connie was not so certain of the answers as she had been that morning and she was taking no chances. Turning about, she hurried along Superior Street—not toward home but in the opposite direction.

Full dark had fallen when she pushed open the door of the blockhouse. Faith gave a sharp cry of relief. Ash gave his daughter a sharp reproof for the scare she had given them both.

"What kept you out so late, my girl?" he demanded. "Did you lose your way? Good lord, don't stand there shaking your head. Give account of yourself."

Connie obeyed, reluctantly, fearfully, for now it was over her knees knocked together and she could scarcely talk. Little by little she managed to tell the whole story, interrupted by squeaks of horror from Faith and Ash's stifled oaths. Ash, incredulous, demanded to see the scalps, and when she told him that she had already collected the bounty, he held out a hand, saying, "Give it to me, my girl. I'll keep it to add to your dowry."

Backing away from the outstretched hand, Connie stuttered, "I —I h-haven't g-got it."

"In heaven's name!" shouted Ash. "Don't tell me you lost all those coins between here and the courthouse! If that isn't just like a female! No head, no——"

Stung into anger, Connie interrupted. "I did no such thing! I— well, if you must know, I went straight to the schoolmaster's house and paid him in advance for the whole twelve-week term."

The announcement left both parents speechless. Faith looked anxiously from husband to daughter, thinking how alike they were —both so headstrong, so stubborn, so set in their own ways which, it was appallingly clear, led in different directions. At the threat of conflict between the two beings she loved best, Faith's loyalty was sorely strained.

As for Ash, while he scowled at his daughter he could not stifle his pride in her courage, the sheer physical courage that carried her into the wolf's den, and the moral courage that made her stand there before him, defying his prejudices and his judgment. But he dared not reveal his pride. Book learning was only one kind of knowledge, Ash knew from bitter experience, and from the same source he knew that youth seldom accepts the wisdom gained by its elders. Youth insists on making its own mistakes, just as he himself had done long ago. Ash had tried to save his sons from repeating his errors, but with ill success. Now it was evident that his daughter was no more amenable. To be sure, she was not of age; he could forbid her the schooling she had earned and paid for. Yet he was reluctant to take advantage of parental authority and by so doing lose her affection and perhaps even her respect. In three months she couldn't absorb much of the learning he honestly believed detrimental to her future welfare.

Suddenly Ash grinned and gave in. "Well, I'm bound to admit you got round me very neatly," he said. "Go to school, if you will. But don't go on any more wolf-hunts. That I strictly forbid; it's too dangerous."

At the moment nothing was further from Connie's desire than to repeat the day's exploit. She did not confess as much, however. All she said was, "Thank you, Pa. And now, if you and Ma don't mind, I'd like to go to bed, for I'm fair beat out."

Not until she had admitted it aloud did she realize just how bone-tired the excitements, the perils of the day, had left her. Yet, after exchanging her linsey-woolsey gown for a night shift and crawling under the coverlet, she could not sleep. Now that she was alone to think it over, she saw how inconclusive was her victory. What she had won was no more than a preliminary skirmish. Pa had agreed to let her attend school only for the period paid for. At the end of that time her education would end also unless she could figure out some other means of earning tuition. Moreover, even if she succeeded in getting more cash honestly, the maneuver by which she had outwitted Pa's demand to hand over the bounty was not likely to meet with success a second time. Pa would warn the schoolmaster in advance to accept no more fees from a minor. Pa held the whip hand; that is, he had it until she turned eighteen, or married.

Married! Constitution cringed at the thought. Not that she was so abnormal as to shrink from the marriage bed or its natural result—childbed. What she shrank from was the idea of being tied for life to some clod so absorbed in tilling the earth and gathering the fruits thereof, that he would never lift his eyes to the stars.

Chapter 2

THROUGH the schoolhouse door Constitution Field entered another world. A world of wonder and enchantment spread out before her eyes on the big map hanging on the wall behind Teacher's desk. Teacher himself was a little gnome of a man with whisps of white hair and the sharp eyes of an eagle under brows as untidy as that bird's nest. Connie saw in him a wizard and in his long pointer a magic wand.

The other pupils regarded him in no such light. To them he was an ogre whose fierce gaze held them pinned between benches and desks. They could not even avoid that compelling glance by looking out of the windows, placed high to prevent just such escape. Foreign countries and capitals, indicated on the map by that pointer, meant even less to these dullards than did the names of those places chalked on the blackboard under the map which, when rolled up, revealed such jawbreakers as Afghanistan, Baluchistan, Constantinople. After spelling each in turn, Teacher called on the class to repeat the letters in unison, syllable by syllable.

Connie's mind absorbed knowledge as newsprint takes ink. When the class was lined up for a spelling match, that ordeal invariably left her standing alone. As girls of her age did not usually attend school, all her classmates were big boys who resented her presence the more because she excelled them in every subject. Even at figures, which no female was supposed to understand, she soon outdistanced the class in long division and threatened the supremacy of the head boy in vulgar fractions.

It wasn't decent for a gal to be so smart. She ought to stay home and tend to her knitting. Oh, yes, she was handsome, they supposed, if you fancied a long-legged filly with mane enough to make a bell rope. Injured masculine pride and smouldering resentment

15

found outlet in pulling that long rope of hair. Connie had grown up with brothers, but their gentle teasing had raised in her no such anger as did these vicious yanks on her hair. Instead of bringing forth screams, however, repeated assaults finally brought humiliation to one of the assailants. Before he could relinquish his grip on her braid, Connie turned and struck him with a fist hard as a bell-clapper, knocking out two front teeth.

The instinct to hit back being stronger than chivalry, the startled boy swung wildly. Dodging his blows, she whirled and hit him again, this time squarely in the eye, and when he staggered off, blinded, she turned to face the other tormentors. None of them cared to take up the challenge, however, and risk the ignominy of being bested at fisticuffs by a girl. Muttering threats and insults, they retired leaving the tomboy victor.

That triumph cost Connie dear. Hitherto the only places of public entertainment had been the taverns where no respectable female would show her face. But with the schoolhouse free of an evening, Faith saw no reason why her daughter should not make merry with the other young folks under the watchful eyes of elders. Faith inserted gussets in the bodice of Connie's best gown and let down the hem, but still it stopped short of her ankles. Modesty forbade the display of stockings in public; frugality forbade discarding any wearable garment. Faith solved the dilemma by adding to the hem of Connie's gown a ruffle which, although of a different shade and texture, nevertheless lengthened it discreetly. Faith's own "good" gown, the same drab garment she had spun, woven, cut and sewed a dozen years ago, still fitted her figure kept trim by hard work and short rations in wartime. Her thin fair hair had turned as drab as the gown, but although her flower-blue eyes too had faded, they looked out of her worn face with the same steadfast sweetness that had won and kept the devotion of the man whose name and children she had borne through thirty years of marriage.

Ash no longer enjoyed dancing, but to please his wife and daughter he took the family lantern and lighted their way along the dark streets. Inside the schoolhouse the row of family lanterns, hung on the pegs designed for schoolboys' caps, illuminated the festive scene. All the desks had been piled in one corner and the benches

16

pushed back against the walls where girls who had never gone to school whispered and giggled together. Bright-eyed and red-cheeked with excitement and further beautified by beads, breastpins and spit curls, they preened and palpitated under the appraising gaze of prospective partners.

These beaux, too, had beautified themselves after their own fashion. Beardless faces had been scrubbed with soft soap until they shone like copper kettles, and home-cropped hair was plastered flat with bear's grease. Most of them wore buckskins, some new, others patched where worn thin by a saddle, but a few bold spend-thrifts dazzled the belles with coats of many colors and those new pantaloons which were slowly replacing knee breeches. Patched or pantalooned, the pomaded beaux caused a flutter among the petti-coats. Although males still outnumbered females on the frontier, there was always the risk of being claimed as partner by some clumsy bumpkin who trod on toes, tore flounces, or became con-fused in the intricate figures of a reel or square dance. Even worse than being trampled upon was the fate of a wallflower. For some lads were so conscious of their own awkwardness that they claimed no partner at all.

The hubbub of greetings drowned the scrape of strings as the fiddle was tuned. But when the caller shouted, "All right, fellers! Pick yer pardners," the beaux made a beeline for the benches, bowed before the belles of their choice, and whirled them away to the tune of "Hi, Betty Martin! Tiptoe Fine!"

Constitution Field, alone of all the maidens, was left seated among mothers and grandmothers whose dancing days were over. As though frozen, she sat there, two red spots on her high cheek-bones the only sign of humiliation too deep for tears. As she had neither gloated nor gabbled about her defeat of these same boys in class or on playground, Connie wondered what was wrong. Faith was equally at a loss to account for this awful situation. Was it that pieced-out petticoat? No. Many of the flying figures on the floor flaunted additions even more incongruous. The trouble was not Connie's clothes. Was it, perhaps, because she was so tall, so angu-lar, looked so top-heavy with that great braid coiled about her head? Nothing could reduce her height, but maybe she would look more like other girls if she did her hair up in rags every night

17

and practiced saying *prunes* and *prisms* to purse up her lips into the shape of a crumpled rosebud. If something wasn't done, and soon, Connie was doomed to spinsterhood. And the only prospective husbands in Cleveland were these young jackanapes kicking up their heels in company with foolish flipperty-gibbets who couldn't hold a candle to Connie. Faith's heart was heavy, for she knew that more matches were made at play-parties than ever were made in heaven.

Ash knew the real cause of his girl's lack of partners was neither her clothes nor her looks. It was her behavior—the behavior that was the talk of the taverns. He had never been what folks called "a drinking man," but there was no place equal to a tavern for hearing grievances aired by someone who was in need of a lawyer. Among the complaints Ash had overheard in Mowrey's taproom were those of two tipsy old men who resented their grandsons' discomfiture at the hands of "that Field gal."

She was "a vixen, a beldame, a bad'n bound to come to no good end," in the opinion of one grandsir. "What's her pa thinking of, anyway, sending a great gal like her to school?"

"Hanged if I know," replied the other old man. "Field must be teched in the head."

Silently, Ash agreed with him. He should never have given in to the girl's preposterous notions. Well, the term she had paid for would soon end and with it this nonsense. No doubt she would be disappointed, but she would soon get over that if provided with more suitable employment.

The thought recalled his promise to replace his wife's spinning wheel so that she might initiate their daughter in that art. In the press of professional problems he had forgotten that promise. Now he determined to make it good. He'd send to Pittsburgh for a woolwheel, and while he was about it, he'd order a flaxwheel as well. Hang the expense! He'd find the wherewithal to pay for the tools on delivery, even if it cleaned out his cash drawer.

Faith planned to provide another kind of poultice for the pain of disappointment and at the same time further the girl's matrimonial chances. She had pointed out the way to win a man's heart, but had not followed up the statement with precept. Somehow, Connie never seemed to be around when it was time to stuff and truss a

18

fowl, or when the bread was ripe for kneeding. But when school "let out," Faith determined to school the girl for marriage.

The school term had yet a week to run when the wheels arrived by goods-wagon, and in order to keep them as a surprise until the right moment, Ash stowed them away in the office. He did not know that the book-hungry girl pored over his tomes of Torts whenever he was busy in the courtroom. It was while in pursuit of knowledge that Connie discovered the wheels, the big one marked with her mother's name and the smaller one, *Constitution Field, her wheel*. Hope that high marks in class would lead to further schooling died at sight of that inscription; to the girl it spelled *finis*. All the good her education had done her, so far, was to provide classic comparisons. Pa was as firm as the Rock of Gibraltar; his opinions were as unalterable as the laws of the Medes and Persians. It was well she realized this before the term ended, otherwise she would have been unprepared to accept her father's ultimatum with good grace and his gift with at least a show of gratitude.

Learning to spin did, indeed, absorb all her time and attention, for like many people of superior intellect, Connie's fingers were less nimble than her brain. She had great difficulty in mastering the motions of spinning and often broke the thread. A break could be spliced, but too many knots in a skein resulted in cloth of poor quality. Flax was scarce and Faith was a frugal woman; she decided that weaving would be a better occupation for the girl at this time. For years she had saved all outworn garments to make a carpet when Ash got around to replacing her loom. As she had never reminded him of the lack, it had slipped his mind. Now when Faith explained the need of a loom, Ash agreed to bargain with a joiner, who owed him for legal services, to build the frame and beams. Smaller parts, bobbins, quills and so forth, Ash himself could whittle out during the long winter evenings.

While Ash plied his jackknife, Faith took over the flaxwheel and spun the stout warp for the carpet. Connie was set to cutting rags into strips for the weft. This was a chore calling for little or no skill and, long before the loom was ready, she had cut and wound into balls enough rags to make six feet of carpet.

Idleness in the company of such hard-working parents was shameful and the girl looked about for some new occupation. The search led her into the front room, sacred to weddings, christenings and funerals, none of which had ever been celebrated in this house. What she discovered was the family Bible, unused since Granny Marvin went to live with Uncle Silas down on the Muskingum River. Granny always read a chapter of Scripture aloud every night, and Connie recalled just enough fragments of those readings to whet her curiosity. The front room was cold, so she carried the Book into the kitchen and set it on the table beside the candlestick, turned back the leather cover and began to read to herself: "In the beginning——"

It was a faintly remembered story, how the Lord God made heaven and earth in six days. What an incredible accomplishment! No wonder even He felt the need of rest on the seventh day before attacking the creation of man! Connie read on, fascinated, how Adam was fashioned out of the dust of the earth and made free in the Garden of Eden, except for one tree. The fruit of the tree of knowledge of good and evil was forbidden. Without explaining this taboo the story went on to say that, since it was not good for man to live alone, the Lord God put Adam to sleep and then from one of his ribs made Eve. This, indeed, struck Connie as so remarkable that she read on into the next chapter until the wag-on-the-wall struck nine. Bedtime!

The following evening temptation entered the garden disguised as a serpent and coaxed Eve into sampling the fruit of the tree of knowledge. It tasted so sweet that Eve wanted to share the treat with her husband. Adam took a bite and then put all the blame on Eve when the Lord God accused him of disobedience. (Was that fair or just?) However, the pair did not pay with their lives, as was threatened, but were merely driven out of the garden.

Connie pondered the story, wondering whether it was because Eve was the first to eat the forbidden fruit that females were now denied the knowledge men freely enjoyed. But perhaps a better reason would appear later on in the Book. What chapter four related was the birth of Cain in verse one, and that of his brother Abel in verse two. Within the chapter both boys grew up, quarreled, and in a jealous rage Cain killed Abel. Murder was exciting! Connie read on, breathlessly, how Cain lied to the Lord God concerning his crime and in punishment was condemned to live out his life a fugitive and a vagabond.

Well, anyhow he didn't live long alone. Somewhere in his wanderings, Cain acquired a wife and a son, Enoch. Ignoring the father, the next verse recorded the fact that "unto Enoch was born Irad; and Irad begat M-e-h-u-j-a-e-l." Connie's lips moved as she spelled out the strange name, letter by letter, before reading on: "and Mehujael begat Me-thus-ael; and Methusael begat Lamech." That ended the chapter, ending at the same time Connie's pursuit of knowledge for another night.

Next evening chapter five went back to Adam who, it seemed, lived over nine hundred years during which he begat many more sons, and assorted daughters not one of whom was mentioned by name. Adam's son Seth lived a hundred and five years and begat Enos. And Enos begat Cainan, who begat Mah-al-al-eel, who begat Jared. Here at last was a familiar name; the boy Connie had hit in the eye was called Jared. But what about that word *begat* so often repeated? Although she had never seen it chalked on the blackboard, Connie found it easy to read, easy to spell, easy to say, but nevertheless incomprehensible.

"Begat," she said, aloud. "Pa, what does it mean?"

Startled, Ash gouged the smooth surface of a bobbin. He glanced up, saw the girl bent over the Book and told her, "Oh, that! Well, it's just genealogy. Pretty dull subject. Better omit it."

"But, Pa," she persisted. "What does *begat* mean? What did Adam *do* when he begat Cain and Abel and the rest of them?"

Ash had explained such matters to his sons in turn, and he had taken for granted that Faith would do so to their daughter at the proper time. She had neglected this duty, it seemed. Well, she must do it now. "Ask your mother," he told Connie shortly.

Brilliant young eyes met faded blue eyes enquiringly. Faith turned away, red and embarrassed. "Some other time," she said. "Time now busy folks was in bed." By morning, she hoped, Connie would have forgotten the matter.

But this avoidance of straightforward answers only increased the girl's curiosity. After breakfast, when she and Ma were doing the dishes, Connie repeated the question.

Words never came easily to Faith, and her flustered effort to explain her own exalted feelings about the most sacred of human relationships left Connie more confused than ever. Quite early in life she discovered that chickens were hatched from eggs and demanded to know how the chick got into the egg.

"That," Faith had replied, "is something you are too young to understand."

Connie hadn't been too young to keep her eyes open. While further observations in the barnyard led to knowledge of where kittens came from, she remained as much in the dark with regard to what made the kittens grow inside the cat as to what made chicks grow inside eggshells. As time went on she came to some conclusion not too far from the truth, and had asked no more delicate questions about the facts of life until now. Had the strange Bible word been explained to her in simple everyday language, she would have said, "Oh!" and dropped the subject. But no, Ma had to go and bring the Lord God into it without making clear just what was His capacity. And the more Connie tried to pin her down, the more vague, the more flustered Faith grew, until she was driven to say again, "You are too young to understand."

When Faith reported the conversation to Ash, he nodded slowly. He himself had never been a close Bible student, but he knew that men who spent their lives in its study did not always see eye to eye on its interpretation. Indiscriminate Scripture reading was not to be encouraged in the young.

"Select passages suitable for mixed company," he told his wife, "and read them aloud yourself each evening, like your mother used to do." He was unaware that Jerusha Marvin had not actually read those nightly chapters; after her eyes grew too dim for fine print she had repeated from memory favorite Psalms and Proverbs. Faith had never been a ready reader, and she shrank from revealing this deficiency before her clever daughter. Therefore she practiced in private and then read the same verses over and over aloud to her family. Ash believed this was due to a fondness for these particular passages. But Connie, aware of her mother's difficulty, took it as just another proof of man's unfairness in denying females an education. Determined not to grow up in such ignorance, she vowed she'd go to school, somewhere, sometime, once she came of

age. Meanwhile her hands were tied—tied up in carpet rags—
while Ma stumbled and mumbled through a few verses Connie
could have read in a matter of minutes, but was forbidden to scan.

By the time the weather turned warm enough for work in the
unheated loft, the loom frame and beams arrived, ready to be assembled. Connie, whose recollections of the lost loom were hazy,
thought the new one looked like that four-poster bed, a family
heirloom recently reclaimed from Connecticut. As Pa put the
loom together, however, the likeness diminished. The four-poster
had been filled by a feather bed, but the loom was fitted with a web
of those coarse linen threads Faith had spun. The strands of this
warp ran through a pair of heddle bars, suspended above the
loom-bed, to the cloth beam, alternate threads going through each
heddle so that when the foot-treadles were worked below, the
strands separated to form a shed.

When the harnessing of the loom was completed, Faith bade Connie climb up on the bench before the cloth beam and showed her
how to tramp on each treadle in turn, then through the shed
throw the weft-wound bobbin from her right hand to her left,
bring down the heavy batten to set the threads firmly and then re-
verse the performance, bringing the bobbin back from left to right
and the batten down again with another thump.

"There!" said Faith. "That's all there is to weaving. Just you
keep at it, my girl, and if the carpet comes off neat and firm, I'll
larn you to weave something finer. Maybe a linen sheet for your
hope chest."

Left in the loft, Connie seemed to hear those words over and
over as her long legs pumped the treadles and the heddlebars
chattered. Hope chest, hope chest! Hope for what? Connie knew
the answer. Hope for a husband, Ma meant. It was the hope of all
the girls she knew, girls whose company bored her because they
never talked of anything but beaux, weddings and babies. Was
there nothing in life for a woman except the bondage of wedlock?
Men married and went on with their business, whatever it happened to be—farming, hunting, trading or the law, like her own
father who never discussed legal matters with his womenfolk.

Thwack! Thwack! The monotonous chatter of the heddles and
the thump of the batten accompanied these thoughts, emphasized

23

the monotony of the only life open to women. Raising a family was important, of course. It always had been, according to Scripture. Why else was Genesis filled with begats? Yet all that genealogy, as Pa called it, all but ignored the distaff side. Who was Cain's wife, the mother of Enoch? Who was the mother of Irad who begat Mehujael? Her name was not mentioned, nor was the name of her who bore sons and daughters to Methusael. Adam lived nine hundred and thirty years, but the length of Eve's life was not recorded, nor was the name of a single one of her daughters. Why, when man was born of woman, was she accorded so little importance?

Why, why? The question hatcheled the girl's mind until the chattering heddles seemed to repeat, "Why? Why? Why? Why?" The thwack of the batten was the only answer—a dull hopeless thud that provided no answer at all.

Chapter 3

AMONG Cuyahoga County lawyers, the most active of Ashbel Field's young rivals was Alfred Kelley. The two men were very different in appearance. The aging Ash stood six feet tall in his moccasins, while young Kelley's bootheels did not raise the crown of his sleek head level with Ash's broad shoulders. Kelley's narrow shoulders, however, were held so straight, and his head set so stiffly upon them, that he looked as though he were carved from stone. There was a flinty quality about his character also—a quality Ash shared so that they had much in common. For one thing, they were in agreement on local problems.

Although Cleveland had doubled in size since the war, the rival town on the southern border of the state was nearing five figures in population. Field and Kelley agreed that the difference was caused by the difference in transportation. Cincinnati had access to world markets by way of the Ohio and Mississippi Rivers.

Cleveland, located on the Cuyahoga, close to the confluence of that crooked stream with Lake Erie, was handicapped by the sand bar at the river mouth which blocked shipping. Sloops and schooners were forced to anchor offshore in all sorts of weather and cargoes loaded, or unloaded, by small boats. Furthermore, at the eastern end of the lake, passage was blocked by the cataract of Niagara.

Kelley, who hailed from New York State, knew of the governor's scheme for getting goods around the falls and into the Hudson River without the long overland haul. Even before De Witt Clinton had succeeded in financing this project, Kelley and Field envisioned wealth pouring into Cleveland by way of the Erie Canal. Another local man who shared their views was Leonard Case, a cripple with courage and brains and ambition. He had bought a house on a corner of Superior Street, and in his front room opened Cleveland's first bank. Cleveland's first carriage belonged to Kelley who had bought it in Buffalo to bring his bride to the West. And when Case needed transportation to bring his bride from adjoining Portage County, he borrowed the Kelley carriage.

Another welcome addition to the population that same year brought, not a bride, but an old printing press, a font of second-hand type, a meager supply of newsprint, and a boundless supply of optimism. Andrew Logan brought the tools of his trade in a wagon all the way from Pittsburgh. Where he got the brash idea that a frontier settlement could support a newspaper is not recorded. However, the machine was set up in a cabin on Superior Street, and under date of July 31, 1818, the first issue of *"The Cleveland Gazette and Commercial Advertiser, Andrew Logan editor and proprietor"* came off that antiquated hand press. Although the masthead did not include the information, Andy was also reporter, ad-getter, typesetter, pressman and printer's devil.

As a matter of course, Ashbel Field was one of the first subscribers. He was not, however, the first member of his family to read that first issue. A client held him late in the office, and when he came home he found Connie bent over the newspaper, devouring it by the light of a candle.

Ash sat down at the table, poured molasses on his hasty pudding, and over it glanced at his daughter, wondering what she found so absorbing.

Suddenly she burst out, "Pa, are females people?"

Ash's spoon paused between bowl and mouth. "Certainly," he said. "Why ask such a foolish question?"

"Because," she replied, "it says here 'the Constitution of the United States and the sovereignty of the people assure their liberty.' If that's true, Pa, and females are people, then why aren't we just as free as you menfolks?"

"But you are," Ash asserted, unguardedly.

"That," retorted his daughter, "just isn't so."

Horrified, Faith gasped, "Darter! How dare you contradict your pa!"

Ash was more amused than angry. He said, "It is unwise to make such sweeping statements unless you can prove them." The wrinkles at the corners of his eyes invited argument.

Head on, the girl met his challenge. "Well, sir," she said, "if womenfolks were just as free as menfolks then I'd be free to go to school same as a boy."

Ash kicked himself mentally for provoking the same old argument. Begging the question, he reminded her that she wasn't a woman, legally, and wouldn't be for two more years. "Meanwhile," he added to clinch the matter, "you are a child, and children are obliged to accept the judgment of their parents."

Connie, however, did not accept that as final. "If a girl isn't of age until she's eighteen," she demanded, "then what does it mean that fourteen is the age of consent? Consent to what?"

"Good Lord!" Ash exploded. "Where on earth did you pick up that expression?"

"Why, in your law books, of course," she told him. "I must say I found them very dull, but there's been nothing else to read around here since you forbade me the Bible; nothing until now."

"And from now on," Ash told her, drying, "I also forbid you to read my law books. Is that clear?"

"Yes, Pa," she replied. "It's quite clear that you want me to grow up a dunce."

"I want nothing of the kind," he retorted with asperity. "You know very well I want you to grow up to be like your mother—an accomplished housewife. I've provided the tools; see that you make good use of them and stop wasting your time over books. Now, my good girl, hand me that paper."

As she obeyed in silence, Connie made note that Pa referred to the *Gazette* as "that paper." It was not, then, in the same class as books. She was free to read it every week, after Pa was done with it, of course.

Editor Logan proved to be a great freedom lover and often quoted Tom Paine. One of his editorials echoed Paine's assertion that "Where liberty dwells, there is my country." There was, it seemed, more than one country in the Western Hemisphere presently fighting for what Connie's grandfather Marvin had fought and died for, what her father and three brothers had fought to keep—freedom. But it was freedom for men only.

While the editor of the *Gazette* expressed his opinion freely in print, to keep free from debt he was forced to print advertisements. From these Connie learned that Elisha Taylor would shortly open a new store where groceries, dry goods, paints, dyestuffs, drugs, crockery and glass could be obtained for cash, or in exchange for grain, salt meat or peltry. Leonard Case, who eked out his banker's stipend by dealing in real estate on the side, advertised ninety acres of land in exchange for cash, or for salt, flour, rye or whiskey. There was the announcement of a new stage to leave Cleveland every Thursday for points all along the Buffalo Road and due in Buffalo in a matter of eighteen hours. A rival means of transportation, a strange new kind of craft propelled by steam instead of wind and sail, and named the *Walk-on-the-Water,* promised to make the lake trip between Buffalo and Detroit in ten days, with a stop en route off Cleveland.

Constitution Field had never seen a steamboat, nor had anyone else among the crowd that gathered on the bluff one summer day to watch for the first sign of smoke on the eastern horizon. While men argued whether the side-wheeler was two hundred and forty tons burden, or three hundred and forty-two, a small boy sighted the steamer and gave a shout. The cannon left over from the war had been brought down to the bluff, and by the time the new craft hove to, a salute of welcome rang across the water. Town officials rowed out to inspect the wonder and rowed back to report that, besides cargo, she could carry a hundred first-class passengers and as many more in the steerage.

It was not by steamer, however, that half a hundred homeseekers arrived together later that summer. The schooner *American Eagle* landed the party on the lake shore where they were met by the sheriff, whose duties included prying into the private affairs of all newcomers. After questioning these fifty-odd arrivals, he ordered them to camp where they were for the time being.

Back in the village the sheriff summoned other officials into his office where he told them, "These folks just come off the *Eagle* are poor as Job's turkey; not a copper amongst the whole lot. It being my bounden duty to keep off vagrants, I told the *Eagle's* cap'n to take these paupers back where they come from."

The old storekeeper nodded approval. It was the new storekeeper, Elisha Taylor, who wanted to know, "What's all this about then, sheriff? If the crew's gone, why call us fellers away from business?"

"Because they *ain't* gone," replied the sheriff shortly. "Seems this crew, as ye call 'em, come a fer piece; clean across the ocean from Ireland, in fact. The *Eagle* cap'n swears that when he picked 'em up in Buffalo, they paid their passage here, and how was he to know it cleaned 'em out, complete? Soon's I was over the side, cap'n he give orders to set sail—I mean to reve up the engines, or whatever the lingo is. What I'm trying to tell you is the *Eagle's* made off without—left these paupers on our hands. Now then, what are we goin' to do with 'em?"

The men assembled looked at one another for suggestions. Finally the old storekeeper said, "If they was our own kind, with kinfolks in New England, I'd be willin' to give 'em credit till they could send home for money. But I'll be derned if I'll trust furriners. We want no furriners here."

Ashbel Field rose to differ on that point. "If we want our town to grow," he said, "we can't pick and choose our fellow citizens for their place of origin any more than for the color of their eyes, or skins. The only requirements should be an honest desire to earn an honest living, so long as they don't interfere with other men's right to do likewise."

"That's all very fine," remarked the tavernkeeper, in a tone as sour as his mash. "But if these fellers is honest, why did they leave wherever 'twas they come from?" Without waiting for an answer, he went on, "And if they *had* to leave, what's the reason they didn't get work in New York, or wherever 'twas they landed?"

Mr. Case believed he could answer that question. "Prejudice against foreigners," he said, "is not confined to our western frontier. Perhaps the port of debarkation passed the buck to Buffalo."

"And Buffalo," said the tavernkeeper with a snort, "passed on to us this penniless bunch of buckaroos."

Alfred Kelley, who had not entered the discussion hitherto, now remarked, "If that is true, then Buffalo was very shortsighted in view of the large number of laborers that will be required to dig the big ditch clear across New York State. Friends, let us prove we are smarter than Buffalo. Let us make these Irishmen welcome and make work for them by building a canal of our own, a canal linking Cleveland, not only with Zane's Trace and the National Road, but with the Ohio River as well."

Part of the company called Kelley a fool. The idea of digging a canal up the Cuyahoga Valley was crazy. Can you make water run uphill? You know darned well you can't. And even if you could, digging up the swampy approaches to the lake would stir up the devils of ague. So spake men who were "agin" the project.

The "fers" argued that the "agins" were the fools. Had they never heard of locks? No, not the kind you put on doors to keep out rascals; the kind you put in canals to raise the water level. An undetermined number of locks would carry barges up to the height of land; once there the water would find its own level and carry the barges down to the Ohio River. As for those devils of ague, the canal would drain them off into the lake and drown them forever.

"Speakin' of devils," remarked one of the agins, "supposin' a canal could be dug, as you say—which I ain't convinced—who the devil will pay for all that diggin', not to mention them—what do you call 'ems?—locks."

Kelley suggested that the State of Ohio might follow the example of New York State and finance the enterprise.

This raised a howl that any such fool idea would raise taxes. If the taxpayers paid for the canal, would it pour money into their pockets in the long run, or drain the state treasury as dry as the bed of the Cuyahoga in August?

So it went with sharper and sharper contradictions in the debate. Kelley believed he had all the answers. And Ashbel Field believed Kelley and backed him up as did also a few others, including the banker. Although they were in the minority, they had the gift of gab and kept the arguments going until the candles burned down, guttered and threatened to leave the company in darkness. A hurried motion was made to adjourn.

"Wait a minute, men," Ashbel Field interposed. "We haven't settled what's to be done about these Irish emigrants. I move they be allowed to stay."

"Second the motion," said Kelley quickly.

In all probability a new debate would have developed had there been time. But time was running out with the candle grease. In all haste the question was put to a vote, and the "ayes" had it, by a narrow margin. How these destitute folk were to keep body and soul together until the canal question was settled in the General Assembly remained to be discussed at some future time.

Meanwhile the six Irish families, left to their own devices, squatted among the rushes on the west shore of the river near the lake. Here was a piece of land considered so worthless that when a handful of the original owners ventured to return, after the war, the Indian tribal remnant was not disturbed. Presumably these Indians taught the "furriners" how to live off the land and water, for no Irishman came into Cleveland to beg. Now and then some rawboned, sandy-haired male would appear at the general store with peltry to trade. In exchange, he would take salt to be used for fish caught through the ice, rabbits snared, or deer shot with bow and arrow. On such fare, and corn given them by the Indians, Cleveland's first Irish settlers faced their first winter.

Since Ashbel Field did all his family's trading, Connie saw nothing of these squatters. Then one evening, as she was reading the *Gazette,* her eye was caught by a new advertisement. Cleveland had a new store, one devoted entirely to books and stationery. Below the notice a line of smaller type stated: *Rags! Rags! Two cents a pound, payable in books, will be given for rags.*

Connie was ignorant of the process of papermaking, and she

wondered what on earth a bookstore wanted with rags. But what did it matter? What did matter to the girl was the waste of time and energy making the family hoard of rags into rugs when deerskins and bearskins were so plentiful and made so much softer floor covering.

Next day, she bundled up all the old linen she could carry and went to the new store. The proprietor weighed the bundle with care and announced that it was worth one book. "Take your pick, miss," he told Connie, waving a hand toward his shelves.

The meager contents of those shelves were, for the most part, theological works, histories of foreign countries, and travel in distant lands. Conscience whispered that she ought to select something religious. But her thirst for more knowledge of far places, known to her only as dots on the schoolhouse map, drove the girl to settle on *The Adventures of Marco Polo.*

Connie came out of the bookstore so preoccupied with her treasure that she failed to see a lad whose nose was pressed against the window.

He saw her, however, and barred her way. "Ma'am," he said, bowing from the waist as no Yankee bowed to man or woman, "would you have the kindness to read me off the names of thim books in the window?"

A quick glance showed her that the glass was fogged by his breath and, believing he sought a pretext for picking acquaintance, she told him sharply, "Sir, if you can't see through that glass, how do you think I can?"

" 'Sir,' she calls me!" exclaimed the lad. " 'Sir,' like I was a laird. Can it be me britches? The britches the laird gave me when he busted out of them from living on the fat of his land whilst his tenants starved?"

"If you are hungry," Connie said, "I'm sure my ma will give you something to eat." To her astonishment the gangling boy stiffened and turned red under his freckles.

"Ma'am," he said. "I want no charity. Me hunger is not so much of the belly as of the mind. I crave book larnin'."

Connie warmed to this stranger who shared her own longings. She asked if he went to the village school, and when he shook his head she pried no further into what, after all, was none of her business. As she was about to pass him, however, the lad blocked her way.

With another pull at his forelock and another stiff bow, he said, "Ma'am, the glass is clear now. Please, ma'am, what does that card say?"

Connie halted, stared hard at him, then demanded, "Can't you read?"

The boy, reddening afresh, confessed, "No, ma'am, I can't. You see nobody ever had time to larn me letters."

It was the girl's turn to be embarrassed. "Oh, do forgive me," she cried. "I—I—didn't mean to be rude. Of course I'll read the card for you. It says the same thing as the advertisement in the paper, that you can get books in exchange for rags."

The boy whistled his wonderment. Then he said, "So they spoke the truth, thim lads I asked in passing. And I mistrusted they was just making game of me ignorance." His glance traveled down a frayed sleeve to the hole through which a chapped and cracked elbow protruded. "Sure, and I'm rich in rags," he said. "But even in a free country a body can't go about naked." He grinned, raising one sandy eyebrow.

Connie did not return the smile as she told him, "We still have the old buckskin breeches and jerkins my brothers used to wear. I'm sure my pa would give them to you. But if you traded your—huh—clothes for a book, what good would it do you, if you can't read?"

"A fair question," replied the boy. "Well, you see, I figured that once I'd got me a book, *it* would larn me to read."

The girl looked skeptical. Then, remembering her own first lessons, she smiled. "Oh," she said, "you mean a hornbook. Maybe our old one is somewhere up in the attic. If it is, maybe pa'll give it to you. Come on home with me and I'll ask."

The ragged boy made another bow, as though about to ask her to dance. But what he said was, " 'Lead on, Macduff.' "

Connie halted. "That's not my name," she said. "It's Field. Are *you* Macduff?"

Grinning widely, he replied, "Mick, yes, but not Duff. He was a Scot in a play by the only Englishman me grandsir could abide. You see, grandsir was educated for the prastehood, but just as he was ready to take orders, he set eyes on me grandmither. Oh, she wasn't anybody's grandmither then. She was just a fair colleen who stole the heart out of him. Before he knew what was up, she married him and that was the end of the Church for grandsir."

Connie was confused. The only church she knew was very strict about marriage, and she was at a loss to understand why a wedding should have made an end of the church for. . . . Aloud, she asked, "What was the name of your grandsir?"

"Seumas McSeumas," replied the boy, "same as me own."

"Well, then," said Connie, a twinkle adding brilliance to her black eyes, " 'Lead on,' McSeumas."

"What?" He cried, in mock horror. "Do you take me for an ill-mannered lout who would walk ahead of a lady? Do you lead on, Lady Field, to your father's castle."

Connie laughed outright. What a droll boy! So polite! So ready of tongue! So different in speech and manners from the bullies she had bested at fisticuffs. With the memory of that victory came a question. Was McSeumas a coward? Did he give the schoolhouse a wide berth out of fear of those bullies? Almost she repented her offer of help, but as her scorn of folks who went back on their words exceeded her scorn of the fainthearted, Connie took the ragged boy to the blockhouse.

Faith took one look at the boy and asked no questions at all. She gave him one of her sweet smiles and an invitation to share the midday meal. He backed off, repeating what he had told Connie—that he wasn't hungry. But the way his mouth watered and his blue eyes bugged out at sight of the steaming platter of hot food on the table convinced both mother and daughter that the boy was half starved.

When Ash came in he listened to no excuses. Anybody who happened to come by at mealtime was expected to take potluck. "So sit down, my lad," he commanded, "and no more nonsense." The tone was the tone of a man accustomed to command respect and obedience.

Seumas obeyed without further argument. The restraint with which he ate disturbed Faith until, having cleaned his plate, he told her, "Ma'am, you are the queen of cooks. That is by all odds the best meal I ever ate in my life."

33

Faith, pleased but embarrassed, remarked that she had no doubt his ma could cook victuals equally well.

"Belike she could," agreed Seumas, "but you see, ma'am, I never knew me mither. She died of me borning."

Faith murmured sympathy while Connie, always restive at the mention of death, changed the subject by asking about the old hornbook. Ash inquired why she wanted to know, since she already knew how to read.

Connie glanced at the boy, reluctant to reveal his ignorance. Then she said, "I promised Seumas he might have it, if you're willing, since he can't, I mean he doesn't go to school."

"Why not?" Ash directed the question to the boy. But sight of that protruding elbow, the ragged coat, and breeches torn off at the knees, seemed answer enough. "If your father cannot afford to send you to school, my lad," he said, "the town will pay your fees."

Seumas studied his empty plate for a moment, then looked up to say, "I've no father, either. The folks I come with are not kin at all."

"That," replied Ash quickly, "makes no difference. The town will pay for your schooling and I, personally, will see that you have slate, pencils, and such textbooks as needed."

Seumas got up from his stool, pulled his forelock and bowed, just as he had bowed to the girl. "Thank you kindly, sir," he said. "But I'll be putting you to no such expense. I figure on trading me rags for books, just as soon as . . ."

Ash interrupted, "Rags! Books!" Then his face cleared. "Oh, I see. You read that ad in the *Gazette.*"

"No, sir," Seumas replied. "I can't read at all, at all. It was the young lady here read me what the card in the window said, after she come out of the store with her book."

Ash turned a frown on his daughter. "You," he said, "have no permission to make purchases. If you bought a book on credit, you can march it straight back to the store."

"I didn't," Connie protested. "I traded some rags for it."

"And where," Ash demanded, "did you get the rags?" When the girl admitted having taken them from the attic, he glanced at his wife inquiringly. Faith shook her head, and Ash turned back to their daughter, telling her, "You took those rags without leave. They are of no value. But honesty is beyond price. To make sure you remember that, my girl, I order you to return that book, whatever it is." While Connie gasped, speechless, he went on. "The bookseller need not return the rags, however. He can credit the amount to this lad here."

Finding her voice, Connie began, "But Pa——"

"Be still!" Ash commanded. "Bring me that book."

His fierce black gaze clashed with the defiant gaze of the girl. After a moment her long lashes drooped in surrender. Slowly she left the room. Slowly she climbed the stairs, came down with the *Travels of Marco Polo,* and laid the little volume on the table before her father. Then she looked up at him with wet eyes, eyes that implored him silently to relent, to say that she might keep her treasure. But Ash was not looking at her. He was smiling at the strange boy in that friendly, understanding way he used to smile at his sons.

Stifling a sob, Connie turned and ran up the stairs to fling herself down on her bed and pull a pillow over her head to cover the sounds of her grief. There were wide cracks between the floor boards, and had it not been for that pillow over her ears, Connie would have heard more of the boy's story. The pity of it would have transmuted her resentment into partisanship, for she hated tyranny in any form.

Ash was questioning the orphan as to how and why he had come across the ocean with people who were no kin. Were they old neighbors, friends, perhaps, of his family?

"No, sir," replied Seumas. "They didn't even come from the same corner of Ireland." He went on to explain that his grandmother had been an Ulsterwoman, and it was in that county his grandparents settled down to raise a family on what the apostate postulant could earn with his hands, there being no opportunity for him to put his education to that use. "Keeping body and soul together took all of grandsir's time and strength," the boy continued, "so me father grew up in ignorance, and me likewise. Soon's I was knee-high to a duck, I was bound out to a farmer. 'Twas in a rebellion against such conditions that me father was killed and grandsir

wounded. He lived just long enough to bid me get out of Ireland—
to a new country where every man is free to pull himself up by his
own bootstraps, so to speak."

The boy paused for breath and Ash asked, "But how did you get
here without money? Did you stow away?"

"Indeed, I did not," replied Seumas. "I sold the gold cross grandsir
wore all his days under his jerkin. I sold his books and the wedding
band of me grandmither. These things provided just the price of
me passage. I worked me way up the Hudson and on the *Eagle,*
cleaning the scuttlebutts." He paused again, and as Ash made no
remark, finally mustered the courage to beg, "Please, sir, let the
young lady keep her book. I'm not afraid of hard work. I'll find
some way to earn me own books, and pay me school fees, too,
before I'm done."

Although Ash admired this show of independence, he refused to
retract either his promise to the boy or the verdict given his daughter. Independence in a girl was dangerous. Connie needed discipline
as much as the Irish lad needed encouragement. Ash shook his
head. "When I make a bargain I stick to it," he said. "However, I
myself will take this book back to the store where you can make
your own selection when you learn your needs." A gleam of humor
lighted the somber black eyes as he added, "One thing you'll not
learn from books, my lad, is that a schoolyard has much in common with a barnyard. Young cockerels are quick to pick on
strange birds."

An answering gleam of mirth lighted the blue Irish eyes as the
McSeumas said, "Sir, I'm not the lad to pick a fight. But neither do
I turn me tail on a challenge."

Ash laughed. "So I surmised," he said. "Well, good night, me
brave buckaroo and good luck to you. Drop in again soon and let
me know how you get on. My latchstring always hangs out."

The first flood of grief having passed, Connie felt smothered under the pillow and threw it off in time to hear that boyish boast
and the man's amused response. Bitterness surged over the girl
afresh. So this was the result of her kindly impulse to help that
ignorant boy! He had wormed his way into her father's heart, replaced her, robbed her of her first book, the only book she had ever
called her own. Worse than that, he was to have the schooling she

36

was denied. She vowed that if this McSeumas took advantage of that invitation from the master of the house, he'd get no welcome from the daughter.

Chapter 4

A FEW DAYS LATER Ash brought home a stranger to take potluck. Mr. Hannibal Jones, it seemed, had recently come to Ohio and had taken up a quarter section of land west of the Cuyahoga only to find the title in dispute. Therefore he had crossed the river to Cleveland to get legal advice and assistance in pressing his claim.

As Connie set a plate of hot victuals before the visitor, she noticed that the crown of his head was bald. Poor old man, she thought, hoping he had strong sons to help him fight the wilderness.

As though Mr. Jones had read her mind, he said, "My oldest boy's no more than knee-high to a duck, and whilst my gals is older, ain't one of them can bake a proper loaf of bread or a pot of beans. This here is what I call a fust-class meal, best I've et in a month of Sundays." He transferred his gaze from his empty plate to the girl. "You cook it, miss?" he enquired.

Before she could disclaim full credit, Ash interposed, "If she didn't, she could have. Her mother is training her well."

Mr. Jones helped himself to more beans, remarking that Field was a lucky man to have two prime cooks in his household.

Connie was aware that not every female was a good housekeeper, and she leaped to the conclusion that Mrs. Jones must be an easy going slattern. This conclusion was strengthened when, having wiped his mouth with the back of a horny hand, Mr. Jones rose, saying, "I know it ain't polite to eat and run, but I got to make tracks for home. No telling what them young 'uns is up to."

When the guest had gone, Ash explained that Mr. Jones had

brought letters of introduction from several substantial men in Connecticut who vouched for his integrity, both financial and personal. "A sound citizen," was Ash's further comment. "We need more of them here. To make sure Jones stays, I shall leave no stone unturned to see that his title is cleared."

Attorney Field must have been as good as his word, for some weeks later Mr. Jones came to dinner again, this time looking several years younger, despite his bald crown.

As he warmed his hands before the fire, he told Connie, "Smart feller, your pa. He's brung me out of the woods, so to speak, in jig time. Howsomever, there's woods enough on my place to keep me choppin' for the rest of my natural life." Mr. Jones grinned at his attempt at a joke, thus exposing long crooked teeth stained with tobacco.

Those teeth fascinated Connie. Store teeth, when folks could afford them, were as white and regular as a row of china cups in a cupboard. On the strength of those repulsive teeth, she revised her estimate of his age; he couldn't be as old as she had thought on first sight. On this second meeting, however, she liked him even less. Not that he wasn't polite. In fact, Mr. Jones's awkward attempts to be agreeable were so forced that she wondered if he was preparing to beg off from his bill for legal services rendered.

After dinner the two men went back across the street to the office. When Ash came home to supper he brought the astonishing, the astounding news that what Mr. Jones had begged was leave to court his lawyer's daughter.

Connie gasped, "But Pa! You must be mistaken. Mr. Jones *has* a wife."

"*Had* a wife," Ash corrected. "She died bearing their tenth child on the journey. Jones blames himself for not postponing the start until after the boy's birth. But he was most anxious to get here before winter and get a good quarter section before all the best land was gone. Now he's sure of his land, he needs a strong healthy young woman to raise his children."

Mr. Jones's need was obvious enough. What Connie could not understand was her father's obvious eagerness to marry her off to this hard grasping widower. "You want to get rid of me," she burst out.

"I want nothing of the kind," Ash contradicted. "What I want is to see you well settled for life. As Jones's lawyer, I have every reason to believe him a sound man of good principles and prospects. A *settled* man. Not one of these callow young fellows who may or may not turn out well. When I am gone, you will come into considerable property, my girl. I want to see you wed to a man who can be counted on to take good care of you and your heritage. Hannibal, I believe, is the man to do both."

This lengthy speech gave Connie time to recover her breath, time to gather her forces to protest. "But Pa, Mr. Jones is an *old* man. I'd be sure to outlive him."

Ash nodded. "Quite probable, although he is not nearly so ancient as you seem to think. What's more to the point is that, having considerable property of his own, Jones does not want you for your prospects."

Connie said, "What Mr. Jones wants me for is to cook and wash for his children."

"Granted," Ash agreed quickly. "But doesn't that prove my point? A man determined to do his duty by his children can be counted on to do his duty by the woman he makes his wife."

Connie's thoughts must have been written on her face, for a gleam of humor lighted Ash's black eyes as he told her, "You claim you want to be a schoolmarm. Well, I have no doubt Hannibal will be more than pleased to have you save him the expense of schooling ten children."

The answering gleam in the girl's eyes was not mirth; it was a danger signal and before she should burst forth in words, Ash asked hurriedly, "You haven't taken a fancy to some young whippersnapper, have you? That Irish lad, for instance?"

"No!" the word burst from the girl. "No! no!" she repeated. "I hate him! I hate all men, young or old." She might have added *including you, Pa,* but the words stuck in her throat and left her gasping.

For a moment Ash felt a twinge of compunction. Then he said soothingly, "Well, well! You'll get over your hatred of men in due time. Possibly I should have prepared you for this proposal before putting it to you so bluntly. If I wasn't so sure, my girl, that you'd never get a better chance, I'd not urge this marriage. Take a little time to think it over and you'll see what I mean. But don't take *too* much time. Hannibal must have a new helpmate by spring. He'll spend the winter clearing as much land as possible, and as soon as it is dry enough to plow, he'll be too busy to spend time for anything except raising a crop."

Connie made no comment. How Mr. Jones spent his time was no concern of hers and never would be, if she could help it. But could she? She was uncertain as to whether or not a father had the power to force a daughter into marriage against her will before she came of legal age. And since she had been forbidden those law books, there was no way she could find out. What she did know, however, was that sooner than become the slave of this long-toothed widower and his large family, she would do what her second brother had done before he was of legal age and his own man.

Jedediah Field had been no such scholar as Malachi. Jed hated school and loved ships. But when he begged Pa to apprentice him to one of the Marietta shipbuilders, Pa had tried to force Jed to remain in the Muskingum Academy. The result of this attempt to make a silk purse out of a sow's ear was that at sixteen Jed ran away to sea. Wide watery spaces did not call Connie who had never even seen the sea. What she shared with Jedediah, whom she scarcely knew, was a determination to be free to fashion her own future.

That night the first frost of the season gripped the lake shore. Connie, shivering under a blanket, heard the far-off howl of a wolf and shivered afresh. What chance of survival had a girl alone in the forest at night? What were her chances of survival even by day with winter coming on? Practically no chance at all, she was obliged to admit.

As though further proof were needed, she woke to find the ground white with the first snowfall which, light as it was, served as a grim reminder of deep drifts to come. Well, she had until spring and much might happen in the meantime. While she dressed, shivering, Connie thought of what might occur to save her from Mr. Jones. If she could make Ma realize how much she detested the man, Ma might talk Pa into relenting. Mr. Jones himself might come to the conclusion that he'd been too hasty, that he'd better take more time to reconsider the choice of a stepmother for his children.

Each evening when her father came home from the post office, Connie waited for him to announce the receipt of a letter from the widower withdrawing his offer of marriage. There was no such announcement. Nor did Mr. Jones write his intended bride to tell her more about her prospective stepchildren, such as their names and ages. To the girl this seemed to confirm her belief that he'd lost interest in her and was looking over the matrimonial field nearer home before coming to Cleveland to beg off from his contract with Lawyer Field.

Connie's conviction that such was the case grew as the weeks passed. And one afternoon when a knock fell on the door, a ceremony dispensed with by neighbors, the girl answered the summons prepared to help Mr. Jones through the awkward business of freeing himself—and her.

When she opened the door, however, it was not a man who stood on the step, but a boy—the hated boy who had deprived her of her book. "You!" she exclaimed. "Well, what do you want now?"

"Nothing," replied Seumas. "I come not to get, but to give." He brought a hand from behind his back and held up a fine string of fish. "Caught through the ice," he explained. "And, knowing Mr. Field had no time for such sport, I figured these beauties would be a treat for you, I mean for you folks here in the blockhouse."

However much Connie disliked the boy, good manners obliged her to ask him in.

Seumas said, "Thank you kindly, me lady, but I'll be stepping around to the woodpile, first, and ready the fish for the pan." Bowing, he backed off the step.

Connie closed the door, wondering why he had not "readied" the fish before presenting them. Curiosity drove her to the rear window, and she saw Seumas trying to scale a half-frozen fish with the axe. It must be he owned no blade of any kind! Catching up the butcher knife, she opened the back door and called, "Here! Take this before you chop off a finger."

Faith, who had been up in the loom room all afternoon, came down at dusk to find the Irish lad warming chapped hands before the fire. When she learned what had brought him, she insisted that he stay and eat some of his own fish for supper. Seumas' protests were overridden. He was not to go out again in the cold until he was warmed, fed and properly mended. For the longer she looked at him, the thinner, the hungrier and the more ragged he looked to the motherly woman.

"A body would think," she observed, "that some female in your company would look after an orphan."

In defense of his fellow emigrants Seumas explained that most of them were men; what few wives had come with their husbands were hard put to keep them respectable. "Six of us men batch it together in a wigwam and do for ourselves as best we can." Then lest he appear to be asking for sympathy, the lad launched into a humorous account of his own efforts to cover the yawning gaps in his garments with scraps of buckskin as Mrs. Field had suggested.

"But I had me trouble for me pains," he concluded. "For me hands were so cold I run needle and thread through me own hide which was colder, and never discovered me mistake till I tried to get out of me britches at bedtime. It couldn't be done till I'd ripped off the patches." Cocking a humorous eyebrow, the boy finished his tale. "So here I am, no better off than before."

Faith regarded him in horror. "Do you mean to say you tried to patch your own clothes whilst they were *on you?*"

"How else?" he inquired. " 'Twas too cold to sit round in me birthday suit and I've got no other besides these duds."

"Then march yourself straight up those stairs," Faith ordered. "You'll find some old clothes in the attic to wear while we mend yours. Here, take a candle, but mind you don't set the house afire."

" 'We,' " thought Connie. "Not me, Ma. Do you think I'd prick *my* fingers for that fellow? I see through him, if you don't. The fish he brought were bait to catch more help from this family." When the boy had disappeared with a lighted candle, as ordered, Connie wondered what she should do if ordered to fry his fish.

Faith, however, did not trust so delicate a chore to the girl, but directed her to warm up some beans left over from dinner.

While these preparations were in progress Ash came in. "Do I smell fresh fish?" He exclaimed. "Where did they come from in this weather?"

Before Faith could reply, the angler reappeared in shabby old buckskins and with his own threadbare garments over an arm. The warmth of Ash's greeting atoned for his daughter's cool reception and served to increase her dislike for the boy. It was hard to hear Pa press for a report on his studies, harder yet to hear how he was learning to read from the reader for which her own precious book had been exchanged. Hardest of all did Connie find it to listen to the boy's report that he stood at the top of the class in addition, a bit of information Ash had to pry out of him, like the meat from a nut.

But when Ash inquired how he got on with his schoolmates, Seumas became even more laconic. All he would say was, "All right."

He showed no signs of conflict, no black eye, no bruises or broken knuckles. Therefore Connie leaped to the conclusion that the Irishman had failed to live up to his boast of never turning tail on a fight.

Ash, however, knew better, for like the tomboy's victory, that of the "bogtrotter" was the talk of the taverns. In Ash's opinion, it was Seumas himself who was "all right." He liked the lad all the better for reticence regarding his prowess at fisticuffs. But it was not in Ash's nature to be fulsome in praise. All he said was, "Good."

After the meal Connie escaped from the table to the dry sink where she hid her hurt in the dishpan. When Faith set about mending the visitor's garments, Ash noticed for the first time what his protégé wore.

"Let the lad keep the buckskins," he said. "Don't waste your time on those rags, wife; let the lad swap them for books, and if he needs more rags for that purpose, let him make up the poundage from our supply."

A wooden bowl fell from Connie's hand and clattered on the floor. No one seemed to hear or heed.

Faith said, "Let us supply all the rags needed to keep the boy in books. When I've patched these clothes proper, he can wear them under the buckskins. A body needs double protection 'when the days begin to lengthen and the cold begins to strengthen.'"

Connie took comfort in the ancient adage. Long months of cold weather ahead meant that spring was far off. After Seumas had gone off in the buckskins and the Fields had gone to their beds, the girl warmed herself with thoughts of all the things which might happen that winter to prevent the hated marriage. Although there was no longer any danger from Indian attack in Ohio, the state was still filled with dangers. Bears had been known to come on a hunter from behind and hug him to death before he could turn and take aim. And the bite of a rattlesnake was nearly always fatal. Both these creatures hibernated in winter, however. The chief winter danger was from wolves and from falling trees. Mr. Jones was engaged in tree cutting. Connie caught herself with a gasp. Did she actually wish the widowman would be crushed to death by one of his own trees? No, oh *no!* Such a thought was sinful. Besides, there were his children. Thought of ten little Joneses being left fatherless as well as motherless wrung her heart. She might hate the father, but she could not hate the children about whom she knew nothing except that the older ones were all girls. The girls were not much younger than herself, perhaps, which was much too young to nurse toddlers and a cradle infant through croup, measles, lung fever and other winter ailments. This fact strengthened Connie's belief that, before spring, Mr. Jones must surely see for himself the necessity of wedding an experienced older woman rather than a girl just turned seventeen in November.

Chapter 5

WILD BEASTS multiplied in the forest much faster than domestic animals in the settlements. For flocks and herds continued to be depleted in spite of the liberal bounty paid for wolf scalps and the redoubled efforts of individual hunters.

In December the citizens of Cuyahoga County got together with those of adjoining Medina County in organizing a general hunt.

On the day set for the start of the Cleveland hunters, Ash was cleaning his rifle in front of the hearth while his womenfolk prepared a lunch to pack in his saddlebags. All three Fields were startled when a heavy hand pounded on the door. Before Ash could rise to answer the knock, the door opened and Mr. Hannibal Jones came in, stamping the snow off his boots on the bearskin rug.

With a curt nod for the women, Mr. Jones said, "Well, Field, here I be. Reason I ain't been around sooner is I've been so all-fired busy. Now, seein' the chance to kill two birds with one stone, so to speak——" he broke off to wink at the girl.

Connie's blood seemed to congeal. Her hand shook so, that when she laid down the bread knife, she cut herself instead of the loaf.

It was the loaf Mr. Jones eyed as he said, "Looks to me like fust-class bread. You bake it, my gal?"

Connie supressed a desire to cry, *I'm not your girl, yet* and said instead, "Yes, sir."

Proud of her daughter's culinary progress, Faith added, "She baked a pie, too. It looks fine. We'll have it for supper, if you'll stay."

"I was countin' on doin' so," replied the visitor, "and sleepin' here, too, if it's agreeable." Again he winked at the girl.

"Of course it's agreeable," said Ash. "Aren't you practically one of the family? By the way, Hannibal, how is *your* family?"

Mr. Jones replied that all the "young 'uns" were in good health. Indeed, "the colts" were growing so frisky "the fillies" couldn't keep them in the paddock; they were forever running away into the woods. "It ain't nowise safe. That's one reason I figgered on jin'in this hunt."

Both hunters fell to discussing arrangements. It seemed that advance preparations had been made over in Medina County by Judge Hinkley, one of the largest landowners there. The Judge had hired surveyors to blaze the forest trees in a wide circle around the county seat where all the hunters were to foregather for the attack in force.

While the menfolks were absorbed in this subject Faith slipped upstairs to prepare a bed for the unexpected guest. When the wagon-on-the-wall struck nine, she reappeared to say that she hoped Mr. Jones would sleep warm and comfortable.

Mr. Jones replied, "Sleepin' alone is cold comfort, ma'am, no matter where. I figgered on gittin' spliced today, gittin' me a nice warm bedmate. Then it slipped my mind when Ash and me got to gassin'. But it ain't too late now, I presume to say. If the justice of the peace has gone to bed, we could wake him up. How about it, Ash?"

For once Ash was taken aback. He gasped, then reminded Hannibal that certain legal steps were necessary before the ceremony, such as posting notice of intent to wed.

"Ye mean banns?" said Mr. Jones, looking annoyed. "I figgured folks out here was free of such nonsense."

Connie sat as though frozen to her chair. Until his remark about the cold comfort of lonely nights, it had not occurred to her that Mr. Jones expected her to share his bed as well as his burdens. In all her short life Constitution Field had never fainted. Now the room seemed to spin round like a flaxwheel. Her eyes grew dim, and through the roaring in her ears she heard her mother's startled voice.

"Ash, quick!" Faith cried, "Get down the bottle and give the girl a drop."

When the heady draught had revived her daughter, she said, "I could do with a drop myself. Matter of fact, a nightcap would do us all a world of good; help us get a good night's sleep."

There was no sleep for Connie that night. If Mr. Jones considered banns nonsense, did he perhaps look upon marriage vows as equally senseless? Fears of her maiden chamber being invaded finally subsided when loud snores came through the closed door from the chamber across the hall. Nevertheless that raucous trumpeting kept Connie awake and shuddering at the thought of future nights closer, much closer, to the source of those dreadful sounds.

She was still shivering under a pile of blankets when she heard Mr. Jones clomp down the stairs. Other sounds from below, the snapping of fresh fuel thrown on the coals, the rattle of chains on the crane, announced that breakfast was in the making. Ordinarily, Connie would have hurried down to help. But this morning she only cowered deeper in the feather bed until sounds outside assured her that the hunters had ridden away. She breathed a little easier then. For a day or so, at least, four or five at most, the blockhouse

46

would be free of menfolks. But they would return, and what then? Would Mr. Jones insist on having the banns published at once? Or would Pa insist that he wait until spring, as originally agreed?

In her extremity, Connie appealed to her mother. What did Ma think of Mr. Jones's remarks last night? What had Pa said about those remarks after Mr. Jones retired?

Faith replied with caution. Menfolks sometimes forgot to weigh their words before womenfolks—spoke a bit rough. She admitted that Mr. Jones's words had been ill-chosen, indelicate. Faith chose her own words with the utmost delicacy; she spoke of "wifely duty," of "resignation to woman's lot," and wound up with something about "God's will."

At the moment Connie was more concerned about Ashbel Field's will. "Ma," she pleaded, "couldn't you talk Pa out of this idea?"

Faith shook her head. "I'd no more think of questioning your father's judgment than I'd question God's," she said.

Connie said no more. But when Pa came home she meant to put in her own plea for a change of mind. And if she failed, what then? All she could think of was Granny's old saying, *Sufficient unto the day is the evil thereof.*

Several days later Ashbel rode into his barnyard alone. The limp body of a deer was draped across his cantle, and on the pommel he steadied a magnificent pair of moose antlers. Hannibal, he said, had taken the moose meat and two more deer straight to his own smokehouse. "With all those mouths to fill, Hannibal needs more meat than we do," Ash remarked as he went about the business of skinning the deer.

While he worked, he related the tale of the great hunt. Dark had fallen by the time all the hunters arrived at the rendezvous in Medina. "It was like war days," he said. "We made camp and received orders. The men were told off in pairs or small bands, each assigned to a post on the blazed circle. Next morning the company broke up, all squads going to the places appointed on the perimeter. It took all day, for that circle enclosed an enormous amount of territory. All the posts were established by dark, however, and at this season when the forest was bare of foliage, the circle of campfires could been seen stretching away for miles. You could hear the songs and laughter of the men even further, for the night was cold and still; men took turns keeping their fires alive, else nobody would have lived to see the dawn."

Ash broke off to hold up the hide of the deer, stripped from the carcass. "Look at that, my girl," he said. "Stretched on the sunny side of the barn all winter, it will be well cured by spring and make you a nice rug for your bridal trip across the river."

Connie did not want to be reminded of that journey and to change the subject, she said, "Tell us more about the hunt, Pa. What happened next morning?"

Nothing loath, Ash took up the tale. Orders were to be ready to start before dawn at the signal. "We heard the shot on our left and fired once in reply, heard the sound repeated on our right and then more shots further off, growing fainter and fainter until the last one died away. It was time to go. And go we went, back toward the center of the circle, men and dogs and guns all making an unearthly racket to scare the game out of holes and caves and hollow trees, bears and deer and——"

"And wolves," Connie put in, holding up a scalp pulled from one of the saddlebags.

"Lots of wolves, yes," Ash said. "We killed so many of the varments that the sheep of both counties will be a lot safer from now on. And travelers, too. By the way, my girl, you'd better take all those scalps in my bag to the courthouse right away before the rest of our men come home and clean out the county treasury. The bounty on those scalps would buy a wedding gown."

Connie protested, "But Pa, I don't want a wedding gown, or——"

Faith interrupted in haste, "You needn't to go to that expense, Ash. Remember that lovely lutestring Margaret Blennerhassett gave me to wear at the ball on the island? Well, I never wore it again. I've saved it careful all these years for our darter to wear when she's wed. But she will need some other things. A good stout calico dress, or two. And a bonnet and shawl. If," she added, doubtfully, "you can afford so much."

"Get whatever you think needful," Ash replied, "and charge it to me, provided the total is no more than the bounty on these scalps." Then, scarcely glancing at his daughter, he ordered, "On your way, girl."

As her feet carried her obediently toward the counthouse, Connie's mind was a riot of insurrection. It was clear that any further appeal to her father was hopeless. But what he had said about the success of the Hinchley hunt gave her fresh hope that escape was possible, after all. Now that the danger of being killed by wild beasts was greatly reduced, just as soon as the danger of freezing to death was past, she would run away.

Connie's plans, perforce, had to be carefully concealed. Faith's plans, on the contrary, were known all over Cleveland by nightfall of the day mother and daughter made extensive purchases at Taylor's Store. Had Connie expected to wear these purchases, she might have pleaded for a voice in their choosing, pleaded for something prettier than the drab and durable bonnet and shawl better suited to her mother's age. As it was, she did not even raise an objection to a brown bombazine dress length or speak for a gayly flowered chintz instead of the ugly striped calico.

When the calico was cut, basted together, and tried on for fit, Faith herself was dismayed to see how those stripes accentuated the girl's height and thinness. Why, folks would think the bride was pining away! This would never do! In her anxiety to correct this impression, Faith sheared off the long full skirt at the knees, ripped apart the bottom section, and set Connie to stitching it up again with the stripes running the other way. When both sections had been rejoined, the effect was a bit odd, even in Faith's eyes, but at least it did reduce Connie's resemblance to a beanpole.

Although the girl had not expected ever to appear in public in that gown, she was obliged to wear it at several sewing bees given in her honor that winter. For as soon as it became known that she would be a spring bride, every female in town took a hand in the preparations. Hitherto "that Field gal," whose notions were as unorthodox as her first name, had considered odd. As a prospective bride, however, she was the center of friendly interest. Mr. Jones was not known, personally, to any of these women, but their husbands reported him to be a man of substance. The "Field gal," it seemed, was doing very well for herself. Later, when it became known that she was to acquire a ready-made family as well as a husband, the majority of her mother's contemporaries still con-

49

sidered the match a good one. The care of ten stepchildren (and doubtless a brood of her own, in due time) would knock those notions about book learning out of the foolish girl's head.

Connie was showered with good wishes and with gifts for her hope chest. There were homespun linen bolster slips edged with knitted lace, towels marked with the letter F, or with F and C intertwined, and sundry intimate garments. Some half-dozen generous souls pooled their cherished collections of bright silk and wool scraps for a crazy quilt.

The actual quilting of this work of art was the occasion for the largest party of all. And because Alfred Kelley's new stone house had the largest front room, it was there the frame was set up in advance. On that frame was stretched the kaleidoscopic result of the joint project. Over it was spread a thin old blanket, and this was covered with a length of "boughten" material known as "Turkey red."

On the day of the party all female Cleveland converged on the Kelley house bringing needles, thread, thimbles and shears, together with "covered dishes" of goodies for the feast to follow when the quilt was completed.

Constitution, as queen bee, was not expected to bring anything or to do any of the quilting. She was given the seat of honor close to the frame and then ignored while fingers flew and tongues ran on and on about what beau was "sparkin'" which "gal," and which of the recent brides was "expectin'."

It was not until these absorbing topics had been exhausted that the hostess introduced another subject currently being discussed in the taverns. Not that young Mrs. Kelley ever visited such low resorts. Goodness no! But as the wife of the new prosecuting attorney, she felt well qualified to give account of the trial going on in the courthouse.

The bare facts of the case were well known. It concerned two runaway slaves whose Virginia master, convinced they were headed for Canada, had advertised widely in Ohio newspapers that he would pay five hundred dollars reward for the return of his property. Joseph Keeler, a Cuyahoga County farmer, had caught the fugitives in his corncrib and started to take them back to Virginia. But the trio had gone no further than Hudson when Keeler himself was arrested for kidnapping. As this was the first trial of a slave hunter in Cleveland, public opinion was varied and confused. The prosecutor's wife, naturally, considered Keeler guilty as charged. Other quilters questioned his motives. Was Joe taking those blacks back to Virginia as a matter of principle? Or was he doing so purely for the sake of that reward?

For some time Constitution Field held aloof from the controversy. None of these women knew what it was all about; their opinions were formed in their hearts and not in their heads. Connie's own heart went out to the fugitives. She too hated bondage in any form. But she had been brought up to respect the law and the law said——

Involuntarily, she repeated aloud, "The law says fugitive slaves must be returned to their legal owners. That's in the Ordinance of 1787 which governs the frontier. And when Congress passed the Fugitive Slave law in 1793, it made anybody who harbored runaway slaves liable to five hundred dollars fine." Turning toward her hostess, the girl went on, "Mr. Kelley is prosecuting Mr. Keeler under that law, I presume to say."

The prosecutor's wife stared, then stammered, "I—I w-wouldn't presume to say."

Then one of the older quilters regarded the guest of honor sternly. "You presume too much, gal," she asserted. "What do *you* know about the law?"

Tone and look goaded the girl into saying, "Not nearly so much as I wish I did. But I do know about those two laws, for I read all about them in my father's law books."

All the quilters were staring at Connie now, staring coldly. And Faith, chilled by this sudden change in temperature and fearful that Connie might reduce the social atmosphere still lower by further unwise confessions, said hastily, "Ash has forbid our darter to read any more law books."

"Well!" ejaculated a plump matron, "Well, I should hope so!" She continued to stare at the culprit with disapproval as did all the other quilters. Their thoughts were plain to read. Mothers of sons were sincerely thankful their boys hadn't taken "a shine" to the Field gal. The sooner this Mr. Jones took her away from the vicinity of her father's law office, the better for all concerned.

51

Connie was thankful that her own thoughts were not equally transparent. She knew very well what the verdict of these home-bodies would be if they knew she was planning to run away from home. For all their sympathy expressed for the runaway slaves, there would be none for a runaway bride.

The verdict of the court, the following day, freed Joseph Keeler of the kidnapping charge. But Black Sam and Martin were not set free. Under an officer of the law they were escorted back to Virginia. The whole affair convinced Constitution Field that she must stop only dreaming of escape and take immediate action to that end. Already the first signs of spring were in the air: the sound of running waters, the cawing of crows, and the honking of wild geeses, northbound. A girl, however, could not take wing, like a bird. Nor, in petticoats, could she set off on foot with any hope of outdistancing pursuit.

Connie was at home in the saddle, and a mare and a gelding occupied stalls in the Field stable. Both animals belonged to her father, however. If she rode one away and was overtaken, she was liable to arrest for horse-stealing—a criminal offense. And while she had no fear that her father would prosecute her to the full extent of the law, even he might not be able to save her from the penalty—hanging. Connie had no intention of taking that risk. What she did intend to do was to discard her petticoats in favor of her brothers' discarded buckskin breeches. Those given that brash Irishman couldn't have cleaned out the supply, for Ma never threw anything away.

Connie did not dare search the attic by day. It must be done at night after Ma and Pa were abed, and only then with great care not to wake them. As the girl was never given more than an inch of candle to light her to bed, each nocturnal exploration was brief, and more than a week passed before she had collected all the old tunics and breeches under her bed. Then they had to be tried on for fit. This took more time, for although she was as slender of hip and leg as any boy, the girl was far less flat as to chest. Eventually, however, she found a tunic with a deep collar, heavily fringed, which concealed the swelling curves of her young bosom. These two articles of apparel, together with a battered old tricorn hat,

Connie hid between her feather bed and the bedcords, and she returned the remainder of the shabby old garments to the attic.

There was only one more thing to do. She must cut off her beautiful hair. Connie was pardonably proud of that hair, but the sacrifice seemed essential to the success of her masquerade. A shorn head would call for explanation, however, so that the supreme sacrifice must be deferred until the very last moment.

Chapter 6

THE APRIL NIGHT when the full moon rose and set late offered the best chance of escape. Even the village watchman was apt to doze in some doorway toward morning, and by sunrise, when her absence was discovered, the fugitive would be many miles from Cleveland.

Connie knew that discovery would terrify her mother, and to set Faith's fears at rest to some extent, she scribbled a note saying that she was bound for Athens, but "please don't tell Pa." Then, realizing the futility of asking Faith to keep any secret from Ash, she burned the note in the last flickering flame of her candle. It was not until she was left in darkness that the girl remembered what she had put off until the last possible moment—the final sacrificial rite. Well, now she would have to wait until moonrise to sever her braid —sever the pride of her girlhood and the life she was leaving.

For hours she lay wakeful, waiting, waiting for what seemed an eternity, before the moon peered in at her window flooding the bare little room with eerie light. The room was cold as she pulled on her brother's breeches and tunic, thrust her feet into moccasins, and padded across the rag rug to stand before the little cracked mirror over the chest of drawers. But it was not the cold that made her shiver as she picked up the shears. What she was about to do now seemed more than a sacrifice. Wrought up as she was, it seemed a sacrilege. Was there no other way? No way she could keep her hair concealed? What about that moth-eaten coonskin cap left hanging too long on the peg in the attic?

Connie laid down the shears, tiptoed into the storeroom and returned with the disreputable relic of frontier days. But when she pulled it down over her head until the fur touched her eyebrows, that long braid still hung several feet below the animal's tail. She tried winding the braid around her head, but over all that bulk the cap would not go. With a sigh, the girl picked up the shears again, and again laid them down, loosened her hair and replaited it in two sections, then wound them around her head, one at a time. Now, indeed, the cap could be pulled on. It was a tight fit far from comfortable, but a glance in the glass made certain that it completely concealed every strand of black hair.

Connie felt in the pockets of the tunic to make sure fishline and tinderbox were there, hung an extra pair of moccasins around her neck by the thongs, and cautiously felt her way down the stair. In the moonlit buttery she cut johnnycake, crammed it into another pocket, and was about to thrust the bread knife through her belt, when she realized that a bare blade would be far too dangerous to carry. Ash's hunting knife in its sheath hung from a peg beside the back door and, seizing it, Connie crept out, feeling like a thief— a thief in the night.

Dawn found her walking swiftly along the southbound road many miles from home. As her feet padded forward, her thoughts went back to the blockhouse where, by now, her flight must have been discovered. Even without that note she had burned, Pa might very well surmise her destination. Indeed, the more she thought about it, the more certain Connie grew that he would pursue his runaway rowan intent on taking her back across his saddlebow, as he had brought home the dead deer. Only she would be alive and suffering all the torments of those captured blacks returned to bondage.

No one afoot, however young and fleet, could outdistance a horseman. Connie took to the underbrush, out of sight of the road, but never beyond earshot. From time to time as the day wore on, she heard voices, a horse's whinny, or the creak of a cart. But none of

54

these sounds disclosed the identity of the travelers or whether they sought a fugitive. Her fellow-feeling for those runaway slaves increased toward dusk when she came over a rise to see a cleared common surrounded by log cabins. This could be no other place but Hudson.

The natural thing to do at that hour was to look around for a sign marking some place of public entertainment. But not only was Connie penniless, she was afraid, afraid to test her disguise in a taproom filled with men. Candles flared up behind windows as she hurried past, unseen at this time of day when womenfolks busied themselves at hearths, and menfolks in barns. The moon, which had lighted her escape that morning, would not rise again for many hours, and after leaving the settlement she could no longer see the road. The only thing visible was a ruddy rectangle in the distance. Overcome by a sudden pressing need of human companionship, the girl stumbled along a lane toward that open doorway.

In breeches, she looked much younger than seventeen, and when her voice cracked with agitation as she asked leave to sleep in the haymow, the settler's wife took her for an adolescent lad. The request was not an unusual one on the frontier, nor was the woman's insistence that the traveler must first take potluck. Refusal would arouse suspicion, and Connie sidled into the cabin where the only light came from the fire smouldering under the kettle on the crane.

Almost at once three men stamped in to sit down around the table without removing their headgear. This lack of good manners encouraged Connie to come out of hiding and bestride a vacant stool.

As the woman dipped rabbit stew from the kettle, she poured out a stream of questions to which the menfolks replied with grunts. Connie aped them, mumbled something unintelligible when the woman inquired her name. And when the woman said, "Lookin' for yer folks, sonny?" the girl grunted, "Aye. Brudder, Athens."

"My stars!" ejaculated the woman. "That's an awful fer piece from here. Better git straight to bed and make an early start t'morrer. Sorry we ain't got no extry bed in the house, but the hay's clean and dry, and yer welcome to come in to breakfast."

"Thanks, ma'am," muttered Connie, and she escaped to the barn where, worn out with fatigue and excitement, she fell asleep at once. The crow of a cock woke her. Fear of facing these folks by daylight was greater than hunger and, scrambling down the ladder, she was off toward the main road before the cabin inmates were astir.

If Pa had followed her yesterday, he would now be ahead instead of behind her. When would he reach that conclusion and turn back? For turn back he would, rather than wait to waylay her, Connie was sure. Ashbel Field was not a patient man. Therefore she walked warily, close to the side of the road, keeping a sharp lookout for approaching horsemen and both ears cocked for hoofbeats in the rear, wondering how far the news of the runaway bride had spread from Cleveland. Such news must reach every corner of Cuyahoga County in a matter of days. Then those folks back in the cabin would remember a strange "boy" in buckskins. She must risk no more cabins, no more haymows, in this part of the world. Better to risk a night alone in the woods, without a fire, than curious eyes in clearings.

As sunset reddened the sky above the treetops, Connie climbed wearily into the crotch of a giant beech, munched her last crumb of johnnycake, and settled herself for the night. Fear of falling kept her from sleeping soundly, but she did doze off from time to time between squeaks and rustlings nearby and the far-off weird cry of an owl.

Next day she trudged on until, at length, she came to a deep ravine cut by a rushing torrent. This must be the Cuyahoga deflected from its course by the height of land. Wheel tracks disappearing into the foaming stream indicated a fording place, useless at this season of high water. Connie sat down to rest and gather her wits. A line of rocks sticking up through the flood suggested that other spring travelers might have crossed here on foot. The girl rose, hunched herself, and leaped. She leaped again and again like a deer, landing breathless on the further shore.

That afternoon she came to a lake, small in comparison with the great inland sea at Cleveland, yet a body of water large enough to convince her that it was one of the chain forming the headwaters of many rivers. The trail, for such it had now become, followed the marshy shore, and, rounding a turn, Connie stopped short, her heart beating wildly. Coiled in the narrow path was a reptile. Small green gliders held no terrors for a girl who had caught many of them by the tail and snapped off their heads. But this creature was neither small nor green; it was large and scaly and of a repulsive mottled yellow and brown. Although the head was tucked out of sight among the coils, the protruding tail told her that the ugly thing was a rattlesnake.

Could she get by without rousing it? Connie glanced about, saw that the trees on either side of the trail were rooted in water, and knew that if she left the road it would be at the risk of treading on the rattler's mate. Even if she managed to creep up on this one without rousing it, and could seize that tail with all its rattles, it was far too big to be snapped like a garter snake. With a gun, or even a bow and arrow, she might have shot the sleeping menace from a safe distance. But her only weapon was the hunting knife; to use the knife she would have to stand directly over the creature and strike quickly, faster than it could strike her with its deadly fangs. Connie was swift in all her motions, but snakes were swifter —swifter than lightning.

With great caution, she backed away. Cautiously she felt about for a good-sized stone, found one and hurled it with all her might upon the snake, not with any hope of killing it, but hoping that, startled, it would slither off into the swamp. Her aim was good. The stone landed squarely on top of the coils, and when the snake began to thrash about she realized that, for the moment at least, it was powerless to do her harm. Connie could have leaped over the writhing coils to safety, but some innate hatred of Eve's ancient enemy made her leap upon it, slashing madly with the hunting knife. Then she ran and ran until faintness forced her to drop upon a fallen tree. As her head cleared, she realized that the odd feeling at the pit of her stomach was not due entirely to the danger just escaped. She had eaten nothing all day. At this season there were neither berries nor nuts in the wilderness, nothing edible except— slowly something remembered from childhood came back to her. Pa had told about one of his trips through this very region and how, at a trader's cabin, he had dined on broiled rattlesnake and found it good.

Connie retraced her steps slowly. Yes, there was the snake, sprawled motionless across the trail—dead. She had skinned many an eel, yet shuddered while handling this scaly reptile. Gritting her teeth she finished the loathsome chore, piled pieces of the fine white flesh on a bark, and carried it off beyond sight of the mutilated carcass. It was a matter of moments to gather twigs for a fire and set her supper over it on a forked stick. It looked good; it smelled good. And when she sampled the meat it tasted delicious. Nevertheless, she hoped her first meal of rattlesnake would be her last of the kind.

When, where, and how she would find further sustenance Connie had no idea as she trudged on past the last of the lakes. Now all the streams ran the other way. She was over the height of land, out of Cuyahoga County at last. As danger of discovery decreased, danger of wild beasts grew, for this was deep wilderness beyond the circle of the Hinchley hunt, beyond clearings or cabins—the very back of beyond. Deer never attacked human beings unless held at bay. Nor did wolves fall upon travelers by daylight. But what if, rounding a turn, she came face to face with a bear?

Fortunately, Connie met no such dilemma. What she was forced to face was a choice between sharing a cave with some forest denizen or spending a wet night in the open. For rain came at twilight. Although later in the season the foliage would form a protecting canopy, as yet the young leaves were just a thin green mist through which the drizzle dripped steadily. The best refuge Connie could find was between the roots of a giant elm where she managed to scrape together enough dry dead leaves and twigs for a tiny blaze. A fire would keep wolves away, provided she could keep it alive. This chore kept her awake and busy and, if neither warm nor dry, at least free from overwhelming loneliness.

Rain ceased with dawn, and wet and famished she trudged on until the trail disappeared into a stream swollen by the night's downpour. No log bridged the torrent, nor were any stepping stones visible. Wheel-tracks led to a fording place, however, and Connie sat down to wait until the flood should subside or a cart come along. As the wait might last for days, she would have to catch a meal or starve. An overturned stone revealed a crawler with which she baited her hook and cast it into the stream. Almost at once something tugged at the line, and in a few moments she pulled in an ugly-looking thing with a blunt nose and cat's whiskers. This fish, cleaned and broiled, was less toothsome than rattle-snake, but food of any sort was more than welcome.

Welcome, too, after the rain was sunshine, and Connie pulled off the cap and let down her hair to dry. Birds, also drying plumage, raised such a loud chorus of joy as to drown the creak of cart wheels. It was a belated sense of something at her shoulder that made Connie turn—turn to look squarely into the face of a patient old horse. Over the animal's drooping head she saw the driver, an old man, moonfaced and rotund of body.

"Off der road, squaw," he shouted in thick gutturals.

Squaw! So that's what I look like with my hair down, thought Connie. But who and what was he, and where did he come from? Certainly not from New England where folks talked through their noses instead of swallowing their words. Dimly, she recalled hearing that a remnant of Tuscarora had come back to ancestral hunting grounds where Pennsylvania Dutch folks had set up a mission. Surely any missionary could be trusted. Raising her voice, Connie called after the cart.

The Dutchman checked his horse and looked back. Then, evidently concluding that she was harmless, he said, "Koom! Get der cart in."

When she had clambered over the high wheel, he slapped the reins on the rump of the horse which obediently waded into the stream. When they were safe across, they went on in silence, broken only by the creak of the cart wheels. Connie was wondering what she should do on reaching the Indian village where she could not hope to pass as a squaw. The old man seemed to be pondering some problem of his own.

At length he turned to stare at the girl. "You milk cow, yes? Churn, maybe?" And when she nodded, he explained, *"Meine frau ist krank.* What you say? Seek? You bring der butter, I pay you."

Pay! Did he mean money, *cash* money? It did not seem likely, but at least she would eat, and well from the look of him. His small china blue eyes were upon her and she nodded agreement.

"Gut!" grunted the Dutchman and he prodded the horse into a trot.

Where the trail was joined by a narrower green track the horse turned in of its own accord, and after awhile the cart emerged from the forest into a considerable clearing. The driver drew rein before a small cabin, and when the girl got down, the horse went on to the big barn. Inside the cabin Connie found a gaunt old woman lying in a bunk, face to the wall. At the sound of footfall the woman turned, stared wildly, and screeched.

For a moment Connie thought the creature demented. Then she realized that the sick woman, too, had taken her for an Indian and was afraid. These folks, then, could not be missionaries, but were simple settlers. Connie tried to smile reassuringly, but the woman pulled the blanket over her head and lay still.

Connie abandoned the silence that was her own protection and shouted, "Don't be scared, ma'am. I'm no Injun. Your man brought me to take care of you."

The sick woman peered out from under the blanket. "He went fer *unsere Tochter*," she said. "You be'n't her."

At that moment "he" came in to explain that their daughter was tied down with a sick baby, so he had brought "dis squaw" instead.

"Squaw," repeated the woman. "Her be'n't no squaw." Then, to the girl, "Who be you? Where you belong? Vat you do here?"

Connie confessed then, trusting these folks would not trouble to report her whereabouts. The tale was punctuated with grunts of amazement from the simple old pair who, obviously, did not believe a word of it but were quite willing to accept her as an answer to prayer.

For a week the girl worked hard, preparing meals, waiting on the invalid, and tending the dairy. At the end of that time the old folks' daughter appeared on horseback with the infant, now well enough to travel.

True to his promise, the Dutchman, whose name Connie never could pronounce or remember, gave her a handful of copper coins and the suggestion that she might get a ride with the cheese merchant, due any day now. Through gestures, rather than words, the old man explained that the merchant made a regular circuit through the countryside buying cheese to resell in the Cambridge market. This town, situated on Zane's Trace, was some distance east of Zanesville, where Connie was headed, but with money in her pocket, she had no doubt she could get a stage there for points west, perhaps even as far as Lancaster, if the money held out.

Neither the day nor the hour of the merchant's arrival was certain, and it so happened that he came on her in the milkhouse without her cap. She was further flustered to find that he was not, as she had expected, just another kindly old Dutchman, but a big brawny young man with a look in his eye she did not like. On the spur of the moment, however, she could think of no better excuse for delaying her journey than the worn state of her moccasins which, the merchant pointed out, with a guffaw, was no excuse at all. The Cambridge cobbler would make repairs while she waited for the stage.

Connie cast an appealing look at the Dutchman, hoping he would beg her to stay on. But his candid countenance betrayed his eagerness to be rid of this vagrant, now that she was no longer needed. There was nothing for the girl to do but clamber aboard the cart.

The road was so filled with stumps and potholes as to require all the driver's attention to avoid overturning the cart. He paid not the slightest attention to his companion, and gradually her fears subsided. After some time the road ran into deep forest, and here the man brought his horse to a stop. Connie expected him to get down, perhaps to inspect the animal's hooves. What he did was transfer the reins to his right hand and throw his left arm around the girl.

When Connie struggled, he laughed and hugged her tighter. "Playin' hard-to-get, hey?" he said. "Don't try to make me think a gal travelin' by her lone, and in britches, ain't lookin' for a lark!" With that he kissed her full on the mouth, bruisingly, brutally.

Rage, revulsion and sheer terror gave the girl strength to fight free, leap over the wheel, and run into the forest. When she paused for breath behind a tree, she heard him shout, "Come back, gal! Don't be a fool! You'll only git yerself lost in there."

Connie neither obeyed nor replied. Better to lose her way than her virtue. That fear made her heart beat so fast that she could not run, could only take refuge behind another forest giant, draw her knife, and wait. If the brute followed her, she would defend herself or die in the attempt. The thud of her heart was so loud in her ears that she thought surely the sound must lead the man to her hiding place. Then, as the moments dragged by, her heart slowly quieted, and she heard the cart creak away in the distance.

What should she do now, Connie wondered. Should she return to the farm where she was no longer wanted? Should she follow the cart to Cambridge—at a safe distance? Or should she trust her own sense of direction and strike out across country toward the Muskingum River and follow it down to Zane's Trace?

Connie decided to take this third course even though the soles of both pair of moccasins were worn through and her feet were, literally, on the ground. The ground was rough, making travel painful, and she managed to endure the pain only by focusing all her thoughts on holding to a general southwesterly direction through virgin forest, guided by the moss on the north side of the trees and by rivulets running toward the river. As fear of becoming lost diminished, fear of encounters with more strange men grew. Until now her experience with males had been limited to schoolboys and respectable middle-aged citizens, but the cheese merchant's brutal kiss had awakened awareness that no female was safe with all men. The chances of avoiding men in the forest were better than her chances of avoiding bears, but if she lived to reach Zanesville, more rough characters were certain to be encountered there.

Could she pass for a boy, if she kept her head covered? Instinctively Connie put up a hand. What she felt was not coonskin. It was her own glossy hair. The cap must have fallen off during her scuffle with the cheese merchant. Anyway, it was gone—gone for good. Well, that settled one question at last. She sat down on a log and uncoiled her coronet. Then she unsheathed the knife. Killing that snake had been easier. A serpent was a woman's natural enemy. A woman's hair was a part of herself.

Connie drew a long breath, took a firm grip on the knife with one hand, in the other a braid, and slashed it off close to the nape of her neck. A moment later the second braid lay beside the first across her knees. The girl stared at the ruin, overcome with a sense of having committed a crime—a crime against her womanhood. Then she laid her cropped head down upon her lost glory and wept —wept with all the abandon of a strong nature too long repressed.

Chapter 7

DAYS LATER a bone-weary, footsore girl reached the Muskingum River. The road that followed its meanderings was well traveled but, still shy from her experience with the cheese merchant, she shook her cropped head at all offers of a lift and limped on. Toward evening the roar of the falls at Zanesville was audible, and following the road through outlying farms, she came at length to the long covered bridge which carried the Trace over the broad stream into the town.

The wide main street was crowded with goods-wagons, all larger and fancier than any seen in Cleveland. Blue bodies mounted in huge red wheels were arched by dirty white canvas that rose at either end and sagged in the middle like a sway-backed old horse. The teams being detached from these wagons were young and husky, and although all of them must have come far that day, a few frisky horses were still hard to manage. Long whips cracked sharply while drivers cursed these recalcitrant beasts, other drivers, the vile roads, and life in general.

Cleveland was never like this! The courage which had sustained the fugitive through the wilderness quailed at sight of so many rough men and the sound of their loose language. None of the teamsters gave her a glance, however, and with a quaking heart she entered a door under a swinging sign offering *Refreshment for man and hors.*

The taproom was blue with tobacco smoke through which she saw men seated, eating and drinking and pounding on the tables with empty mugs as they called for more beer, hard cider or Monongahela whiskey. The smell of liquor and human sweat was strong and acrid, but Connie had eaten nothing for days and hunger overcame disgust. She slid into a vacant chair, wondering how to order the smallest quantity of drink with the largest amount of food she could pay for.

This problem was settled by a slovenly barmaid who set a mug of beer before Connie, then a nicked crockery plate loaded with steaming meat and vegetables. "Two bits," she demanded, holding out a dirty palm.

Connie could only stare, speechless. She did not have that much money.

"I said two bits, boy," repeated the slattern. "If ye ain't got it, what business ye got comin' in here a-tall?"

A man at the next table turned and, over the steaming food, Connie stared into the face of her third brother. It was six years since she had seen him, but his face was still the Field face—dark, heavy-browed and handsome. During the interval he must have prospered, for instead of faded homespun, Ezekiel Field wore a fine greatcoat of puce broadcloth with big brass buttons, and on his black head a fawn-colored, bell-crowned beaver hat sat jauntily.

"What's the matter, bub?" he inquired. "Broke?" Then, without waiting for the obvious answer, he tossed a coin at the barmaid, telling her, "Scat, gal."

Famished though she was, Connie longed to trail the slattern from the taproom before recognition should light Zeke's black eyes. Then, as he returned to his own supper, she began to gobble hers in haste to be gone while meat and drink absorbed her brother's attention.

Zeke, having been served first, finished his meal first and came over to inquire, "Heading west, bub, to jine your folks?" And when Connie nodded, he said, "Well, bub, I'm going your way as far as Chillicothe. Be glad to give you a lift in my wagon tomorrow."

Connie managed to stammer, "Th—thanks, sir, but——"

"But me no buts," said Zeke. "Always give any lad a helping hand. Four of us teamsters will be sharing a two-bed room tonight. You can sleep betwixt me and my bedmate and it won't cost you a cent."

Wide frightened black eyes came up to meet the man's black eyes. Evidently he had not suspected her identity. But did he guess her sex? Was Zeke no better than the cheese merchant?

As startled as she, Zeke gasped, "Connie! What the deuce! Come on out of here and give an account of yourself."

Night had fallen. But the lanterns of late arrivals provided light for unhitching. When the last team had been led away to the stable, the glow from the tavern windows guided brother and sister along the row of wagons to the one belonging to Zeke.

"Now my good girl," he said, "tell me how come you're here, alone and in britches."

When she had explained, Zeke roared with laughter. "What a rum joke!" he said. "Jed ducked out because Pa was bound to make him a scholar. Now you've run away because Pa's bound you *won't* become a scholar." Then, sobering, he told her, "I admire your spunk, Sis, but not your sense. Don't you know you're taking an awful risk? Still, with that head of hair chopped off as though Ma had clapped a pumpkin shell over it and trimmed round the edges, like she used to do us boys, I never suspicioned you was a gal till you stared at me out of them black Field eyes." Zeke pushed back his hat and scratched his head, adding, "But what the Sam Hill am I going to do with you? I got no time to take you back to Cleveland."

Connie thrust out her chin as she told him, "You couldn't, anyway. I'm going to Athens and you can't stop me."

"Can't, hey?" Zeke retorted, thrusting out his chin in turn. For a moment two Field wills clashed in a silent tug of war. Then Zeke chuckled. "Well," he said, "looks like I can't without raising a rumpus and landing the both of us in the calaboose for disturbing the peace. Looks like I'll have to give you a lift toward Mal's place tomorrow. But that's no answer to the question what to do with you tonight."

When Connie suggested that the tavern might have a room reserved for ladies, like the hotel in Cleveland, Zeke said, "Same here. But I can scarcely ask the landlord to put you into it."

"Not if you explained that I'm your sister?" Connie asked.

"Gosh, no!" said Zeke. "Don't you know there's a law against females going about in pants?"

Connie had never chanced on any such statute, but as she could not refute her brother's statement, she asked, "Is there any law

65

against sleeping in wagons? Any reason why I can't sleep in yours, Zeke?"

"Why, none that I know of," he replied, "provided Elmer has no objections."

"Elmer!" Connie repeated. "Who's he? Your partner?"

"No," said Zeke, "Elmer's my dog. I've trained him to guard my goods, but if you can make friends with him—make him understand you belong to me, Sis, he'll take good care of you, too."

At the sound of his name, an ugly-looking brute crawled out from under the wagon to lick his master's hand. Zeke fondled the huge head for a moment, then turned it toward the girl, saying, "Look, feller. This is one of my family. Shake hands, Elmer."

The dog sniffed Connie all over, then sat down to offer a paw.

Zeke said, "There! What did I tell you? Elmer knows a Field when he smells one. Climb in, Sis. Elmer always sleeps under the wagon. Inside, you'll sleep as snug as a bug in a rug."

There was scarcely room for a good-sized insect on top of the cargo, but somehow Connie wedged herself in between the bales and the canvas cover. She soon drifted off to sleep, undisturbed by the gentle rain that fell all night so close overhead.

Elmer's joyous barking awakened her to see, framed in the puckered canvas opening, what she took for the full moon. It turned out to be the light of Zeke's lantern.

"Go wash yourself in the hoss-trough, Sis," he ordered. "Then hurry and eat whilst I harness up. I've already et and paid for your grub and I want to get on the road by daylight."

The night's rain had left the Trace deep in mud and the hooves of Zeke's four horses, flogged to top speed, flung up clods of wet earth to bespatter wagon and passengers. Zeke cursed the ruin of his finery, but Connie's buckskins were already so disreputable that a little more mud and mire did not trouble her.

When the wagon was clear of the town and the confusion of other early starters, Zeke said, "Athens is scarce a day's journey from here, as the crow flies, but seeing you haven't sprouted wings yet, Sis, I'm taking you on to Lancaster. After supper I'll see you settled in the wagon again, then take your shoes to the cobbler's and have them resoled. Tomorrow I'll take you as far as where the river road turns off from the Trace. All you got to do is follow the

Hockhocking; it's crooked as a dog's hind leg, but it passes right through Athens. Once you're there, you'll be Mal's problem."

"Mal," Connie asserted confidently, "will see things my way."

"Maybe so, maybe not," replied Zeke. "Remember, Mal's got a conscience." Then, after a moment, "He's also got a wife. A married man ain't always his own master, which is why I never got hitched."

Connie fell to musing about both married brothers and their wives. Neither Mal's wife nor her mother were strangers, for they had lived in the Field blockhouse during the war. How such a saintly soul as Serena Pomeroy came to have such a selfish, empty-headed fool for a daughter was as incomprehensible as was Mal's devotion to Mercy. Nobody in the family knew anything about Jed's wife except that the couple had met and married in New Orleans. The fact that the bride neither spoke nor understood a word of English kept the Fields from getting acquainted with Anastasia when Jed brought her to Cleveland on their honeymoon. At that time Ash had given them his Marietta property, since it was worth more to his sailor son than any of the others. A year later Jed had written to say he was the father of a daughter, but since then nothing further had been heard from him.

"Zeke," said Connie, "do you know anything about Jed?"

Zeke shook his head. "Jed and me both take after Ma's folks," he said. "None of the Marvins ever was any hand with a pen."

It was true, Connie knew. Since Granny died down at Uncle Si's place, Ma hadn't heard from her only brother. As for Faith's sisters, long ago she had lost track of both of them, although once in a while she spoke of the one named Hope.

Connie said, "Zeke, do you remember our Aunt Hope's married name?

For a moment Zeke made no reply. Then he said, "Seems like it was Bennet. No, that's not it." The black Field brows drew together as he struggled with memory. Then his face cleared. "Benedict," he said. "I remember now. He was a hatter from Danbury, Connecticut, who come out here with the Marvins, married Aunt Hope, and took her on further west, but where to I've clean forgot. It all happened before Pa brought us out here."

67

Connie mused. "I wonder. Do you suppose we've cousins we never even heard of?"

"Like enough," said Zeke absently, giving all his attention to his team.

For at this point the Trace was crossed by a rivulet swollen with last night's rain. Zeke halted the wagon and got down to help Elmer clamber aboard. "The old feller can swim," he said, "but I don't want to chance he'd drown tryin'." Getting back on his seat, Zeke drove slowly down the bank and into the river.

At midstream the water swirled about the hubs, but all four horses kept their footing, and when they neared the further shore, Zeke drew rein and let them drink. By now the sun was directly overhead, and when the wagon was once more on dry land, Zeke gave the horses their nose bags, Elmer a bone, and then produced a basket of victuals brought from the Zanesville tavern.

When the journey was resumed, he brought up a new subject of conversation. It was a rumor he'd heard regarding a canal to connect Lake Erie and the Ohio River. "You hear any such nonsense in Cleveland, Sis?" he asked.

Connie said the matter was, indeed, under serious consideration. Mr. Kelley and Mr. Case and Pa were all strong for a canal, but plenty of other men were against it. "So," she concluded, "nothing's been done except talk."

"Talk," asserted Zeke, "is cheap. A canal would cost millions, provided it could be built at all hereabouts, which I misdoubt. At all events, the money would better be spent on roads than experimenting with waterways." To prove his point, he told how the National Road, slowly pushing west through Pennsylvania, was being paved with stone and crossed all streams by means of stone bridges. When the road crossed the Ohio, it would follow the Trace. "So don't it stand to reason paving this mudtrack, and building a paved road down from Cleveland to meet it, would make more sense than digging a big ditch just to float flatboats?"

Zeke was just airing his personal opinion, Connie knew, not asking hers. Nevertheless, she agreed with him, for after covering so much of the proposed route of the canal afoot, it did seem to her the wildest and most impractical of projects.

And so the day passed, intervals of talk alternating with intervals of silence which grew longer and longer as the shadows lengthened across the Trace. Now and again they passed other teams, more rarely a clearing, but no settlement until toward dusk when Zeke drove his Conestoga wagon into Lancaster.

The second night under canvas passed like the first, with the tired girl sleeping soundly until roused by Elmer's bark at dawn. She looked out to see Zeke with a lantern in one hand and her footgear in the other. A very short time later, Zeke set his sister down at the parting of their ways and drove off along the Trace.

Soon the sun rose to redden the waters of the Hockhocking, and beside it she trudged south hour after hour. Whether Zeke had miscalculated the distance or his sister's capacity to cover it afoot, at any rate she had not reached her destination by sunset. Zeke had not thought to provide her with lunch, and she was faint with hunger, enough so to catch, cook and eat fish again, and once again spend a night in a tree. Connie was thankful that no rain fell that night, thankful, too, for another fish for breakfast.

Then she resumed the journey beside the crooked stream. Late in the afternoon the Hockhocking rounded one more bend, and she saw ahead a low bluff in a curve of the river. There were houses on the bluff, and from among them rose a gaunt three-storied building that could only be the goal of her long hard journey.

Snatches of song led the girl to the steps of the college where a group of students lounged in the gathering dusk. When she interrupted the chorus to inquire if anyone knew Professor Field, the answer was a shout of laughter.

Then one of the lads said, "Know old Field? How can we help knowing all the profs when there are only four of them all told?"

Another student who had been staring at Connie remarked, "A fellow whose voice hasn't changed yet can't be ready for college. You come to take the prep course, bud?" And when she asked what he meant, the whole crowd roared, "Preparatory school, greeny!" After the laughter at the greenhorn's expense had died down, one of the older lads gave directions for finding "old Field's hangout."

It was little better than a cabin. In fact Connie suspected it *was* a log cabin clapboarded over, and with the old batten door replaced by a new one with panels. Her knock on the panels brought to the door a slight, stooped man whose fair hair was already receding from a dome of a forehead.

Peering through thick horn-rimmed spectacles, he inquired kindly, "What may I do for you, lad?"

"Mal," cried Connie. "Oh, Mal, don't you know me?"

"Not in this light," he replied, "although the voice is familiar."

"Well," she exclaimed, "it ought to be! I'm your sister."

The high balding brow reddened with embarrassment. "Constitution!" ejaculated Malachi Field. "I should have known, even in those clothes and short hair, for we've been expecting you."

It was her turn to be taken aback. *"Expecting* me?" she repeated.

Mal nodded. "Yes. Pa wrote he was sure you were headed for Athens and would turn up sooner or later. But do come in, my dear! You must be completely exhausted."

Connie followed him into a shadowy room where one female bent to stir a steaming kettle while another female looked on. Firelight illuminated both faces, the older one worn, sweet and resigned, the younger pretty, petulant and empty. Marriage had not made the spoiled child into a woman. Mercy still left all the work to her mother.

When Mal's wife caught sight of his sister she screamed, "Heavens! What a mess you're in, Connie. You'll have to wash and change your clothes before supper."

Connie said, "I'll be glad to wash, but I can't change because I've nothing to change *into."*

The older woman had risen and now came toward the traveler with both arms spread wide in silent welcome. As Connie went into the warm embrace she cried, "Mrs. Pomeroy! Dear Mrs. Pomeroy, I—I——" She choked and stopped, breathless.

Mercy, concerned with her sister-in-law's disreputable condition, cried, "What? Do you mean to say you brought no decent clothes?"

"Not a stitch," Connie replied. "I could scarcely walk all the way from Cleveland with a pack on my back, like a peddler, now could I?"

Mercy screamed, "Walk! You *walked* all the way?"

"Except for a couple of lifts—short lifts," replied Connie. "But

I'll tell you about everything later, after I've made myself a little more respectable."

During this interchange between the two young women, the older one had filled a basin from the steaming kettle. Now Connie saw her bearing the basin toward the dry sink. "Please!" she cried, "let me do that. You mustn't wait on me, Mrs. Pomeroy."

While the traveler made herself tidy, Serena Pomeroy dished up the porridge and Mercy Field brought a pitcher of milk from the buttery. When Malachi had lighted the single candle on the table, the family sat down.

Serena said "the blessing," then after a moment of silence told Connie, "I've not been able to rest easy in my bed since your pa's letter came. He said your dear ma was sick with worry about you and I've been half sick, worrying about you both."

Connie was contrite. "I'm sorry," she said, "sorry to cause so much trouble, I mean. Tomorrow I'll write Ma and beg her forgiveness."

Mal said, "You do that, Constitution, and I'll enclose your letter with mine to Pa. He asked me to be sure and let him know the moment you arrived and then, after you'd rested a few days, send you straight home."

"Home!" Connie gasped. "Do you think I'll go back and marry that dreadful man?" Seeing the bewilderment on all three faces, she explained about Mr. Jones. Then she told Mal, "I came here expecting you to understand and help me get an education so I'll never need to wed for my bread. I'm good and strong. I can work —cook, scrub floors, chop wood, feed pigs, clean stables—do anything respectable to earn my way through school."

While Mal admitted that some lads did get an education in this manner, Athens offered no such opportunity to females for the simple reason that none were accepted as students either in the preparatory department or the college.

This was no more than Connie expected and she said, "But Mal, even those boys who directed me here never suspected I wasn't one of them. Do you have to tell anybody I'm your sister? Why not your brother?"

Professor Field regarded her sternly. "Putting the question of ethics aside," he said, "I doubt your masquerade could be maintained indefinitely. Females are famous for inability to keep secrets."

"I could keep mine," Constitution asserted.

"Possibly," replied Mal. His gaze turned toward his wife. Although he made no further comment, it was clear that he did not give her the same benefit of the doubt.

Serena said gently, "Anyway, you could never live a lie, deary."

Mal agreed quickly. Constitution was too forthright by nature. "And even if she had no integrity," he added, "my own would never countenance such deception. I'm afraid, Sister, there is nothing for you to do but obey our father and return to his house."

Connie drew in her breath quickly, then burst out, "So you're on Pa's side, too. Oh, Mal, and I was so sure——"

Malachi interrupted, "I have not said I agree with our father with regard to female education, quite the contrary. I believe that any female with sufficient wit and desire for study should be given a classical education. Unfortunately, few men agree with me, and at present I know of no college open to women. Perhaps, a few years hence——"

His sister took the words out of his mouth. "A few years hence will be too late for me, Mal. If you make me go home, Pa will make me wed that horrible old man."

"From your description of Mr. Jones and his situation," Mal comforted, "I find it difficult to believe that he will wait for your return. By now I would not be surprised if Mr. Jones had already found himself a more suitable mate."

Connie's face brightened. Then her eyes darkened again and she said, "Pa won't let him. You know Pa, how set he can be. Pa picked Mr. Jones for my husband and he's sure to hold Mr. Jones to the bargain."

For all his mild blue eyes and gentle manner, Malachi had more than a little of the Field inflexibility of purpose. He said, "I promised to send you home, Constitution, and I'm a man of my word. However, I shall intercede on behalf of your freedom of choice in the matter of marriage."

This assurance was small comfort to Connie, for she well knew that, although Ashbel Field held his eldest son's scholarship in high regard, he did not think much of Mal's judgment on matrimonial matters.

At the look of utter dejection on the girl's face, Serena exclaimed, "You're fair beat out, deary. After a bath and a good night's rest in a decent bed, things will look brighter."

Professor Field took the hint, and after putting fresh fuel on the fire, disappeared up the steep little stair beside the chimney.

Mrs. Pomeroy went into the woodshed and returned with a wooden washtub which she set on the hearth and then went out again. When she came back lugging a heavy bucket of water, Connie seized the bail, saying, "I can't bear to have you wait on me, Mrs. Pomeroy. While I'm here *I* shall wait on *you.*"

Serena smiled gently, but she did not release the bail. "Tomorrow you can help with the chores, if you like, deary, but not tonight." When the girl gave in rather than argue, the tired little woman filled the kettle, then said, "Now! While the water warms, I'll go find you something to sleep in."

Left together, the sisters-in-law were silent. Mercy evidently felt no more obligation toward the guest than she felt to lighten her mother's labors. As for Connie, she was so angry that she could not trust herself to speak lest she tell Mal's wife exactly what she thought of her.

Soon Serena returned with a night shift over one arm, and over the other, part of an old blanket. "The minute you step out of the tub, deary," she said, "wrap yourself and come straight to bed before you catch a chill. I'll rid up here in the morning. Come, Mercy, I'm sure Connie wants to be alone."

When mother and daughter had vanished, Connie tempered her bath with the contents of the kettle, stripped off the filthy buckskins, and stepped into the tub to scrub herself until the water cooled. Then she stepped out, shivering, to ply a towel hastily, pull on the shift, wrap the piece of blanket around herself and go up the stairs, as Serena had bidden, without ridding up the kitchen. Morning would be time enough to empty the tub and tidy the room when she came down to dress before anyone else was astir.

The stair ended on a little landing with two doors, one of which was closed. The other door stood ajar, and through it Connie carried her candle into a bare little room with a chest of drawers, two

73

slat-back chairs, and a four-poster with a strip of rag carpet on either side.

From the bed Serena spoke. "Blow out the light, deary," she said, "and then hop in with me quickly. I'm sure the good Lord will forgive you for saying your prayers in bed, just this once."

While the girl acted on this suggestion, Serena was silent, and after a moment, slow regular breathing told her that her bedmate was fast asleep.

Indeed, Connie slept so soundly that she did not wake until the sun shone into her eyes. When she became aware of being alone in the bed, she leaped up in dismay and ran downstairs without waiting to cover the shift with the blanket. A fresh blaze burned brightly in the fireplace. The tub was gone and the hearth swept and tidy.

Coming in from the buttery Serena saw the girl and exclaimed, "Oh, deary, I meant to get back upstairs and find you something to wear before you woke."

"Don't bother," Connie told her. "I'll just slip into my own clothes for now and——" She stopped and exclaimed, "What's become of them? I'm sure I left them right here."

"So you did, deary," replied Serena. "But they were so filthy I carried them out with the fire tongs and burned them in the yard first thing this morning. Oh, I know buckskins *can* be washed, for I've done it, but these were past mending. Besides, deary, you couldn't go about in britches here. I haven't many gowns, but what I have I'll be glad to share with you."

Consternation held the girl speechless for a moment. Mrs. Pomeroy was a small woman, and although the voluminous shift had served for a night, Connie was sure she would be unable to button on any bodice belonging to the dear little lady. As for Mal's wife, she too was small-boned and dainty. Suddenly Connie chuckled inwardly at the thought that now Mal would be obliged to give her some of his own garments and perhaps, before feminine gear could be fashioned to fit her big frame, he would give in—agree to let her stay on and enter college, not as his sister, but as a younger brother. These thoughts Connie kept to herself, however. What she said aloud was, "Dear Mrs. Pomeroy, don't look so disturbed. Mal will be needing his breakfast before going to class. I'll just go back

74

to bed until he has gone. Then we can talk about something for me to wear." Despite protests that she, too, needed food, Connie returned to the upper room.

Soon she heard her brother and his wife go down the stair, and after an interval Serena came up bearing a bowl of porridge. While the girl breakfasted in bed, the little woman rummaged through her meager wardrobe and produced a faded indigo calico. "I've grown so much thinner since I made this," she said, "that it ought to fit you, deary, if we let out all the seams."

When Connie had slipped the bottom section over her head, the waistband did, indeed, come together, but even with the hem "let out," it was clear it would not reach below her knees. As for the bodice, it could not by any stretch of imagination be made to cover the girl's full bosom. For the first time Serena realized that Constitution Field was no longer the little girl she had loved. Her cry of dismay brought her daughter to the door.

"Oh, law!" screamed Mercy. "You've no idea how silly you look, Connie. I never saw anything so absurd."

"This is no joke, daughter," Serena reproved. "If my gowns won't fit Connie, neither will yours. Dear, dear! I can't think what to do!"

"I can," Mercy asserted. "Just rip apart two of my oldest gowns and put them together. You're so clever at make-overs, Ma, I'm sure you can manage."

Compliments from this source were so rare that Serena beamed. "How clever of *you* to think of a way out," she said. "Such an idea would never have occurred to me."

It occurred to Connie that something was behind Mercy's generosity, but she could not imagine what, and refrained from comment.

Whatever Mercy's motive, she produced two butternut homespun gowns, not of identical weave or dye, but at least both were shades of saffron. Serena's mild doubts were ignored as Mercy set about ripping the gowns apart. She even helped her mother to refit the pieces to Connie's figure, but this done, she left the stitching to others. This chore kept both Serena and Connie busy throughout the day with only a brief pause for a snack. The professor had taken his midday snack with him and did not come home until after his last class of the day. Then until sundown he worked in the garden. The extra food he grew eased the strain on a meager salary, all too often in arrears.

Brother and sister did not meet until he was called to supper. If Mal noticed what Connie wore, he made no comment until after the family was seated and grace said. Then he remarked, "I've been thinking about you, Sister, and on more mature consideration——" the Professor paused to sip boneset tea.

Connie held her breath, expectantly, until Mal set his cup down and repeated, "——On more mature consideration, I realize that it will not be safe for you to travel alone in female garb, and so——" he stopped for another sip of tea. Tantalized by these delays, Connie could scarcely keep from finishing the sentence for him, so sure was she that Mal meant to give her some of his own clothes. But what he said finally was, "——And so I have advised our father that although you have arrived safe and sound, I shall not start you back immediately. You will remain here until after college closes for the summer and I am free to escort you home to Cleveland."

This was not at all what Connie had hoped for, but at least it was a reprieve. Several weeks remained of the college year; time for further "consideration" on Mal's part, and if—— "Mal," she said, "until your classes are over, will you teach me in your spare time, like you used to do?"

A rare smile made Professor Field look years younger. "I will, Sister," he replied, "provided you help me in the garden, like *you* used to do, in order that I may *have* time to spare."

Mercy, piqued that her generosity to her sister-in-law should be ignored, spoke up to say, "If you can spare the cash for a journey, Mal, then you can well afford to buy yardgoods for at least one new gown to replace the *two* Ma put together to cover Connie."

Mal gazed from his pretty little butterfly wife to his tall stately sister. "I presume," he remarked dryly, "that a mere college professor is not qualified to pass judgment on feminine apparel. Nevertheless, it seems to me new material might better have been provided to clothe Constitution. However, since it is too late for that, may I suggest that you also provide her with a bonnet? Manifestly, she can not expose that cropped head on the journey. It would cause comment—most unpleasant comment, to say the least." Reminded that his wife possessed only one bonnet, he replied, "You need not *give* it to Constitution; merely loan it for the journey. I will bring it back and in addition——"

Mercy interrupted, "But Mal, I shall need that bonnet myself on the journey."

A stern look replaced the professor's habitually mild expression. "It was not my intention, Mercy, to take you to Cleveland. The additional expense would be quite unwarranted. Besides, as you know very well, Satan is no longer a young horse; he could not carry three persons so great a distance." When Mercy opened her lips to protest, he told her with decision, "The subject is closed."

The following weeks passed all too quickly. By day Connie helped Serena with household chores and, before supper, helped Mal plant, weed and hoe. Then every night after supper, she and her brother bent over his books in the flickering light of a single candle and the clearer light of his learning. Connie passed quickly from *amo, amas, amat* to recitations in elementary Latin. On starry nights they went out together and Mal taught her the names of the planets, their relation to one another and to the one called Earth, thus opening to the girl the wonders and the vastness of the universe. Sketchy as these lessons were, perforce, they whetted her appetite for a regular diet of books and raised her hopes afresh that when Mal realized how sincere was her ambition and how worthy she was of an education, he would alter his decision to take her back into bondage.

Meanwhile Mal's wife had not altered her determination to make a third on that journey. And because she would need her one bonnet, Mercy set about concocting headgear for Connie out of such material as was available. Indolent and selfish though she was, Mercy could use her fingers to good purpose when so disposed. The creation fashioned from last year's cornhusks, cut into strips and braided, then sewed into what she called "a shape," was a fair substitute for a "boughten bonnet." For trimming, Serena suggested fresh flowers and foliage, a wholly impractical idea vetoed by Connie in favor of hen feathers.

While she did not once suspect what Mercy had in mind, by the time college closed Connie was convinced Mal's mind was made up

77

and could not be changed. It was with a heavy heart that, on the morning of the day set for departure, she tied on the new bonnet in Serena's room. Outside she heard the old black gelding stamping off flies at the horse block. Then she heard Mercy go out, followed by voices raised in argument.

What now, thought Connie, hurrying down. Through the open door she saw Serena wringing her hands on the step. Mal stood on the horse block. Mercy, bonneted and shawled, was seated in the pillion, to which she must have managed to climb, unassisted, while Mal was busy in the barn and Serena in the kitchen.

Now Mal held out a hand to help his wife descend so that Connie might mount. Mercy, however, ignored the hand and continued to clutch the cantle, vowing she'd not budge—that she too was going to Cleveland.

"But that is not possible," Mal reiterated patiently. "As I explained, it would be an extravagance even if Satan could carry three persons, which is one too many."

"Well, then," said Mercy, "let Connie walk. If she could walk all the way here, she can walk all the way back, can't she?"

"No doubt she could," retorted Mal, "but she is not going to do so. Come, Mercy, be reasonable and allow me to assist you down without more ado."

Mercy's response was a tighter grip on the cantle as she shook her head until the flowers on her bonnet bobbed wildly. That his butterfly wife could be persistent Mal had good reason to know, and he usually gave in to her over trifles to save unpleasantness. But when convinced indulgence was wrong, he set his course and rode out the storm. The present tempest, however, could not be permitted to blow itself out. A start must be made without further loss of time if lodgings were to be reached by nightfall. Malachi Field looked delicate, but he was quite equal to tearing his wife from the pillion and carrying her upstairs to lock her in her room. However the thought of laying violent hands on any female was repugnant. Moreover, Athens was a dull place for a pleasure-loving young woman; perhaps Mercy did need a change. He had intended to bring her a present from Cleveland, but perhaps the trip would please her more. Mal surrendered, telling his wife, "You may go if you will release your hold on the cantle and allow me to help Constitution into the saddle. It will not be the first time she has ridden astride, I presume to say."

Connie demurred only at depriving Mal of his saddle; she could walk just as well as he.

"Do you think I would permit any female to travel afoot while I rode?" he demanded. "Come, come! Have done with argument. Let us start without further delay."

The summer day was fine. Mal knew all the maze of cowtracks that cut the forest between Athens and Zanesville, so that before dark the three Fields arrived at the tavern where Connie had encountered Ezekiel. No inn, with the exception of a very few in the larger cities, could offer private apartments. Even high government officials were accustomed to sharing a room, and often a bed, with total strangers. It was a foregone conclusion that Professor Field should take whatever accommodations the men's dormitory afforded, while his wife and sister passed the night in the ladies' chamber. Had the party arrived on stage day, that feminine retreat might have been overcrowded. As it was, Connie and Mercy could have a bed to themselves in a room shared by only two other guests.

All four females hung their gowns on the wall pegs and preserved their modesty by pulling on nightshifts before letting body linen slip to the floor. Then Mal's wife and sister climbed into their bed and lay down, back to back, separated in body by an inch or so of coverlet, but in spirit miles apart. Having become accustomed to strange places, Connie soon fell asleep until toward dawn, when she was roused by unmistakable sounds of illness. Mercy was being very sick in the communal chamber pot. Connie's first thought was that something eaten for supper had disagreed with her sister-in-law.

The matrons in the other bed, also awakened by Mercy's retching, attributed it to another cause and were duly sympathetic.

"Mornin' sickness be nothin' to fret about," comforted the younger matron.

"Jes so," agreed the elder stranger. "I've borned ten, and every last one of 'em give me a bad time the first few months they was under my apron. But ye hadn't orter be travelin' in your condition, ma'am. It ain't nowise safe fer ye or the child."

Mercy made no comment. When the paroxysm had passed, she climbed over Connie and lay down again, facing the wall.

In a whisper Connie inquired whether their chambermates had reached the correct conclusion. And when Mercy admitted that they had, Connie lay still recalling old wives' tales of pioneer mothers prematurely brought to childbed in covered wagons. Mr. Jones's wife, for one, and for another, a Putnam wife who insisted on coming west with her husband even though she was three months pregnant. After riding a gentle old white horse clear across the mountains, Mrs. Putnam had lost her baby and come very near losing her own life as well on the banks of the Monongahela.

"Mercy," whispered Connie, "how long have you known about this? I mean that you are going to have a baby?" And when Mercy reluctantly admitted to having known for two months, Connie cried, "Then what possessed you to insist on coming with Mal and me?"

In the gray dawnlight, Mercy turned over to stare defiantly. "If you *must* know," she said, "I hoped I'd lose it on the way."

"Lose it!" Connie repeated, scarcely crediting her ears. "You mean—you *can't* mean your—your baby!"

"What else?" retorted Mercy. "Do you think I want a nasty brat spitting on my bodice and messing my petticoats? Well, I don't!"

Such vulgarity, such wickedness, left Connie speechless with disgust while both matrons cried out against this revolt from females' sacred duty.

Mercy turned on the strangers, crying, "You two keep out of this; its none of your business."

"Well, it certainly is *Mal's* business," remarked Connie. "Had he known, he would never have brought you along. You've got to tell him, Mercy, just as soon as we go downstairs."

"I'll do no such thing," retorted Mal's wife. "And don't you blab either, Constitution Field." Repeating "It's none of your business," Mercy turned her face to the wall once more.

Ordinarily Connie had no use for a talebearer, but this was no ordinary circumstance. She could not keep Mercy's secret and let Mal continue the journey in ignorance of the risk to his wife and to their unborn child as well. Very quietly she slipped out of bed, slipped into her clothes, and opened the door. The rasp of rusty hinges made Mercy turn. But even a frantic female could not rush down to the public taproom in her night shift. By the time Mercy Field, clothed but scarcely in her right mind, reached the lower floor, her husband was already in possession of the news.

Anger, disgust and exasperation struggled for mastery of Professor Field's candid countenance. His voice, however, was low and controlled as he said, "You and I are returning to Athens directly after breakfast." He said no more for the taproom was fast filling with strangers.

His wife, heedless of interested onlookers, shrilled, "I couldn't swallow a mouthful, and I'm not going home. I'm going on with you and Connie."

"Connie," asserted Malachi, "will remain here until I have placed you in your mother's care. Then I will return for my sister and resume our journey. If you have no appetite, neither have I. I will go and saddle the gelding immediately."

When he had gone out, Mercy turned on her sister-in-law, berating her, making a scene in which Connie, like Mal, refused to join. The professor soon returned to find his wife weeping with helpless rage. Picking her up bodily, he set her, not on the pillion from which she might slip to the ground while he mounted, but on the pommel where he held her and climbed into the saddle. Mercy sobbed and struggled. Mal picked up the reins with his free hand and paused only to tell his sister that he had settled with the innkeeper and would pay any additional bill on his return. Then a touch of his heel on Satan's flank started the black gelding homeward.

Embarrassed by the stares and grins of onlookers, Connie escaped to the bedchamber where she found the two matrons hanging out of the window. At her entrance, they turned, curious to know why she had been left behind.

When Connie had explained as much as seemed necessary, but no more, the elder matron introduced herself as Ma Betts and the other female as her daughter, "Widder Birdseye."

The widow remarked, "If yer brother leaves that critter, she's apt to try some other trick to bring on a miss. It wouldn't surprise me none if, instead of comin' back, he sent ye word to take the stage wherever 'tis yer goin'."

Before Connie could point out that there was no stage from Zanesville to Cleveland, the older woman interposed, "Now darter, ye know as well as I do, it ain't safe fer a young unpertected female to go trapsin' about. I'll ask Pa to give this gal a lift in our wagon, if it be she's bound our way."

Connie was already convinced that Mal ought not to leave Mercy to the sole care of the mother who had never been able to control the self-willed creature. As for her own safety, no one knew better than Connie the perils of travel. Even disguised as a boy she had not escaped them entirely. Alone and in petticoats, she would face further insult, greater danger. And if she did arrive safely in Cleveland without Mal, it would be to face an irate father and a hateful marriage. While these thoughts raced through Connie's mind, the two matrons stood watching her, waiting to learn her destination.

Instead of a direct answer, she thanked them for their kind offer of protection and inquired which way they were bound.

"South," replied the widow. "We're goin' to visit Ma's folks in Marietta."

Suddenly, like the sun coming from behind a cloud, the way of escape opened before the Field rowan. "What a coincidence!" she exclaimed. "I'm going to Marietta, too. My second brother lives there."

"Well, don't that beat all!" said Ma Betts. "Pity ye didn't say so last night. Then that brother who brought you here could have gone off easy in his mind, knowin' we'd see ye safe on yer way."

Connie said that she would write Professor Field before leaving the inn, if the Betts party was not in too much of a hurry.

"We don't aim to start on empty stomachs," Ma replied, adding, "You've already et, I presume to say."

Connie was reluctant to admit she had had no breakfast, for she was not sure whether it had been included in the bill Mal had paid. She did beg a sheet of foolscap from the landlord, however, and the loan of his quill pen to write Mal a few lines, just enough to say that he need not return as she was going on with "those two respectable females who shared the ladies' chamber last night." Conscience hurt her a little for withholding part of the truth, but she knew that if Mal knew her whereabouts, *his* conscience would never permit him to withhold it from their parents. Their failure to reach Cleveland together would, of course, have to be explained later. But not now. Having composed the letter, Connie made a copy of it to leave with the landlord, in case Mal left Athens before the arrival of the post. He would have to pay the postage, but that cost was small as compared to the cost of the journey she hoped to save him.

Upstairs in the chamber, Connie folded her night shift and the change of body linen she and Serena had contrived out of the best parts of an old sheet. She rolled up the garments together with her hair comb in the fragment of blanket that served the double purpose of shawl and portmanteau. Then she glanced out of the window, saw that her traveling companions had already climbed into a covered wagon, and hurried down to join them.

While the wagon swayed and bumped along the road beside the Muskingum River on its way to join the Ohio, there was plenty of time for the fugitive to weigh her chances of success in this fresh adventure on which she had embarked in such haste.

How welcome would she be in Jed's home? What did she know of his wife? Nothing more than that she was young and handsome in a queer foreign sort of way and spoke only French. The bride's maiden name had not been mentioned by the bridegroom who called her Stasie which, he explained, was short for Anastasia. What, indeed, Connie asked herself, did she know about Jed—what manner of man he had turned out to be, or how he earned a living. Presumably, he was engaged in some business to do with shipping, since Pa had given him the homelot on the banks of the Ohio River. Connie's recollections of her birthplace were vague, for she had been a very small girl when the family moved from Marietta.

On the outskirts of that town she parted with the Bettses and trudged on past rows of shipyards and ropewalks separated by a long open common from the homes of their owners. These were not the log cabins Connie remembered, but fine mansions of brick or white painted clapboards. Looming among them, however, was a large gaunt building she recognized as the Muskingum Academy where all four of her brothers had gone to school. As she trudged on past, she saw herself attending classes there now, and her heart lifted.

At the Picketed Point, meeting place of the two rivers, she

turned east to follow the main stream a little way to the spot where the Field cabin had burned down after the family had departed. Connie had expected to find a new house on the lot, Jed's house, but the entire water front had changed almost beyond recognition. Only the river looked the same, the big bend and the island which had been visible from the kitchen window, but these landmarks convinced her she was not mistaken. This was the place—the original Field homelot. But what had replaced the log cabin wasn't any sort of residence; it was a large warehouse. Connie's not unnatural conclusion was that the warehouse belonged to Jed, and she entered the door marked office with every expectation of finding him inside.

A man, seated on a high stool, bent over an open ledger on a high desk. He was lean and stooped, with a bald head and spectacles, an old man who bore not the slightest resemblance to Jedediah Field.

In reply to the visitor's questions, this man said he knew the name, for it was on the deed to this land purchased by him a few years back. Where the previous owner was now, he had no idea, but he did know that no Fields lived in Marietta. The only means of locating the missing man he could suggest was a visit to the post office where a forwarding address might have been left.

Connie acted on this suggestion and retracted her steps to the Picketed Point where the post office was located on the wharf, handy to the river craft which carried the mail. The postmaster did recall Jedediah Field, but had no record of his present whereabouts.

Panic seized the runaway girl. Here she was, penniless, far from any of her natural protectors and friendless except for chance-met travelers, dependent for food and lodging on kinfolk whose name Connie had not learned. She could not even recall the location of the farm where she had parted from the Bettses. How, in the name of common sense, had she got herself into this mess? Why had she not considered that a man with an itching foot, like Jed, was likely to move without notice? This journey down the Muskingum was proving as mad as leaving Cleveland in the first place, madder, in fact, for she had left home confident of finding sanctuary with her best-loved brother.

Dear Mal! His refusal to harbor the defiant minor, and his insistence that she must return to bondage until released by law at eighteen, although a bitter blow at the time, had increased Connie's respect for him and his integrity. The cross-country distance between the Muskingum and Hockhocking could not be great, and even in petticoats Connie would have faced the trackless wilderness on foot in an attempt to reach the pioneer college again. What she could not face was Mal's disappointment in her, should she appear on the heels of her misleading letter. Sooner or later he must learn how she had deceived him, but before they met face to face again, Connie must justify her deception.

At the moment, facing an angry father seemed her only alternative. She would have to return to Cleveland, after all. At least she would have to set out on that long return journey, alone and unprotected. Whether or not she ever arrived, Connie was too dejected and too distraught to care.

Chapter 8

THE DESCENDING SUN reddened the wide waters of the Muskingum as the girl started back along shore feeling more lost, more alone here in the midst of the little town than ever she had felt in the forest. It was not until Connie came abreast of the shipyards again, and saw the workers emerging with empty lunch baskets on their way home to supper that she realized part of her empty feeling was caused by hunger. Sight of shipwrights and apprentices furnished food for thought and revived her spirits. As a lad Jed had worked in those same yards during summer vacations; some of these men might very well know where he had gone.

Connie accosted one workman after another with no success. Then, just as she was about to abandon hope, she saw a face that looked vaguely familiar, the face of a man who turned out to have been a schoolmate of her brothers. This man had heard that Jedediah Field had "gone down river," but how far down, whether the young Fields had gone back to New Orleans or settled somewhere along the way, he had no idea.

Pursuit of one Field wanderer by another might well prove a wild-goose chase under any circumstances, Connie was well aware. Nevertheless, she would not have hesitated to board the first southbound boat and ask for Jed at every landing as long as funds held out, *if* she had possessed any funds at all. Penniless as she was, the mere thought of such a project was fruitless. She'd better be thinking about food and lodging.

The last rays of the setting sun glinted on the windows of the fine houses fronting the common. Surely, some of these houses must belong to folks who remembered the Fields. That big white house near the Academy, for instance, seemed familiar. The tired, hungry girl prodded childhood memories, and slowly there came to her the name of the builder. If the house still belonged to her father's lawyer friend, he was not apt to turn Ashbel Field's daughter from his door. Connie approached that dignified door and plied the shining brass knocker. After a moment the door opened a crack, through which a female eyed the stranger with suspicion. Yes, she said, the owner was the Honorable Return Jonathan Meigs, but he "wa'n't to home." Since his appointment as United States Postmaster General, the Meigses had resided in the national capital.

The girl turned away with a sinking heart. The sun had sunk below the hills on the western shore of the river. Dark was deepening on the common. A strange young female found wandering about after curfew by the town watchman might well spend the night in jail as a vagrant. Connie turned up a lane with no set purpose beyond finding some more frequented place. Suddenly she paused at sight of two more buildings that looked a little familiar—a small one-room cabin on one side of the lane, and directly opposite, a dwelling house perched on a low bluff. Connie kept staring at the house, and after a moment she knew it for General Rufus Putnam's log cabin clapboarded over and painted white. The old general and her father had fallen out over something to do with politics, she couldn't remember what. But she did know that the coolness between the two men had not broken the friendship between their wives. Perhaps, for the sake of old times, **Mrs.** Putnam would welcome Faith Field's child.

Connie remembered Persis Putnam as an old lady with a kind wrinkled face framed in a frilly cap, and it was a surprise to find her looking exactly the same after ten years—no older, no less benign. That her welcome was somewhat less than warm was soon explained by the fact that the General, at eighty-two, was bedridden.

"Could I be of any help?" Connie asked eagerly.

The lined face brightened. "If you could," said Persis, "just give me a hand changing his bed linen. He's well-nigh helpless and I'm not as spry as I once was." As they went down the hall and through the kitchen into the adjoining chamber, the old lady spoke of her own daughters, all wed and living at a distance with children of their own. "I always lent my gals a helping hand when they had need of it," she said. "Now I need *their* help, *their* hands are overfull with their own families." Burdened with personal problems, she showed no curiosity about those of the Field rowan.

Rufus Putnam had never been a handsome man and now, with loss of teeth and hair, his big nose stood out from his shrunken face like a headland. Separated by that promontory, however, his blue eyes were as alive and alert as when, thirty years earlier, he had built this house as part of the old frontier fort, now vanished.

When his wife spoke the visitor's name, he said testily, "No need to tell me! I know those black Field eyes." He made no further remark while Connie lifted his wasted frame and his wife deftly changed the under sheet. But when Persis had gone out to prepare supper, he demanded, "What brings you here, gal, without your folks?"

Connie dropped into a hickory rocker beside the bed and poured out the whole story, from the time Pa came back from Fort Meigs to the night she had run away from home, and why.

At the end of the tale the old man lay, looking thoughtfully at the young woman in the flickering firelight. Finally, he told her, "When I first set eyes on Ash Field, back in 1796, he was a man of one idea, and that was to bring up his sons in greater freedom than New England offered."

Connie said, "Yes, I know."

87

"*How* do you know?" Rufus Putnam demanded. "That was before ye was even thought of." Then he chuckled. "Will I ever forget how your coming into the world delayed your pa's arrival at the Constitutional Convention! That pleasured me mightily at the time. But the bill making Ohio a state passed without Ash's vote; it was that issue he and I fell out over—immediate statehood. He was all for it; I was agin it in those days."

The old man paused and the girl, feeling that some comment was expected, said, "I never knew what the trouble was."

"Well, you know now," Rufus told her. "However, once the bill was passed, we were all agreed that Ohio must always remain a free state, that is, us New Englanders stood together against those Virginians who were bent on making slavery legal here."

Again Connie interjected, "I know, sir," wondering whether the old man was just talking to hear himself talk, or whether his reminiscences were leading up to something definite.

" 'History repeats itself,' " Putnam continued. "It seems that your pa and I are at odds again. To my mind, if Ohio is to live up to its constitution, every soul, black or white, must have equal chance to make something of himself. Or *herself*," he added with emphasis.

Connie's eyes widened. "You mean——" she began.

"I mean," he interrupted, "that what's sass for the gander is sass for the goose. Maybe it was because I'd not chance at much schooling as a boy, that a school was one of the first things I helped plant here. Muskingum Academy was the first schoolhouse built this side of the mountains. They built another in Cincinnati that same year, but ours was the first. However, Cincie's gone ahead of us now."

Puzzled, wondering what took the invalid's mind off on another tangent, Connie inquired, "Just what do you mean, sir?"

"I mean," he replied, "their Lancaster Seminary has just got a college charter. What's more, it will be open to females."

At that, Connie was sure the old man's mind wandered. Surely, Professor Field should be better informed on educational matters than any bedridden invalid. Doubt must have been visible in her eyes, for the old man said, "You think I don't know what I'm talking about? Well, I do. Our local representative in the General Assembly just came back from Columbus and brought me the news, knowing my lifelong interest in education. If I had my way, gals could stay in our Academy as long as their brothers, instead of only long enough to larn the Three R's, although," he added, "I never yet saw the female with any head for figures."

Connie said, "Well, sir, you could see one now, if it wasn't so dark in here."

Putnam chuckled. "Go ahead, light the candle. Time it was lit, so Ma won't stumble over the rug when she brings my supper. Supper!" he repeated testily, "all I get is pap."

By the time the girl had touched a burning brand to the wick, Persis appeared bearing a bowl of gruel. "I set your supper on the kitchen table," she told Connie. "After I've fed Pa, I'll join you and we'll have a good talk."

Whatever manual dexterity the old man had lost, his hearing and wits were unimpaired. "You two will do your talking in here," he asserted. "I've got more to say myself to the both of you."

Hot food raised the girl's spirits and the hope that, among the things the general had to say, was the offer of a night's lodging.

What was offered her, when she returned to the sickroom, left her speechless with relief and gratitude.

"I got so interested in telling ye about that college in Cincie," remarked the old man, "that it slipped my mind to say as how your brother Jedediah come to bid me good-bye before he went there to take a job in some shipyard, although I disremember which——"

Connie interrupted, "Jed in Cincinnati! *Now?*"

"So far as I know," replied Putnam. "Anyhow, you can write to him there, and if your letter don't come back, you can be sure that foot-loose brother of yours has settled down, at last."

Connie was about to point out that she, too, was foot-loose, perforce, and would be gone long before a letter could reach Cincinnati, much less return.

The keen old man must have surmised what was in her mind, for he told her, "If you'll stay here and help Ma tend me till we can find somebody else, I'll pay your way to Cincinnati in the care of some river cap'n."

When, almost overcome with gratitude, Connie stammered thanks, Persis told her, "It's Pa and me who are thankful, thankful to the good Lord for sending you here in our hour of need."

For several weeks thereafter Connie milked night and morning, chopped and carried fuel from the woodshed and water from the well. She lifted the heavy iron kettles on and off the crane, and the heavier weight of the invalid from bed to chair and back again twice a day. Of an afternoon, while Mrs. Putnam rested in an upstairs chamber, the girl sat beside the old man listening to endless reminiscences about the Revolution when he helped his cousin Israel keep the Hundon River free of redcoats and how, a few years later, he had come out here to help free the Ohio Valley of hostile redskins.

"Freedom," he told the girl on one occasion, "sometimes goes to a feller's head, like whiskey does when he takes aboard more than he can carry. A drunken man gets big notions about his rights, forgettin' other folks also got rights to 'life, liberty and the pursuit of happiness.'" Putnam paused to peer at the girl. "You got any idea what I'm quotin', missy? Or does your pa believe history is beyond female understanding?"

Connie replied that her brother Malachi had taught her the text of the pact signed by the nation's founders. And in proof, she repeated the entire document from memory down to the final sentence, "'. . . for the support of this declaration, with firm reliance on the protection of Divine Providence, we mutually pledge each other our lives, our fortunes and our sacred honor.'"

The old man sighed. "Great words, those," he said huskily. "Great words of great men who risked all for freedom. Many men died for it."

"My Grandsir Marvin was one of them," Connie whispered. "He died at Fort Griswold. And my brother Remember died at Fort Meigs in the war to keep us free."

"Dead heroes are soon forgotten," remarked the hero of many battles. "What's more important to remember is what they died *for*. We who won freedom in the first place are growin' fewer and fewer; soon the last of us will be gone. Freedom will die, too, unless future generations are taught to value it enough to protect it with *their* lives, if need be. Just you keep that in mind, missy, and teach it to your children."

Connie heard herself asserting, "I'm never going to wed, sir. If I can get an education, I shall be a schoolmarm. But I won't forget what you've said, sir, or let my pupils forget, either."

"Good!" said the old man. "But you'll change your mind about stayin' an old maid once you meet the right feller. Meanwhile, I see no harm in your improvin' the good mind the Lord gave you, Ashbel Field to the contrary not withstanding, and you can tell him I said so."

Connie had put off informing her father of her whereabouts, but that night she wrote him and included the general's message. To forestall any further orders to return home, however, she concluded with the statement that, by the time this letter reached Cleveland, she would be on her way to join Jed in Cincinnati.

Assurance that he was there was not forthcoming, however, and after weeks of waiting Connie wrote Jed again. The Marvin laxness might account for Jed's failure to reply, but Connie was less certain than the general that, if Jed had gone on elsewhere, the unclaimed letter would be returned to Marietta.

Rufus Putnam, convinced that both letters had been delivered, told Connie one evening that arrangements were complete for her to board the steamboat *Washington* on its next trip down-river. Protest that she was still needed here was silenced by the announcement that arrangements had also been made for her replacement as nurse and general helper. Nothing remained for Connie to do but accept the situation with a mixture of regret and relief.

The hour of departure found her standing on the wharf at the Picketed Point, looking upstream. Soon a plume of smoke appeared above the island. Then around it on the channel side came the pride and wonder of the river. Connie had heard that the *Washington* was frigate-built, whatever that meant, and that she was one hundred and fifty feet long, twenty-four in the beam, and capable of carrying two hundred tons of cargo below spacious accommodations for passengers. But she was not a side-wheeler, like the *Walk-on-the-Water*—the only other steamboat Connie had seen—and what propelled the approaching vessel remained a mystery even after the *Washington* pulled alongside the wharf. The two engines were plain to be seen, situated on the main deck, but it was not until Connie stood on the afterdeck and the steamer got under way again, that she observed the single wheel at the stern kicking the water into a foaming white wake.

The summer afternoon was warm, and Connie remained on deck unaware that she was the only female in the crowd of loud-mouthed males who spit tobacco juice. When she became annoyed at their bold stares, she turned her back and, leaning on the rail, kept her gaze on the passing scene. The wide tawny river wound its way between banks where willows and sycamores leaned forward, as though to admire their own reflections in the still waters.

The girl's contemplation of these beauties was disturbed by a voice, a bass voice, saying, "Beg pardon, ma'am, but are you Miss Field?" Startled, she turned to face a young man stiff and straight in a gold-braided uniform. That uniform gave her confidence to reply that Field was, indeed, her name, whereupon the young man explained that he was the first mate. "The captain's orders, ma'am, were to find you and escort you to the ladies' quarters."

Impressed by the gold braid and the word *orders,* Connie dared not refuse to leave the lovely scene for the interior of the ship, and the mate led her into a long narrow apartment lined with rich velvet curtains which, parted here and there, revealed three tiers of berths. Through the thick haze of tobacco smoke, Connie caught a glimpse of an open door at one end and heard sounds of broken glass and ribald laughter. A man lurched out of the barroom to leer at her, then lurched away at a sharp word from her escort. Then the mate took her arm and hurried her to the other end of the main saloon and left her before a curtained doorway above which was the sign "Ladies' Cabin."

The heavy curtains, falling together behind her, muffled the sounds of masculine profanity and revelry as her own light footfall was muffled by the thick carpet. Females of all ages and sizes sat about in armchairs or reclined upon sofas. Although they all stared at Connie, none spoke to her when she dropped into the only vacant seat, wondering whether she would be allowed to sit here all night. Soon one by one, the other females disappeared through another pair of curtains. After a time Connie ventured to follow and found herself in a cabin lined with berths similar to those in the main saloon, berths into which all her companions had retired. While she hesitated, not knowing what to do, a mulatto in cap and apron approached to say that most ladies disrobed in the adjoining washroom. And when Connie had done the same, the maid produced a ladder and helped her to climb into a third tier berth. As it was impossible to sit up, she stretched out, feeling suffocated behind the velvet curtains, to toss until lulled into uneasy slumber by the steady threshing of the paddle wheel as it drove the steamer downstream under the summer moon.

Hours later Connie was awakened in the dark by a dreadful din, a din so like that of the alarm sounded on Cleveland public square by a crowbar beating an iron hoop, that she was certain the steamer was on fire. In a panic to escape from the berth, she slid down the curtains like a cat from a tree. Outside the din ceased abruptly and a rich masculine voice intoned, "Fust call foh breakfas'! Fust call foh breakfas'!" Then the racket broke out again, and diminished as the man went on his way through the ship.

Connie, feeling foolish, became embarrassed when other females emerged from their berths to stare at her as though she were some strange animal. At first she thought it was her night shift that attracted attention. Then she realized the object of scorn was her cropped head. She escaped to the washroom to dress, resume her bonnet, and then seek the empty parlor as a refuge from those cold suspicious eyes. For all its elegance, the unaired place was intolerable, and Connie tugged open a porthole to let in the fresh morning breeze. She wasn't sick, exactly, but there was a queasy feeling in her stomach. Suddenly she realized that she had gone to bed without the supper which must have been served somewhere while she was on deck. Should she follow the dishpan beater to breakfast, or——

As though in answer to her unspoken question, a kinky black head poked through the entrance hangings which then revealed a portly Negro with a white cloth over the white sleeve of his jacket. With a respectful bow to the only female present, the steward spread the damask on the center table, then with another bow departed.

Presently all the fine ladies appeared, clothed but unbonneted, each head wreathed in sleek braids or a cascade of curls. Queer as she felt, Connie kept her head covered—that shameful head cropped like a boy's. Only hunger kept her from fleeing to the deck immediately, and she forced herself to sit down at the table among the other females and wait. Soon the steward returned balancing a huge tray on his head, a tray loaded with delicate china and fragrant food. And such food! Connie was accustomed to a breakfast of hasty pudding and milk, hasty pudding and maple sirup, or as a special treat hasty pudding and imported molasses. Now she gazed wide-eyed at hot beaten biscuits wrapped in a napkin, crisp bacon and tiny brown sausages in addition to fried chicken. These rich victuals were accompanied by a silver pot of steaming hot beverage which, at her first sip, Connie found bitter, at the second delicious.

When, of the table at large, she inquired the name of the beverage, a dozen pair of eyes turned toward her in silent surprise, curiosity and scorn of such ignorance. It was the steward who told her, "Coffee, ma'am. Would you-all feel to have a second cup?"

Connie shook her head. Under those icy stares her appetite had evaporated. Any company, even that of whiskey-soaked males, seemed preferable to that of tight-lipped females with noses wrinkling as though at a bad smell, and she left the cloistered retreat for the open deck. The mate, pacing up and down, lifted his cap, expressed the hope that she had had a good night, and passed on. But as none of the other men on deck approached her, Connie was sure that official recognition saved her from annoyance.

The scenery, although lovely, was monotonous. Bend followed bend as the Ohio wound its way between wooded hills, broken now and again by a clearing where some hamlet nestled under a cliff, or huddled between shore and deep primeval forest still untamed. The forest furnished fuel for the *Washington* which, after whistling for a landing, paused to take wood while cargo and passengers were discharged or taken aboard. A blast of the whistle also warned smaller craft—arks, broadhorns, flatboats, pirogues, sloops and schooners—to make way for the queen of the river. The white flume of smoke preceding each blast fascinated Connie as did the twin flumes of black smoke constantly floating from the tall stacks to shower the deck with cinders. Despite the protection of her bonnet-brim, one of these particles got in her eye and could not be dislodged until she went below and washed it out with the help of the colored maid.

By the time that was accomplished, dinner was served in the parlor, and Connie forced herself to sit again with her critics. This was her last chance for a square meal before landing and then— what then? After dinner she returned to the deck to watch the ever-winding Ohio, ever widening as tributary after tributary joined the main stream. Hour after hour the *Washington* threshed steadily down-river until, toward sunset, rounding a sharper curve than usual, the steamer passed a low wooded point on the port side and made another sharp curve around a treeless promontory to starboard. Ahead, the valley opened out and, shading her eyes with a hand, Connie saw bathed in the sunset glow the red city of Cincinnati. Warehouses spread along the water front while row on row of close-set dwellings climbed the steep bluff to spread out over a wide plateau backed by higher hills, dark and somber.

To the child of the wilderness, the river metropolis looked enormous. Suppose Jed were not on the wharf to meet her, how should she ever find him in this teeming city? Suppose he no longer lived here? What should she do? Return to Marietta at the expense of the kind couple who no longer needed her? And if she did, would General Putnam send her back to Cleveland, like a runaway slave?

Fear must have been written on her sensitive face, for the mate came up to reassure her that as soon as the captain was at liberty after the ship docked, he would escort her ashore in person and put her in care of the dockmaster.

As the *Washington* edged closer to the landing, Connie saw with astonishment that the whole area was paved with brick, over which drays and teams clattered and clomped amid shouts and curses of drivers. The warehouses and the dwellings too were entirely of brick, which doubtless accounted for the peculiar color of the city as seen from afar. There was not a tree in sight, although at intervals barkless stumps thrust up along the edge of the wharf.

At a series of queer sharp cries, deck hands put coiled ropes over these posts while other crewmen hung out bumpers to protect the white flanks of the steamer as she was warped to the dock. Not one, but two gangplanks were pushed aboard, and while roustabouts rolled or trundled boxes and bales over one of them, passengers streamed down the other. Connie lingered on deck, straining her eyes for sight of a familiar broad back and shoulders, but while men greeted other female arrivals it soon became clear than none had come to meet her. The captain, now at liberty, fulfilled his promise to the extent of leading her ashore to the company office, then excused himself and rushed back to his bridge leaving the girl alone. With another wild shriek of her whistle, the *Washington* chugged off downstream. When the commotion of her arrival and departure had died down, the dockmaster entered his office frowning, obviously disgruntled by orders to look after a strange young female.

He was a paunchy middle-aged man in a linsey-woolsey coat and breeches sadly in need of repair at knee and elbow. "Be hanged if I know what to do with you, miss," he growled. "Since my wife died on me, I've been batching it so I can't put you up at my house for the night."

Those fears, briefly quieted by the mate, sprang up afresh as Connie said, "Then you don't know my brother, Jedediah Field?"

The dockmaster snorted, "In a city of ten thousand population, I can't know every Tom, Dick and Harry." And when Connie ventured to remark that Jed was engaged in the shipping business, the man snorted again, "So are more than half the menfolks in town. I got no time to take the census of all the shipyards, sail lofts, ropewalks or boiler factories, not to mention every firm that ships goods to New Orleans or Pittsburgh."

Connie caught at the straw and said, "My brother married a girl from New Orleans named—I don't know her maiden name; he calls her Stasie."

A louder snort suggested that females, named or nameless, were no clue to any man's whereabouts. But when Connie went on to say that Jed had worked on Commodore Perry's fleet at Presque Isle and fought aboard the *Lawrence* in the battle of Lake Erie, the dockmaster's expression grew less dour.

"That being the case," he said, "some of the veterans hereabouts are liable to know whether your brother's in town or gone to sea again."

"To sea!" echoed the girl, aghast. Why hadn't she considered that possibility? Would even a wife and child anchor a sailor in love with blue water?

"Well," said the dockmaster, "I can't stay here all night. What do you aim to do, young lady?"

For the moment Connie forgot she was penniless and said, "In a big city like this there must be respectable places where a lady can hire a bed."

"There be," he replied, "but a lone female of your age and looks would be turned away from any 'respectable' place."

Three months earlier Connie would not have caught the implication. Since then she had learned much not found in books and her face burned in the shadow of her bonnet. She turned away and saw through the dirty window that night had already fallen. Thought of wandering about strange dark streets filled with men, drunk or sober, filled her with terror.

"Tonight," she told the dockmaster firmly, "I aim to stay right here in your office."

"But you can't do that," he expostulated.

Connie retorted, "Indeed, I can. Who is going to stop me?" The gleam in her black eyes challenged him to pick her up bodily and carry her out on the public wharf.

The dockmaster knew himself equal to doing exactly that, for he was accustomed to moving much heavier baggage. This human baggage, however, looked quite capable of putting up a fight—a fight sure to bring a jeering crowd to the wharf, not to mention the constabulary. Even if the justice of the peace accepted his version of the affair, the tale of it would make him the laughingstock of every water front tavern for years to come. Furious at the girl for putting him in such a position, the dockmaster was forced to give in.

"Stay here, then," he told her, "at your own risk. I'll not be held responsible whatever befalls you."

"Nothing will," she asserted with more assurance than she felt. "I can take care of myself."

Angry as he was, the man could not stifle respect for her courage. "I believe your story!" he ejaculated. "Heaven help the bum who breaks into this office between now and daylight! Until then, Miss Wild—I mean Miss Field— *Good* night!"

When the door slammed behind him, Connie went to turn the key against intruders. But although there was no key, no bolt, and no bar, the door would not open. Had she been locked in to prevent her from making off with company property, or for her own protection? Connie made sure of the latter by pushing the heavy desk across the entrance. Then, as she stood panting with exertion, the oil lamp flickered and went out. Total darkness increased her terror. Distant voices raised in rowdy song caused her to hold her breath, listening. Every footstep on the brick pavement sent shivers of apprehension along her spine, lest the approaching male be some drunken bum. When the footsteps passed, she comforted herself with the thought that they had been those of the night watch. Nevertheless, the next sound of footfalls gave her goose flesh again. Sounds of revelry died down gradually, followed by silence in which the far-off voice of a clock told the hour of one. After what seemed years, the same clock struck two. The sleeping city was still. At last the voice of the river, lazily lapping the wharf, lulled the weary wanderer to sleep, as she sat upright in a chair.

Chapter 9

THE EASTERN HEADLAND shielded the city from the rising sun, and what roused the girl at daybreak was the clop of many hooves, the rattle of wagons on the brick pavement, and loud altercations between drivers and roustabouts as cargoes were shifted from carts to craft. Connie got up stiffly from the chair to search for water, found none, and was trying to open the window when she was startled by banging on the door. Then she recognized the dockmaster's voice raised in profane demands for entrance.

When she removed the obstruction, he stamped in, scowled and told her, "Well, miss, to make sure of getting rid of you, I located your brother."

"Oh, where!" cried Connie. "Do you mean Jed actually is right here in Cincinnati?"

"What else could I mean?" retorted the dockmaster. Then, without troubling to explain that, by making the rounds of all waterside taverns the previous evening, he had finally obtained the address, he scribbled it on a scrap of paper. "Here," he said, "take this and make yourself scarce!"

Connie was only too glad to go. Between moving drays, horses' heads and rough men she made her way across the common to the sidewalk which ran along in front of ship chandleries, grog shops and warerooms. The street name, or rather number on the paper, was no help to a stranger, and with some misgivings the girl entered a hole-in-the-wall where a man sat repairing a boot. Her question remained unanswered until the cobbler had removed several pegs from his mouth, one by one, and pounded them into the sole of the boot. Then, twitching a thumb to the left, he mumbled something. Connie caught only one word, but thanking the man she went east to where Broadway ran inland at right angles to the river. This main thoroughfare, in even wilder confusion than the water front, was crowded with horses, carts, wagons and workmen shoveling earth out of a long trench. Stories about the building of Fort Meigs led Connie to the conclusion that some new fortification was underway, and she asked a passing carter if Indian attack was expected.

"Injuns?" said the man, pushing back a battered felt hat to stare at the girl. "There ain't been nary redskin hereabouts for years." Then, as she glanced toward the ditch, he roared with laughter. "That, missy," he told her, "be the new waterworks. 'Tis gumwood pipes we'll soon be puttin' underground, not corpses."

Connie felt foolish, too foolish to ask directions and she edged between cart wheels into a side street. This street ran uphill between unbroken rows of attached two-story houses, all exactly alike. Each house had three windows upstairs, two below, and a door that opened directly upon the crowded sidewalk. For here, too, people were on the move, all bearing baskets. Connie smiled into the first friendly face and extended the paper.

The plump matron smiled back as she shook her head. "I never larned to read, missy," she said. "Ax somebody as can."

Connie said, "I can. It says Number One Hundred and Sixty-Four, Second Street. Is that anywhere near here?"

"Close by," replied the matron, "but ye ain't like to find nobody to home. This time of day, menfolks is at work and womenfolks gone to market."

Nevertheless, Connie continued along the street to the proper number. As she knocked her heart pounded, but it seemed to stop beating when the door was opened by what she took to be a complete stranger.

Then she cried, "Stasie! It *is* you, after all! Thank goodness!"

Anastasia Field stared at the visitor with lackluster eyes devoid of recognition. A thin nose with wide flaring nostrils above full red lips gave her the air of a nervous horse ready to shy at the unfamiliar.

When Connie realized that her own face was hidden by her headgear, she snatched off the bonnet.

"La petite belle-sœur!" exclaimed Anastasia, *"Mais, se faire couper les cheveux! Pourquoi?"* Then, seeing Connie's brows knit in puzzlement, she said brokenly, "Ze hair! You have cut eet! Why?"

"Oh, that!" said Connie. "If you will let me come in, Stasie, I'll explain—everything."

Jed's Creole wife must have understood more of her husband's native tongue than she spoke for, standing aside, she said, *"Entre donc!"*

Connie followed her down a short dark hall into a disorderly kitchen where a small dirty child played on the floor surrounded by pans and potlids. Although there was nothing of the "Field look" in the little girl's tangled brown curls or brown eyes, Connie felt the pull of the blood tie. She dropped to her knees and held out both hands, saying, "I'm your auntie, dear! Won't you give me a kiss and then tell me your name?"

The child stared blankly and continued to suck her thumb. Suddenly she smiled and held up her mouth to be kissed.

Catching the child in her arms, Connie gazed over the tangled curls, inquiring, "What do you call her, Stasie? My, isn't she sweet?"

The mother made no reply. Perhaps she did not understand, for she was gazing at the pair with a speculative expression in eyes at once like and unlike her daughter's, for where the child's gaze was clear and confiding, the woman's resembled that of a fowl looking for worms.

When the question was repeated, Anastasia started, then said, "Ah, *oui! Le nom.* She is call Julie. You like *les enfants, ma belle-sœur,* no?" Then, seeing again that she had not made herself clear, she asked, "You like baybees?"

"I like this one," replied Connie. "I guess I'd love any child who belonged to any of my brothers. Mal's wife is going to have one and she hates the very idea. Can you imagine that?"

"Mal?" Stasie repeated, knitting delicate brows. Then, brightening, *"Mais, oui!* He ees Jed's *frère.* Has these Mal much familee?" And when Connie explained that the one expected was the first child, Jed's wife said, "One keep me busy. We have no sairvant. Wat weel I do with two children?"

At that, Connie regarded the shapeless wrapper more closely and realized why she had been so slow to recognize Stasie as the slender bride of a few weeks Jed had brought to Cleveland. "Oh, you'll get along all right," she comforted. "Nobody I know keeps help and most families have from five to ten children."

"Oo-la-la!" shrieked Stasie, throwing out both hands in a gesture like the flapping of wings. "Zat ees what Jed say, *mais,* I do not believe. *Moi,* I demand zat he buy *une négresse, mais* he weel not."

"He can't," Connie explained. "I don't mean my brother can't afford a slave; I don't know about that. But I do know that slavery is against the law in Ohio."

"Zat Jed also tell me an' I do not believe," was Stasie's retort. "Across the river, everybody keep slaves." Before Connie could explain that across the river was Kentucky, a different state with different laws, Stasie raved on, "Jed say hees mother scrub ze floor, wash ze clothes, cook, do everysing, so-o-o, *moi,* I mus' do ze same."

Connie said, "Well, right now you'd better not, Stasie. I'll scrub this floor. But first, could I have a bite to eat? I'd no supper and no breakfast, and I'm fair famished."

The meal Stasie set forth on the dirty kitchen table was far from appetizing, but Connie was too hungry to be squeamish, and while she ate underdone bacon and overdone bread, Anastasia continued to inveigh against a husband too stingy to provide a domestic, but who made a slave of his wife. "All ze day I do nuzzing but work, work, work!" she complained.

Connie was moved to ask "what at," but curbed the impulse and inquired about the Lancaster Seminary.

Instead of supplying this information, the Creole launched into a eulogy of the convent where the good Sisters had taught her to embroider and play the pianoforte, a word that had to be demonstrated with finger exercises on the edge of the kitchen table.

By then Connie had finished the miserable meal and rose to wash the dishes. Both kettle and bucket were empty, and she opened the back door to visit the well. A rain barrel, fed from the roof by a length of wooden pipe, was green with scum and alive with insects. The only other object in the yard was an outhouse at the end of a path. Over its roof Connie caught sight of a breath-taking panorama—the lower level of the city with its wharves and warehouses, and across the wide river a hamlet nestling in the blue folds of the Kentucky hills.

"Water for wash and scrub, eet come een ze cart," she heard Stasie saying. "For cook, eet is *nécessaire* to visit ze poomp *au coin.*"

As Connie had seen on the corner a tall wooden contraption painted blue and worked by a long red handle, she took the hint and went out the front door with the bucket.

On her return, the kitchen was empty. Evidently Stasie had taken Julie upstairs for a nap. Connie spent the remainder of the morning on hands and knees, scrubbing the filthy floor to whiteness. Surely, she thought, I can earn my keep here! Earning cash to pay tuition fees was the problem. For between classes there would be little time to seek gainful employment elsewhere, and it was too much to expect that Jed, in addition to the cost of her victuals, would pay his sister's schooling.

However, Connie resolved to cater to her brother's love of food by giving him a better supper than her own breakfast suggested Stasie was in the habit of providing. But when she went into the buttery, she found it as bare as Old Mother Hubbard's cupboard. Did this mean that Jed was actually poverty-stricken, or merely as stingy as his wife claimed?

These questions seemed to be answered in part when Stasie came downstairs with a purse and explained in garbled French and English and many gestures, how Jed had refused to do the day's marketing before going to work, and in retaliation she had refused to prepare any evening meal. Now, however, *la belle-sœur* could do both chores.

More than willing, Connie took purse and basket to market. It was her first trading experience, for Ashbel Field's clients paid his fees largely in produce. Now his daughter carried a heavy sense of responsibility to the public place of trade and barter. It was located between Third and Fourth Streets, where a long narrow roof sheltered a narrower stretch of brick walk to which scores of farm wagons were backed up, tail gates lowered to form counters for the display of produce.

Prices struck Connie as outrageously high. Beef and mutton at six cents a pound! Fifty cents for a turkey would empty the purse! After making the rounds, she finally purchased a pair of fat fowl for two bits. A dime bought a peck each of onions and turnips with a large head of cabbage thrown in. Five cents provided a loaf of bread and a pat of butter. A dime still remained in the purse, but as the basket was full, Connie returned to start supper preparations. As the first step, she looked in the woodbox, found it as empty as the buttery had been, and visited the outhouse, dismayed to discover that it did not serve the usual double purpose. Where then, did Jed keep his fuel?

Stasie, asked that question, replied that fuel was not kept; it was purchased as needed from a vendor. Today, however, she had missed the woodcart as well as the water cart. In consequence, Connie was obliged to go to market a second time and spend the last dime for an armful of logs and lightwood. She had been accustomed to filling the blockhouse woodbox from the nearby woodpile, but by the time fuel had been lugged from Fourth Street to Jed's kitchen, Connie was completely winded. Cincinnati, for all its huge size and market facilities, lacked some wilderness conveniences, it seemed. Jed's house, for instance, had no clock at all, much less one contrived to turn the spit like the clock in the Putnam kitchen. When the fire Connie kindled was reduced to the right amount of glowing coals, she placed the pair of fowls on the spit and sat down to turn it slowly by hand. This was a chore even a pregnant female might have undertaken with safety. But Stasie was nowhere around, and Connie left the spit only long enough to put the kettle on the crane at the proper time and boil all three vegetables together.

Dark had fallen outside when the front door opened with a bang and a heavy tread announced that the master of the house was home. As Connie looked up from the hearth, her face was in shadow while that of her second brother was illuminated by the flames.

Jedediah Field at thirty was a handsome man, as black-browed and lean-hipped as his father, but perhaps because he held his broad shoulders more erect than Ashbel did these days, Jed looked much taller. When he caught sight of the crouching female, he boomed, "Well, I'll be hanged! Cooking a square meal after all, for a change, hey?"

Connie rose to her feet, saying, "I'm not Stasie, Jed. I'm——"

Jed interrupted, "Well, I'll be hanged if it ain't the Field tomboy! No wonder I didn't recognize you at first sight of that cropped head. How come, Sis?"

She took the question literally and replied, "By steamboat, like I wrote you I would. And when you didn't meet me at the dock, I——"

Jed interrupted. "You sent me a letter, Sis? Well, I never got it. Fact is, I never stop at the post office, seeing folks who don't write can't look for letters. Stasie gets 'em from her pa, though. I wonder——" He broke off to shout, "Stasie! Stasie, where in heaven are you?"

His wife, awakened from a long nap, came down yawning and sleepy-eyed. She confessed that she had, indeed, brought home a letter addressed to her husband, weeks ago, and another more recently. But when Jed demanded to know what she had done with them, Stasie replied, "I forget. I keep them safe, Jed, *mais* where I cannot remember. I weel make search."

Connie said, "Wait until after supper. It's ready to dish up. Anyway, there was nothing in either letter I can't tell quicker than you can find them. Sit down, both of you, and we can talk while we eat."

It was she who did most of the talking and Jed the eating. By the time his appetite had been appeased, little was left of the hearty meal, but Jed was left very kindly disposed toward the cook. "Just how old are you, Sis, anyway?" he inquired, and when told, he exclaimed, "Don't seem possible! Why, I remember the night you were born like it was yesterday, and here you are, already an old maid. How come? A gal who can cook victuals fit for a king, had ought to have her pick of husbands."

The assertion that what Constitution Field wanted was not a husband, but a man's education, left Jed well-nigh speechless. All he could say was to repeat, "Well, I'll be hanged." He continued to stare at her so fixedly that Connie grew uneasy, fearful that Jed was about to repeat Mal's injunction that she must return home. What Jed did say, finally, was, "Well, now, being all Field, you won't change your mind, I presume to say, 'twixt now and the day you become of age and your own man—I—uh—mean your own mistress." When Connie shook her head, he went on, "Such being the case, you might as well stay here now, provided you and me can strike a bargain. You help Stasie keep house, learn her to cook and speak United States in return for your keep and your schooling."

This was so much more than Connie had dared hope for, that easy victory left her speechless. It was Stasie who spoke up to protest any cash expenditure on projects other than her own, but fear of losing this willing slave finally overcame cupidity and she agreed to try harder to learn "these Eenglish." She balked at housework, however, declaring it beneath the dignity of any white female born and reared in New Orleans. "Con-nee," she insisted, "mus' do all ze wash, ze cook, ze scrub."

Fear that argument on this point would end in her own loss of this heaven-sent opportunity, drove Constitution to agree in haste, and on that basis the bargain was concluded.

Jed rose, picked up the candle to light a second candle for his sister, and then led the way upstairs to bed. The second floor, like the first, consisted of two rooms, and when the door of the rear chamber closed behind the family, Connie entered the front room. It was bare except for a trundle bed without linen or coverlet. She set the candle on the floor, hung her gown on a wall peg, and stretched out on the husk mattress. After the restless night in the stuffy steamer cabin and another on a hard chair in the dockside office, the tired girl fell asleep almost at once.

The next thing Connie heard was pounding on the door and Jed's voice shouting to her to get up and get his breakfast. Connie hurried down, found Jed making the fire. There was no sign of his wife, and after putting the hasty pudding to boil, Connie put the remnants of last night's meal in Jed's lunch basket. After breakfast he took the basket, gave her fifty cents for provisions, and hurried off to the shipyard.

One thing Connie had made up her mind not to do was lug fuel from the market place again, and she entered the front room to watch for the vendor. A chair by the window suggested that Stasie did not usually miss both wood and water carts. While Connie sat gazing out of the window, Stasie appeared with a soiled peignoir over her night shift to drop down on the only vacant chair. The bareness of this room, as well as the one above it, was not due to Jed's inability to pay for furnishings, his wife said, but to his refusal to buy the kind Stasie wanted. If she couldn't have a plush-covered parlor set, a marble-topped center table, and a rosewood piano, she'd have "nuzzing."

Connie was saved necessity for comment by a short sharp cry that came nearer and nearer down the street. By the time wood was purchased, the water cart rumbled into view—a huge hogshead mounted on wheels. With the day's supply of water in the house, Connie set out for market.

She did not proceed there directly, however, but went up Walnut Street to Fourth for a look at the magnet which had drawn her down the Ohio Valley. The boast that Lancaster Seminary was the finest building west of the Allegheny Mountains seemed to her well warranted. It was indeed a handsome structure of brick, with two long wings connected by a pillared portico topped with an octagonal tower. It was in that tower, no doubt, that the class in astronomy met to explore the firmament and study the stars.

No classes of any kind were presently in progress; the seminary was closed for the summer. Jed had explained that "Commencement" came in September when students who had completed the preparatory school might enter the college. Connie could not

106

resist the urge to peer through the tall windows of the portico into the vast empty hall and dream of the time when she would climb those broad stairs into the heaven of her dreams. There was an exalted look in the black Field eyes when she finally tore herself away to go about the mundane matter of marketing.

When she returned to Second Street and had deposited the heavy basket in the buttery, Connie went upstairs to do the bed work. Stasie, still in the peignoir, was holding up a gown for inspection before the window. Amid a jumble of garments on the bed sat Julie, unwashed, uncombed, playing with a doll. At sight of her aunt, the little girl gurgled with pleasure.

Stasie turned. "Oh, Con-nee!" she cried. "Come een! Come een *et regardez!* These robe have I outgrow. See weel eet fit you."

Compared with the makeshift she had on, the garment Stasie held out looked to Connie very elegant—far too elegant to be discarded. It would fit Stasie again when her slim figure had been regained, Connie reminded.

Stasie shrugged. The gown was already out-of-date, she intimated. *La mode nouvelle* would be displayed in New Orleans. After bearing Julie among strangers, she craved for her second confinement the services of a family slave skilled in the art of midwifery. All this Stasie communicated to her *belle-sœur* more by gesture than by words, for her limited English was almost as incomprehensible to Connie as French.

Anxiety to bear the coming child in Louisiana, however, was something Connie could well understand, for it was an old New England custom for young wives to return to their parents' home for such blessed events. What troubled her was Ma Betts' warning to Mercy, and she could not keep from protesting, "But Stasie, is it safe for you to go so far, now?"

Stasie stared for a moment, then said, *"Ah, oui!* I understand. But ze trip on ze new steamboat—eet ees—what you say—a gentle journey." Her only concern for the voyage was that she could not look *chic*. *"Apres l'accouchement,"* Stasie asserted, *"mon* papa weel buy me manee costume *à la mode.* Alreadee he haf send me *une papier pour le bateau à vapeur."* In proof she held out a slip of paper.

At first glance Connie took it for a steamboat ticket, such as

General Putnam had given her. The strip of parchment, however, bore a legend to the effect that it was a draft on the Bank of New Orleans. She knew what a bank was. Had she not heard Pa and Mr. Kelley discussing the prospects of financing a canal through Mr. Case's bank in Cleveland? Jed, who gave the impression of knowing everything under the sun, could be depended on to know what to do with a bank draft.

That he had no knowledge whatsoever of this particular draft became evident when Connie mentioned it at supper. Jed scowled across the table at his wife. "I thought I had made it clear that I want no help from your father," he asserted. "When I married you, I didn't know you were a rich man's daughter."

Stasie blazed back, *"Mais, toi,* you lead me to theenk you are a reech man's son. All time you talk beeg how *votre père* own haf ze citee of Cleveland! City! Poof! *Un endroit sauvage!"* Tone and gesture alike expressed contempt for the crude settlement on Lake Erie.

It was no surprise to Connie that Jed had talked "beeg." Always he'd been a braggart. But that Stasie might have married him for his prospects was a shocking thought.

More shocking was the way he shouted at his wife, "Shut your mouth, woman!"

Stasie's response to this command was a grimace. Whereupon Jed leaped up and closed the provocative lips with a kiss—a kiss so fierce that it looked to Connie like the bite of some wild beast. Yet Jed's wife seemed neither hurt, frightened nor revolted by the savage caress, but pressed her body against her husband and, reaching up both hands to clasp his head, returned his kiss with equal passion.

Such forthright display of powerful emotions embarrassed the girl, and she escaped into the buttery to stand in the dark, her heart beating fast with this sudden revelation of what drew men and women together in spite of differences of language, race and upbringing. But how long would it *hold* Jed and Stasie together, Connie wondered. She had kindled too many hearthfires not to know that the hottest blaze burns out soonest and turns to ash unless fed with care, little by little, until the logs are reduced to a bed of coals that radiate a steady warmth and glow. A marriage, like a fire, must call for constant tending.

That Jed, bred in the New England tradition of thrift and hard labor, would ever conform to the easier, more luxurious way of life in which his Creole wife had been nurtured was doubtful. Was it any more probable that the combined efforts of Jed and his sister would succeed in making a New England housewife of Anastasia? Once she had returned to the comfort and indolence of her father's house, would she ever tear herself away from it again and bring Jed's children back to Cincinnati?

On that score Jed seemed to have no doubts. At any rate he raised no objections to Stasie's return to Louisiana to bear their second child. What he balked at was the use of her father's draft to defray the expense of the journey. Employees of Shreve's Shipyard, he asserted, were entitled to cut rates on Shreve steamboats. When the time came for Mrs. Jedediah Field to embark, her husband would foot the bill.

Meanwhile Mrs. Field's preparations for the journey consisted of setting her *belle-sœur* to work letting out the seams of several gowns for shipboard wear. As a reward for this service, Stasie gave Connie a brown bombazine gown and its matching bonnet. When tried on for fit, the slim skirt covered Connie but left her well-worn moccasins exposed. The contrast between the wilderness footgear and the product of the French *modiste,* however outmoded, was so marked that Stasie rummaged out a pair of scuffed satin slippers with run-down high heels. But into these hand-me-downs Connie could not force the feet which had gone unshod every summer since childhood. As going barefoot in the city was unthinkable, it was decided that she must wear the disreputable moccasins until they could be replaced by the local cobbler. If it occurred to Stasie that the cobbler would have to be paid, that matter was not mentioned.

Her *belle-sœur* having been made halfway *présentable,* Stasie proposed a promenade, for which she proceeded to make herself as *présentable* as possible under the concealing folds of a handsome Paisley shawl.

Connie took the basket, Stasie took Julie by the hand, and the three Fields set out for Fourth Street. Opposite the entrance to the market place a poster plastered on a housefront caught Stasie's eye, and since she could not read a word of the legend, Connie had to explain that wild animals from foreign parts were on view within. Nothing would do then, but to expend a dollar to see the elephant, the jaguar and the dromedary.

Only Julie was impressed, for the elephant turned out to be an old wrinkled creature that looked moth-eaten. The loose curling lower lip of the dromedary gave it a pessimistic expression, excusable in a humpback, but nevertheless depressing to look at. As for the jaguar, in his native wilds he might have been as fierce and frightful as claimed, but in captivity he was just a big sleepy cat. Mrs. Jedediah Field complained loudly that she had been cheated, but to no avail. The showman merely kept shaking his head at her voluble French, although he could scarcely have misunderstood her gestures. As for Connie, who had disapproved the expense in the first place, now the market money had been spent, she refused to demand a refund from the showman, even though with nothing left from last night's supper the one in prospect would be meager indeed. Still, at the risk of Jed's withdrawl of his promise to a cook who did not live up to specifications, Connie agreed to suppress the real reason Jed must go hungry to bed.

Julie, too, was cautioned not to "tell papa." But what child could keep silent regarding so remarkable an experience? Jed had scarcely sat down to the supper table when his little daughter burst into an excited description of a huge creature in a "gray overcoat" with bed blankets for ears and a snout as long as the hose on the new fire-wagon.

Jed stared at the child, then at his bowl of hasty pudding, and drew his own conclusions. He did not reproach his sister, however, but turned on his wife a torrent of blame for foolish extravagance. Eyes flashing, Stasie called him an *avare* and a pinch-purse. But the quarrel ended like that of the previous evening with husband and wife locked in a passionate embrace.

Next day when the womenfolks went to walk, however, it was Connie who carried both purse and basket. For entertainment she suggested seeing such sights as were free, for instance the remains of ancient works similar to those she had seen in Marietta which were presumed to have been constructed by some race of man long vanished.

With gestures more expressive than words, Stasie explained that she had already seen those "beeg croquets" left by the mound builders. The works she wanted to visit were the pianoforte works. And it was there the Field females proceeded. Fiddles, flutes and bassoons were the only musical instruments Connie had ever seen. Now at first sight she took the piano for an unusually handsome table. But when Stasie raised the lid, a long row of ivories, like a set of false teeth designed for a giant, seemed to grin in derision at the country girl's ignorance.

Seating herself at the instrument, Stasie ran practiced fingers over the ivories. The beautiful box responded with a series of tinkles that reminded Connie of a brook running downhill to join a river. Her regard for her sister-in-law's accomplishments rose accordingly. But when it became clear that Stasie's reason for visiting the works was the hope of enlisting her *belle-sœur* as an advocate for the installation of a piano in the Field parlor, Connie could not be moved from the opinion that anything so elegant would be out-of-place in a poor man's home.

On the way back toward the market, they passed the post office where Stasie wanted to mail a letter to her papa. While she waited at the window, Connie, looking about, discovered a door marked "Reading Room." As the door was open she ventured to enter. A long trestle table in the middle of the room was covered with neat piles of newspapers, over which Connie's gaze moved quickly to the book-lined walls. Then, catching sight of a pair of pantaloons below an open newspaper, she inquired if she were trespassing.

At the girl's voice, the newspaper fell, revealing a bespectabled old man who cupped an ear with a wrinkled hand. When Connie repeated her question, he replied that the room, tended by the postmaster, was open to all citizens for an annual fee. At mention of money, Connie was about to withdraw when he mentioned that reading room privileges were extended to visitors, free of charge.

Stasie, searching for her companion, found Connie's nose buried in a book and only got her away with the reminder that the day's marketing still remained to be done.

Fortunately, that evening's meal was of the sort to put any man in good humor. It was fortunate, because although Stasie had failed to win the support of Jed's sister for her purchase of a piano, his little daughter unexpectedly put in a plea for "a beeg music box." When her father's black brows drew together in a puzzled frown, Julie demonstrated on the edge of the supper table. The pantomime was very expressive.

Turning the frown on his wife, Jed began, "How many times do I have to tell you——"

Stasie interrupted, *"Mais,* eef you buy ze ticket on ze steam *bateau,* why for can I not spend *le papier de mon papa* for zee piano?"

"Because," Jed informed her, "when a female weds, any property she has or gets afterward belongs to her husband."

Although Connie sympathized with the rebellion in the dark Creole eyes, although her own heart cried out that it was neither just nor fair, for the sake of peace she felt obliged to assure Stasie that such was, indeed, the law. And when Jed, surprised by this corroboration, demanded to know how and where Connie had come by this information, she replied, "Why, in Pa's law office, of course, before he forbade me his books."

Jed ejaculated, "Well, I'll be hanged," staring hard at his sister.

In order to keep his attention from returning to his wife at the moment, Connie said, "You men! You're forever bragging about how this is a free country."

"Well, so it is," he retorted, "thanks to Pa and the rest of those old fellers who fit the Revolution, and to us who fit again to keep us free, me and Zeke and Rem. Rem died for it, remember?"

Connie said, "As though I could ever forget Rem. What you seem to forget, Jed, is how the Declaration says 'All men are created equal' with equal rights. Not a word about womenfolks rights to 'liberty and the pursuit of happiness.' No female is free."

Once again Jed ejaculated, "Well, I'll be hanged. How do you figure that out, Sis?"

"Isn't it perfectly clear?" she replied, and when Jed shook his head, she told him, "If females were free to pursue their own happiness, in their own way, I'd have gone to school in Cleveland. Then Pa would have sent me to the East to some Ladies' seminary, like he sent Mal to Yale." When Jed reminded her that Mal had worked his way through college with a minimum of help from their father, Connie reminded Jed, in turn, of his bargain. "If you aren't going to keep it," she told him, "I can cook and scrub for somebody else. In a big rich city like this, there must be plenty of folks who hire help."

Before Jed could comment, Stasie broke into voluble protest against being parted from her *belle-sœur*. And although it was clear to Connie that what Stasie feared losing was a willing drudge, she did not pursue the subject.

Jed pushed back his chair, sighed the sigh of a well-fed male, yawned and said, "Time working folks went to bed."

That night, after weeks of drought, rain fell heavily and continued all next day. Connie went alone to market, returned wet and depressed to find Stasie very gay and excited. Her torrent of French, explaining the cause of this sudden rise in spirits, left Connie bewildered and no wiser.

It was Jed who explained, over supper, that during the summer season of low water, steamboats could not run the rapids at Louisville, always a problem for large craft. But with all this rain the Ohio was rising fast, making certain that the *Washington,* due from Pittsburgh shortly, would continue downstream. Jed had come home by way of the company office where he had booked a berth in the ladies' cabin for his wife and daughter.

After supper, he asked Connie to carry the candle into the attic and light his way down with the traveling trunks.

And now the house Connie had tidied was turned upside down again as Stasie packed, unpacked and repacked with each change of mind over what garments to take and what to leave behind. Several times she gave her *belle-sœur* a gown, a shift or a pelisse only to reclaim it again. Until the trunks were out of the house Connie could not feel sure of being left with any wearing apparel at all except the clothes on her back.

On the day of departure, Jed came home at noon, hurried through dinner, strapped all the trunks, and went out to hire a dray. When the drayman arrived, he had to help restrap a trunk which Connie had been obliged to tug open so that Stasie might change from one traveling gown to another. Then it was discovered that Julie, left alone downstairs, had got into the jampot, so that another trunk had to be opened and the besmeared pinafore replaced.

Despite all these delays and time lost in argument over them, the entire Field family was on the wharf when the steamboat whistled for the landing. Now that the moment of parting was at hand, Stasie, whose idea it had been in the first place, cast herself upon her husband's breast with wild protests that she could never leave him. Whereupon Julie burst into tears, threw both arms around one of her father's legs, and wept upon his best pantaloons.

Jed proved equal to the situation. He detached his daughter, hoisted her to a shoulder, seized his wife's elbow, and took his family up the gangplank, followed by the drayman trundling the baggage.

From the wharf, Connie watched the gangplank half expecting to see all three of them stream down it to shore. Then, as the moments passed with no sign of her brother, she watched the gangplank being pulled in. All lines had been cast off when Jed appeared on deck, alone. The water was fast widening between deck and wharf, and Connie gasped as she saw her brother prepare for a leap which, surely, must land him in the river.

A moment later Jed landed on his feet beside her, grinned into her frightened face and said, "Forgot I used to be a sailor, didn't you, Sis?" Sobering, he went on, "In those days I had a gal in every port. I'd love 'em and leave 'em. Now the only gal I ever really set any store by has left *me*." When Connie reminded him that it was not for long, that before the leaves fell, Stasie would return with Julie and the new baby, Jed muttered with unwonted piety, "God willing."

Ashamed, perhaps, of showing sincere emotion, he added, flippantly, "And God knows what else beside. I scotched her wasting her pa's draft by buying her ticket with it, but there's no telling what she'll honeyfuddle the old man into buying for her in New Orleans."

Connie ejaculated, "Jed! You didn't! Surely you didn't use that draft for the ticket after all you said about paying for it out of your own pocket!"

"Why not?" Jed retorted, not at all embarrassed. "Wasn't that what the old man sent the money for?"

Connie was too shocked for words. It was as though she saw her brother in his true character for the first time. She had known him for a bumptious braggart, but nevertheless she had believed him to be a man of his word. If he wasn't—— There on the wharf, Connie seized Jed's arm. "Tell me," she demanded, "have you—will you keep your word about paying my tuition fees?"

Quite without shame, he grinned down into her perturbed face. "To tell you the truth, Sis, I won't have to. The seminary has an endowment that pays the cost of educating poorfolks' children. Well, Stasie keeps me poor, God knows, and seeing it will be years before Julie goes to school, I figure I'm entitled to free schooling for my sister."

This answer to her question, this confirmation of her fears regarding her brother's ethics, brought Connie face to face with fresh problems. Jed might consider his sister entitled to free schooling, but would the school committee agree with him? And even if it did, how long could she attend school free of charge? Within two months after Commencement Day, she would be eighteen— free of parental control, to be sure—free to stay with Jed and earn her keep as his wife's drudge, but just as certainly, legally no longer anybody's child.

Chapter 10

SUPPER TABLE conversation, hitherto revolving around Stasie, was now monopolized by Jed. Connie found these discourses more interesting than his wife's complaints and prattle, for Jed's talk was man-talk, the kind of talk she had sometimes overheard in her father's office and remembered after the gossip of her mother' friends was forgotten.

Jed talked about his work. Black locust, plentiful hereabouts, was superior to any timber available in the Pittsburgh neighborhood and just as good for hulls as Jersey oak, used by shipwrights on the Atlantic seaboard where construction costs were higher than out here in the Ohio Valley. This was only one of the reasons Jed believed in Cincinnati's great future.

The valleys of the tributaries—the Great and Little Miami— were richly productive and poured their golden harvests into every sort of bottom navigating the rivers. Hitherto the voyage to New Orleans, under sail, pole or drift, had been much too long to show a profit, for wheat, corn and flour often spoiled before reaching market. Steamboats made the trip in far less time, but increased speed increased the danger of running foul of submerged logs, roots and branches that infested all rivers. The resulting loss of larger cargoes was all the greater, not to mention the loss of craft, any one of which cost more than a whole fleet of sail or flatboats.

"But we've figured out how to get rid of those hazards, now," Jed asserted. "Hen—he's the feller I work for, Cap'n Henry Shreve, has invented a host of contraptions, and the one we're building now is sure to keep the channel clear of obstructions. Just as soon as our snag boat gets to running, money will pour into this port the way grain pours out of it. Just you wait and see."

Connie doubted that she would be in Cincinnati long enough to see this dream of her brother's materialize. Nevertheless, she put aside her own problems for the moment and reminded Jed how long their father had dreamed of a great future for Cleveland, a dream now revived with this talk of building a canal to link Lake Erie with the Ohio River.

"There's talk of digging one hereabouts, too," said Jed. "Talk of linking the lake with this river by way of the Great Miami and the Maumee."

"The Maumee," Connie repeated. "Wasn't that where Pa and Zeke helped build Fort Meigs?" And when Jed nodded, she remarked that it was still wild unsettled country and did Jed believe it would pay to dig a canal through the Black Swamp?

Jed said, "I do, but most of the talk hereabouts is of building a canal only from here to Dayton. That would bring down more crops and livestock raised in the back country than it pays to cart over roads as can't rightly be called roads, and that's nothing to sneeze at. Why," he went on with growing enthusiasm, "last year fifty thousand tons of produce went out of here. And we exported more'n a half million dollars worth of flour alone, not to mention ten thousand barrels of pork worth a hundred and fifty thousand dollars and whiskey worth forty thousand. With a canal and more steamers on a river free of snags, export figures will reach—well, the sky's the limit."

He seemed to have forgotten that his listener was a mere female, and carried away by his own confident hopes, Jed confided that what made him a penny pincher was neither poverty nor his wife's extravagant notions. As foreman at Shreve's shipyard, he was well paid. For two years he had been banking the bulk of his wages, and now had accumulated enough money to buy several city lots in the section out beyond Northern Row where the only present building was the county courthouse. Jed was gambling on Cincinnati's future as the capital of the West, if not of the entire nation.

"If Pa would only sell out in Cleveland for whatever he could get," Jed asserted, "and invest in land here before prices go sky-high, he'd leave all of us fortunes, Mal and Zeke and me. And you, too, Sis," Jed added, remembering that Ash's daughter was also one of his heirs.

Connie had no such long-range expectations. Her concern was the immediate future. This revelation of what absorbed most of Jed's thoughts and earnings convinced her that she would look to him in vain for financial aid. If she was to start school in September, somehow before then she must earn her own books and tuition. Now that Stasie was gone, *la belle-sœur* was free many more hours each day, and after marketing next morning, Connie set out for the better residential district where household help was likely to be employed.

The first place she visited was a handsome mansion with a mistress to match. This lady took for granted that the deeply tanned, black-eyed applicant was an octoroon and asked for proof that she was free.

Connie took the question for reference to her age and replied that her brother, a master-shipwright at Shreve's, would vouch for the fact that she would be eighteen in November.

"That was not my meaning," said the lady. "I mean, I must have assurance that you were either born free, or have been freed by

117

your master. Harboring runaway slaves is against the law in Ohio."

Connie knew that, and now she also knew that the lady had made a mistake—a mistake Connie corrected quite frankly and without offense.

"I beg your pardon, miss!" exclaimed the lady, "But you see, we've never had a *white* servant. They come too dear." She went on to explain that "colored" cooks, nurses and housemaids were content with a few pennies a day and "pickin's." Leftovers from whitefolks tables were toted home to their homes, becoming the only meal of the day for large families of children.

Jed was close, but his sister was sure the idea of eating the residue of wealthy men's tables would be as repugnant to him as it was to her. Laundry work would be preferable, she said. It was explained to her then that in summer when wells often went dry, Negro women carried huge baskets of linen down to the river for washing and were glad to take old clothes in payment.

Upon this information Connie abandoned any idea of entering domestic service. She had been brought up to regard any honest labor as respectable, but her stiff New England pride balked at carrying on her head a heavy basket of strangers' dirty linen through the public streets to cleanse the laundry in public in exchange for strangers' old clothes.

She did not abandon hope of attending the seminary, however. Although Ash had not replied to the letter sent from Marietta, she clung to the hope that when he had cooled off and become convinced that her eagerness for education was no childish whim, he would give in, give her his blessing, and even a little material assistance.

After Stasie's departure, Jed had taken to calling at the post office on his way home. But the letter addressed to him, which he tossed across the table one evening, did not come from New Orleans.

"Well, Sis," he said. "You sure cooked your goose. Here, read the bad news for yourself."

The document, for such it resembled more than a family letter, stated in legal language that unless Constitution Field complied with the terms herein set down, she need expect no share in the Field estate. Said terms were: immediate return to Cleveland and marriage with Mr. Hannibal Jones, as agreed, before her eighteenth birthday. In less formal words Ash wrote that Hannibal had shown remarkable patience and forbearance under very humiliating circumstances, but he could scarcely be expected to wait indefinitely for his promised bride to come to her senses. "Tell your sister," Ash concluded, "that my will to the above effect has been drawn and signed. But that if she returns to do her duty by the date stipulated, I shall destroy said will and write another including her among my beneficiaries."

The threat of disinheritance struck no such terror to Connie's heart as did this renewed threat of wedlock with a man she loathed. The mere thought of returning to the trap escaped at cost of so much hardship and peril turned her sick and cold.

"Seems to me if Pa and this Jones are so set on this match, one or the other of 'em might have come after you, Sis," Jed remarked. "I've got no time and no cash to spare for such a journey. However, if you aim to go back alone, like you came, I can spare a pair of old britches. But you'll have to start soon, if you want to get home before November."

Connie found voice then to assert, "I don't aim to go back to Cleveland at all, *ever!*"

"What?" cried Jed. "Do you mean to say you'd throw away your share of Pa's money just for a crazy notion?"

"I do," she replied, "only I don't consider it crazy to want an education."

Jed shook his head. Clearly, he did not understand his sister.

She, however, was quite sure she understood what made Jed accept her decision without trying to desuade her from it. Her disinheritance would mean a greater share of the Field estate for the other heirs.

Both brother and sister were silent for a moment. Then Jed asked, what she *did* propose to do.

"Stay here with you and work for my keep," she told him. Then, before he should repudiate the rest of his bargain, she made haste to add, "I'll find some way to earn what little cash money I shall need. Just because Cincinnati womenfolks don't hire white help, doesn't mean it isn't employed in shops."

"Hoh!" Jed hooted. "Whoever heard of a female clerk?"

Not Connie, certainly, but she wasn't prepared to take Jed's word on that matter as final. And the following day she set out to canvass the business district. Inquiry made at the fanning mill, several tobacco shops, five hatter's shops, two upholsterers, fifteen bakeries, and a pottery all met the same answer, accompanied by a look of astonishment that a female should ask so foolish a question. When Connie came to a bookbindery, her flagging hopes rose afresh. Surely, this was one establishment where a bookish girl would be welcome. But here, too, she was turned away with the statement that females were never employed. At the end of a long disappointing day Connie had to face the fact that the only shops where a girl could find work were grogshops. Every tavern kept one or more barmaids. She hesitated outside one half door after another, trying to screw up courage to enter. Each time she was driven away, like a sloop before a stiff breeze, on a blast of profanity and coarse laughter. She felt suffocated, contaminated. And in search of pure air she turned off Broadway into Fourth Street and followed it east until the way was barred by a fence, enclosing acres and acres of young vines. As she stood there, breathing in the fragrance of ripening grapes, a group of old crones limped, stumbled and crawled past to disappear around a corner of the fence. The last straggler stumbled and fell, and Connie rushed to her side.

"Are you hurt much?" she asked softly, bending down.

Rheumy, sunken eyes gazed up at her as the crone mumbled, "He'p me up, missy. If'n I ain't on hand, I'll have no loaf all week. This be the day Misser Longworth gives away bread." Clinging to Connie's arm, she tottered after her companions.

When the oddly assorted pair turned the corner, Connie saw the other crones clustered around a gate. Beyond the gate a stocky middle-aged man, carelessly dressed, was advancing down a graveled driveway followed by a younger man carrying a basket.

All the old women bobbed, babbling shrill greetings. Their benefactor returned the greetings and listened to their woes while the servant doled out loaves of bread from the basket. When Connie's crone tried to get a second loaf, the stocky man interposed.

"With such a strong healthy young kinswoman," he said, "you shouldn't stand in need of any charity at all, mother."

At that the crone cried shrilly that the gal was a stranger she'd never set eyes on till a minute ago.

Nicholas Longworth's shrewd gaze was turned on Connie as he inquired, "Then what the deuce brought you here, my good girl?"

"Work," she replied. "I need it."

Longworth's gaze traveled from the fresh young face inside the modish bonnet down over the well-cut gown which, to him, did not look old-fashioned. "You don't strike me as a needy person," he said shortly.

Connie hastened to explain that her fine clothes were a gift from the wife of the brother with whom she lived—a brother who wouldn't, or couldn't pay her tuition in the Lancaster Seminary. But when Longworth thrust a hand in a pocket and brought out a fistful of dimes, Connie drew back, flushing, to protest that she was not a beggar.

"And I," he returned tartly, "was not about to offer you alms, my good girl. But these old dames won't leave until they get their usual handout. Wait, I want to hear more about you."

When the dimes had been distributed, the crowd drifted away, mumbling prayers for the long life and continued prosperity of the most generous gentleman in Ohio.

Longworth shrugged off these blessings and stared across the gate at the girl. "Now," he said, "Who are you? And why on earth should you want to go to school at an age when most girls want to find a husband?"

Connie felt obliged to tell once again her whole story. And although Nicholas Longworth found it hard to believe that any young and attractive female should prefer to teach other folks' children to raising a family of her own, he was a man of liberal ideas who had a genuine desire to help people.

"If you really are willing to work," he told her, "and by that I mean long hours of labor too heavy for my ancient pensioners, I can offer you fair wages here in my vineyard. The catawbas are beginning to ripen, and from now until frost I shall need extra hands to harvest the crop and get it into the presses."

At the girl's look of bewilderment, he chuckled. "Not *printing* presses—*wine* presses. Grapes are too perishable to ship to distant markets, but the wine made from catawbas is equal to any imported vintage and ships well. I can afford to pay careful pickers well. But you will have to earn your money."

That evening when Connie reported where she had found work, Jed said, "Queer dick, Longworth. Got a finger in pretty near every pot that's boiling hereabouts, including shipyards. He owns more real estate than you can shake a stick at, yet he goes about in duds most poor men would give away to colored folk."

Connie recalled their father's struggle to pay taxes and she suggested that Mr. Longworth also might be "land poor."

"If he is," Jed replied, "then why the deuce don't he plant quick crops to pay taxes whilst waiting for land values to rise? You put in corn as soon as frost is out of the ground, and before snow flies you can turn your corn crop into whiskey. It takes years to bring vines into bearing, and then what have you got?" Without waiting for Connie to say *grapes,* Jed said, "Wine! That's all you've got. Weak stuff, fit only for females and parsons. You know what I think? Longsworth's crazy as a coot."

That term had been applied to Connie herself so often for nonconformity that she rose in Mr. Longworth's defense. Far from being crazy, he was smart. Someday folks who poked fun at his odd ways would find he'd been a lot smarter than they. "Anyhow," she concluded, "I mean to pick grapes in his vineyeard until school opens."

Jed found no fault with this decision provided he found a good hot supper waiting for him each evening. And, beginning with the following morning brother and sister left the house together, Jed going west and Connie east to the day's work.

Under the sun which ripened the grapes her cheeks grew browner. Under the basket of grapes balanced on her head to the end of the row where the cart waited, her gawky girl's figure took on the grace and stately carriage a duchess might well have envied. And the money earned increased her self-confidence. As all labor began at dawn and ended at sundown, the public markets remained open until curfew to catch working-class trade. By the time Connie reached the produce wagons, however, the vegetables had wilted and the best cuts of meat were gone. She had to take what remained and hurry home to get the kettle on before Jed's arrival. Had he been forced to wait for his supper, Jed might have grumbled that his sister wasn't earning her keep. But during these days he never failed to stop at the post office, and Connie always managed to have hot food on the table by the time Jed sat down.

One evening he came home not only late but drunk; something unheard of in a tightfisted man who wasted no money in bars. He tried to explain that this was a very special occasion and called for treating all hands. Connie suspected what the occasion might be before the letter he tossed at her confirmed her suspicions.

Stasie, unable to write in English and aware that Jed could not read French, had called in an amanuensis to inform her husband that he was the father of a son, and that mother and children would return to Cincinnati as soon as the long voyage was advisable.

In his cups Jed confessed what he would never have admitted when sober; he'd been none too sure of eventual family reunion. His relief and joy made it easy for Connie to forgive Jed's lapse from sobriety and help him to bed.

The good news did not end Jed's visits to the post office. For now he was impatient for further news as to when and by what steamer to expect his family. So it was that in the post office Jed saw notice, and reported to Connie that entrance examinations would be held at the Lancaster Seminary the following afternoon.

Thought of such an ordeal had not entered Connie's mind. Now, faced with the necessity to prove herself worthy of education, self-confidence failed. After all, Mal's tutoring had been brief, and aside from it she had enjoyed only one term of school. How could she expect to fill scholastic requirements in this center of learning? That night she tossed sleepless. But morning found her bound for the vineyard as usual, to work until noon and then beg leave of absence for the rest of the day.

When Connie reached the judgment hall, the door she had so often gazed upon with so much longing now stood invitingly open. Yet she approached the open door with no sense of elation, but with dread lest the sacrifice of home, mother-love and inheritance had been in vain. What should she do in event of failure to pass the examinations? Could she, perhaps, return to Athens after she turned eighteen and became free? Could she beg Mal's charity when, for long, she had failed to write and beg his forgiveness for flouting his judgment as well as their father's commands?

Constitution put these questions aside and entered the long room where examination papers were being distributed among the little handful of applicants. Malachi Field had entered Yale at an earlier age than Connie was now, but Mal had enjoyed the sound preparation denied his sister. What Connie requested in a husky whisper, was to be examined, not for college, but for the preparatory department.

She felt rather than saw her way to a desk, and upon it spread the sheet of foolscap. Slowly her heart quieted and her eyes cleared so that she could study the questions. It was a surprise to find how many answers came readily to mind. There was an inkhorn and quills on the desk. Connie dipped a pen and slowly, deliberately, and with infinite care, proceeded to fill in the blank spaces between the questions. Time seemed to stand still. Yet, when the last line had been filled, she looked up bewildered to find the room had grown dim and empty except for the master in charge. When Connie apologized for having been so slow, he took her paper, saying that the results of the examination would be posted in the portico at the end of the week.

That night Connie tossed sleepless again, sure that all her answers had been wrong. Next morning she returned to the vineyard thankful for something to do, anything to keep hands, feet and mind occupied. After the evening purchases of provisions, she entered a cobbler's shop to be measured for her first pair of "boughten" shoes. Whatever happened, whether she attended school here, or was forced to walk all the way to Athens before winter, stout new footgear was a prime necessity.

The remaining days of that week seemed longer than all the weeks since her arrival in Cincinnati, but at last the sun set on Saturday. Yet Connie did not rush to the Seminary to learn her fate. The verdict was too important to be faced with the sweat and grime of the vineyard upon her. After Jed had gone to bed, she got out the washtub and filled it purely for her own personal use— an extravagance not indulged in since she came to live in this house with no well. In Cleveland, where there was no meetinghouse for religious services, water was free, and the New England tradition that cleanliness was next to godliness was religiously observed every Saturday night.

Cincinnati had several Houses of God before a public waterworks was so much as thought of. A place of worship was another of the things Jed and his wife could not agree upon. Therefore they attended no religious service. And since young unwed females never attended meeting alone, Connie too stayed home on Sunday.

The First Presbyterian Church, located on Main and Fourth Streets, stood back to back with the Lancaster Seminary, and as Connie approached the fateful portico on Sunday morning, the strains of the doxology followed her up the schoolhouse steps. Eagerly, breathlessly, she scanned the lists of those boys and girls who had been accepted as students. The top and smaller list, under the heading of "College," she gave no more than a glance in passing down to the longer list of successful aspirants to the preparatory department, arranged in alphabetical order. No Constitution Field appeared there!

Connie thought she had schooled herself against this bitter disappointment, but it was so overwhelming that she wondered if folks did actually die of a broken heart. A sinking sensation made her knees tremble, and lest she collapse and roll down the stone steps, she sat suddenly upon the top step and buried her face in her hands. When the first wave of grief had subsided a little and her mind cleared, she realized that the names she had read were family names. How silly she had been to look for her own name among the C's! If it was there, it would be further down the list. Getting to her feet, she drove herself back to the bulletin board and braced herself to face further disappointment, the harder to bear since, if her name did not appear among the F's, she had indeed failed beyond all possible question or doubt.

Her eyes blurred and she dared not believe what she thought she saw. The girl winked hard and looked again. And now she knew she was not just dreaming her name was there—it *was* there! *Field, Constitution* had passed!

Neither her mother's family nor her father's had any ear for music. Ash rather prided himself that he did *not* know "Yankee Doodle" from a psalm tune. And deep as was Faith's maternal love, it had never found outlet in lullabies. Nor had Connie ever felt any urge to lift up her voice in song until now. Now, although the strains of the doxology had died away in the nearby church, the words still rang in her ears, rose to her lips, and she burst out, off key, "Praise God from whom all blessings flow!"

Chapter 11

THE FRUITS of many weeks' labor in the vineyard paid for one term's schooling in advance, but left little cash to buy the books listed on the paper given Connie with the receipt for tuition.

The bookseller, deceived by the brown bombazine gown and matching bonnet, took Connie for a young lady able to buy new books. The prices made Connie gasp. She murmured an apology and turned toward the door with such an air of dejection that the bookseller suspected he had made a mistake.

"Wait a minute, miss," he said. "If you don't mind used books, I can supply your needs at less than half the cost of brand-new volumes."

Connie turned back and after doing sums in her head, purchased a dog-eared Latin grammar and an English rhetoric minus the cover. Just enough money remained for ink, paper and pens. A French grammar and reader were superfluous, anyway, since French was an extra course she could not afford. For geography she would have to depend on the wall maps at school for the present, and young ladies did not study arithmetic anyway.

With the two secondhand textbooks under her arm Connie set out next morning for the Lancaster Seminary. When she turned the corner into Walnut Street it was to see a swarm of boys of all ages, with a scattering of little girls, converging on the pillared portico. Some young fellows and three older girls lagged behind while their juniors stormed through the open doors. Then the dig nified elders, Connie among them, entered the stair hall to part company, young gentlemen to head up the right-hand staircase. With her three female companions Connie climbed the left-hand flight toward the heaven of her dreams.

She entered it, not through pearly gates guarded by an angel with flaming sword, but through a substantial oak doorway—unchallenged. The room held no fleecy clouds for the elect to recline upon, and the young ladies sat stiffly on hard straight-backed chairs facing a platform. Instead of Jehovah's throne, the platform supported a table and another stiff chair occupied by a very human figure wearing a neat but well-worn coat and knee breeches and a learned expression. No sound of harps broke the academic stillness; only the shuffling of several pair of uncomfortable new shoes. Connie had once heard a benevolent old parson make the unorthodox statement that heaven is where the heart is. This then, this bare unadorned chamber on the upper floor of the Lancaster Seminary was indeed, for Constitution Field, a veritable heaven of bliss.

That first day in such rarified atmosphere retained much of the dreamlike quality. And to convince herself of reality, Connie wrote on a sheet of her precious paper, *This is me. I'm in school. I'm going to stay in the preparatory class until I'm ready for college. Then I'm going to college and earn a diploma, like Mal, if I can manage to earn the money.* That little word *if* had importance out of all proportion to its size. *If* represented so many problems that Connie pushed them all out of her mind, crumpled the paper, and opened her Latin grammar.

After school she carried her books home to face the immediate problem of where and when next day's lessons could be prepared. Certainly it could not be in the kitchen with Jed talking a blue streak. Dared she ask him for another candle and leave to take her books into the parlor?

Jed settled this question before it was asked. Directly after supper he mumbled something about having to "see a man" and went out, leaving his sister to wonder if this were just an excuse or real business.

On subsequent evenings Jed made the same excuse again and again. He never stayed out late during the work week and never came home drunk, which proved nothing beyond the fact that if he actually met a man on business, it wasn't very profitable business for any bar. Connie made the most of these quiet evenings, knowing they would cease when Stasie returned. No further word had come from New Orleans since the birth announcement. But although she kept reminding her brother that "no news is good news," Connie herself was not convinced that this was true.

As the weeks passed the weather grew colder, a little too cold to go coatless to school. The brown dolman that matched the gown and the bonnet still hung on a peg in Jed's room, but Stasie had not included the wrap in her gift, and Connie would not ask Jed for it although she knew her lack of warm outer clothing increased the suspicion of queerness with which she was regarded. She had not forgotten the look in her classmates' eyes that first day when she hung up her bonnet and exposed her shorn head. She must have looked, to those ringleted maidens as odd and strange as the elephant and the dromedary had looked to the Fields.

Connie had said nothing of her ostracism to Jed. And when he asked how she was getting on, she replied, "First rate," even though he did not refer to her studies.

Whereupon Jed asked if, among her new friends, was a lad named Harrison. Connie said there was a college student of that name, but he wasn't a friend, exactly.

"Well," said Jed, "ask him anyway if his pa's the general our pa fought under. Zeke and Rem fought under him too and Red was his favorite scout. You remember Red, Sissy?"

Connie nodded without comment. What Field could forget their strange half-wild kinsman who, as a baby, had been stolen by Indians and dubbed Wisawanik, meaning Red Squirrel, because of his auburn hair? After the war, Red had lived in the Field block-house until Mal came home from Yale. Then Red left and Mercy with him. Connie had been too young then to understand what made the mild Mal so angry, or what made Mercy so meek after Mal brought her back home. During the years since then Connie had come to suspect what lay behind this matter which was never mentioned among the Fields.

Nor did Jed refer to that old scandal now. All he said was, "Red wasn't a bad feller at heart. He was just ignorant of whitefolks'

128

ways. I always wondered what became of him. General Harrison might know. Ask Young Harrison, will you Sis?"

Connie was reluctant to approach the college student, but she was anxious to please Jed and forced herself to step into the path of Young Harrison next day. From the lad's expression she saw at once that he suspected her question of being a bold pretext to scrape acquaintance. Before she could explain that Red was her cousin, Harrison gave a curt answer and turned his back on her. Even then it did not occur to Connie that the general's son had heard that old gossip of Red's elopement with a female named Field and that Young Harrison had leaped to the conclusion that this bold short-haired female was that Field. What troubled Connie at the time was the fact that her female classmates had witnessed her rebuff by the most important young man in the whole Lancaster Seminary.

As an immediate result of that humiliation, Connie was able to report to Jed that Red was presently Indian agent on the Wyandot Reservation at Upper Sandusky. She did not mention the price she had paid for that information. Indeed, it was a long time before Connie herself realized how great was the price she had paid.

Meanwhile, Jed's passing interest in their cousin was forgotten on receipt of a letter from New Orleans. A brief letter announced that the next voyage of the *Washington,* from that port, would bring the Field family. Each evening thereafter, Connie brought extra water from the corner pump, not only to wash the day's dishes, but a window or two, or scrub a floor before sitting down to her books in the quiet kitchen until Jed came home from wherever he spent his evenings. The whole house was in apple-pie order by the date the steamer was due.

That day Jed left work early and came home to change from blue jeans into his best clothes. Connie too cut her last class in order to do extra marketing in preparation for a festive meal. Jed, however, insisted that she accompany him to the wharf "to lend a hand."

"You know Stasie," he said. "She'll bring so much stuff I'll have my hands full getting it all together and finding a dray. Stasie's hands will be full of the new baby, so you've got to be on hand,

Sis, to look after Julie—keep her from getting underfoot or falling into the river."

So it was that brother and sister stood together when the *Washington* was warped alongside the dock. The usual confusion followed. Townsfolk who had come to meet friends or relatives, or merely for the entertainment of "steamboat day," blocked the shore end of both gangplanks. Roustabouts cursed and shouted "gangway," while excited females screamed greetings or just screamed.

Jed left Connie to watch the passenger exit and pushed his way up the baggage gangplank to make sure his wife's trunks and boxes were unloaded and not carried on upstream by mistake. After a time the crowd of disembarking travelers thinned out and Connie was beginning to wonder if, at the last moment, Stasie had changed her mind as usual and had not boarded the steamer at all. Then her gaze was caught by a fashionable female figure which she did not recognize until she heard Stasie's voice, crying her name. Jed, too, must have heard the cry for he pushed his way back to the foot of the passenger gangplank.

In spite of the impediments of parasol, reticule and a froufrou of ruffles to which her small daughter clung, Stasie rushed down the gangplank to throw herself upon her husband's broad chest. Between laughing and weeping, she sputtered French endearments so that it was several minutes before Jed could get in a word.

Then he demanded, "Where's my son?"

Stasie cried, "Ah, *oui!* I have forgot!"

"What?" roared Jed. "Do you mean to say you left my son behind, like an old shoe?"

"No-no-no!" sputtered Stasie. Then with a glance over her shoulder, *"Regardez!* there she come now."

"'She,'" Jed repeated. "But the letter said it was a boy! What the devil do you mean saying 'she.'"

"Delphine," Stasie retorted hotly, "she ees no devil. *Regardez!* Here she come weeth *les enfants.*"

Obediently, Jed looked and saw a tall, bandanna-crowned mulatto coming forward with a bundle in each arm. Under his breath Jed muttered again, "What the devil—"

Stasie heard and interrupted, "I tell you she ees no devil, *mais* my ol' *bonne* weech my papa have give me for to—what you say—nurse *mes enfants."*

By then the mulatto was holding out a sleeping baby in each arm. Jed shouted, "Twins, by heck! And you never told me! Why?" he turned to scowl at his wife, demanding, "Is anything the matter with one of 'em?"

"No-no-no!" Stasie cried again. "Nuzzing! Bof boys are *parfait.* See!" She extended a gloved finger to poke her offspring. Whereupon the mulatto stepped back, muttering softly deep in her throat like some jungle creature in defense of its young. Stasie laughed. "See!" she said, "Delphine is devoted to my two little boys. *Vite! Vite,* Jed! Take us all *à la maison* before zey wake and—what you say—raise ze devil. Doz boys, Jed, have *les voix terribles,* like you. Zey make ze great beeg noise."

As a matter of course, Jed had intended taking his family home on foot. But he was so surprised, so rattled by the extra member that, forgetting the baggage, he bundled the *bonne* and the babies into one landau, his wife and daughter into another and, climbing to a seat beside the driver, ordered the man to drive up the hill with all speed.

Connie, overlooked in the excitement, followed on foot. There were sounds of angry voices upstairs when she opened the door, and roars of infantile rage came from the kitchen. It was in the buttery, however, that she found the *bonne,* holding both wriggling babies in one arm while her free hand lifted one lid after another from the row of crocks. At sight of Connie she burst into a torrent of words.

The only word Connie understood was *lait,* and she said, "Oh, I'm so sorry; there isn't any milk. I took it for granted Stasie nursed the baby or I'd have bought milk at the market. I'll run back there as fast as I can."

When Connie returned from this errand, the confusion in the house had become bedlam. She held the squalling infants while their nurse warmed the milk in a pannikin, pulled a pair of bottles from a bag, filled them, and then retrieved her charges. Their roars subsided so suddenly that the voices of their parents abovestairs rang out like pistol shots.

"How often do I have to explain that it's against the law, before you get it through your thick head?" Jed shouted. "I *know* you didn't buy the wench. It makes no difference that she was borned on your papa's plantation and he gave her to you for a present. Nobody can keep a slave in Ohio. It's against the law."

The cause of this tempest in a teapot continued to feed her charges as oblivious as they of anything amiss. Suddenly the screams and shouts ceased abovestairs and a heavy tread was heard descending.

Jed came into the kitchen and stared down at his sons. Both boys gave him back stare for stare, black and brilliant. Now that their bonnets were off, he saw that their heads too were black as a raven's wing.

"By gad!" breathed Jed softly. "As like as two halves of the same nut and all Field, every inch of them. By gad!" Pride swelled him visibly, as he continued to look at the twins. But when he reached a hand toward them, the mulatto emitted again that maternal feline growl. Instinctively, Jed's hand dropped to his side. Then he looked up sheepishly into the black Field eyes of his sister. "Hanged if I know what to do," he confessed. "Stasie nursed Julie, but she's got no milk for these brats. And you know, Sis, as well as I do, Stasie's got no sense about feeding grown folks, let alone babies. This woman seems to know what kind of pap to fix for 'em, but I can't keep her here without running foul of the law. Looks to me like you'll have to give up school, Sis, and turn nursemaid."

The words *I'll do no such thing* rose to Connie's lips, but she bit them back and instead reminded Jed, "You could keep Delphine if you freed her and paid her wages. As Stasie's husband, you have control of her property, you know." Before Jed could protest that he couldn't afford hired help, Connie reminded him that no law set a minimum wage for free Negroes. Consequently they took what was offered and were grateful.

Jed nodded slowly, the expression on his face showing plainly a rising opinion of his sister's intelligence. "A sound idea," he told her. "I'll see to the matter at once. But," he cautioned, "not a word of it to Stasie. She wouldn't understand any better than this woman would," he jerked a thumb toward the *bonne,* now softly crooning over his sleeping children.

132

Connie promised to hold her tongue although she wondered how such a transaction could be kept secret. Moreover, would Jed actually pay Delphine a weekly wage, however small? Aware of Jed's weasel ways with money, his sister had a feeling that, until the mulatto learned to speak enough English to mingle with her own kind here, she would remain ignorant of her freedom. Between loyalty to her brother and loyalty to the law of the land Connie felt pulled two ways, like a stone at an ox-testing contest.

The immediate problem posed was sleeping accommodations for the extra arrivals. Connie had expected to take Julie into her bed so that the crib might be free for the new baby. Two babies could not be crowded into that crib, and where was their nurse to sleep? When this question was put to Stasie she shrugged it off. At her papa's place there were slave quarters. Since there were none here, Delphine would of course occupy the front chamber with the twins, for whom a double cradle had been brought from New Orleans. This statement reminded Jed that he had forgotten the baggage and he left in a hurry.

Connie took for granted that if the front chamber were to be converted into a nursery, a bed for her would be set up in the bare unfurnished parlor. When Jed came back with two heavily loaded drays, however, she watched the room being crowded with a red plush parlor set and a rosewood piano. There was no space to spare for a bed, and although the set included a love seat two people might share if they sat very close together, even one person could not stretch out upon this fancy piece of furniture.

After considerable fuss and fuming on the part of husband and wife, Connie went to bed in her own bed, but not to sleep, for Delphine, who occupied the trundle, snored half the night. And the other half the twins cried in their cradle on the other side of Delphine. Until midnight there was no sleep in the backroom, either, for continued altercations were audible through the thin partition.

"Lancelot!" Jed roared, "What kind of a name is that for a he-man? Or Lafayette, either, for that matter. Oh, I know a feller by that name helped us win freedom from Britain, but he was a frog— a Frenchman."

Stasie reminded Jed that she herself was French, and so was her papa for whom one of her sons had been christened. It was to

133

please her husband that the other twin had been christened in honor of the great patriot.

By no means mollified, Jed retorted that while he admired the marquis, there were any number of native patriots he'd prefer to honor thus, including his own father, or the grandfather for whom he himself had been named. Had he dreamed that Stasie would take such a step without consulting him, he would have forbidden her her voyage down-river to bear their sons in what, despite the Louisiana Purchase, Jed still looked upon as a foreign country.

How much or how little of this Stasie understood, she was subdued temporarily by the tone of Jed's voice, and soon the noise of battle died away. Throughout the tumult and the shouting the *bonne* had snored on, undisturbed. But at the first hungry whimper from the cradle, Delphine awoke instantly. Big as she was, she crept out of the room and down the stairs in the dark as silently as a wraith to return with two bottles of warm milk. From then on the house was quiet until dawn when the twins woke again like a pair of famished young robbins. While Delphine prepared more bottles, Connie prepared breakfast for all adults and did the daily marketing before going to school.

She found study difficult, however, for her mind was a muddle from lack of sleep and worry about the future. With hired help in the house she felt superfluous—a feeling augmented by Stasie's lack of consideration for her comfort. Connie was determined to put up with anything for the duration of the term already paid for, but beyond that she could not stay on, unwanted. The question of how to make herself indispensable under these new circumstances posed a problem. Renewal of her effort to teach Stasie to speak English would please Jed, but would Stasie make the effort now she had Delphine to converse with in their native tongue? Was Delphine a fixture? Or would Jed decide to send her back to New Orleans rather than assume the added expense of wages, however small?

On this matter, at least, Connie's mind was set at rest that night when Jed took her aside and confided that he had taken legal steps to make the mulatto a free woman. "But don't let on to Stasie," he warned. "Not that I'm not within my legal rights, you understand,

Sis. But Stasie never will understand, so there's no use getting her back up over it."

In that Connie concurred. Then she inquired how Jed proposed to make Delphine understand her new status.

"I sh'n' try," replied Jed. "What I aim to do is open a bank account in her name and pay her wages into it. You keep the book, Sis, and show it to any officer of the law who calls to check up on me. But if any abolitionists poke there noses in here, you tell them to go to—I mean to mind their own business."

Delphine soon made clear by shrugs and gestures that *her* business was minding babies, not *cuisine*. She'd never been trained to cook. This relieved Connie's mind regarding her own continued usefulness in her brother's family. After the household had settled down to the new regime her chief problem became a quiet place to study. Even when Jed went out after supper, the noisy crowded kitchen was no place for a student. When Connie suggested going across the hall, Stasie objected: her precious parlor was for company. Reminded that they never had any, Stasie asserted that they would have now that she had a proper place to receive callers.

For once Jed sided with his wife, although he gave a different reason. Oil for the new astral parlor lamp was costly, and fuel for the new Franklin stove a needless expense. If Connie was bound to pore over her books all night, she could do so in the kitchen after the fire was banked and the family retired.

Heat radiated from the hearth and kept the quiet room warm longer than the stub of candle provided light, and it was darkness rather than cold that forced Connie to close her books and feel her way up to bed night after night. Perhaps this was just as well. Otherwise she might have overtaxed even her robust good health, for she had to rise before dawn and go down to build the fire and get breakfast for herself and Jed. His wife did not join them for this meal. She liked to sleep late and breakfast in bed. To the child of industrious New England parents, this habit seemed the height of indolence. Yet had Stasie demanded that her *belle-sœur* serve her, Connie would scarcely have dared refuse. Luckily, Stasie never rang her bell until Connie had gone to school so that it was Delphine who carried up the tray.

135

Although *la belle-sœur* and *la bonne* continued to sleep in the same bed, communication between them was so difficult that Connie undertook Delphine's instruction in English. It was uphill work. Connie did finally succeed in getting through the mulatto's head the impropriety of referring to the mother of three children as *Ma-amselle*. She should address her mistress as Mrs. Field and the head of the household as Mr. Field. The young lips found the strange words so hard to form that Connie ceased insistence and compromised on Missy and Misser. It was some time before the *bonne* called the self-appointed teacher anything at all. Finally, when it dawned on Delphine that Misser's sister, for some inexplicable reason, had never been married, the title *Ma-amselle* was transferred to Connie.

Jed made no attempt at all to communicate with the mulatto, and since she seldom spoke unless spoken to, it was some time before Jed became aware of Connie's efforts. Then he advised her to leave well enough alone, lest learning the local language lead the ex-slave to learn that she was no longer in bondage. Jed said, "Did the woman get it through that kinky head of hers that she's not bound to stay here? If so, she's like to skedaddle, in which case, you'd have to leave school, Sis, and tend those twins."

Repetition of this threat did not disturb Connie. "You're wrong, Jed," she told him. "You couldn't drive that woman away. She loves those boys better than——" Connie broke off. What was the use to point out that the *bonne's* love was deeper, more maternal, than that of their own mother? "Better than anything," she concluded. She no longer had any illusions about her brother's wife. Love, as described in the Bible, was something Stasie was incapable of feeling, Connie was certain.

That Stasie was capable of learning English, if so inclined, Connie was equally certain. But Stasie never tried except when involved in a quarrel with her husband. Now that the couple had ceased to bicker over the *bonne* and the names of the babies, Stasie took to berating Jed for staying out nights. She didn't believe he went "to see a man" on business. It was some woman he went to see, Stasie insisted, in spite of her husband's angry denials.

It was Connie's private opinion that Stasie was driving Jed away from home to escape those eternal rows in which he never came off victor. But her attempt to convince Stasie that this was so was no more successful than was her attempt to teach the local language to the two Creoles, black and white. Connie herself fell into the habit of using French terms picked up from her housemates. It was so much easier than talking English to blank stares and ears that would not hear nor heed.

Stasie whiled away the time reading novels brought back in her trunks. And although Connie had no time to waste, she stole a little from her textbooks to peek into those same yellow-backed novels out of curiosity. They were fascinating, Connie found, as she spelled out the foreign words with less and less difficulty. It was by way of being recreation, her sole recreation, she told herself to quiet conscience, never dreaming what effect such self-indulgence would have upon her future.

Chapter 12

IN NOVEMBER a warm outer wrap became a necessity and one cold morning Connie went to school swathed in a bed blanket. This, together with her black eyes and straight hair set afoot a rumor that she was half Indian and had escaped from the Wyandot Reservation through the connivance of the agent. The rumor no doubt stemmed from the other rumor that she was the Field with whom the agent had eloped.

The blanket brought about a happier result at home. At sight of it on Connie's shoulders, Stasie screamed, "Oo-la-la!" Waving her hands she demanded, *"Pourquoi?* Why for you not wear ze *manteau* wheech go *avec la robe* wheech I haf give you?"

"Because you didn't give me the *manteau,"* replied Connie. And when Stasie frowned, she repeated, *"Parceque vous ne m'avez donné le manteau."*

Stasie whirled about then, rummaged through several layers of

137

new frills and furbelows in her new mahogany wardrobe, and from the depths pulled the brown dolman and flung it toward Connie, saying, *"Voila! Maintenant, je me rappele!* I haf save eet for *ta jour de naissance.* Happee birfday, *ma belle-sœur!"*

Connie was so unaccustomed to gifts of any kind that she was grateful and did not blame Stasie for selfishness in failing to provide some new trinket bought in New Orleans for the occasion. Her heart was warmed by proof that somebody remembered she was about to turn eighteen, and her pride was revived by the handsome outmoded garment as a substitute for the bed blanket.

Jed proved to have remembered the important date also, not with a gift, but by some facetious remarks. Connie had hoped that Jed might open his heart and his pocketbook sufficiently to pay for one of the books she had been unable to buy for herself. But she managed to hide her disappointment and joined in the general laughter at her expense when Jed said that now, indeed, she was a *regular* old maid.

That night when she was alone in the kitchen she sat down, not to study as usual, but to mark her coming of age with a very unusual occupation. She had never replied to her father's ultimatum, nor did she write Ash now. The letter was addressed to Faith Field, for Connie was sure her mother's continued silence was due to her father's injunction against any communication with their disobedient daughter. The letter was no plea for a change of heart, no change in the will from which she was excluded. All Connie asked for was forgiveness. All she said about her life was to report good marks received in the Lancaster Seminary. Then, certain that Jed had not written to report the addition to his family, she added news of the twins' arrival and the fact that both were, to use Granny's expression, "the 'spittin' image" of their grandfather. This, Connie hoped, would soften Pa's annoyance at their fancy French names. After biting her pen in deep thought, Connie concluded the letter with the suggestion that, since she would not participate in the Field estate, her share might be divided between Ash's twin grandsons.

Somehow, Connie had expected that coming of age would bring a new sense of freedom. And it was with considerable disappointment that, as November passed into December, the only difference was increased sense of fear for her future. More now than ever that future depended upon her own efforts, upon getting an education at all costs in order to support herself. The Lancaster Seminary employed only male instructors, but once in a while some wealthy family made application there for a qualified governess.

The term paid for in advance would end with the midyear vacation, and she was faced with the problem of how and where to find funds enough to keep her in school until summer when she was reasonably sure of securing employment again in the Longworth vineyards. It did not occur to Connie that a man of Nicholas Longworth's interest in education might be willing to advance a little cash against her future earnings.

The only thought that occurred to her was one she had had before and discarded as unthinkable. Now, as her last resort, she considered it again with the result that one cold January afternoon on her way home from school, Constitution Field entered a grogshop for the first time in her life.

To her great relief, she saw that she was not the only female. A middle-aged woman sat at a table with a middle-aged man, while three younger women mingled with the crowd of men at the bar. As no barmaid seemed to be in attendance, Connie screwed up her courage to ask the bartender for that position. In reply, the paunchy red-nosed man told her to "see the boss," and jerked a thumb toward the seated couple.

The man was a hawk-faced, shrewd-eyed individual who wore an expensive suit of broadcloth and a fancy vest. His companion was a brassy-haired, hardmouthed female in a plain black gown. Connie approached the pair with diffidence and forced herself to ask for employment.

The couple scrutinized her face, then her clothes for some minutes. Finally the woman said, "Sit down, deary, and have a beer on the house."

Connie accepted the chair pushed forward, but declined the drink on the grounds that she wasn't thirsty. Whereupon the woman reproved her. Girls engaged here were expected to drink with the customers. Despite the woman's neat and inconspicuous garments, there was something about her that repelled the girl who had grown up in a village where no respectable female frequented taprooms, much less drank in them. But since she herself had entered this bar, Connie suppressed her instinctive revulsion and asked the woman politely if she hired all the female help for her husband.

At that the proprietor gave a queer snort of amusement, followed by the statement that "the madame" was not his wife. She was, nevertheless, "the gals' boss." He stared hard at Connie. And she, determined to win his approval, stared back with what, perhaps not unnaturally, he took for boldness. At any rate he nodded, saying, "You'll do. A gal as good-looking as you ought to make plenty here. Madame will explain how we work it." He rose then and left the two women together at the table.

Connie was silent, waiting for the promised explanation while "the Madame," equally silent, looked her over as though she were a filly or a heifer on sale. Finally the woman nodded, as though convinced that her partner's estimate of the applicant was sound.

"Play your cards right, miss," she said, "and you'll do well by the house and yourself, too. You see, you get a percentage on all the licker you can honeyfuddle partners into buying for the two of you." Connie was on the point of repeating her assertion that she did not drink when the madame went on, "But don't take aboard more'n you can carry. After you've had enough, you can spill your licker on the floor when your partner ain't looking. If *he* gets drunk, the better your chances of getting him to part with his last dollar, one way or another. Like I said, you get a percentage on whatever your partners spends in this house, down here or upstairs." She nodded toward a flight of steps at the back of the room.

To the innocent girl, that last remark suggested only another bar on the second floor, very possibly an exclusive place where gentlemen of quality could drink in more refined company than down here. And she said, "I think I'd rather work upstairs, if you don't mind. But it will have to be in the evening, because——"

Madame cut her off with a short laugh, followed by the information that evenings were the only time the upper floors were ever open for business. Then she rose and dismissed Connie with orders to report that evening prepared to stay "as long as business holds good."

Connie went on home, uncertain how Jed would take the news

of her new employment. It seemed certain, however, that Stasie would object to her *belle-sœur* spending free time outside the home, and therefore Connie said nothing at all about her plans at supper. Afterward, it was taken for granted that she would spend the evening in study, as usual. But Connie remained in the house only until Jed had followed his wife to bed. Then she stole out, feeling as she had felt on leaving the blockhouse—like a thief in the night.

The appearance of a handsome new girl in the barroom drew plenty of attention, plenty of customers only too eager to buy hard liquor in her company. Connie forced herself to ignore bold glances, and all innuendoes went over her innocent head. It was well after midnight when she started home, heartened for the trip through the dark streets by the feel of hard money in her pocket. The front door creaked as she entered and one of the stairs creaked under her light step, but both small sounds were drowned by Delphine's snores.

The second night the madame introduced Connie to a sailor who soon suggested going upstairs. Connie's preconceived idea of a better bar on the second floor led her to hint that a visit there might prove costly.

"Hang expense!" shouted the sailor. "What do you take me for? A tightwad? Come on!"

Connie went with him then, up the steps at the back of the barroom. Although no bar was visible in the upper room, men sat drinking and playing cards at little tables. Another and larger table was so surrounded with men, sitting and standing, that what went on there was not immediately apparent. Attracted by the crowd, the sailor led Connie to the edge of it and she saw, between the shoulders of the men in front, a sort of spinning wheel in the middle of the table. There was neither flax nor wool-wound spindle and no spinstress, however, although this wheel whirred and clicked round and round and then ran down, like a clock left too long untended. The wheel was started again, not by a key but by a snub-nosed stick in the hands of a pasty-faced man with curiously expressionless eyes. The men seated around the table tossed down disks like checkers, some on red- and some on black-painted squares. When the wheel stopped spinning again, the blank-faced man pulled in all the checkers with a short-handled rake and then pushed coins toward some of the players.

The sailor said in Connie's ear, "Bring me luck, gal, and I'll divide the take with you. Do I lose, will you make it up to me in some way?"

For a moment Connie wondered what the sailor could mean, then she saw him glance toward a second flight of stairs and concluded that there must be still another game room above, perhaps where stakes were higher, too. When she made no reply, the sailor said impatiently, "Well, gal, are you ready to play the game, or ain't you?"

Madame's injunction that the customer must always be pleased came to the girl's mind and she said quickly, "Yes, oh, yes, of course I'll play."

"Good!" exclaimed the sailor. "Now, which shall I bet on, the red or the black?"

For no better reason than a love of gay colors, Connie replied, "Red."

The man with the rake touched the wheel. It whirled wildly, then gradually turned slower and slower until it stopped. In a flat voice the man with the rake announced, "Red wins," and pushed a pile of coins toward Connie's companion.

He let the pile lie and looked at the girl over it, raising one eyebrow. "Well, how about it, gal?" he demanded. "Shall we call it quits? Or shall we bet the hull caboodle? What'll it be this time, red or black?"

And again, without giving the matter any serious thought, Connie said, "Red." She had no knowledge of the habit in such places by which a new customer was permitted to win a few times until he was ready to wager all he possessed—and lose. Connie caught the contagion of victory and urged the sailor to keep on playing the game. He was still winning when something prompted Connie to shake her head at him when he raised that questioning eyebrow. It was not suspicion that their "luck" was about to turn that prompted her to shake her head. It was remembrance of the old adage about the folly of "flying in the face of Providence."

Over the face of the man with the rake flashed a fleeting look of venom that made Connie think of the snake which had barred her path in the forest. Then the looked faded as quickly as it had appeared and the colorless voice chanted once more, "Red wins."

The face of the sailor turned red with anger and he shouted, "Look what come of your hunch, gal. It was no good. We could just as well have won again."

Connie, hastily scraping her share of previous winnings into her reticule, replied, "Maybe." That fleeting flash of venom suggested that if the sailor had bet on the red again, the black would have won. Something was wrong here, so wrong that she couldn't get out fast enough. Before the sailor was aware of her intention, Connie flew down the stairs and out through the swinging doors, determined never to enter them again.

She had not gone far when she began to have an uneasy sense of being followed. The double row of houses was silent and dark. The empty street between them was dark except for the light of the waning moon, and silent except for footsteps that slowly drew nearer and nearer. Heavy footsteps were coming up from behind. Turning into Second Street, Connie began to run. Her pursuer leaped forward then and grasped her elbow.

A beery voice rumbled huskily, "Don't yell, miss. I ain't no thief. I'm yer friend. Ye lit outa that joint so fast, ye dropped sumpin'. Here 'tis, miss."

The beery voice was strange to Connie's ears, the article he held out strangely familiar. It was the reticule she had not missed until now. "Oh, thank you!" she said and reached for her property.

It was withdrawn quickly. "Not so fast," said the man. "What about the reward?"

"Mister," said Connie, "You can't need a reward half as much as I need every cent of that money."

The shadowy man chuckled. "You," he asserted, "kin git plenty more where that come from. Yer a mighty enticin' baggage. Hanged if I wouldn't ruther have a kiss than the cash. How's that for a bargain?"

For answer Connie gave him what she had given the cheese merchant—a blow so swift, so strong, so utterly unexpected, that the grip on her elbow relaxed and the shadowy figure staggered back with an oath. Before he recovered from the surprise attack, his assailant had run down the street and disappeared.

143

Connie had entered her brother's house to close the door and lean against it, breathless. It was not until her heart quieted that she realized that she had left the reticule in the hands of the stranger.

All next day she went about her usual occupations in a fog of doubt and uncertainty. When she had dashed out through those swinging doors last night, it had been with the determination never to enter them again. The loss of the reticule caused her to reconsider that determination, for the thought of the beery-voiced man guzzling on the money so desperately needed for books and school fees was unbearable. Connie had no idea what the man looked like, but she was certain she would know that voice again. The city was full of grogshops, but already Connie had learned enough about such places to surmise that drinking men had their favorite hangouts. Her only chance of getting her money back was to return to the place where it came from on the chance that the beery-voiced man would do likewise.

It was the measure of her necessity—the crying need for money to pursue the course for which she had already sacrificed so much —that gave Constitution Field courage to suppress her repugnance and enter those swinging doors again next evening.

For a time she sat at one of the little tables forcing herself to smile brightly at one patron after another, allow some man to fill her glass and then, while he drained his liquor, dispose of hers under the table. And all the while that she smiled at her current companion, Connie was deaf to his silly talk because her ears were strained for the sound of a voice roughened by years of tippling. As the evening wore on, she realized her hope had been misplaced. Either the man who had her money was spending it elsewhere, or her memory for voices was not dependable. With the growing certainty that her precious reticule was gone for good came the necessity for replacing the contents. And when her current partner, a tall lanky Kentucky tobacco grower from across the river, made the suggestion that they go upstairs together, the force of her need was so compelling that she agreed.

Beside the table where the wheel whirred and clicked, Connie saw with relief that the man holding the rake was a different man from last night. When the tobacco grower asked her to pick their color, she spoke once more for the red to win. It did, not only once, but again and again as it had the previous evening.

"Gal," exulted the Kentuckian, "You-all sure are a wonder. I'm going to bet my shirt on the red to win again."

Connie slipped her share of their winnings into her petticoat pocket, saying, "Do as you please, sir, but for me 'enough is as good as a feast,' as my Granny used to say."

"Granny yourself!" retorted her partner huffily. "Lookit, if you-all have turned lily-livered, I ain't! Here goes!"

Yet, when the wheel stopped on the black, he grew furious and blamed the girl because, as he said, he'd "lost his shirt." The game was crooked, the gal a decoy, a come-on, a thimblerigger, a sharper, and like enough, a pickpocket to boot."

Aghast, and now thoroughly frightened, Connie stood beside the table unable to defend herself against these accusations because of her conviction that the Kentucky man was right about the wheel being crooked. The noise he made brought up from below a brute of a fellow who seized him by the coat collar and hustled him down and out in short order. The row had drawn the eyes of the card players at the smaller tables, and through the haze of tobacco smoke Connie saw her brother's face, slack-jawed with amazement as black Field gaze met black Field gaze. Then Jed blinked, passed a hand over his forehead, and turned back to his game. It was evident he did not credit what he saw, believed it a hallucination.

Connie gasped and turned to escape before Jed should glance again in her direction. At the top of the stairs, however, her way was barred by the brassy-haired female.

"What's your hurry, miss?" inquired the madame. "Business is good upstairs tonight. You'll make more up there than you are like to do here, if you play your cards right."

Cards! The word conveyed only the literal meaning—that the third floor, like the second, was furnished with card tables. She would have preferred to go down rather than up, but the set of the madame's jaw made plain that she could not pass without argument, loud and noisy argument sure to attract the attention of every man in the room, including Jedediah Field.

At the moment there was nothing Connie feared so much as

145

discovery by her brother and to escape the risk, she took what she felt to be the lesser evil—the stairway to the third floor.

To her surprise there wasn't a table in sight. What she saw was a narrow corridor between a double row of doors, some closed and some open. Muted sounds of revelry came from behind the closed doors, and through one which stood open Connie saw that the cubicle was a sparsely furnished room. Now she knew beyond any possible doubt what until then, in her innocence, in her ignorance, she had not so much as suspected—what the purpose of this floor was. The knowledge came with such a stunning force that she stopped, as though frozen in her tracks. Then a hot and sickening wave of revulsion swept over her, freed her feet to turn back toward the stairhead.

Again her way was blocked by the hard-eyed madame. "What's wrong with you?" she demanded.

"Wrong?" echoed Connie. "With me? Nothing, except that I've been a fool, a blind silly fool. It's this dreadful place that's wrong, all wrong. I never dreamed——"

The madame interrupted, "Don't try to put any of that stuff over on me. You can't be no spotless lily or you'd never of come in here in the first place. So far, you've cost the house plenty by not playing our game, like I told you. Well, you'll play it now until you've made good our loss. Up here's where my place does the best business. And it's my business to see that it goes on. Get yourself into that room yonder, missy, and I'll send up a sailor as bespoke your company last night and was mad as a wet hen when I couldn't locate you for him nowhere."

Pleas for compassion, Connie realized, would be as useless as argument with this hard-eyed purposeful female. There was only one thing for her to do, and that was treat the woman as she had treated the beery-voiced man. Connie struck out at the mean aged face so swiftly that the woman, caught off guard, staggered back. Connie was halfway down the flight when the madame, furious and frightened lest the girl rush into the street screaming for the constabulary, overtook the fugitive. She threw one muscular arm around Connie's waist and clapped her free hand over the girl's mouth.

Desperation gave Connie strength to turn her head and scream,

"Jed! Help!" just once before the talon-like fingers cut off speech.

The sound of his name in that familiar voice brought Jedediah Field to his feet, his gaze to the open staircase and the pair of fighting females. Without that earlier glimpse of a handsome black-eyed girl, Jed might not have recognized one of the struggling women as his sister, for men nearer the scene were climbing on chairs for a better view of "the fun." Shouted curses and profanities mingled with cries of encouragement, now for one combatant, now for the other, as though the place were a cockpit.

Jed forced his way toward the stair, ran up and thrust a brawny arm between the girl and the woman.

The madame had seen the black-browed man before, although he had never shown any interest in her or her games. Now she leaped to the conclusion that this handsome new girl had made a conquest. Since Jed had every appearance of affluence, she released her hold on Connie, smiled at the customer, and stood back. The smile gave place to astonishment, then to frustrated rage, when the man hustled his companion not upstairs, but down. The furious woman might have followed them had not the stairhead been blocked by the other customers, shouting jibes and jeers after the pair.

Out in the frosty night Jed cursed under his breath, but his sister's throat was too full for words. Suddenly the strength went out of her and, clinging to him, Connie laid her head on her brother's shoulder and wept with long shuddering sobs.

He patted her back clumsily, as he told her, "By rights, I'd ought to wallop you, Sis. But somehow I've a notion you've already been punished plenty for your foolishness. What in heaven possessed you to go into such a place?"

Connie gulped, then replied, "Same thing as possessed you. Money. Only you've got a good job that pays steady wages, so you've less excuse for gambling."

In the dark she could feel Jed bristle as he growled, "Don't you start preaching to me, Sis, not after what you've been up to!"

The tinderish Field temper flared. "What I've been up to," she retorted, "is no worse than what you've been up to. Like old General Putnam said, what's sass for the gander should be sass for the goose."

Jed snorted. "Only it ain't, as you well know."

Connie did know, none better. Despite her assertion about the equality of the sexes, she was painfully aware of the restraints, the taboos, the rules, imposed upon females by the male of the species. It was useless to argue the injustice of the law, written or unwritten. This man of her own blood would no more sympathize with her revolt than he sympathized with her ambition to rise above the ignorance imposed upon her sex. Her reason for battling with the madame needed no explanation—it spoke for itself. Jed's sympathy on that score led Connie to dare ask the reason for his timely presence.

"Tell me," she said, "were you put to it to find the money to buy Delphine's freedom so Stasie could keep her here? Is that what drove you to gambling?"

"Lord, no!" he replied. "All I had to do to make that woman a free Negro was sign a paper at the courthouse, and then sign another paper agreeing to pay her wages. You know I've kept that bargain, Sis. I told you, too, awhile back as how I've been gambling in real estate for several years. But now land values are going up so fast here in the city that saving out of my wages is too dern slow. Why, just tonight I won enough to buy another lot out beyond Northern Row. Likely I'd have won four lots, if it hadn't been for you and the pickle you got yourself into. For saving you from that wicked old harpy, you ought to reward me with *your* winnings, Sis—if any."

Connie did not deny having been lucky "at that spinning wheel," but she wasn't going to give Jed a cent to invest in city lots. She was going to invest her ill-gotten gains herself—in books and school fees. What she was prepared to give Jed was her word that she would never again resort to such means of getting hold of money.

Jed chuckled. "From the look on your face when I stuck my fist betwixt you and the madame," he said, "I figured you'd larned your lesson. Like Granny used to say, 'Least said, soonest mended.' And that," Jed added, "goes for the goose as well as the gander. Keep your trap shut about my doings, Sis. I've had the devil of a time convincing Stasie I really do 'meet a man' of an evening, and not a woman. If she knew the sort of place I meet men in, she'd

148

never believe that she's the only woman in my life, even if I swore it on a stack of Bibles."

"You don't have to swear at all to convince me," Connie told him. "I know you love Stasie, in spite of the way you two quarrel. And I wouldn't for worlds start another quarrel between you."

Chapter 13

ON THE SURFACE, life in the Second Street house went on as usual. Of the undercurrent, Connie at least was conscious. When Jed was moody and silent at breakfast, she felt certain he had lost money the night before, just as she was sure he had won when he acted pleased with himself of a morning. Once she ventured to suggest that he ran grave risk of serious loss in that "tricky place."

To which Jed replied, "Don't worry, Sis. I wasn't borned yesterday. I've larned a few tricks of my own."

Connie made up her mind then to drop for good and all the subject which she had refrained from mentioning to Stasie. She also kept her own counsel on the subject of Delphine's altered status, much as she would have liked to tell the devoted *bonne* of her freedom.

That Delphine was content to slave for what she called *"ma famille,"* was plain to read on her broad smiling face and in the strange melodies she crooned over the sleepy twins and while going about her work. Although the mulatto made no more effort to learn to cook than she did to learn what, to her, was a foreign language, Delphine did more and more of the household chores as time went on. From the start she had washed all the childrens' clothes and those of their mother. Later she added those of Misser and Ma'amselle. When Jed complained of the cost of extra water bought from the cart, Delphine literally shouldered the yoke that carried buckets at both ends to and from the corner pump where water was free. Connie felt the devoted creature should have some extra reward for this service, and when Jed refused to do more than agreed, Connie used one of her own precious coins to buy a bright bandana. The big mulatto was as pleased with the gift as a child and wore it wound around her woolly head as though it were a crown.

For herself Connie bought nothing but books—Caesar's *Gallic Wars,* a volume of English history and, on being admitted to the boys' class in mathematics after the midyear recess, an algebra. The other three girls took French and prattled proudly and ungrammatically among themselves, certain that "awful short-haired girl" did not understand what they said about her. Connie wondered if she ought not to let them know that she could speak French more fluently and more accurately than they because she was obliged to use that language so much of the time at home. Her decision to keep still was due to what she overheard—what accounted for the fact that the girls ceased speaking *to her* at all.

It was clear from their remarks that one of them was cousin to the college boy who had seen "that Field squaw" in the gambling room, witnessed her struggle with the madame and her final exit from the place on the arm of a big bold man. That the man might be the girl's brother, taking her safely home, never occurred to these "nice" young people. The only girl in the algebra class, her presence also affected her classmates according to their natures. Boys, spoken of by their mothers as "such *good* boys," shunned the "black-eyed baggage" as a menace to morals. Bad boys, glorying in their badness, approached her with suggestions which would have gone over Connie's head a few weeks earlier. Now, with her new knowledge of the world and its wickedness, she caught the implications in the unfamiliar words not found in Johnson's *Dictionary.* Time was when the Field tomboy had defended herself with her fists against the attack of schoolmates jealous of her superiority at spelling and figures. She soon led the algebra class as easily. But these new classmates were not adolescents. They were young men she would be no match for at fisticuffs. Her only weapon was a furious glance from the brilliant Field eyes. After a few such encounters, the members of the algebra class left her as severely alone as did their cousins and sisters.

Constitution felt her friendlessness deeply even though, in any case, she could not have spared time for society. Neither the days nor the nights were long enough for all she had to accomplish. And it was not until spring that she took time to write her best beloved brother.

Steamboats were laid up during the winter months when rivers were fast-frozen or else filled with floating ice dangerous to shipping. And mail, routed overland by vile roads, rutted and icebound, was slow and uncertain. The letter, posted in Athens soon after New Year's Day, did not reach Cincinnati until the last day of February. Professor Field's relief and pride shone through the stilted announcement that he was the father of a boy, and that both mother and child were doing well. This was Mal's only reference to his wife. Of his son, he wrote, "Mother Pomeroy says he is as fine a child as she ever delivered. And even I, who know less than nothing about infants, can see my son's resemblance to our mother's family. For that reason I have named him Marvin."

The letter was addressed to Jed. In a postscript he added, "I have just learned from Pa that Constitution has been living with you and attending the Lancaster Seminary. Had she so informed me, I would have offered her what assistance I can in this laudable purpose. Of money I have none to spare. My stipend barely supports my family with nothing left over to lay away for the future education of my son. However, if I knew what textbooks our sister needs, and have them in my little private library, I would be only too happy to loan them to her. Pray ask Constitution to keep me informed in the future of her progress toward the goal she has so courageously set for herself."

Connie's heart swelled with happiness. Dear Mal! How happy she was that he had a son—a son born in his image and not that of his butterfly wife. Connie was happy, too, at his generous offer which proved that he held no resentment against her for flouting his judgment. The letter Connie wrote Mal to tell him how happy she was, thanked him for the offer of books and explained that, so far, she had been able to buy what was needed. She made no mention of the price she had paid in pride and bitter experience. "Give my love to dear Mrs. Pomeroy," she concluded, "and all my best to you, Mal, now and always."

When the letter was sanded, folded and sealed, Connie stared at it, wishing she had some gift to send the new baby. But, like Mal, she had no money to spare. Her wish, however, fathered the thought of something she might do for that baby's future.

The message sent to Cleveland this time was not through Faith, but addressed directly to the father who had ignored her existence since the day she had ignored his final orders. Instead of dividing her share of his estate between his twin grandsons, she asked that Jed's boys be put down for half of it, and the other half earmarked "for the college education of Marvin Field."

Concerning her own education, Connie wrote briefly and strictly in accordance with the rules set down in her new rhetoric, but she could not bring herself to close with the conventional "your obedient servant." She was, literally, nobody's servant and certainly not obedient to Ashbel Field. Nor could she, in all honesty, sign herself "your loving daughter." He had hurt her too deeply and the wound would not heal. The old spirit of revolt swelled afresh and drove her to end the letter with the words "your refractory rowan."

When the letter was gone, Connie regretted this futile flash of Field temper. It was as childish and as senseless as Stasie's jabs at Jed. Contrition for her own folly made Connie less inclined to criticize her sister-in-law. And when, one blustery afternoon, she came in to find Stasie seated at the pianoforte tinkling tunes while Julie danced and sang for the twins' entertainment, Connie suppressed her impulse to cry out that the floor was too cold for creepers and little girls in satin slippers.

Julie had the sniffles by night and before morning both baby boys came down with the croup. Their mother took no blame on herself, but flew at their father, calling him names for providing only fuel enough for the kitchen fire. Stasie demanded a second fire be kept in the parlor. She was sick of lying abed to keep from freezing.

"If you got up and dressed yourself decently," Jed retorted, "and then hustled around like other poor men's wives, you'd be warm enough. And if you were busy in the kitchen, the boys could crawl about the hearth with Julie to keep them out of the fire. I've got no money to waste on extra fuel just so you can sit in that parlor playing that blasted contraption like a rich man's wife, and that's that."

Secretly, Connie had hoped Stasie might get her way in this matter as she had in so many others. Even if the parlor fire died down before supper, the Franklin stove would radiate some heat for hours. She could study in there directly after the supper chores were done, instead of having to wait until Jed went out or the couple took their quarrels upstairs to bed.

As it was, Connie herself never went to bed until she could no longer keep her eyes open to scan the printed page. The house still lacked a clock. Stasie, to whom hours and minutes were all alike and of no importance, had not coaxed any sort of timepiece out of her papa. Connie would never have known just how late she sat up studying, except for the voice of the clock in the Seminary tower. Often, before she slept, she heard that bell strike one, and sometimes two o'clock in the morning.

On Sabbath mornings Jed lay abed until late. But Connie rose at the usual time in order to get in a few more hours undisturbed study in the kitchen. After the family came down the place was a bedlam for the rest of the day. As soon as dinner duties were done, Connie escaped from the noise and confusion to walk the streets until dark drove her home again. She could not seek peace and quiet in the sanctuary since all the city churches were closed between morning and evening services. And she had no friends to visit. The object of these lonely Sabbath walks was Drake's Drug Store. It, too, was closed on the Lord's Day. But in the window, between a tall glass bottle of red liquid and a matching bottle of blue, books were displayed for sale. Just reading the titles was exciting: *The Journals of Lewis and Clark, Cook's Voyages,* and *The Complete Works of William Shakespeare.* The better to read the list of these "works" one Sunday afternoon, Connie found herself pressing her nose against the window. Some memory stirred in her, but of what or whom she did not know immediately. Then she remembered that ragged Irish lad pressing a freckled nose against the window of the Cleveland bookstore. The lad who, although unable to read or write, could recite long passages of Shakespeare from memory. By now Seumas McSeumas must have learned to read in the Superior Street School, and she wondered what book he had chosen in exchange for the one Pa had made her return. The thought revived the old resentment of the boy whose education her father fostered at her expense.

Connie soon forgot both of them as she strolled on, for as she approached a hat shop other memories flooded her mind. The shop was not new to her. It was one of those she had visited in vain during her search for employment. Nor was there anything novel in the sight of stovepipe hats on a row on stands inside the window. What caught Connie's attention was the glistening new sign over the door: Danbury Hat Shop. Solomon Benedict, proprietor."

Immediately her thoughts went back to the day she had bounced and splashed along Zane's Trace in Zeke's Conestoga wagon. That day she had learned that their mother's sister had married a man named Benedict from Danbury, Connecticut, and had settled on a section of land in the Miami Country, north of Cincinnati.

Could there be any connection between these facts and that sign? Or was that combination of names mere coincidence? The question could not be answered on this day of rest, but tomorrow Connie determined to find out.

The first thing that met her eye next day when she entered the Danbury Hat Shop was—of all things—a female clerk! The young woman, a timid colorless creature, appeared to be equally surprised, since there were no bonnets in the window or on the shelves, and womenfolks did not presume to select headgear for their menfolks.

"What can I do for you, miss?" she inquired, adding, "I mean madame or—or whatever you are."

"I'm *Miss* Field," Connie told her and waited to see if the name brought any sign of interest to the pale blue eyes. When the girl continued to look blank and apprehensive, she went on, "Don't be afraid. I didn't come in to steal the stock, or buy any of it, for that matter. A man's stovepipe would scarcely become me, now would it?" Connie inquired with a smile.

The pale girl turned a shade paler and seemed about to burst into tears or go out through the door into the rear of the shop, and before she should disappear, Connie said, "I'd better explain. It's about the sign outside. Are you, by any chance, one of the Benedicts?"

The girl nodded, then whispered, "Yes, I'm Faith."

Connie's heart leaped. "That's my mother's name," she said. "Ma was a Marvin, and if your ma was Hope Marvin, then we're cousins."

Slowly Faith smiled as she nodded again. Further urging brought forth more information, including the fact that Hope Benedict had borne children at the traditional rate of "one for the house and two for the hill." It was easy to understand then how the bearing and burying, or rearing of so large a family had contributed to the Marvin neglect of letter writing and loss of contact between the sisters.

"There's six of us left, three of each kind," Faith disclosed. "Ma didn't think much of me coming to the store to sell hats to menfolks. But Pa said the other two gals were enough to help Ma with the chores and *he* needed both the big boys in the factory. Pa's just bought it you see, and he can't afford hired help." Under Connie's prodding, Faith went further back in the family history to explain that, before the Revolution, Benedicts had been hatters in Danbury, Connecticut. "After that war, Pa came out here because he could get land for—well, I never did understand all of it."

Connie did, at least enough to explain that many veterans of the Continental Army got land on the frontier in lieu of back wages the new government was unable to pay.

From there Faith went on to say, "It didn't take Pa long to decide he'd never make a farmer. So, as soon as a hat factory was opened here in Cincinnati, down he came to get a job in it, leaving the boys to work the land just enough to hold title and feed us. But the boys didn't like farming either. So, when the owner of this shop died last summer, Pa sold the farm for enough to buy out the heirs, and brought Ben and Amos down to learn the business from the bottom up. But listen to me run on! You'll think I'm a regular clapper-tongue, Cousin—why, I haven't asked you your name!"

Before it had been given and explained, another Benedict came in from the back shop, drawn by the chatter out front.

He was a gaunt, stooped old man, entirely bald. The color of the hair he had lost was suggested by a pair of sandy eyebrows drawn together in a frown over faded blue eyes.

"What's going on here," he asked brusquely, "a quilting bee?"

"Pa!" Faith exclaimed. A flutter of words followed until halted by a bony uplifted hand.

"Save your breath, gal," said Solomon Benedict. "Now I get a good look at this other gal, nobody needs to tell me she's Ashbel Field's darter." Then addressing Connie directly, he pressed her to stay until closing time and accompany the Benedicts home.

Connie replied that she was sorry, but she couldn't do that because she had to get supper for her brother's family. However, she asked where her new-found kin lived and promised to call on them the following Sunday afternoon.

The report of her discovery roused less interest in Jed than in his wife. Stasie saw in his relatives an excuse to give a play-party, show off her fine clothes and stylish parlor. But first, she and Jed must go with *la belle-sœur* to call upon his kindred. Connie, concerned at the idea of taking uninvited guests along, hoped Jed would veto the suggestion. Jed merely shrugged. Evidently he did not regard the matter as worth an argument.

It was the weather which intervened. Sunday dawned cold and wet. Rain fell steadily all the morning, and there was no sign of clearing at dinnertime. Stasie, who did not come down until the meal was on the table, pecked at her food between bitter remarks about *le bon Dieu* for withholding His sunshine. Since it was unthinkable that a lady should go out in her best clothes in a downpour, Jed would have to go to the livery stable and hire a carriage.

Jed retorted that he'd do nothing of the kind. To begin with, he had lived here for years without knowing he had local cousins, so he guessed he could make out without meeting them awhile longer. Furthermore, he wasn't going to waste any money on hacks. "And that's that."

And, for once, that *was* that, despite a torrent of angry tears and name calling. Connie's intervention, with an offer to hold the family umbrella over Stasie so that she would have both hands free to hold up her petticoats, failed to dam the flow of French invective. It was with considerable relief, finally, that Connie set out alone under the umbrella.

The outside of Number Ten, Sycamore Street, looked exactly like that of the house she had just left. And on being admitted,

Connie saw at a glance that the interior arrangement too was the same. But what a difference in the atmosphere!

Faith, who opened the door, greeted the guest with glad chirps, took the dripping umbrella, and thrust her into the front room crying, "Here she is, Ma, after all, despite the rain."

The room corresponding to the Field parlor was equally crowded, not with fine new furniture, but with a homemade four-poster bed and several slat-back chairs. The chairs, drawn in a companionable half circle around the fire, were full of folks—Connie's folks. For a moment her eyes misted, and the faces blurred. And the eager chorus of welcome all ran together in what, to the lonely girl, sounded like a heavenly choir.

Then a harsh female voice said, "You young 'uns, get out of my light so's I can get a good look at my sister's darter."

At that the men, there seemed to be three of them, disappeared into the hall, hastily followed by a half-grown boy.

Connie saw then the woman who had been Hope Marvin and her heart fell. Unconsciously, she had expected to see a replica of her own calm well-poised mother. Why, this was an *old* woman, with faded blue eyes in a face like a dried apple, framed in a ruffled cap such as Granny used to wear.

The girl's disappointment was reflected on that wrinkled face as Hope Benedict cried, "My land! You don't look one bit like your ma! Somehow, I figured you would, despite what Sol said about you having the Field eyes. Maybe, when you take off your bonnet— Take it off, dearie, and then set down and tell me all about your folks."

Removal of the brown bonnet only emphasized Connie's lack of resemblance to the Marvins. For, although these new-found kin did not miss the beautiful long braids sacrificed nearly a year ago, the head revealed was sleek and black. By now the shorn locks had grown out enough to pin up in a bun and no longer excited surprise or distrust.

From under the cap frill the sunken blue eyes continued to stare. "No," Hope said sadly, "You're like Ash. Faith never was handsome, but somehow——"

"I know," Connie said quickly, "Ma's plain outside, but inside she's—beautiful." Then, anxious to change a subject which might prove embarrassing, the girl said, "But let's talk about you, Aunt Hope, you and your family. I'm so happy to have found you." She looked around to include the three plain-faced girls, only one of whom she knew by name.

Faith Benedict introduced one of her sisters as Rooshy, "short for Jerusha," then a slip of a thing called Charity.

Charity! The word was proof that Aunt Hope had not forgotten the third Marvin sister, although she had substituted the other Bible word for love. Connie knew enough of Love Marvin's story not to refer to her now, but she could speak with freedom and affection about the grandmother for whom Rooshy was named.

Suddenly these family reminiscences were interrupted by a sharp exclamation. "Open the window!" cried Ma Benedict. "Shoo it away, girls!"

Connie's gaze flew to the rain-washed window. A pigeon had taken refuge on the sill from the storm. "Oh, let it stay!" she begged. "The poor bird isn't doing any harm."

"Harm!" echoed her aunt. "Don't you know that's a sure sign of death in the house?"

Connie said, "Oh, that! Nobody takes any stock in those old superstitions nowadays."

It was evident that Hope Benedict did so, for she would not rest until the window had been raised and the fugitive driven away. When the commotion had subsided, Connie remarked that she must be going in order to reach home before dark.

As with one voice Hope and her daughters protested against so short a call. She must stay to supper! They'd counted on it. An extra big pot of beans had been baked, New England style. There were four pies in the buttery and a pound cake "with frosting." After supper, the boys would see her home. Why, she hadn't yet met the boys! Faith hurried down the hall to call them "to keep Cousin Con" from "running away."

Warmed by such sincere hospitality, of course she stayed. She met Benjamin, twenty-four years old, six feet tall, and all Benedict. Amos, two years younger, favored his mother's family as did the freckled hobledehoy, Tommy, who exposed two front teeth missing when he smiled at his cousin.

All the family managed to crowd around the kitchen table, and while his wife and daughters passed the victuals, Solomon Benedict took command of the conversation. He had endless questions to ask about his idol whom he persisted in calling "the Lieut," even after Connie had told him that Ashbel Field had been a captain of militia during the War of 1812. Finally, Sol asked the question Connie had managed to avoid earlier. "How come you are living here with your brother, my girl, instead of with your pa and ma until you get married?" Before she could decide how best to explain, Sol grinned unexpectedly, exposing a gap in his teeth like his youngest son. With a playful stroke of his finger, he told her, "I know! Ash always was longheaded. He figured a handsome girl like you stood a better chance of making a fine match in this city than in that Godforsaken end of somewhere up by the lake."

This slur on her home town saved Connie the necessity of confessing the truth about herself. She rushed to the defense of Cleveland. It wasn't nearly so big as Cincinnati, to be sure, but it was growing now and just as soon as the canal was built——

Ben broke in to speak of the Miami Canal which, even if it never reached Lake Erie, would beat the Ohio Canal to completion. Amos bet it wouldn't, and the brothers debated the matter with some heat. Connie watched them, wondering whether Amos really believed what he said or just enjoyed bating Ben. The argument continued until Faith rose and asked to be excused.

"My beau is coming to take me to meeting," she said. "And I want to prettify myself before he gets here."

Ma Benedict beamed approval, and Faith left the room to run up the stairs. Perhaps the rain made the hall darker than usual, or perhaps the girl's eagerness made her stumble. At any rate the sound increased Hope's smile of satisfaction. "There now," she said. "That's a sure sign of a wedding in the house. 'Twan't be long now before Faith's a bride."

Connie was amused by the second proof of her aunt's belief in omens, but out of deference to age she suppressed a desire to laugh and soon rose to say, "I know it isn't polite to eat and run, but really I must be getting back to Second Street."

When the mother asked which of the boys would see their cousin home, both of them volunteered. This started another argument which was settled by Sol ordering them both to go. Amos got in first with his plan that Ben should carry the umbrella over "Cousin Con," while he, Amos, took her arm "to steer her clear of puddles." Before the slower Ben should protest this arrangement, Connie laughingly interposed to inquire whether either of them was prepared to lay his cloak across puddles for her, "like Sir Walter Raleigh."

Although both young men joined in the laugh, neither of them made any rejoinder, and Connie was sure they had no idea what she was talking about. Outside, in the dark street, she was guided by Amos' hand on her elbow and shielded by Ben from the rain which continued to fall, unabated. This double escort gave her a sense of safety, a sense of protection. It was as though she had suddenly acquired two more grown brothers. And she began to ask the boys about themselves, eager to know them better.

Amos spoke for them both. There wasn't much to tell. They worked at the hatters' trade weekdays and went to the First Presbyterian Church Sunday mornings, "with the folks." When Connie inquired whether either of them ever attended evening lectures in the seminary, Amos said they weren't interested in such things. Ben spoke up to add that Amos wasn't interested in anything but gals and dances. What his own interests were, Ben did not say. Hoping to stir this silent cousin into self-revelation, Connie inquired where he had gone to school.

"Nowhere," Ben replied shortly. "Pa larned us to read and write and figure a little. He figured that was all we needed to know outside the hat business."

Amos added, "Pa thinks education is all fiddlesticks."

Connie made no comment. She might have replied that Ashbel Field, too, considered education all fiddlesticks—for females. But somehow this did not seem a good time to reveal her own opinions, aims and desires. Ben and Amos might think her "stuck up," pretentious and proud of the fact that she enjoyed superior advantages. More than anything else at the moment, she wanted to be sure of their friendship. Until today Connie had never admitted, even to herself, just how lonely and friendless she had felt here in this city of opportunity.

The very fact that Sol's sons lacked the rudimentary education

Ash had forced on all four of his sons, then denied his daughter, seemed to draw Connie nearer to the Benedict boys. As she picked her way between puddles Amos pointed out, while Ben protected her bonnet with the umbrella, Connie planned to reward their care of her by providing food for their neglected minds.

She said nothing of this plan, however. The friendship was too new, too undeveloped. But the new warmth in her heart gave warmth to her words as she bade the boys good night on Jed's doorstep.

Chapter 14

WHEN Connie entered the kitchen, she found Jed and Stasie still at the untidy table strewn with soiled dishes and the remnants of a cold meal. Jed showed some interest in hearing about their cousins. But what Stasie wanted to know was how the womenfolk dressed and how the house was furnished.

Except that all four female Benedicts wore heart-warming smiles, and Aunt Hope a frilled cap, Connie confessed that she had not noticed any details. As for the home, it was too full of friendly kinfolk for her to notice the furnishings except for the huge four-poster which took up so much space in the front room. No, she didn't mean the front chamber. She hadn't gone upstairs. The big bed stood in what corresponded to Stasie's parlor. It was there she had visited with her cousins until suppertime. No, it hadn't been cold in the front room, even on this raw March day, because there had been a fire on the hearth.

"*Voilà!*" cried Stasie, turning toward her husband. "You understand zat, Jed? Your cousins are not stingy, like you. Zay haf ze fire in ze *salon*."

"But no piano," put in Connie, in the hope of capturing her sister-in-law's attention and preventing another quarrel. In this she was successful. The statement made Stasie feel very superior. And to demonstrate that superiority, she repeated her intention of giving a party. Connie must go to Sycamore Street again after school next day and invite the entire Benedict tribe for tea on the following Sabbath.

"*Pour le thé,*" she repeated, "*pas* supper. We weel haf afternoon tea een ze parlor." Over one shoulder Stasie made at Jed what she called *une grimace,* and he called a snoot. Then she wanted to know if he wished his cousins to believe him unable to provide a fire in his parlor.

Obviously, Jed did not. Once again his wife had got round him, got the best of an argument.

Although Connie wondered how so many Benedicts could be squeezed into the already overcrowded parlor, she could scarcely refuse to convey the invitation. The flurry of excitement it engendered in Sycamore Street was nothing to the storm that agitated the Second Street house all that week. Connie was ordered to clean the place from top to bottom, to run to market for this and for that, then for something else Stasie suddenly thought indispensable. Rather than add to the hubbub by asking Jed for more funds for these extras, Connie put off buying a needed book and used the last cent of her own ill-gotten gains. In some ways it was a relief to see the last of them.

A silver tea service Connie had not known was in the house came out of its flannel bags as black as the kitchen pots. Polishing the pieces kept Connie busy a whole evening after supper so that she did no studying at all. Among other surprises Stasie exhumed from trunks were fine linen napkins, an elaborately embroidered tea cloth, and a cap and apron, all of which had to be freshly washed, starched and ironed. Since the wearing of a finger ring had superseded the ancient custom of a cap as the badge of a married woman, Connie asked Stasie what she proposed to do with this piece of fancy headgear. Did she mean to wear it herself at the party?

For a moment Stasie did not grasp Connie's meaning. Then she tittered, "Non-non-non! Onlee *les domestiques* wear caps *en maison maintenant.* These cap *et le tablier* es for Delphine when she sarve *le thé.* Moi, I weel—what you call—pour." With the little

162

finger of her right hand extended, Stasie's pantomime was as graphic as it was graceful.

When Connie inquired what part she herself should play, it was to learn her duties would be performed in the kitchen. Many little frosted cakes must be baked beforehand, but fresh *brioches* must be prepared at the last minute. Also, while the party was in progress, she would be expected to keep the kettle boiling for relays of fresh tea and at the same time keep the children in the kitchen with her and out from underfoot in the parlor.

It was this last duty assigned which reconciled Connie for missing the festivities. By the time her nephews woke in the morning, she had gone down to get breakfast. And by the time she returned from marketing after school, the baby boys had been fed their supper and taken upstairs to bed. Seldom did she catch a glimpse of them except on Sundays or when they were asleep. As for her cousins, she had already had her turn in their company and would, she hoped, visit them again and again on future Sundays.

The Sabbath set for the party turned out to be so pleasant that no fire was needed in the parlor. A fire in the kitchen, however, was needed to bake the *brioches* and boil the water for the tea. In these final preparations Stasie took no part. She was upstairs preparing her person to impress the guests. Just before their arrival she came down, looking almost regal in a gown of gold satin, her brown curls piled high on her head and the *chignon* secured by a tall tortoise-shell comb.

Connie, perspiring in one of Stasie's old muslins, wondered how the guests would greet this grandeur. And, despite Stasie's orders to keep the kitchen door closed, curiosity drove her to open it a crack on hearing sounds of arrival in the hall.

The three adult male Benedicts looked stiff and uncomfortable in well-worn broadcloth as each hung his beaver hat on the pegs on the wall. The four females clung to the shabby old shawls on their shoulders and retained the tentlike calashes on their heads. Nothing could have been more completely concealing. When Julie, peering from behind her aunt's petticoats, demanded in a loud whisper why the ladies had carriage hoods on their heads, Connie closed the door hastily.

Almost at once it flew open to admit Jerusha, dragging toothless

Tommy in tears because he'd been sent out of the parlor as too young for the party. He was soon comforted with a cupcake. Julie, of course, had to have a cake, too. Then the baby boys, denied such confections, howled so loudly that Connie was appalled. But Rooshy seemed to know exactly what to do. Scooping a babe with each arm, she bounced them up and down upon her knees until the howls of anger turned to crows of glee.

Connie looked on with interest. All week she had thought more about Rooshy than any other cousin, not only because of the name, but because at first sight Rooshy had struck her as possessing more of what Granny used to call "git up and git" than either Faith or Charity. Somehow, although her face was just as freckled, her straw-colored hair as stringy and straight, she seemed to have more character. Rooshy's pale blue eyes had more light in them. Rooshy's jaw looked more aggressive. Her mouth was more generous, smiled more easily.

She smiled at the twins now as she set them on the floor, poked Julie playfully, and then turned the smile on Connie, inquiring, "Well, what can I do to help?"

Such an offer was so unusual in this house that Connie, caught by surprise, could think of nothing to say. So she said, "Nothing."

Rooshy said, "Oh, come now! There *must be something.*"

Before Connie could reply, the unwatched twins started to scramble across the floor in opposite directions, one toward the fire, the other toward the water bucket. Julie screamed and pursued her fire-bound brother. And while Connie snatched up the other little boy in time to prevent him from overturning the bucket upon himself, the kettle boiled over.

Rooshy laughed. "Looks like I could make myself useful here, after all. At least I can keep these young 'uns out of mischief." Removing bonnet and shawl, she sat down, took a twin on each knee, and trotted them vigorously to the tune of "Ride a cockhouse to Danbury cross." Between verses she told Connie, "Ma used to sing it different. But whoever heard of any place named *Ban*bury?"

Connie said, "I have. It's in England. Not *New* England, *old* England. Banbury is a market town and a long time ago, so the story goes, there was a fine lady——"

Rooshy interrupted. She was not interested in English folklore, but she was curious to know how and where her cousin acquired so much information.

Forgetting how careful she had been to avoid being a show-off, Connie said, "Why, in school, to be sure. I'm taking English history."

Rooshy exclaimed, "You go to school! A great girl like you, old enough to be married! Oh, I know I'm not married myself and neither is Faith, but she's promised and only waiting till her beau has saved money to set up housekeeping."

Hoping to divert the conversation from herself, Connie inquired whether Jerusha also had a beau.

"No, I haven't," was the reply. "Anyhow, I couldn't leave home. Ma's old and sickly and Chary's none too stout. Besides, when Faith weds, Chary will have to go tend the shop." Rooshy hesitated a moment, then burst out, "I can't see why Faith wants to get married, knowing all Ma went through, bearing and burying. I don't want any husband, but I do wish I could go to school."

There was no need to ask the reason for Rooshy's ignorance. Ben had made clear Solomon Benedict's view on the subject of education. Connie said nothing, but she promised herself to include Rooshy in her plans for the Benedict brothers. At the moment final preparations for the party absorbed all her attention and when everything was in readiness, she opened the door and called Delphine.

It was Delphine who had admitted the guests and, from the expression in the faces of the elders, Connie feared something was brewing besides the tea in the china pot. Therefore she left the door open, just in case her presence was needed to save the situation. For a few moments the only sound from the parlor was the tinkle of tea things. Then the silence was broken by Solomon Benedict's harsh voice, demanding to know the status of the female in cap and apron.

"When she handed me that chiny cup," he said, "I asked that colored gal a question. I misdoubt she knew what I was driving at for all she gave me back was gibberish. If your Frenchy wife has brought a slave into Ohio, Jedediah Field, you're liable to arrest.

I don't much like the idea of tattling on kinfolks, but as a member of the Abolition Society it's my bounden duty to report any blacks held in illegal bondage."

Caught between two evils, Jed risked what he believed to be the lesser, for he was certain that his wife would not grasp what he said in self-vindication. He said, "I'm a law-abiding citizen, so directly my wife brought this woman here, I signed papers making her a free Negro." Seeing Sol was about to interrupt, doubtless to demand what wages the manumitted mulatto received, Jed hastened to add that he put a sum of money in the bank in Delphine's name every Saturday. "Sis keeps the book to show any fool busybody who comes snooping around, looking for trouble."

This reference to busybodies forestalled any further questions Solomon might have asked to make sure this nephew of his wife's was, in truth, obeying the law to the last letter.

During this conversation, the subject of it maintained a bland impassive expression. Stasie's expression, on the contrary, revealed the fact that although, perversely, she refused to "speak United States," she had acquired sufficient knowledge of her husband's language to understand every word he had just said. In her opinion, Jed had robbed her of valuable property. And in her anger at him, Stasie forgot caution, forgot her duties as hostess, forgot her boasted gentile manners, and deluged her husband with a hailstorm of French invectives.

The Benedicts, abashed by such behavior, understanding neither its cause nor a single syllable of the downpour, nevertheless comprehended very clearly that their big black-browed cousin was a henpecked husband. Embarrassed for Jed and for themselves, the guests "made their manners" in haste and departed—all except Rooshy and Tommy, marooned in the kitchen.

"My stars!" gasped Rooshy, when she could get her breath. "What was all that about?"

Connie, mortified and distressed, said, "I'll explain some other time. Right now, maybe you and Tommy had better go too, before——" she hesitated, not at all sure herself as to what might ensue. For of all the explosions she had heard and witnessed in this house, this one had a force and fury that boded worse repercussions to come.

This fear was fully justified. Jedediah, better disciplined than his wife, refrained from retaliating in kind until the last Benedict was out of earshot. Then his pent-up anger and humiliation burst forth in a tornado of recriminations couched in language almost as unintelligible to Connie as Stasie's French had been to the Benedicts. But the purport of Jed's remarks was, nevertheless, plain.

The give and take between husband and wife went on, intermittantly, for what remained of the Sabbath day. Even when they had retired for the night, Connie was kept awake by the rumpus in the adjoining chamber. When, finally, she drifted off to sleep, it was to dream of being caught in a storm full of thunder and lightning.

Jed must have roared himself voiceless, for at breakfast when he faced his sister across the table he was glum and grim and finally left the house without speaking a word. How much use he was at the shipyard that day Connie could only conclude from her own utter inability to keep her mind on her studies.

Late in the afternoon she returned home, dreading the backwash of last night's storm and an encounter with the fiery Creole. What struck Connie on entering the house was silence—silence so complete as to be alarming. Stasie, having exhausted herself, might conceivably have slept the clock round. But where were Delphine and the children?

Connie's alarm grew when, after a glance into the empty parlor still strewn with rumpled linen and unwashed china, she went into the kitchen to find it equally empty. As she climbed the stairs, she recalled tales of mothers driven mad by isolation and loneliness who had killed their children and themselves. The door at the head of the stairs stood open. So, too, did the door of the mahogany wardrobe, but within it no limp and lifeless body hung from a hook. In fact the wardrobe was half empty of its usual array of frocks. This was at once reassuring and bewildering. No female, however distraught, would burden herself with extra clothes if bound for the river burdened with three children to drown. Still, what *had* Stasie done with her clothes *and* her children? The most obvious answer Connie refused to entertain. No matter how furious Stasie was with Jed, no matter how determined to make him pay for what she considered dishonesty and double-dealing, she could scarcely have deserted his house, taking *bonne*, baggage and babies, between breakfast and dinner. She must have bundled the boys into their baby-buggy and, with Julie and Delphine, set out to walk off her rage. But no, that would account neither for the half-empty wardrobe nor the state of the bureau drawers when Connie pulled them out, one after another.

On top of the few garments left in the bottom drawer, was a folded paper addressed in Stasie's spidery, convent-taught handwriting to Jedediah Field, Esquire. It was unsealed, yet despite her curiosity and anxiety, Connie could not bring herself to open a note addressed to her brother. She took it downstairs and laid it beside Jed's place at the kitchen table. Then she busied herself preparing the evening meal.

Jed stamped in with his usual air of owning the world, glanced around and demanded. "Where's everybody?"

For reply, Connie pointed to the note. The sheet of paper crackled as he unfolded it. There was no other sound until Jed exploded, "Hang! I can't make head nor tail of this. Here, Sis, see if you can."

Connie understood spoken French much better than she could read that language, and despite the clarity of the penmanship, she read the note with many stops and hesitations which drove the impatient husband distraught.

"Hang, Sis," Jed growled. "Can't you get on with it faster? What the devil has that crazy Creole done with my young 'uns?"

"Taken them back with her to New Orleans," Connie told him finally. "Along with Delphine. She says her papa gave her the *bonne* and you'd no right to give her her freedom, so she's taking her back to Louisiana where she belongs."

In spite of this reiteration of the same pronoun, Jed was at no loss as to which female was referred to. And he overworked the same words, shouting, "The deuce she does! She belongs to me, being as I'm her husband, and I was within my rights freeing her and now she's a free Negro, that woman belongs here in Ohio. I've explained the law to her over and over, but she never listened, just kept yelling about how I'd robbed her, and now that crazy female has robbed me of my children! What I can't understand is how she managed to make off with them when she hadn't a cent to her name."

One solution of that question leaped to Connie's mind and she said, "Stasie hadn't. But Delphine had. I wonder——" Rising, she went into the buttery, then came back to say, "It's gone—Delphine's bankbook. I kept it in that old cracked sugar bowl. Stasie must have understood what you told Uncle Sol, Jed, and ransacked the place for that book until she found it. I'm sure Delphine never understood a word of all the talk about freedom for—for colored people any more than she understood what that book stood for. It would never occur to her to question any order Stasie gave her. No doubt they went to the bank together and withdrew Delphine's wages. But what I can't understand, Jed, is how they got clear away in such a hurry."

Jed could supply the answer to that and did so in four words: "This is steamboat day."

"But all those clothes of hers and the children's," Connie protested. "Even with Delphine's help, how could she get everything and everybody down to the dock in time to board the *Washington?*" Stasie, who was too indolent even to wait on herself, could not be as helpless as she pretended. This evidence of hurried departure proved that she could work, and work fast under compulsion—the compulsion of anger. Through these thoughts Connie was vaguely aware of Jed's voice, going on and on, but she did not actually hear his words until he shouted.

"By heaven! I'll take the next steamer south myself and give that gal the horsewhipping she's had coming to her for years and years. Then I'll bring back my sons. And," he added as though it were an afterthought, "my daugter, too, and that free Negro to raise all three of them."

"Don't!" cried Connie. "Oh, Jed, don't do anything so foolish—I mean so foolish as to follow Stasie and beat her. I know how you must feel and with good reason. But that's not the way to bring her to reason, Jed. Let her alone until she cools off, and I'm certain Stasie will come back. She loves you too much to leave you forever."

Jed snorted. "Love! A snare and a delusion. A feller sets store by his get, his young 'uns, but his woman——" he broke off to begin again. "That female bewitched me. Time was I thought Stasie an angel. Now I know better. She's a devil. I don't want her back.

What I want is those little devils—those little black-eyed he-devils I begot."

Connie knew Jed was not talking to her, that he had completely forgotten her presence and was thinking out loud, letting off steam, struggling to rid himself of his hurt and his heartache.

But after she had left him, morose and silent, gazing into the dying fire, Connie could not put Jed and Stasie out of her mind. Was it, or was it not love, that violent passion which had drawn them together, held them together for a time, yet could not make them kind to one another, could not make them try to understand each the other's widely different habits and points of view.

If *that* was love, Connie wanted none of it. Children of her own she longed to have, but if, in order to bear them, one had to live with a man in a state of constant contention, even hatred, she preferred to live out her life alone. There were worse things, Constitution concluded with wisdom far beyond her years—much worse things than the loneliness of spinsterhood.

Chapter 15

QUIET WITHIN the house, bereft of children and free from parents' quarrels, was offset by noise and commotion outside in the street. That summer of 1821 the new waterworks was pushed to completion, for until every section of the city was piped and the entire network connected with the new steam pumping station down by the river, all the inhabitants continued to depend on the old corner pumps, the horse-drawn hogsheads, or their own unreliable wells for water.

All day long overseers shouted orders to ditchdiggers. Carters swore at one another and at the teams that hauled the wooden pipes to the scene and hauled surplus soil away. Except for these vehicles, Second Street was closed to wheeled traffic. The water vender's cries ceased with those of the wood seller. Each day after school Connie had to lug in from the corner every drop of water and make an extra trip to market for firewood.

Nevertheless, she had more time to herself now, for Jed reverted to his former habit and went out regularly right after supper. And with the street as well as the house peaceful during the long June evenings, Connie could study undisturbed. She also had time to visit several small female seminaries recently opened in the city, with view to possible future employment. It was no surprise to find that proficiency in mathematics and Latin were not required. But it was a blow to discover how much importance was given to fine needlework, piano lessons and French. She knew she could never pass muster in embroidery or music, and although she spoke a little French, it was not with the fluency and correctness needed to teach that language. The time had come, she foresaw, when the added expense of French lessons must be assumed if ever she expected to make a living as a schoolmistress.

Before the seminary closed for the summer, Connie visited the classroom of the master known as Monsieur. He was a dapper little man who, by dyeing his hair and mustache black, deluded himself more than his pupils who considered him older than he was.

At sight of the tall handsome girl, Monsieur rose, bowed from the waist, and inquired to what he owed the honor of her presence.

Confused by such fancy manners, Connie faltered something about fees and how to go about making sure of a place in one of his classes next fall. When he inquired why she did not start at once, she confessed that she had no money for extras. Whereupon Monsieur suggested that she apply for credit and pay later in order to make the most of what remained of the present term, and then enter a more advanced class in September.

An inherent horror of debt made Connie refuse to take advantage of this offer. By September she expected to be in funds again and able to pay the full term in advance.

The expected funds, of course, could only be acquired in the vineyard. But when Connie called at the big rambling stone cottage covered with vines, Mr. Longworth explained as kindly as he could, that females were employed only during harvest. True, there was work in the vineyards all the year round, even in winter when the vines were pruned but this was a chore calling for experience. Other chores called for brawn. Setting out new plants was definitely man's work, much too heavy for females.

"But I'm just as strong as most men," Connie told him. "Even when I was only eleven and Pa was away at the war, I cut and carried nearly all of our fuel. And—and once I killed a full-grown wolf."

Nicholas Longworth did not need to be told that this girl was more robust and more energetic than any female employed previously, for she had done more work last fall than two men. He liked her independence and her courage, and on the spur of the moment decided to give her a trial.

For some days Connie plowed one of the new fields, then drove the harrow back and forth over it until the soil was smooth. The work of setting out cuttings was supervised by an old hand, old in years as well as experience, imported from France. Connie was able to help him as an interpreter, although his French differed a good deal from that taught in New Orleans. But she did manage to comprehend his instructions and pass them on to the other workers. This service, coupled with her tenderness with the delicate young vines, made a friend of the old foreigner. Others might safely plow down the rows between the vines. But only to Connie was entrusted the work of weeding close around the roots. From sunup to sundown she crawled on hands and knees, in pursuit of this duty. As time went on and the vines grew, there was also the task of staking and tying up the new tendrils to keep them off the ground. And as the clusters of tiny green fruit began to swell on the parent vines, they too had to be staked and tied. It was, as Mr. Longworth had warned, very hard work, but Connie kept on because it was, she knew, her only honest means of attaining her ambition.

Even her excellent health felt the strain and she was always bone-weary by Saturday night. But no matter how tired she was, on reaching home she went out again with two buckets to fetch the extra water for her bath. There was ample time and privacy to enjoy this luxury, for Jed never came home until the small hours of Sunday morning. And since he slept late on the day of rest, Connie too had a chance to rest and recuperate.

When Jed finally came down to breakfast, he was either glum or garrulous. When he discoursed at length on the profits to be made in steamboats, in mercantile pursuits, and in land, Connie surmised that he'd been lucky at cards the night before. When he lost, he did not talk at all, and in either case he never mentioned his wife and children. Nor did he give any reason for leaving the house directly after breakfast. The shipyards were closed on the Sabbath. So, too, were the taverns, according to law, but behind drawn curtains on the upper floors, the usual activities might continue for all Connie knew to the contrary. One thing was certain. Jed did not spend the Sabbath in any house of God.

Connie herself became a regular churchgoer through a succession of circumstances. The first Sabbath Jed failed to return at midday, she tried to keep his dinner warm all afternoon with the result that the victuals dried up and were ruined. She made no reference to this during the following week and then on Saturday remarked only on the sinful waste of food that went uneaten. If Jed proposed to take his Sunday dinners elsewhere, he would save money by saying so here and now. Jed did just that, with no apparent interest in where or how his sister secured nourishment.

Since that terrible tea party, nothing had been heard from the Benedicts and, under the circumstances, Connie felt any further move should come from them.

The situation on Sycamore Street was confused. On the matter of Stasie's tantrum the family was in complete accord. All agreed to have no further intercourse with "that fancy foreign female," or with her henpecked husband. There was, however, a difference of opinion regarding Constitution. Solomon, citing the old saying that "birds of a feather flocked together," felt that she could not have escaped contamination in such company. Usually Hope reflected the opinions of her husband, but she was loath to lose sight of her favorite sister's daughter. And because her own second daughter was her chief prop and stay, Hope held a private consultation with Jerusha.

In the course of conversation, Rooshy happened to mention her discovery that Cousin Con, a great girl of her own age, was going to school. This news alarmed Hope. Rooshy had shown signs of dissatisfaction with her lot as household drudge, and Hope feared that further contact with a girl who had "kicked over the traces," might encourage Rooshy to do likewise. After repeating what Sol had said regarding birds of a feather, Hope forbade Rooshy to visit the Field house again.

Jerusha, fearful of losing a chance to acquire a little learning, made haste to repeat the gossip that the "foreign female" had left town, blackamoore, baggage and babies. As for Cousin Con having absorbed any fancy ideas from her sister-in-law, if she had, wasn't it the duty of her blood kin to make an effort to counteract these evil influences and bring their own "back into the fold"?

Being a deeply religious woman, Hope Benedict felt that Rooshy was right. It *was* her bounden duty to save the soul of her niece. And, to that end, she sent Rooshy around to the Second Street house with an invitation to join the family at meeting next Lord's Day and afterward go home with them to cold dinner. In offering this invitation, Hope cautioned Rooshy to be sure and explain why folks brought up in Connecticut and strict Puritan tradition attended the Presbyterian Church. In all Cincinnati, there wasn't a single Congregational meetinghouse.

There were, however, *two* Presbyterian societies, and some confusion between them. The little old wooden building that stood back to back with the Lancaster Seminary, housed the Second Presbyterian membership. The First Presbyterians occupied a splendid new brick structure on Main Street, known far and wide as the "two-horned church" by reason of a fine façade flanked by twin towers topped with elaborate lanterns. It was this famous edifice Connie entered the following Sunday morning. For a moment she stood, abashed at sight of five broad aisles between rows of pews filled with worshipers. Seeing her confusion, a young man stepped up, bowed and asked in what family pew she wished to be seated. Connie followed him up a side aisle until he turned, bowed again and left her at the door of a pew in which she recognized her relations in spite of their Sunday clothes.

As an elder of the church, Solomon sat with his fellow elders in the amen corner. It was Ben, as the oldest son who occupied the end seat in the family pew; Ben, who at sight of his cousin, rose quickly, opened the door and stood outside while Connie went in and sat down. Then Ben squeezed himself in beside her and closed the door just as a deep rumble, like the falls at Zanesville, shook the church. The rumble grew louder, and was joined by what Connie took to be assorted flutes and fiddles and finally by a chorus of human voices. When Ben jogged her elbow, she turned to see that he was offering to share an open book printed with queer symbols between lines of words which read:

> The heavens declare the glory of God:
> And the firmament sheweth his handywork.
> Day unto day uttereth speech,
> And night unto night sheweth knowledge.

The first faint dawn of a new knowledge held Connie breathless, so that she could not join in the hymn as she had once joined in the doxology outside the Second Presbyterian almost a year ago. Then she had been alone on the threshold of new experiences. Now she was crushed between Amos, piping a reedy tenor on her left and Ben on her right, apparently voiceless.

Never before had Connie been in such close contact with young men, and she tingled with a strange and pleasurable excitement. Tall as she was, Ben was taller. From the shadow of her bonnet all that was visible was his hand holding the hymnbook. It was a big hand, hard and horny, with a faint golden fuzz between knuckles and wrist; not a beautiful hand but dependable, like Ben's character, Connie suddenly felt certain. His nearness gave her a sense of warmth and safety even greater than she had known in Serena Pomerey's company. Connie knew that she loved Serena. Was she falling in love with Ben? The possibility was disturbing, not because of the blood tie, for she knew nothing of the prejudice against the union of cousins, but because to her marriage spelled bondage.

Male and female voices mingled in a final *amen*. The congregation sat down. In the cramped pew Connie was crammed between the Benedict boys, but she was scarcely conscious of Amos although he, too, was big in body. Ben's nearness continued to send tremors through her so that she could not keep her mind on the sermon. She seemed to be floating in a kind of waking dream until roused by the preacher's final word, echoed from the amen corner.

The organ pealed forth again and again. Connie held the hymnbook with Ben, although neither of them tried to sing. Glancing sidewise, from the ambush of her bonnet, she saw that the muscles around Ben's jaw were tight, and at his temple, between a sandy eyebrow and his sandy hair, a tiny pulse beat madly.

Connie caught her breath, remembered a similar pulse beat at the edge of Jed's black hair when he looked at Stasie. After witnessing so many scenes between Jed and Stasie, there had been no question in Connie's mind regarding their mutual emotion until Jed's outburst after his wife's desertion. That revelation, coupled with her own brief but illuminating experiences with the cheese merchant and in the gambling room, distorted Connie's judgment regarding the relationship between men and women, and left her in a quandary about Ben.

Her confusion was increased when, at the end of the closing hymn, Ben bent, unbuttoned the pew door, and strode down the aisle and out of the sanctuary.

In a daze, Connie heard his mother's shocked whisper. "I declare!" ejaculated Hope Benedict. "What could of struck Ben to rush off without waiting for the benediction?"

When the family reached home, Ben had not arrived. Solomon advanced the opinion that Ben must have recollected some chore neglected at closing time last night, and gone to the shop. Wherever Ben went, he came in when dinner was on the table, shrugged off his father's questions and sat down. That he scarcely tasted his victuals could not have escaped notice, but only Tommy commented on the fact with a small boy's embarrassing candor. Whereupon, Connie, whose appetite had deserted her too, made a great show of cleaning her plate.

The meal finished, father and sons left the cramped kitchen. Faith excused herself to prink for the beau who "walked" her out every fine Sunday afternoon. When Hope suggested that she and her niece retire to the front room "for a chat," Connie hesitated, then asked leave to help the girls "wash up." The biblical injunction against labor on Lord's Day was not followed to the extent of leaving dirty dishes in the sink. Rooshy bustled about, putting away the remains of the meal while Charity washed and Connie wiped the coarse crockery. Charity, overawed by her handsome cousin, took no part in the conversation between the other two girls. Rooshy took advantage of the opportunity to pelt Connie with questions. Were there any grown girls among the beginners at the seminary? Could a girl, needed at home mornings, attend afternoon classes only? Above all, was schooling free?

The answer was no, except to the last question to which Connie replied that poor folks' children were taught to read and write without charge, but she felt bound to point out that Rooshy had advanced beyond childhood. At the downcast look on the freckled face, she came out with an offer to teach Rooshy during summer vacation.

Whereupon Charity found her voice and begged to be included. It was impossible not to agree, although where and when these lessons could be given Connie was at a loss to say.

Had the younger Benedict girl kept quiet, the more discreet, more resourceful Rooshy would undoubtedly have solved the problem. But no sooner had the three girls joined Hope than Charity burst forth with the news.

For a moment the wrinkles ironed out of the mother's face, then it aged again as she said, "You'll have to ask leave of your pa, gals." Then, to change the subject, Hope began to catechize Connie on her knowledge of Scripture. There was no escape until lengthening shadows offered excuse to hurry in order to reach home before dark. Then again, as on the previous Sunday, Hope insisted that she stay to supper. The boys would be back when they got hungry and would see her safe home.

Sunday supper was a pickup meal, soon over with little ceremony and fewer dishes. Then Connie said that she really *must* be going. Ben, who hadn't addressed a word directly to her all day, quickly offered his company. When Amos also volunteered, Ben turned on him and growled, "Three's a crowd."

Amos agreed. Where they differed was as to which one of them was superfluous. One pair of hot blue eyes glared fiercely into the other pair and the square jaws of both young men bulged with equal belligerence. For a moment they stood motionless as two gamecocks. Then the younger lad looked away.

That Amos' surrender was temporary only, he soon made clear. "Have it your way this time," he said. "But mind you, Ben, next Sunday evening it's my turn to walk her home."

When a fellow walked a girl home after dark, it was usual to take her arm. Ben's failure to follow this established custom might imply ignorance of it, or it might mean that he dared not trust himself to touch his companion. Connie had no real need of assistance, even though the young trees that lined the unpaved sidewalk kept off the light of the full moon, but she did feel the need of light on Ben's behavior. He walked on the extreme outer edge of the walk as far as possible from her and without saying a word. When his silence grew awkward, she tried to speak lightly, naturally of impersonal matters, such as how slowly the waterworks was in reaching completion.

Ben made an effort to follow her lead. He remarked how much labor womenfolks would be saved when the last pipe was laid and water flowed at the turn of a tap in every kitchen in the city.

Connie had taken for granted the water would flow only into the old cisterns below the corner pumps when they went dry. Such luxury as running water in the kitchen had never occurred to her, but she agreed that running water would be, indeed, a wonderful saving in time and strength. This seemed to exhaust the subject and the pair walked on in silence again—silence that grew heavier and heavier, like the air before a summer storm breaks.

When they reached Jed's doorstep, Connie managed to get out a polite word or two of farewell. Ben made no reply. But when she turned to unlock the door, he caught her hand. She made no effort to release herself as she turned back to face him again, and waited, unsure of what he wanted of her and still more unsure of what she wanted from him.

Ben suffered from no such uncertainty. Yet somehow he could not bring himself to deliver the peck on the cheek expected by his sister's friends when he walked them home. More than he had ever wanted anything in his life before, Benjamin Benedict longed to press his lips to this girl's lips. But he couldn't do it. It seemed a sacrilege. Instead he did an unheard-of thing. Bowing his head over her hand, he kissed the fingers, then released them hurriedly and dashed off down the street.

For a moment Connie felt paralyzed with astonishment. Then she let herself into the empty house and went directly upstairs to bed. But it was a long time before she went to sleep. Again, as in church that morning, she wondered what was happening to her, to him. And again she was confused as much by her own feelings as by Ben's odd behavior.

Throughout the week that followed, the question continued to hatchel her. At work in house or vineyard, she often paused to stare at the hand Ben had kissed. The slim brown hand, roughened by toil, looked no different than usual, which struck her as strange, under the circumstances. She had never seen Jed kiss Stasie's hand. And the kisses she had seen the pair exchange were violent, not gentle and shy and, yes, reverent. Still, if the emotion they shared was not love, what was it? And why, if Jed did not love Stasie, did he act so lost and unhappy without her?

The question of what to do with the clothing Stasie had left behind presented a different kind of problem. For weeks Connie had been expecting to hear either that Stasie was returning by the next boat, or that she wanted her personal belongings packed and sent to her papa's plantation. Jed never mentioned the receipt of any letter from his wife and his sister dared not ask. Finally she decided to write Stasie herself for instructions. That had been weeks ago and, up to the day she had gone to church, Connie had received no reply. Before another Sabbath came around, however, Jed brought home a letter and tossed it down by his sister's plate without comment, although he could scarcely have failed to recognize Stasie's spidery penmanship.

After he had gone, leaving most of his supper untasted, Connie broke the seal on the folded sheet. Stasie wasted no words. She wrote merely that she had no intention of ever returning to Cincinnati and never wanted to see again anything in the Second Street house, including her husband.

When, at breakfast, Jed inquired as to the contents of the letter, Connie reluctantly repeated it word for word.

"I never want to see her again, either," Jed declared. And when Connie inquired what should be done with his wife's castoffs, he told her, "What the devil do *I* care? Chuck 'em in the river. Send 'em to the heathen. Or, if you want, wear 'em yourself, but not when I'm around."

Connie did want, and need a replacement for the brown bombazine which was too heavy for summer. And she selected from the assortment of wearing apparel the simplest gown—a plain yellow muslin, then to wear with it a wide-brimmed leghorn hat wreathed with artificial cowslips and tied on with black velvet ribbon. She had little vanity, but a glance in the mirror told her that yellow was her color, and that bow under her chin certainly did make her eyes look bigger and blacker than ever.

As she walked to church next Sunday, she wondered what effect this enhancement of her charms would have on Ben, and her heartbeat quickened. But it was not Ben who opened the pew door for her to enter, it was Amos. Amos was all spruced up in puce broadcloth, his unruly fair hair plastered down as though licked by a cat.

With one less occupant in the pew, Connie was able to edge away from Amos when his arm touched hers. For that, or some other reason, she was also able to listen to the sermon. The subject of the discourse was foreign missions and the duty of Christians to carry the light of the Gospel to heathen lands, especially those far-off islands where the benighted natives had nothing to cover their nakedness except leaves and grass.

Afterward, on the way to Sycamore Street, everybody talked about the sermon. Nobody mentioned Ben, and although Connie continued to wonder at his absence from meeting, she shrank from breaking into the conversation with so irrelevant a question.

Ben wasn't at home, either, and his place at table was still vacant when the family sat down to the cold dinner. Finally, unable to curb her curiosity any longer, Connie commented on Ben's absence.

It was Solomon who explained it at some length. It seemed that the buyer of the family farm had fallen behind in payments which, in turn, delayed the Benedict payments on the hat shop. During the week all three men were too busy to ride up the Miami and back. And, as absence of Elder Benedict from meeting would cause criticism, it was Ben who had gone on Lord's Day.

Connie glanced at Amos, saw the triumphant look on his freckled face, and wondered whether Uncle Sol had ordered Ben to go or left the boys to decide between themselves. Last Sunday Amos had backed down before Ben's determination to walk her home, alone. Had Amos forced Ben to back down in turn? Or—

the thought was disturbing—had Ben seized the trip as pretext to avoid her out of embarrassment over his odd farewell? Was he ashamed of his impulsive action? In Ben's absence there was no way to solve the question.

Over the cold victuals the subject of the sermon was revived. Connie learned that Aunt Hope was a member of the Society for the Propagation of the Gospel in Foreign Lands. Later on in the afternoon, she learned that the female branch of the society met regularly to cut and sew flannel nightgowns to replace grass skirts on Sandwich Islanders.

This reminded Connie of one of Jed's suggestions for the disposal of his wife's wardrobe and she passed it on to her cousins. When Rooshy seized this pretext for returning to Second Street with Cousin Con, Hope could scarcely forbid such a mission, nor could she very well refuse Charity's plea to be allowed to go along and help Rooshy bring home the booty.

As a result, all three girls started at once without waiting for Amos to return from the usual Sunday rounds of the factory.

Jed wasn't at home, either, and his bed was soon strewn with his wife's castoff furbelows. Except for the gold-colored satin Stasie had worn at that ill-fated tea party, and the yellow muslin Connie had on, the Benedict girls had never seen such elegant garments. Charity tore off her faded blue linen homespun to try on one lovely gown after another. Even Rooshy, who was less carried away by the finery, finally succumbed to it and exchanged her coarse pink linen for a green muslin embroidered all over with tiny white flowers.

Connie exclaimed, "Why, Rooshy, it makes you look like a different person. I never thought of it before, but no one of your complexion should ever wear pink."

Rooshy stared at her reflection in Stasie's mirror. "Well," she said, drawing a long breath, "this is one gown no heathen will ever wear. That is, if you'll let me keep it, Cousin Con."

Connie saw no reason to refuse. Surely, these beauty-starved girls needed pretty clothes far more than savages satisfied to go naked. But when Charity suggested that they keep the whole collection, Rooshy reproved her for greediness. One gown apiece would do the Benedicts, although, since Faith was about to get married, perhaps she might be allowed two. It was also decided that Faith should ask her beau to walk her over next Sunday to make her selection and then help carry the rest of the clothes to the church for packing.

It was not Faith who objected to this plan the following Sunday; it was Benjamin. Connie had taken pains to arrive early at meeting so that the Benedicts found her seated in the far corner of the pew when they arrived in a body. And after meeting, she took equal pains to avoid Ben, by walking between Faith and Charity, and then seat herself at the dinner table as far from him as possible. Nevertheless, she was acutely conscious of his burning gaze and ill-concealed agitation.

That these symptoms were observed and diagnosed correctly by at least one member of the family was evident. With a wide toothless grin, Tommy intoned, "Ben's sweet on Cousin Con! Ben's sweet on Cousin Con!"

Solomon silenced his youngest son with a frown. He did not so much as glance at his eldest and, following the father's example, the other Benedicts ignored Ben, although not one of them could have failed to see that Tommy's dart had drawn blood. Ben's face turned white, then red, and he kept his gaze on his plate.

Connie longed to help him, to cover his confusion with some clever offhand remark. But never having faced such a situation before, she too was tongue-tied with embarrassment.

It was Rooshy who rescued them both. Jumping up, she cried, "Come on girls, let's hurry through the dishes and get over to Second Street."

Whereupon Ben recovered his speech. "I was minded to ask Constitution to walk out with me," he said.

This placed Connie in a difficult position. If she pleaded a previous engagement with his sisters, would Ben believe it genuine? Or, suspecting the reason for her early arrival at church, would he conclude this was just another excuse for avoiding him? Before she could decide how to reply to Ben's remark, his brother saved her the trouble.

Amos asserted that, if anybody was going to "walk Cousin Con," he was the man. "It's *my* turn."

"*Your* turn," said Ben. "You had your turn last week when I went to the farm."

Amos replied that the gals had stolen a march on him—made off directly after dinner while he, too, was absent. This statement was corroborated by Rooshy who made haste to explain the purpose of their visit to Second Street last Sunday and also again today. "Both you boys had better come along," she remarked. "And make yourselves useful."

It was clear from their expressions that neither Ben nor Amos was pleased with this solution, but rather than lose Connie's company entirely, both boys accepted Rooshy's invitation without enthusiasm. To avoid further argument, Connie herself elected to walk between the brothers.

On entering the Field house all four girls went directly upstairs leaving the boys to wait below in the parlor or, if they preferred, to take a walk and return later in the afternoon. The idea of walking out together did not appeal to either brother, and although they took scarcely more pleasure in sitting together in the Field parlor, each hoped the other would weary of waiting and go home. There was also the chance that their sisters might not need any help and would leave without them.

And so they sat together in the parlor, but without solving the major problem. Faith's beau joined her brothers shortly and the three young men waited—and waited and waited. At last when the girls finally descended, burdened with bundles, Amos continued his aimless fingering of the piano keys while Ben stared out of the window as though fascinated with the herringbone pattern of the brick sidewalk. But when Connie followed the other girls down the stairs, Ben sensed her presence and turned. Their eyes met. Neither of them spoke, but something in the air diverted Amos' attention from the piano and, whirling about on the fringed stool, he broke into mocking laughter.

Ben spoke only two words, "Get out!" But each word had the force of a powder charge.

Although the Benedict sisters were aware that Ben was not aiming at them, they piled their bundles on Faith's beau, pushed him out, and followed like a covey of frightened partridges.

183

Amos was no coward. Two years younger than Ben and more than two inches shorter, he had never shrunk from battle with his brother even when doubtful of victory. Until now, however, Amos had known he need only cry quits to escape injury. Now the note in Ben's voice—a note of suppressed violence—warned Amos that he'd better obey before Ben became angry. Amos got out of the house without ceremony, without so much as a word of farewell to the cause of contention.

When they were alone in the parlor, alone in the house, neither Ben nor Connie spoke. Nor did they move for some moments. Then, without being conscious of having taken a step, they were in one another's arms. Through his Sabbath waistcoat and her thin muslin, Connie felt the wild thud of Ben's heart, and her own heart responded. Slowly he bent his head. She sensed that he was about to kiss her and was frightened—frightened by sudden memory of the cheese merchant's brutal lips.

Had Ben given way to his feelings and kissed Connie with passion, she would have recoiled instinctively, and repulsed him as forcibly as she had the stranger. But Ben's instinct restrained him, and he merely held her tenderly and laid his cheek against her cheek. When, finally, his lips sought hers, it was with the same gentleness and reverence he had kissed her fingers.

How long it was before he released her, neither of them knew nor cared. It was the distant voice of the seminary clock telling the hour of curfew that warned Ben that he must leave or risk meeting the master of the house and accounting for his presence. Ben wasn't ready to face Jed and declare his intentions, honorable though they were. So he kissed Connie again and let her go, then hurried away.

Gradually her head cleared, leaving her no longer in doubt that she and Ben were deeply in love. What else could it be but love, this blissful knowledge of need, each for the other? Certainly what she had felt in Ben's arms bore no resemblance to the emotion she had so often witnessed between her brother and his wife.

Connie was a long time in going to sleep that night. She was too happy and when, finally, drowsiness overcame her, it brought dreams of greater happiness to come.

Chapter 16

WHETHER or not Hope Benedict's purpose in taking her niece into the bosom of the family had been achieved—the purpose of saving Connie's soul—there was no doubt in Hope's mind, or in Sol's mind, that their eldest son had lost his heart to his cousin.

That Amos, too, seemed smitten was of no consequence, for Amos was given to passing fancies, and both parents believed this one was whetted by a boyish desire to plague his serious elder brother. With Ben it was different. There was not and never had been anything flighty about Ben. In fact Ben's blindness to female charms had become a family joke. But his sudden capitulation to the charms of his newly discovered cousin was no joke. It created an alarming situation. In the privacy of the big four-poster, Pa and Ma Benedict discussed the problem of how best to nip this unfortunate romance in the bud. The decision reached was that no time must be lost. Sol must "talk turkey" to Ben.

Whatever Solomon said to his eldest son, it resulted in Ben's absence from meeting the following Sabbath.

Connie, whose thoughts had been filled with Ben all week, felt let down and stirred by the fear that he didn't love her after all. Recalling the haste with which he had left her, she wondered whether he regretted what had passed between them and left town to avoid another encounter. Had it not been for that tender episode, she would have asked Ben's whereabouts, as a matter of course, but under the circumstances she could not bring herself to mention his name. Nor did any member of the family speak of the absent one, and when, after supper, Connie said it was time she went home, Amos promptly claimed the honor of escort.

There was no moon and the thick foliage on the rows of young trees bordering the sidewalks created areas of darkness between the street lamps. When Amos took advantage of the shadows to steal a kiss, Connie pushed him away with orders never to "do that again." Amos chuckled. But Connie felt no answering mirth, only wonder at the difference between her reaction to that kiss and the way she had responded to Ben's kisses last Sunday. Her mind was so completely absorbed by thoughts of him that on nearing home, she believed her eyes deceived her into taking the shadow on the doorstep for Ben.

Amos halted, muttering, "What the deuce?" And when the shadow moved and materialized into a man, he repeated, "What the deuce are you doing here? I thought Pa sent you upcountry."

"He did," replied the shadow, "and I went. I just got back."

Although she could not see Ben's face, Connie knew it was turned toward her, awaiting her word of welcome. Not knowing what else to say in Amos' presence, she said, "Won't you come in, boys, both of you?"

Ben said quickly, "I will. But Amos won't." And when Amos retorted that he took no orders from his brother, the shadow moved quickly. There was the dull sound of a blow. Then Amos' voice, answered thick with rage, crying, "You'll be sorry for this, Ben, I promise you. And you, too, Cousin Con." The threat was followed by the tread of heavy boots in retreat along the brick sidewalk.

Not until the footsteps had died away did either of the pair on the doorstep move or speak. Then Ben asked, huskily, "Aren't you going to ask me in?"

For answer, she unlocked the door and stepped in, waiting in silence while he entered and closed the door behind him. Then, in the dark hall, they were locked in a close embrace and Ben, breathing hard, was saying brokenly, "I couldn't stand not to see you. So I hired a nag and rode up to the farm instead of walking, like Pa intended. He's set on keeping us apart. But nothing on God's earth can do that, unless——" the agitated voice faltered.

"Unless—what?" prompted Connie, scarcely less agitated.

Ben whispered, "Unless you won't have me." He was holding her body crushed against his so closely that she was conscious of him in a way she had not been before—conscious that, mingled with his reverence of her, was a powerful elemental emotion held tightly in leash.

186

Had Connie never been a third party to those scenes of violence between Jed and Stasie, never come to the reluctant conclusion that what moved them was something less than love, she might have responded to Ben's emotion. As it was, she strained away from him in the darkness, saying, "I—I—don't know. Oh, Ben, honestly, I'm not sure. Last Sunday I was sure, but now——"

Ben interrupted, "If Amos took advantage of my absence, if he's taken you away from me, I—I'll kill him!"

At that she cried out sharply, "Ben! You mustn't say such things. Anyway, I don't care a fig for Amos. Or he for me, really. Oh, I *do* care for you, Ben! I care a lot. Only——" again she could not go on, could not explain her reservation.

He said, "I've scared you! I ought to have waited. Ought to have asked you to keep company with me first, given you time to—to get used to—the idea. Last Sunday I made up my mind to be patient, to court you, right and proper, and I would have, if Pa hadn't forbid it."

Connie exclaimed, "Your father forbade you to—to court me? Why? Has he heard anything—against me?"

Ben himself had heard rumors, wild rumors, and discounted them as spawned by female jealousy. But he did not tell her this, nor did he disclose the real reason for his father's prohibition—the kinship between them. Ben was so deeply in love that he refused to recognize the blood tie as a barrier. Belatedly, it struck him that Connie, aware of the prejudice against the marriage of cousins, might have repulsed him on that account. He had to know now, immediately, and if that was all that stood between them, he would overcome her fear with the assurance that it was just an outworn superstition, like witchcraft.

Words never came easily to Ben, and under the stress of anxiety all he could find to say was, "Tell me! I've got to know—everything."

Everything! To Connie that could only mean that Ben had heard evil reports and wanted assurance from her own lips that they were false. Aware as she was that the gossip was not entirely groundless, she told him, "It's a long story. Wait until I make a light in the parlor and I'll begin at the beginning."

She proceeded to do so—told how she had defied her father and sacrificed her hope of inheritance on the altar of education. She explained how she had even risked her good name to earn money for school fees, and how her brother had saved her from the consequences. At the end of the confession Ben was silent so long that she began to fear he did not believe she could have emerged unscathed from such experiences.

"Ben," she cried, "you've got to believe me. I can't bear it if you don't. I *did* gamble. But I didn't do anything worse. Ben, I'm telling you the truth, the whole truth."

After another silence that seemed endless, he said slowly, "I do believe you, honest I do. But I don't understand you. A girl like you who could have her pick of husbands, what do you want with book learning?"

It was the old question. This was the question which had puzzled Ashbel Field and determined him to settle it once and for all by forcing his daughter into what he believed to be a safe and advantageous marriage. Instead of answering Ben, she asked him if he had ever regretted his own lack of education.

"Sometimes," he admitted. "But that's different. I'm a man. And anyway, I know all I need to know in the hat business."

What the intellectual requirements might be for the making of hats, Connie had no idea. What Ben's view was on the matter of female book learning, however, was something she had to know, and without loss of time. "I suppose Rooshy has told you that I'm going to the seminary and expect to be ready for college next year."

"College!" he repeated. "Girls don't go to college. It's against—well, I don't know as there's any *law* against it, but it's against nature."

"Why?" Connie wanted to know. "Surely, you don't take any stock in that silly old superstition about—about——" she faltered. Modesty forbade mention of the belief that book learning deprived females of their power to bear children. It had been in the back of her mind that someday, far in the future after she had earned a college diploma, *cum laude,* like Mal, she would prove the fallacy of that belief by marrying some good man and giving him sons and daughters. But not yet. She wasn't ready yet. Ben might be that man. Ben was good. He loved her. Of these things she was convinced. And she returned his love, if not in kind, at least sincerely and in her own way. As proof of her love, she longed to inspire him with her love of learning, so that they might travel together the road she had set herself.

Unlettered Ben was, but by no means stupid. He sensed something of what was in Connie's mind and was aghast at the possibility that her love for him was less than her love of books—that she might not be willing to abandon what he considered a foolish idea for the sake of being his wife. That he did not put her love to the test at once with a demand that she chose between him and school, here and now, was due to the fact that he was in no position to defy his father's orders.

Solomon Benedict had warned Ben to relinquish any thought of marrying his cousin, or be disowned, disinherited and forced to find some new means of livelihood. It was the measure of Ben's love for Constitution that, having disobeyed his father's order, he could not bring himself to claim her for his wife until he could offer her the security of her own home in exchange for her school. All this was too involved for Ben to express in detail. What he said was, "I love you. I want you to marry me, but not right now. We'd better wait awhile, if you don't mind."

Mind! It was precisely what Connie wanted—to wait awhile—but had shrunk from suggesting lest Ben doubt the sincerity of her affection. Given time, she believed that she could rouse in him a desire for the education he had been denied, but which he was not yet too old to get here in this city of opportunity. To that end she would gladly help him as she had promised to help his sister, and meanwhile pursue her own education. Such, in her ignorance of human nature, was the new dream Constitution Field added to the old dream she had cherished for so long.

That the course of true love was not destined to run smoothly became evident before the week was out. Amos, making good his threat that Ben would be sorry, went straight to the parental chamber and blurted out how he had found Ben on the Field doorstep and left his brother alone in the house with Cousin Con.

As a result of this revelation, Hope Benedict resolved to "talk turkey" to her niece without delay. To that end she, who seldom left home on weekdays except to attend a meeting of the Society for the Propagation of the Gospel in Foreign Lands, put on bonnet and shawl late the following afternoon and walked over to Second Street.

When Connie returned at dusk, she was surprised to see a female figure seated on the doorstep. On recognizing the visitor, she surmised at once why her aunt had come, and took measures to forestall discussion of the issue while the two of them were alone in the house. After ushering Hope into the parlor, Connie excused herself on the plea of having to get her brother's supper over the fire. It was some time before she returned to ask their aunt to stay and share the meal.

Hope hesitated. Her one brief glimpse of her nephew had not made her eager to extend the acquaintance. Still, so long as his sister lived under his roof, Jed stood to Connie in the place of a father. If informed that his sister and their cousin were "carrying on" in secret, Jed could be counted on to join the Benedicts in forbidding the match, Hope believed. To that end she accepted Connie's invitation.

When Jed came in, Hope felt obliged to apologize for her family's unceremonious retreat from the tea party and extend a belated invitation to Sunday dinner.

Jed, wondering what "the old woman was up to," said bluntly that he was satisfied to take Sunday dinner at home, his sister being a "prime hand with victuals."

This gave Hope the opening she sought, and she was quick to warn Jed that, unless he exercised his authority and laid down the law to Constitution, she was apt to desert him for a disastrous marriage.

"Marriage!" Jed repeated, looking hard at his sister. "I've heard nothing of any marriage around here. Matter of fact, I've not even seen a suitor." Then, realizing how little he himself was "around here," he demanded to know "what deviltry" Connie'd been up to in his absence.

"None," she told him. "No 'deviltry' at all." Nor was she in danger of disaster, as Aunt Hope seemed to fear. It was true that she and Ben had discussed marriage, but they had decided it was inadvisable for——she was about to say "for the present," when interrupted.

"Praise be!" Hope exclaimed. "Praise be, you two have seen reason in time. The wonder is you didn't see from the start that it wouldn't do."

"Why not?" Connie wanted to know.

"Why not?" Hope repeated. "As though you didn't know your ma is my sister and that it ain't right for cousins to wed."

Connie replied quietly that she was aware of some prejudice against such unions, but there was no law against them so far as she was able to determine. There were many other outworn beliefs which fair-minded folk no longer took any stock in, such as the belief that a bird on the window still foretold death in the house, and a stumble on the stairs a marriage.

Faced with her own belief in omens, Hope realized that she was not clever enough to argue the point with Connie and so she turned her back on her niece and looked at her nephew for support.

Although Jed shared his sister's opinion that Aunt Hope was a silly old woman whose prejudices should be disregarded, he was quick to take advantage of her objection to a marriage which would deprive him of Connie's services. With a stern look at his sister, he told her, "I won't have Ben hanging around here when I'm not at home. You hear that, Sis?"

When Connie reminded him that she was of legal age and free to decide her own course of conduct, Jed retorted, "In my house you're not. I forbid you to see Ben, or any other feller, alone in this house. And before long you'll be alone here for a month or more. I'm going down-river to New Orleans."

"Oh, Jed!" Connie exclaimed. "Are you *really* going? I know you talked about following Stasie when she first went away, but I thought you'd given up the idea. I'm so glad you've decided to forgive her and ask her to forgive you and come home."

Jed snorted, "Forgive—nothing! I don't want that she-devil back. I want my boys. Stasie can keep the girl, but she can't keep my sons away from me any longer. I'm bound I'll have those two little devils, those two little black-eyed devils I begat."

A man's desire for his sons was understandable. But did Jed understand what bringing up children involved, Connie wondered. Was he counting on her abandoning her ambition to devote herself to her nephews? She loved the twins, missed their mischief and their cunning ways, but not enough to sacrifice for them what she had already sacrificed so much to gain. Jed must be made to understand this before he set out on his journey. Opposition was sure to get his back up, however, and Connie merely inquired, mildly, how he proposed to bring up his boys without their mother.

Again Jed snorted. "What did Stasie ever do for those brats except whelp them? That black woman can bring them up better. I don't know if she ever got it through her woolly head that she's a free woman, but I've got papers to prove it, although I never left 'em around here for Stasie to find and put in the fire. I'm taking those papers down-river with me and bringing that free Negro back along with my sons."

Connie stared at her brother—at his clenched jaw and beetling brows, at the fire of determination in the black Field eyes, and she was convinced that nothing would stay Jedediah from pursuing his purpose. What the result would be she was less certain.

One possible result only concerned Hope Benedict and she cried, "Land sakes! You can't leave your sister stark livin' alone in this house, Jedediah Field. 'Twouldn't be respectable." In Jed's presence and his objection to the cousins "keeping company," Hope had seen a sure means of averting what she believed to be dire catastrophe. But in Jed's absence she saw grave danger. Desperate to prevent the lovers from meeting alone, Hope was ready to risk exposing her daughter to a lesser danger, and she asserted that Rooshy was to come over and stay with Connie every night while Jed was gone.

Far from having any objection to this arrangement, Connie saw in it a chance to make good her promise to Rooshy and at the same time start Ben on the road to self-improvement. She was, however, careful to conceal these plans lest Aunt Hope believe they covered a plan to enlist Rooshy's aid to abet romance.

Connie's coolness toward the proposal calmed Hope's fears somewhat, and she went home comforted by the thought that while two is company, three is a crowd.

On the *Washington's* next trip south, Jedediah Field was one of her passengers. At the end of that day's work in the vineyard, his sister went home by way of Sycamore Street. The Benedict menfolks had not yet returned from the shop and the two girls protected each other through the dusk to Second Street. Over bread and milk Connie quizzed Rooshy to determine where instruction should begin. A primer seemed essential, and as there was none in the house the two girls soon went to bed.

Next day Connie did not go round to Sycamore Street after work, but down to Drake's Drug Store, instead, to buy the primer. What to provide for her other and unacknowledged pupil was more difficult to decide. A regular school reader would insult Ben's intelligence. He must be set to reading some book likely to hold the attention of a grown man. Connie's gaze wandered over the stock and came to rest on the set of Shakespeare, still unsold. Even as a small boy Seumas McSeumas had listened enthralled to his grandfather's readings from this author, and memorized countless quotations. What better book then could be chosen to whet Ben's appetite for literature? The price of the set almost took Connie's breath away. Seeing her hesitation and sensing the cause, the clerk offered to sell any one of the volumes separately. For no better reason than because it was the source of her own introduction to Shakespeare, Connie bought *Macbeth*.

When Rooshy arrived that evening, accompanied by Amos, Connie did not invite him in, but blocked the doorway until he took the hint and went home. But the following evening when Rooshy's escort was Ben, Connie asked him to share the lesson period.

Absorbed in teaching Rooshy how to spell cat, Connie was oblivious of the fact that Ben's eyes dwelt less often on the printed page before him than on the profile bent over the primer. Even had she shared with him the pages of Shakespeare, it is doubtful that Ben would have forgotten his problems for those of the Scottish lord and his lady.

Legally, he was of age—free to leave his father's business and seek employment with a competitor, or in any other occupation offering work. Ben, however, knew that his skill and industry was essential to the success of the Danbury Hat Shop in which the irresponsible Amos showed little interest and less aptitude. Everything Solomon Benedict had to show for thirty years of hard labor was invested in that shop on which the entire Benedict family depended for a living. Ben had a strong sense of duty. In case anything happened to his father—and fighting two wars had aged

Sol beyond his years—Ben would have to assume the burden of his mother, sisters and younger brothers. Under such circumstances, another man might marry and take his bride to his parents' home. Clearly, this was impossible in Ben's case. His gaze, filled with longing and frustration, was fastened on the object of it instead of upon the book she had given him.

That intent gaze drew hers finally and Connie looked up from the primer. Whereupon Ben made haste to transfer his gaze to the page under his eyes, blind to the immortal lines until Connie cried, "Why, Ben, you've got that book upside down."

Rooshy tittered. Ben, turning red, reversed the volume and tried to focus his thoughts on the contents. Connie, trying to keep *her* mind on the primer, found its contents something less than absorbing. Nevertheless, she listened patiently to Rooshy's slow and painful recitation about how "the cat ate the rat." And when Ben suddenly burst out with a demand to know "what's this all about?" she replied that it was natural history tailored to the reading ability of beginners.

Ben said, "I don't mean that cat-and-mouse stuff. I mean this stuff about a king being murdered. Is that a fact? Or pure nonsense?"

Although Connie had a vague idea that *Macbeth* was, indeed, founded on historical events, she was not sure how much of the tragedy was true and how much the figment of imagination. She blamed herself for not making certain before giving the book to literal-minded Ben. She ought to have consulted the history teacher before buying any book, instead of acting on impulse, moved by the memory of a lad with less education than Ben who, nevertheless, loved Shakespeare. Ben continued to stare at her and she realized that she had not answered his question.

"To the best of my knowledge," she told him, "that play is founded on Scottish history, but I'm not sure how much of it actually happened. I *am* sure, though, that not a word of it is 'nonsense.' It's—it's great literature."

It was clear this clarified nothing for Ben. To Ben a thing was either true or it was false; black or white. He lacked the vision to see and appreciate the rainbow colors, much less believe that any pot of gold was buried at the foot of the arch. For the first time

Constitution realized just how wide was the gulf between them—the gulf she must bridge if they were to travel together the road of her choice. It was not in her to be balked by difficulties. To her a difficulty was a challenge. Ben's backwardness was a challenge to her intelligence, and now that his limited outlook was revealed, it was a challenge not only to her mind but to the love Ben had awakened.

That night, after Rooshy had gone to sleep, Connie crept downstairs in the dark and relighted the candle. Then she set herself to read *Macbeth* and mark passages best calculated to win and hold Ben's interest. As a result Connie herself was so fascinated that she did not close the book until the candle burned down, guttered and went out.

With Commencement in September the seminary reopened. Except for Saturdays, Connie's work in the vineyard came to an end. She continued to attend church Sunday mornings, but excused herself from going home with the Benedicts in order to devote the afternoon to study. Rooshy also continued to come over to Second Street after dark, accompanied alternately by Amos and Ben. The evenings which girls spent alone Connie could set Rooshy a stint at writing or reading, and then turn to the stint she herself had been set by the schoolmaster. But those evenings when Ben shared the study period, Connie found it impossible to keep her mind on her books.

Ben made a pretence of studying the passages marked in *Macbeth*. But when Connie quizzed him on what he had read—as she herself was quizzed in class—Ben either avoided any direct answer, or gave one that convinced her that he kept on reading the book only as an excuse for spending the evening in the same room with his love. This failure of Ben's to find Shakespeare as fascinating as she did, troubled Connie deeply. She had seen their future marriage as marriage of minds as well as of bodies, and Ben's lack of interest in literature was disheartening.

Constitution Field was not one to admit defeat at the first setback, however, and she kept Ben's nose in that book until Jed's return put an end to Jerusha's lessons, and with them Ben's excuse for visiting the Field house.

Chapter 17

JED HAD NOT NOTIFIED his sister as to the date of his arrival, and when Connie came home from school one October evening, she was surprised to find Delphine in the kitchen warming a baby bottle. At first glance this occupation seemed proof that Jed's purpose had been carried out successfully. Then Connie remembered that the twins had been promoted from bottles to porringers before their mother took them away. She could think of only one reason for this return to the bottle and, after greeting Delphine warmly, she inquired whether one of the boys had fallen ill aboard the steamboat.

The *bonne* shook her turbaned head and pointed to the shadows of the ingle nook. Connie looked, astonished to see there the cradle consigned to the attic when outgrown by the twins. Connie stooped, peered under the wooden hood, and blinked. She could scarcely credit her eyes, but yes, it *was* a tiny black head lying on the pillow. And Connie noted the long black lashes and the rosy cheeks of a sleeping baby—a very young baby indeed.

"What's this?" she exclaimed in bewilderment.

"Zat," replied Delphine, "ees *l'enfant nouveau.*" In a mixture of French and broken English, she managed to explain that Missy had known she was *enceinte* when she went away, but kept the fact from Misser to spite him. Misser's unexpected arrival at the plantation had touched off *une grande dispute.*

"I can well imagine!" Connie remarked dryly.

Delphine nodded. *"Oui-oui!* Ver' beeg row. Misser tell Missy for be quiet, and she tell heem go away. *Mais* she do not tell heem about the girl-baby.

"Then how in the world did the baby get here?" Connie wanted to know. "And where are the twins?"

"Zat I weel tell you, Ma'amselle," replied Delphine and proceeded to do so with a few broken words and many graphic gestures. Connie gathered that the situation remained deadlocked up to the very hour when Misser was obliged to depart defeated, in order to catch the steamboat on its return trip for which he had paid passage. Both parents seemed to have ignored the presence of the *bonne* during their argument, and from Misser's repeated accusation that Missy had no right to take a "free Negro" out of Ohio, it finally dawned upon Delphine that the "free Negro" was herself, although just how that had come about she was not at all certain. All she knew was that she was at liberty to leave Louisiana and return with Misser to the free state of Ohio.

Connie had long suspected that Delphine had no idea that the money taken from the bank on Stasie's order was her own wages. What surprised Connie now was Delphine's assertion that she had neither loyalty nor love for the willful creature who had been her mistress. She did, however, love the Field children as dearly as though they were her own, and she also had a strong if somewhat distorted sense of justice. Since Missy had borne four children, Missy was entitled to two of them, but the man who had begotten them was also entitled to two. After mulling over this matter up to the moment of Misser's departure, Delphine had waylayed him at the gate and offered to spirit his sons out the back door and join him at the crossroads provided that he take her, too, back to Ohio.

Upstairs in the nursery which Misser had not been permitted to enter, the *bonne* had been beset with belated qualms, not about keeping her word to Misser, but about giving him both boys. To her mind a fairer division of the family would be a girl and a boy for each parent. And since Julie was much too big to be substituted for one of the yearling twins, Delphine had wrapped one of the sleeping boys in a blanket. Then spreading another blanket on the bed, she had surrounded the month-old baby girl with children's garments until both bundles were of equal size. All that remained visible above the rolled blankets were two identical bonnets. The *bonne* then carried the bundles down the back stairs and slipped out of the house while the other servants were at supper.

When Delphine paused for breath, Connie cried, "Good heavens!" Then, in French she inquired how the substitution escaped discovery before the *Washington* embarked? And what had Misser said when he found that he did not have both boys?

"Misser," replied Delphine blandly, "Do not yet know." Pointing out that he had occupied a berth in the main cabin while the *bonne* and the babies shared one engaged in the servants' quarters, Delphine went on to say that for several days a storm kept them below. Later, when sent for to bring the twins on deck, she had taken up the boy and had managed to convince Misser that she had to keep one hand free to hold on to the stair rail. Misser saw the sense of this and was content thereafter to see one little boy each day, never suspecting it was always the same boy. When the *Washington* docked at Cincinnati, around noon today, Misser had sent the *bonne* and both blanketed babies home in a hack and rushed off to the shipyard.

"Well!" observed Connie at the conclusion of this long and astonishing story, "It's about time for my brother to come home from work. What on earth will he say or *do* when he learns the truth?"

Delphine replied promptly that Misser would curse *le bon Dieu* for whom he had no more respect than he had fear of eternal damnation. Then he would beat the perpetrator of the deception.

"I've no doubt Jed will swear, dreadfully," Connie said. "But he wouldn't dare beat you, Delphine. White folks don't beat black folks up here. It's against the law." Concerning other legal aspects of the case she was less confident. After Jed sailed, she had wondered if he should not have appealed to the courts for possession of his sons instead of taking the law into his own hands. Now she wondered what would happen when Stasie discovered the flight of the *bonne* with two of the children. Would Stasie appeal to the law, and if so with what result? The more immediate question was how Jed would take the discovery that he had a second daughter.

The front door banged. A heavy tread shook the jerry-built house and Jedediah Field burst into the kitchen. With only a curt nod of greeting for his sister, he went straight to the hearth and bent over the cradle. For a moment the snapping of the fire was the only sound.

Then Jed straightened up, turned on the two women, and demanded, "Where did this brat come from?"

"*Pas l'enfer*," Delphine corrected. "*Petite* missy come from beeg missy." Then, conscious of her inability to explain further in words Misser could comprehend, she looked imploringly at Ma'amselle.

As briefly as possible, Connie retold the astonishing story of what Delphine had done. During the account Jed's wrath rumbled in his throat like the muttering of a volcano on the point of eruption. And when his sister ceased speaking, Jed erupted.

He cursed Delphine for the trick she had played on him. He cursed his wife for withholding the fact of the cradle infant's existence. He started to curse the infant, but the words stuck in his throat. After all, the tiny helpless creature was not to blame. It had not asked to be born, nor was it responsible for being substituted for one of its twin brothers. Lowering his voice, Jed demanded to know the whereabouts of the twin he had brought home. And when Delphine, too frightened to speak, rolled her eyes upward, Jed stamped out of the room and up the stairs.

Almost immediately he came back bearing on one shoulder a little boy whose black eyes were still heavy with sleep. Jed scowled fiercely at the mulatto, demanding, "Which one is this feller? I'm hanged if I know."

A shake of the turbaned head was the only answer. Delphine had not yet regained the power of speech.

The little boy, now awake and surrounded by dismayed, angry or frightened faces, began to cry. His father quickly pushed him into his aunt's arms, saying, "Here! Hush him up before he wakes that other brat. I never had any use for the names their mother gave 'em, so what matter whether she called this one Lance or Lafe? I'm going to call him Sonny. What does matter is that you tricked me out of his brother, you——" Jed made a threatening gesture and the ex-slave cringed and ducked.

Connie cried out, "Don't strike her, Jed! Don't you dare. She could have you arrested."

At the warning, the clenched fist relaxed and Jed muttered, "I'll have *her* arrested for swapping those young ones."

If Jed ever took any such action, Connie never heard of it. He might, for all she knew, have found that he himself was open to the charge of kidnapping. Court action was costly, and the expense of the voyage together with the loss of two month's wages could very well have left Jed short of funds.

Lack of ready money could also account for what happened after water from the street main was piped into the kitchen. In consequence of this improvement, the landlord raised the rent. Jed refused to pay a cent more than he had been paying, declaring he hadn't asked for a tap in the kitchen. He was content to go on using water from the corner pump. Connie, who had lugged most of the slopping buckets Jed never touched until they were in the house, spoke up to say *she* wasn't content to go on doing this needless labor. Whereupon Jed confessed that his chief objection to the extra expense was his inability to meet it and at the same time the taxes on those lots he owned out beyond Northern Row. And when Connie asked if he couldn't sell one of those lots for more than the original price and use the proceeds to carry the rest of the property, Jed replied that he could, but he wouldn't. He was going to hold on to every single one of those lots until they doubled in value, "come hell or high water."

It was not high water, but low water that settled the rent question. When the new works finally went into operation, the corner pumps were removed and the cisterns beneath them filled in. The street vendors abandoned their hogsheads and sent their tired old horses to the soap factory. Jedediah Field had two alternatives. He could move or pay the rent demanded by the landlord. When he found that other landlords had raised their rents for the same reason, Jed was forced to dismount from his high horse.

Connie surmised how he met the extra expense. All signs pointed to good luck at the card tables. But what would Jed do when his luck turned, as it was likely to do in the course of time? She had not long to wait for an answer. One evening Jed sat at the supper table until Delphine took the children upstairs to bed. Then he asked his sister if she had any cash.

Except for what she had spent on food during Jed's absence, and for a few books, Connie admitted that all her summer's earnings were safe in the bank.

"Give me the loan of 'em, Sis," Jed said in a tone that sounded less like a request than a command.

"But Jed," she protested. "I haven't one cent more than I shall need to pay my quarterly school fees as they come due."

Jed's tone turned conciliatory. "I'm not asking you to *give* me a copper, Sis, only to give me a *loan* to tide me over until my good luck comes back."

"Suppose it never does?" she inquired. "Suppose I lend you some money and you lose it? No, Jed, I won't lend you a copper to gamble with. But I'll tell you what I *will* do. I'll pay Delphine for awhile. It's little enough she gets and we can't afford to lose her."

Jed snorted. "Wild horses couldn't drag that woman away from those brats," he said. "Why, she loves 'em like she'd whelped 'em herself!"

"She does," Connie agreed. "But she has no love for you, Jed. And now she knows she's nobody's slave, if she fails to get her wages she's apt to appeal to the authorities. You know what that means, Jed, and so do I. And I'd rather pay her pittance than see you dragged into court."

"Good Lord!" Jed ejaculated. "I couldn't afford that! The judge would be sure to learn I'm a property owner. He'd garnishee my lots. You pay that woman for a bit, Sis, like a good girl, and as soon as I can, I'll pay you back, with interest. And that's a bargain."

It was a bargain Connie fervently hoped Jed would keep. If he didn't, she would run out of funds before the winter was over. Jed's shortness of ready money she believed to be the reason he failed to make good his threat to take the cradle infant back to Louisiana before winter set in and get his other son. At any rate, Jed made no further threats of court action, and if any had been made against him, Connie heard nothing of them. It was her opinion that Stasie, deprived of Delphine's services, was finding the care of two children quite enough without doubling the burden.

The two children in the Second Street house roused Connie before daybreak every morning and were put to bed soon after supper. And as their father stayed out late every evening, Connie could study undisturbed until she fell asleep over her books. She was no longer free to attend church on Sunday, however, for out of appreciation of her cooking, or in the interests of economy, Jed resumed his habit of dining at home on the day of rest. To account for her absence from the Benedict pew, Connie wrote a note to her aunt and sent it around by Delphine.

Some weeks later a knock interrupted her studies one evening. When she opened the door, Ben blurted, "Forgive me! I just had to come to find out why you stopped coming to meeting. Are you mad at me, or something?"

Connie replied that she wasn't "mad" at anything or anybody, unless it was his mother for not explaining her absence.

Ben drew a long breath of mingled relief and exasperation. Then he said, "If you don't want me to come in——"

"Oh, but I do," Connie interrupted. "You know I do, Ben, only——"

It was he who interrupted then, to take her in his arms and close her lips with his. How long they stood locked together in the open doorway neither of them knew nor cared until the sound of footsteps approaching along the brick sidewalk startled them apart. Then, as one, they moved into the dark hall.

When the footsteps passed, Connie whispered, "Do you suppose that was Amos, spying on you, Ben?"

"Like enough," Ben replied, "but whoever it was, I don't believe he saw us." Nevertheless, on the chance that his brother might be hanging around the neighborhood, Ben begged leave to come inside "just for a little while."

Connie hesitated. Anything clandestine was repugnant to her. Still, an encounter between the Benedict brothers was sure to result in all kinds of trouble. And so, releasing herself from Ben's arms, she took his hand and led him into the parlor lest, in the dark, he stumble over a chair. Any unusual noise would wake the children and bring Delphine down to warm the baby's bottle. Connie shrank from discovery by Delphine because Ben's presence would call for explanation that they were engaged, but the fact must be kept secret "for family reasons." Secrets with servants seemed wrong to Connie. There was nothing wrong about her feeling for Ben, nor his for her, she was confident. It was his family's attitude that was all wrong. Nevertheless, until the Benedicts could be won around and the engagement announced to the world, Connie wished Ben would not keep putting her in one awkward position after another. All this she sought to explain in whispers, hoping he would agree that their mutual welfare was in jeopardy.

Ben did not see it that way. He said, "You don't love me any more. If you did——"

Connie protested, "Oh, but I do, only—well, since we can't be married for goodness knows how long, it seems to me better we should meet only in public."

In his heart Ben must have known she was right, for he gave in on one condition. He agreed to stay away from Second Street, provided Connie resume her habit of visiting in Sycamore Street on Sunday afternoons.

The condition put Connie in a quandary. Not only was she unsure of a welcome in the Benedict house, but she had promised to take charge of the children on Sunday afternoons in order that Delphine might attend meetings at the African Methodist Chapel. Ben said that was no excuse. She could just as well put the young ones in their baby buggy and wheel them around to Second Street.

The more Connie thought about this idea, the more it appealed to her. What Hope Benedict lacked in book learning, she made up in knowledge about child-rearing. If asked advice on this subject, she could scarcely refuse. And once she saw the little Fields, surely they would capture Hope's motherly heart.

In this Connie was not mistaken. When Hope heard the story of how the Field family had been divided, her horror of the parents' behavior increased her pity for their unfortunate offspring, especially the cradle infant.

"My stars!" Hope exclaimed, peering into the baby buggy. "I never seen a prettier baby. What's her name?"

Connie replied that at present the baby was referred to as Sissy, just as the boy was called Sonny because of uncertainty as to which twin had been brought home. She did not express her opinion that the nurse knew, but for some reason would not tell, nor did she reveal that Delphine *had* told her that the baby was to have been christened Anastasia in the cathedral at New Orleans, on return to town from the plantation. That Jed would never agree to the child bearing the name of his estranged wife was certain. But all Connie considered necessary to tell Aunt Hope was that the baby had not been baptised.

"Then she must be right away," Hope asserted, horrified. "Connie, you must see to it. You must make that ungodly brother of yours agree to bring this blessed lamb to church next Sunday, before anything happens to prevent. Heaven forbid that any grandchild of my sister should die nameless and unconsecrated."

Connie had not been brought up to believe in infant damnation, nor did she believe a godless man like Jed would be impressed with the need of this religious rite now or ever. Nevertheless, she longed to see this ewe lamb safe in the fold of the church, and agreed to take up the matter immediately. This gave Connie excuse to return home without waiting for Ben to come back from the usual Sunday afternoon inspection of the shop.

For once Jed was at home and looking so pleased with himself that Connie did not need to be told he'd been successful at cards. She took advantage of his good humor to broach the subject of the baby's christening.

"By George!" exclaimed Jed, slapping a knee. "That's a good idea. 'Twould pay Stasie back for christening the twins without consulting me." But when Connie asked what name should be bestowed upon the infant, Jed shrugged. "I don't give a hoot," he said, "just so long as it ain't a French name, or a name belonging to Stasie's folks, or mine for that matter. You pick a name, Sis, some good old Yankee name that'll slip as easy off the tongue as hasty pudding slips down the gullet."

The selection of a name for a baby had never fallen to Connie before and she felt it to be a grave responsibility. For all Jed's violent assertion that he had no interest in the choice, so long as it was easy to say, Connie had become convinced that he had become more attached to the little girl than he was willing to admit. Upon studying a dog-eared old book of names in the seminary library, Connie found a traditional New England name never worn by any Field or Marvin; a name meaning "her father's joy."

As she had surmised, Jed resisted all attempts to get him to take his daughter to church. And it was his sister who, after the final *amen* the following Sunday, bore the youngest of the Fields up the aisle of the First Presbyterian and saw the baby given the Christian name of Abigail.

The boy, who was just beginning to talk, promptly reduced his sister's name to 'Gail. And Gail she was thereafter, quite in keeping with the Field tradition of nicknames.

Jed's problems had overshadowed those of Constitution for a time, but as fall turned to winter she was faced with a new problem in school. The difficulty had begun to develop with her entrance into the French class. French, being one of the few studies deemed suitable for the female mind, but too fancy for boys, the class consisted entirely of young ladies, all of whom had "taken French" for years and considered themselves accomplished linguists because they could read forbidden French novels in secret and interlard their conversation with a few fashionable French phrases. But grammatical construction and the vagaries of idiom were quite beyond them, and there was not one young lady who could put a whole sentence together in reply to Monsieur's questions until Constitution Field joined the class.

To be sure, she had her own difficulties with irregular verbs. But she had listened to torrents of colloquial French for two years, and had also been obliged to make herself understood in that language. A keen ear, quick wit, and a naturally facile tongue helped, and now when Monsieur put a question to the class, she was able to answer promptly, if not always with complete accuracy.

The little Frenchman's interest in a promising pupil was natural enough. So too, perhaps, were his flowery compliments. It was equally natural that older, duller and less industrious pupils should resent his partiality for the new classmate. Growing antagonism troubled Connie who had hoped to find friends among these girls. Yet every friendly move she made met with cold and haughty repulse. Connie was sure of the reason for this enmity, and she decided to ask the master to cease singling her out for praise.

This visit of his smartest and handsomest student after school hours flattered Monsieur. Like many undersized men, he was inordinately vain and construed the girl's act as a tribute to his personal charm. Moreover, he had heard rumors that she was not always as prim and proper as she appeared during school hours. Therefore, he leaped to the conclusion that the reason she gave for "intruding" was a cloak to conceal a purpose by no means scholastic. Whoever heard of a handsome female begging a man to ignore her and pay more attention to less attractive members of her sex? It was absurd.

Appearances must be preserved, however, not so much for the sake of the girl whose morals were already suspect, as for the protection of his own reputation. Cincinnati was not Paris where *les affaires du cœur* were not of necessity circumspect. This was a straight-laced community where one breath of scandal might well cost a schoolmaster his means of livelihood. Therefore, Monsieur appeared to accept Connie's request at its face value. Having thanked her for bringing the situation to his notice, he added that it seemed a pity to retard her amazing progress for the sake of catering to dolts and dullards. Monsieur paused, cleared his throat, and then ventured to suggest that Mademoiselle Field might like private instruction.

"Oh, I haven't any money for private lessons," Connie said quickly.

Again Monsieur misconstrued her words and as quickly replied that he wanted no monetary remuneration. The pleasure of her society would be sufficient reward.

The remark sounded innocuous enough, albeit a bit fancy, but there was a gleam in the little man's eyes that reminded Connie of the cheese merchant, and for a moment her throat contracted so that she could not speak. Then, with an effort, she managed to say, "Thank you, Monsieur, but—well, I've no free time except evenings, and then I have to study my other lessons." With this excuse, she fled.

Left to draw his own conclusions, the conceited little Frenchman believed the girl was drawing him on, playing hard-to-get. It was a game self-confident females delighted in, just as confident males delighted in the chase. The experienced hunter, however, did not rush into open pursuit. First he stalked the quarry, spied out the lay of the land, and then mapped his campaign.

Connie's instinctive distrust of the Frenchman was quieted when he stopped singling her out in class, and she chided herself for thinking his offer of free instruction covered any ulterior motive. Never once did she so much as suspect that he trailed her at a distance many times as autumn passed into winter, or that he took a nightly promenade through Second Street.

As a matter of fact, those promenades ceased when Monsieur saw no evidence that Mademoiselle had lied to him about the way she spent her evenings. Not once had he spied a caller on the Field doorstep or a light in the parlor. For once he must have been wrong in his estimate of a female. This one, astonishing as it seemed, actually had no use for men.

With spring, however, Connie was forced to visit Monsieur again after class and report that delay in collecting a debt owed her, compelled her to drop French. Certain now that the quarry had been brought to bay through no effort of his own, Monsieur determined to profit by the girl's poverty. That night, as he stalked through Second Street, he was encouraged by sight of the door to Number One Hundred Sixty-Four wide open, as though in invitation. But as he approached nearer, he saw just inside the dark hall two figures, recognizable only as male and female, blended into one shadow. There could be no question as to the identity of the female, locked in that amorous embrace, and it was equally certain that the man was not her brother.

Still cautious, the Frenchman continued his nocturnal patrol for a fortnight and then, assured that the lover was not a regular visitor, he ventured to knock on the Field door.

Connie, of course, believed the caller was Ben and went to the door prepared to greet him fondly and then chide him for breaking his agreement not to seek her in secret. Words prepared for Ben did not fit the situation Connie confronted on opening the door. And when the Frenchman bade her, *"Bonsoir,"* she could only echo, *"Bonsoir."*

He said then, "I have come, Mademoiselle, to inquire how makes *progrès à langage française* since you leave my class." A neat move, he thought—not too obvious. Now it was her move to invite him in.

Connie made no such move. The last caller she wanted to see in Jed's absence was this foreigner she had never quite trusted. She said, "It is kind of you to ask, Monsieur. I progress very well in *all* my studies when they are not interrupted." She meant, of course, interruptions from uninvited callers. The hint was so blunt, so impolite, that she chided herself for lack of good manners.

The man, however, interpreted the remark as reference to the cause of interruption in her French studies and a hint to renew his offer of free instruction. "I quite understand, Mademoiselle," he told her, "and I shall be *enchanté* to continue your lessons, gratis. *You* do not need money, Mademoiselle."

Ignoring the emphasis, Connie said again, "Thank you, Monsieur. You are most kind. But as I told you before, I can't accept—charity. However, I still have hopes that the money owing me will be paid, and when it is, I will come back to class. Until then, Monsieur, I shall keep up my French conversation here at home."

The presence in the house of the New Orleans *bonne* was, of course, unknown to the French teacher who chose to interpret the remark to his own advantage. "By all means, Mademoiselle," he said, "let us say no more about lessons, but merely chat together— in your *salon*."

Connie was beginning to wonder if she would be obliged to shut the door in the little man's face. But first, she made one more attempt to get rid of him. "Monsieur," she said, "I do not like to entertain gentlemen, except in my brother's company."

"A-h-h-h?" drawled the Frenchman. "Pardon me if I do not believe you. One evening while promenading through this *rue* some weeks since, I perceived—"

The sentence was cut short by an angry voice at the Frenchman's elbow. "What you saw, you confounded snoop, was none of your business. Have I got to knock your nasty insinuations down your dirty throat to make you 'perceive' you're not wanted?"

Startled, the Frenchman whirled on the doorstep to face the speaker. "A-h-h-ha!" He said, slowly, "Mademoiselle's *other* lover, no doubt. He, in whose arms I did perceive her enfolded *le dernier soir*."

The word lover held no double meaning for Ben. But he did resent the implication that this nasty little man shared his girl's affections. "If you saw me kissing Connie," he said, "I'll have you know we're promised, engaged to be married." In Ben's code that clarified the situation. The man would apologize and get out.

In the Frenchman's code, Ben's assertion provided an opportunity to pay off Mademoiselle for, as he believed, leading him on. "So-s-s-so!" he drawled. "We-e-l, Monsieur Amant, had you delayed a moment longer, you would have seen *me* kissing *votre*——" He never finished the sentence. The last insulting word was knocked down his throat, along with two expensive false teeth. The blow also knocked the little man off the doorstep, across the sidewalk, and into the gutter.

Picking himself up, he hissed, *"Cochon!* Peeg! *Moi,* I refuse to soil my hands weeth you. There are other means of *représaille.* Sir, I shall have you arrested for assault and battery."

"You do that," Ben retorted, undismayed. "There ain't a judge in town, nor in all Ohio as would convict a feller for defending the honor of his promised wife. Get out of here, you polecat, before I knock the rest of your teeth down your dirty throat."

Ben's tone carried conviction that he would make that threat good. The Frenchman was convinced also that his own threat could be made good and that he'd better leave the punishment of this big brute to the law. Bowing with mock politeness, he said, "Farewell, Mademoiselle. *Et vous, Monsieur Amant, au revoir—* until we meet again—in court."

Ben, sure of his own rectitude, was content to let the Frenchman have the last word. As for Connie, she was too completely overwhelmed to say anything. While she deplored the whole episode, the woman in her gloried in Ben's action. How could she turn him away now, as she had been determined to do when she answered that knock, believing it his? How could she reproach him for revealing their secret engagement, under such circumstances, even though that revelation was almost sure to have dire results?

She was still silent, still undecided what to say to Ben when he said, "Let me come in, Connie. We can't talk here on the doorstep, and this thing has got to be talked out now, tonight."

"Yes," she said then, "You're right. Come on into the parlor."

When they were seated, not side by side on the love seat, but on opposite sides of the marble-topped table with the lighted astral lamp between them, Ben said, "We've got to get married at once. Then, if that nasty-minded Frenchman brings suit against me, he won't have a leg to stand on."

"Will he, anyway?" Connie inquired.

"I dunno," Ben replied, and hesitated, unwilling to reveal the reason he was less sure than he had asserted to the Frenchman. He hoped that Connie need never know that she was spoken of as a "fast woman." Ben believed her version of that episode in the gambling room, but too many other men had witnessed the fracas on the stair leading to the rooms above. If this brawl on her doorstep became public knowledge, Ben knew her good name could best be defended by her husband.

Connie was by no means unaware of what this unpleasant episode might cost her. She was less sure that Ben realized what his involvement might cost him. "Ben," she said, "if we wed, your mother and father will never forgive you."

"I know," he replied, "but I'd never forgive myself, if I let that nasty little squirt drag your name in the dirt. If we were man and wife——"

Connie took the words out of his mouth, "If we were man and wife, you'd be out of a job. How would we live? *Where* would we live?"

That his father would certainly turn him out of the house, out of the shop, Ben was obliged to admit. But he was a journeyman hatter and stood a good chance of finding employment in some other shop. As for a place to live, "Does your brother ever use this parlor since his wife left him?" Ben inquired. And when Connie shook her head, he went on, "Well, then, what's to hinder us setting up our bedstead here, like Pa and Ma done in their front room?"

Instead of answering that question, Connie asked, "Ben, would you really work for one of your father's competitors? Work to get your father's trade away from him?"

Ben scowled, chewed his long upper lip, and finally agreed that he probably couldn't bring himself to do that. But an able-bodied, industrious fellow should have no trouble finding work if he wasn't too fussy. "Like enough your brother could get me a job at Shreve's," he said. And when Connie reminded him that he wasn't a shipwright, and that common laborers worked very hard for very little money, Ben exclaimed, "Why beat around the bush? Why not come straight out and say you ain't willing to wed a common laborer?"

She saw that he was hurt, distrusted her love, believed she was simply seeking excuses to avoid immediate marriage. Well, it was true that she was opposed to their union at this time, not because she did not care for him enough, but because she cared too much to jeopardize his whole future. All this Connie endeavored to make clear.

Ben was not easily convinced and the argument was still going on when the master of the house came home. The parlor door was open and Jed looked in to protest the burning of midnight oil because of the expense. At sight of Ben he exclaimed, "What are you doing here at this hour?"

"Courting Connie," replied Ben, bristling. "Got any objection?"

Had Jed's luck been bad that evening, he would certainly have retorted, "Yes," with equal belligerence. But unusually large winnings, and their celebration in wine, made him mellow, kindly disposed toward all the world for the moment. Going around the table he offered Ben a hand.

"Good luck to you, feller," he said. "High time that gal got married. Matter of fact, I'll be glad to get rid of her. Seeing I got to pay my young ones' nurse wages, she might as well do all the chores and save me Connie's keep. When do you aim to take her off my hands?"

"Just as soon as she sets the day," Ben replied quickly. Then, while he had Jed's ear, this seemed to him the best possible time to ask Jed's help in finding a new job, any kind of a job that would enable him to pay for food and lodging, "Of course I'd expect to pay you rent for this room."

Jed's mellow mood vanished. Adept at avoiding payment for value received, he suspected Ben of harboring similar motives. After all, what did he know about Benjamin Benedict, except that their mothers were sisters? In the blood-tie he saw no bar to marriage, but the double relationship would make it doubly difficult to turn out the couple for nonpayment of rent, once they were wed and installed in his parlor.

He said, "No house is big enough for two families. You know what happens when folks get married. My two brats are plenty. Besides, for all I know, my wife may decide to come back with the other two."

So far, Connie had kept out of the argument. Although she did not believe Jed expected, or even desired Stasie's return at this late date—that he was just seeking excuse to avoid becoming involved in his sister's problems—Connie did not voice this opinion. It was better that Ben should blame Jed for obstructing his plans, rather than herself, and at this point she interposed to say, "You see, Ben, we'll just have to be patient a little while longer, provided Monsieur doesn't raise a row. And now, dear, it's very late, and all three of us have got to get up early."

Ben took the hint and went home, but not before he had kissed his girl good night right in front of her brother. That act, and the fact that Jed failed to interfere with the love scene, encouraged Ben to hope Jed might change his mind, or else help find a job that would enable Ben to pay rent elsewhere, and solve his own problems.

Connie, on the contrary, realized that the night's events increased her personal problems. Whether or not the French professor carried out his threat to make trouble, he had already done so, inadvertently. It was clear to Connie that if Jed ever had intended to refund what she had paid Delphine, he had changed his mind. Now that he could assume the ex-slave's wages himself, he was bent on getting his money's worth, and at the same time on saving himself the cost of his sister's food. A man as mean as that—a man set on getting on in the world, even at the cost of his own integrity— was capable of paying almost any price to that end.

Jed might not go so far as to turn her out of the house, but Connie made up her mind not to put him to the test. She would *get* out as soon as possible. And since she would be unable to complete the school year anyway, she would also get out of Cincinnati. The question was—where could she go? Certainly not back to Cleveland! Nor to Athens. Although she was now of age and could count on Mal's welcome, she wasn't going to add to Mal's problems —Mal's burdens.

The only alternative that occurred to her was an appeal to old General Putnam. He, and he alone, had encouraged her ambition— had told her about the educational opportunities in Cincinnati and paid her passage there. From time to time, Connie had reported her progress. No reply had been received, nor was one to be expected of a helpless invalid who, by now, might well have passed on to his reward. But if the old man was still alive, and still clear of mind, he might be able to help her again. A man of such wide acquaintance, and a well-known advocate of education, should know folks in communities too poor, or too parsimonious, to build a schoolhouse. In such places there must be some families among which a girl could rotate, teaching little folks their letters for board and lodging.

The chances of success were slim. Nevertheless, after the house was quiet the next evening, Connie wrote a long and carefully worded letter to her old friend and benefactor. That letter never reached Marietta.

Chapter 18

THE REASON the letter from Constitution Field to General Rufus Putnam never reached Marietta was that it never was sent. When the girl took the letter to the post office, the sign over the inner door gave her an entirely new idea. Since that day when she visited the reading room while still unsure of remaining in the city, she had never ventured in again because the room was not free to regular residents. Now she peered in, saw the room was unoccupied, hesitated, and then, feeling guilty of trespass, slipped in and went straight to the table with its neat piles of newspapers.

Jed, with no more taste for reading than for letter writing, was not a subscriber to either of the local newssheets, but once in a while Connie had found in a trash barrel or in the gutter a crumpled copy of *The Western Spy* or *Liberty Hall,* so that she knew both papers published a column headed "Personals." Her dream of one day being engaged as governess in some well-to-do local family had been relinquished after she finally became aware of the gossip about her. Now, wondering why she had not thought of it sooner, Connie consulted the "Personals," hopeful that some residents of distant towns, unwilling to send their children away from home, might desire to engage a student from the famous Lancaster Seminary. Although Connie lacked a diploma, and was none too sure of a recommendation under the circumstances, she spread the *Spy* on the table and eagerly scanned its pages. The only "help wanted" seemed to be journeymen shipwrights, boilermakers, coppers or blacksmiths. Nobody wanted female "help" of any kind. In *Liberty Hall,* however, someone who signed himself "A Congressman," advertised for "a young lady of education and refinement" to serve as governess for his daughters. Ability to speak French fluently, not just read that language, was a prime requisite. Applicants for the position were advised to write, setting forth all their qualifications and addressing their letters to a certain post office box in Chillicothe.

Connie went home, threw her letter to General Putnam into the fire and wrote another to "a Congressman." When posting that letter, she made inquiry as to how long it would be in reaching its destination.

And when double that time had elapsed, she began to ask every day at the post office if there were any mail for her. Evening after evening, she turned away, disappointed, trying to comfort herself with the fact that, although Congress had adjourned, the journey from Washington was long and subject to all manner of delays. And even when this particular congressman reached home, no doubt he would find mountains of accumulated correspondence of all kinds, including many other applications for the post offered.

Then, when she had about given up hope, an impressive-looking letter was handed to her through the post office window. The letter advised Miss Field that the writer was about to visit Cincinnati on business and would grant her an interview at the stagehouse at a stated hour of a given day. The signature on this terse communication was—Duncan McArthur.

Where had she heard that name? For Connie was certain that she *had* heard it, not seen it in print. Slowly there came back to her the memory of her third brother's angry excited voice recounting a tale of ignominious defeat. It was Major General Duncan McArthur's contingent of the Ohio Militia which, under orders from Governor Meigs, had been rushed to the defense of Detroit only to surrender before reaching that border outpost.

Could Congressman McArthur be the same man, Connie wondered? And, if so, would he remember a private soldier named Ezekiel Field? Zeke had stoutly defended his commander, asserting that McArthur had been elsewhere on a scouting expedition at the time. He had known nothing of the surrender until a British officer demanded his sword. In a rage, the Ohioan had drawn the weapon and broken it with bare hands rather than give it to the enemy. Nevertheless, he had been taken prisoner along with Private Field. After an exchange of prisoners had been effected, the officer and the private both returned to Michigan and joined the force that drove the British back into Canada.

These facts added to Connie's excitement as she dressed for the all-important interview. Thanks to Stasie's stylish discards, her *belle-sœur* presented a very genteel appearance in a simple summer muslin and a leghorn hat tied under her chin with wide ribbon. When she asked at the stagehouse for "Mr. McArthur," the clerk nodded toward a door marked "Ladies' Parlor." Connie hesitated. She had not counted on meeting this stranger alone and behind closed doors. Still, this room opened off the public hall into which she could retreat in haste, if necessary. Connie knocked timidly and then, in response to a gruff voice, turned the knob and went in, leaving the door open behind her.

At a marble-topped table in the middle of the room sat, not one man but two, both of whom rose at her entrance. Connie did not so much as glance at the stranger because the other man was the last man in the world she wanted to meet—the little Monsieur. For the life of her, she could not have uttered a word. Fortunately, she was not called upon to do so, for Mr. McArthur began immediately to explain that it was his wife who had bespoken a governess proficient in French which he himself did "not know from Hottentot." For that reason, he had asked the Lancaster Seminary "to send around" the professor. "So, if you'll just jabber with him a bit, miss, I'll take his word for it whether or not you'll fill the bill."

Connie forced herself to look at the little Monsieur then, and saw he was equally taken aback. He, however, being a man of the world, was the first to recover composure.

Scraping a bow he said, *"Bonjour, Mademoiselle."* Then, in the silkiest of tones designed to give the impression of polite small talk, he gave his prize pupil an ultimatum—in French. If she held her tongue regarding his behavior in Second Street, he in turn would hold his tongue regarding certain gossip which had spread from taverns to sewing circles. Under the elegant phrases, it was clear to

Connie that Monsieur was as eager to get her out of town as she was to go.

Her contempt was so hot that it burned away her timidity, her self-distrust, and Connie replied in the same language with a fluency she had not known she possessed. She would stoop to no such bargain. Whatever she had done amiss had been done in all innocence, and she was not going to sacrifice her self-respect for the sake of suppressing the garbled accounts of busybodies, male or female.

When the Frenchman started to argue, Mr. McArthur interposed, brusquely, "No need for more of the same. The young lady has proved she can jabber your lingo, professor, and since you've already been paid for your services, you may go. I'll proceed with this interview myself and in my own language."

When he inquired as to her skill at embroidery, Connie must have looked her astonishment, for he chuckled, then told her, "My wife bade me ask. Personally, I see no sense in females putting their eyes out working chair seats and antimacassers. To my mind, my girls' eyes could be better employed over books."

Much relieved, Connie admitted that she was better at books than at any sort of needlework, and she asked what studies the general wished his daughters to pursue. When he mentioned history and geography, she remarked that Drake's Drug Store offered textbooks on both subjects, including Doctor Drake's own recently published *Picture of Cincinnati.*

Whereupon McArthur thrust a hand into a breast pocket, pulled out a wallet, and from it took a crackling piece of paper currency. "One of Piatt's new bank notes," he said. "Good as gold. Get that book of Drake's and any other you deem desirable. Get your own duds together and get back here tomorrow morning in time to take the stage."

By that Connie knew she was hired, but not on what terms. When she hesitated, the general must have surmised the reason, for he said, "You will, of course, have to make your home with us in Chillicothe. In addition to your keep, you will receive ten dollars a month—in cash." Mention of the former state capitol proved that Mr. McArthur was, indeed, the famous general.

Ten dollars a month! A princely stipend! Dazzled by the prospect of such riches, Connie could only stammer acceptance.

"Good," said the general. "Glad to have one thing settled. But I've a great deal more important business to get through, so if you'll excuse me——" he paused. Then, when Connie took the hint and started for the door, he called after her, "Make sure you're here promptly at five, miss. I've no patience with dawdlers, as the stage drivers well know. The stage will start on time whether you are here or not."

Connie assured him that she would be and left. This man, to whom every moment was precious, had wasted his time on that warning. Nothing short of a cataclysm would keep her from leaving town tomorrow, she vowed as she carried the general's bank note to Drake's Drug Store.

The schoolbooks purchased there went into the little pigskin trunk Stasie had abandoned with part of her wardrobe. With these castoffs Connie also packed her own dog-eared textbooks and her Johnson's *Dictionary*. But when it came to the only other book she owned, she hesitated. *Macbeth* was her chief treasure, and for that very reason she decided to give it to Ben. Telling him that she was going away, for his sake even more than for her own, would be difficult. In fact, she dared not tell him. The news must be conveyed in a letter, and if a gift went with it, Connie hoped that would soften the blow. The letter she wrote Ben was a long one, stressing her love for him as well as her wonderful good fortune in securing so rare and remunerative a position. With no expenses worth mentioning, she could save practically the entire one hundred and twenty-five dollars a year for——she started to write "college," hesitated, and substituted "future needs."

Book and letter, wrapped together in a piece of clean butcher's paper, could be delivered by Delphine on the way to market with the children. She comforted herself that they were too young to miss her as she would miss them, and that Delphine could be trusted to take good care of them. Something of this kind Connie told Jed over the supper table after disclosing her plans. His approval was so quick and complete as to convince Connie she had been wise to get out before she was put out. Jed himself went out, as usual, directly after the meal and without so much as a word of farewell or an offer to escort his sister to the stagehouse next morning.

Far too excited to sleep after going to bed, Connie lay long in the dark, seeing in her mind's eye the little Monsieur—hearing again his polite voice threatening exposure. Had he, perhaps, returned to the stagehouse later? For all her assertion of rectitude, Connie knew the evidence was against her. She might find it impossible to convince the general that her worst offense had been the winning of a few dollars on the turn of the wheel that was not a spinning wheel. General McArthur might gamble himself upon occasion, but that did not mean he would countenance a female gambler as companion for his daughters. Connie had about reached the conclusion that it would be useless to keep that appointment in the morning. Then common sense reminded her that, despite her refusal to bargain with Monsieur, indeed, because of that very refusal, he would be only too glad to have her leave town. Connie finally fell asleep after deciding to make a clean breast of the whole story after she had won the general's trust and respect.

The other inmates of the Second Street house were still sleeping next morning when Connie crept down the stairs in the dark with the little pigskin trunk on her shoulder. She had carried weightier loads of wood and water, yet somehow the trunk seemed to grow heavier and heavier as she staggered along the dark streets to the stagehouse.

General McArthur was standing in the door of the hostelry when she arrived. "Good lord!" he exclaimed, at sight of her burden. "Couldn't you find any man to carry that? Here, let me set it down while we go into the taproom. Or have you already had breakfast?"

Connie hadn't. In fact, she'd been so afraid of missing the stage that she hadn't given food a thought.

McArthur chuckled, then confessed that he'd named an earlier hour than necessary to allow for the proverbial tardiness of womenfolks. There was plenty of time for a good breakfast. "And I mean *good*," he repeated. "Best make a hearty meal, miss, for it's a long journey with bad food and worse beds."

The girl's heart seemed to stand still. It had not occurred to her that Chillicothe would be an overnight journey by stage, and she said so when she could get her breath.

Evidently her misgivings were written on her face, for McArthur said, "Bad food and bad beds don't mean the inns aren't respectable. Chambers reserved for ladies are safe enough, although you'll probably have to bunk in with strange females, just as my wife has to do when we're traveling."

By now they were seated at a taproom table, and when steaming plates of food had been set before them, the general ceased talking and devoted all his attention to the food. Although Connie had not thought she was hungry her appetite returned in the reassuring company of this middle-aged family man. Before the meal was finished, a horn announced that the stagecoach had come around from the stables.

When the general led his companion out, Connie saw her trunk being put into the boot—a sort of leather pouch hung at the rear of the vehicle. The body of the coach hung suspended by huge leather straps between arched supports, one pair resting on the rear axle and the other pair on the front one. All four wheels were so high that Connie had to scramble up a set of folding steps into the coach where she found three other females already seated. No female could, with decorum, scale the top of the coach where all the male passengers took seats.

In spite of the hundreds of miles Connie had traveled on foot, wagon and boat, she had never before ridden in a stagecoach, and she found this one close and stuffy. Yet, when she opened one of the windows the merest crack, her fellow passengers protested. The heat, they agreed, was oppressive, but the dust would be worse. Although Connie thought nothing could be worse than suffocation, she suffered in silence while the three women chattered like sparrows. From this conversation Connie gathered that their husbands, above on the roof, were bound for Dayton on some business to do with the proposed Miami Canal. Mention of that town, situated almost due north of Cincinnati, roused Connie's fears that, somehow, she had boarded the wrong stage. This fear increased when, on venturing to ask if Dayton was the end of the route, she learned that it was only one of the stops on the regular mail route to Columbus.

Columbus! From her study of local maps, Connie knew that the present state capital was situated at the forks of the Scioto, a long way above the former capital which was to be her home. Would any man to whom time was as precious as it was to General McArthur, take such a long way round? Where was he now? Seated atop this coach, or another one Chillicothe-bound as the crow flies? And what should she do if, when this coach reached tonight's destination, she found herself alone and penniless in some strange town?

The question was still unanswered when, two hours later, the stage stopped to change horses at a relay station. When the door was opened from the outside, Connie did not immediately recognize the man in the long duster and disreputable old slouch hat. The sound of his bluff voice reassured her, as did his hand on her elbow as he helped her down. It was a relief to breathe fresh air and to stretch cramped limbs. And during the brief wait, Connie confessed how disturbed she had been on finding the stage was bound for Columbus.

Duncan McArthur was contrite. He should have explained that. Although just under a hundred miles separated Cincinnati and Chillicothe, there was no direct stage route between the two cities. A road of sorts, there was, but one so rough in fair weather, and so frequently under water in bad, that no man with any respect for horseflesh would drive over it. In consequence, he had left orders for his private carriage to meet him in Circleville at the end of the week.

"That was one of my reasons for making such a point of taking this stage," he concluded. "Should the carriage return to Fruit Hill without me, my folks would worry."

This solicitude for his family increased Connie's trust in the general. She would have liked to ask him about that family, the names and ages of her pupils, and how far they had progressed with their education. But at that moment the horn warned that the stage was ready to leave, and the general hurried her back to her seat.

The heat increased as the day wore on, and the interior of the coach became an oven. Nevertheless, the other ladies insisted on keeping the windows closed although, for lack of air, they grew drowsy, ceased to chatter, and finally fell asleep. Connie, too, dozed fitfully through the long summer afternoon. She had slept little the night before and now, with the passing scene obscured by clouds of dust, there was nothing to keep her alert.

She woke with a start when the rocking of the coach ceased and the door opened on lantern light. When she asked if this were Dayton, one of her companions exclaimed, "Goodness no! We don't get there before this time tomorrow. This place is Lebanon."

More than twelve hours had passed since breakfast and Connie felt famished. Supper in the new brick hotel to which the sign of the Black Horse had recently been moved from Hathaway's old log tavern, was better than Connie had expected in view of the general's remarks that morning. Whether the beds were also better than those in other public houses, she never knew because she slept soundly in spite of snores coming from two nightcaps between which her head lay on the bolster.

The second day out was a repetition of the first, with breakfast by candlelight in the taproom and a start before sunrise. Even with daylight Connie saw little of the countryside through which the coach rocked, bounced and swayed amid clouds of dust, and she did not so much as catch a glimpse of the sun until noon when a stop was made to change horses. During the wait, McArthur explained that the terrain between the Great and Little Miami was fairly flat so that this road did not follow the river beds as did roads through rougher and hillier country. A shower during the afternoon cleared enough dust from the air to reveal fertile fields alternating with dense woodlands and an occasional little bridge over which the coach dashed to the accompaniment of rattling boards. Dusk was falling when the vehicle rattled down the wide main street of Dayton.

Upstairs in the inn, Connie poured water from a china pitcher into a china bowl in the Ladies' Chamber and removing her gown, washed away some of the dust and grime that had penetrated the coach in spite of those closed windows. The brown bombazine gown felt dirty, but its color concealed that condition from sight and Connie went down to supper feeling more respectable.

The meal made good the general's prophesy of bad food and he expressed surprise at his companion's failure to complain.

Smiling, Connie replied, "As my grandmarm used to say, 'Hunger is the best sauce.'"

McArthur's surprise deepened. "What?" he exclaimed. "Don't tell me your grandmother read Cervantes!"

"I don't think she ever read anything except her Bible," Connie replied. "But Granny used to read a chapter from it aloud every night as long as she lived with us."

If the general was beginning to question his judgment in hiring a companion for his daughters so hurriedly, this discovery that she had been brought up in a God-fearing household was reassuring. To make conversation, he inquired about her traveling companions and was surprised when she quoted them on the subject of the Miami Canal, adding that her father had long been interested in a similar project to link Cleveland with the Ohio River. She regretted the remark the minute it was out, for the linking of the name Cleveland and Field brought the question she had dreaded. Was she, by chance, related to Captain Ashbel Field?

And when she nodded, McArthur said, "Well! Well! How is the Captain these days?"

For a moment Connie was at a loss for reply. Admission that she did not know, that she was completely out of touch with her parents, would strike her employer as peculiar unless she told him the whole story, and a story so long and so personal would only bore a busy man. Yet he was looking at her expectantly and so she said slowly, "I haven't heard directly from my father in years. He's a very busy lawyer, and my mother is no hand with a pen. None of her folks ever were." As a case in point, Connie mentioned her recent discovery of her mother's sister, lost track of for over a quarter of a century.

By then the general had finished his meal and, seeing that Connie had done the same, he said, "Since we leave at four in the morning, perhaps you'd like to take a look at this town by moonlight before retiring."

As they strolled along the main street, he told her how Dayton had been the gathering place of troops during the War of 1812, and how, afterward, it had grown rapidly owing to its situation at the confluence of four rivers, the Stillwater, Mad River, Wolf

Creek and the Great Miami. "For some miles about here," he went on, "the Miami is, or rather was navigable for keelboats until recently. Now so many milldams have been built across the stream that Dayton is in grave danger of losing its trade with New Orleans, unless the canal project can be pushed through. But come, I'm keeping you up too late, Miss Field. Let us turn back. I trust you will rest well, for we still have three more days travel ahead of us."

Despite a lumpy bed, none too clean, shared with a lumpier and frowsier female, Connie did find herself somewhat refreshed when roused at cockcrow. That day the route turned away from the river, crossed the height of land, and turned southeast to Washington Courthouse where it arrived at nightfall. Wilson's Tavern, which was also the stagehouse, stood nearly opposite the county courthouse—an odd octagonal-shaped building, the like of which Connie had never seen before.

Yet the very next night, on getting out of the coach after another hot dusty day, Connie thought the heat must have affected her mind, for she seemed to be facing the same octagonal courthouse. No, it was not the same one because this octagon formed the hub of a giant wheel, the rim of which was a broad circular thoroughfare. Of course! This was Circleville, so named because of its peculiar layout.

General McArthur amended that theory somewhat when he joined her in the taproom after a visit to the stable to make sure his team had arrived. The founders of the present town were not responsible for its layout. They had merely appropriated that from prehistoric inhabitants. Here, it seemed, was another of those ancient mounds, similar to the ones at Marietta and Cincinnati, and the village had grown up around that mound. On becoming the county seat, the courthouse had been built in the center of the mound.

Connie was much interested in this local history, and even more in the proposal to construct a viaduct over the Scioto River at this point to carry the Ohio and Erie Canal.

"This," McArthur went on, "is only one of several proposed routes under consideration, but in my opinion the best one. I, for one, will work to have it adopted by the next General Assembly.

The people of Ohio are tired of all this talk-talk about canals and are clamoring for action. But I fear I'm talking too much myself, Miss Field, about matters of no interest to a female."

Although Connie politely denied lack of interest, she did wish the general would tell her more about his family, so that she would be better prepared to meet them and her new duties. She made up her mind to ask some questions at supper, but she had no opportunity because she ate alone while the general went out to the stable again to make sure his horses were properly watered, fed and bedded down for the night.

Those horses, a splendid pair of bays, were tied to the hitching rail before the inn when Connie emerged next morning. From the general's mention of a carriage, she had expected to see a light open vehicle similar to those in which the wives of wealthy Cincinnati merchants took the air. The McArthur bays, however, were hitched to a miniature coach on top of which Connie saw her trunk securely strapped along with many boxes. And when the general helped her from the horse block into his coach, she found it so filled with more boxes and bundles that there was space for only one passenger. After saying that he always rode with his coachman, the general closed the door.

Alone for the first time in days, Connie felt free to open a window. She closed it again when the horses started, for although rain during the night had laid the dust, it had also filled the potholes with water. Either the mettlesome bays could not be restrained, or the general could not restrain his own eagerness to reach home, for the carriage windows were soon so covered with mud that Connie saw nothing of the Scioto Valley.

It was dusk when the carriage passed through Chillicothe, and the bays, now as weary as the travelers, slowly climbed the long hill west of the town. Full dark had fallen by the time the team turned in between tall stone gateposts, circled a drive, and stopped before the door of a large stone mansion.

In the central hall, dimly lighted by a pair of astral lamps under glass shades, Connie met the mistress of Fruit Hill. From behind the general she had only a glimpse of his wife who, after greeting him warmly, remarked that "the girls" had already retired, and doubtless their new governess would be glad to do likewise.

Although the room into which Connie was shown by a colored maid was small, an easy chair covered in flowered chintz stood by the single window draped in ruffled white muslin. A wardrobe occupied one wall, and on another a mirror hung over a chest of drawers. The little space that remained was filled by a low post bed with a coverlet matching the chair. By the time Connie had taken in these details, her trunk appeared on the shoulder of a colored manservant who was followed by the colored maid with a tray. It was a silver tray set with delicate china dishes of hot soup, buttered biscuits, a chicken leg and fresh strawberries. Connie had cooked and eaten many meals more bounteous, but never one served in such style.

The bed was equally luxurious, and the scent of roses coming in through the open window so sweet and soothing that the weary traveler was soon dreaming that she was in paradise.

Chapter 19

HABIT WOKE Constitution Field at cockcrow, and she put one foot out of bed before realizing where she was and that there was no need to rise so early. As the light grew, she lay gazing around the pretty room, luxuriating in this unaccustomed leisure and privacy until the voice of a clock somewhere in the quiet house warned that the time had come to prepare for new duties. After bathing in the adjoining washroom she was to share with her pupils, Connie drew on a fresh chemise and over it her favorite yellow muslin, for she was anxious to make a good impression at breakfast.

Anxious, too, not to keep the meal waiting, she hurried down to find herself alone in the dining room. Several massive, high-backed chairs covered in worn and faded needle-point were drawn up around an oval center table. A crystal bowl of fresh roses centered the table which was covered with a damask cloth and set with fine china and small pieces of silver that flashed in the sunshine. More and larger pieces of silver ornamented a massive sideboard in one corner, and in another the glass doors of a cupboard revealed more delicate china. Lillies filled a marble urn on a smaller table between two long windows opening on the flower garden.

From these evidences of gracious living her attention was diverted by the entrance of three young women. Connie was taken aback. For some reason, perhaps because Duncan McArthur had referred to his daughters as "my girls," Connie had expected little folk. Why, the tallest of these fair-haired, blue-eyed belles must be nearly her own age! Before she recovered from surprise and dismay, the eldest of the trio spoke.

"You must be our new governess," she said. "I'm Effie, and these are my sisters, Eliza Ann and Mary, our baby."

Thirteen or fourteen was a bit beyond infancy, in Connie's opinion, but she remarked only that her name was Field and that she was happy to make the acquaintance of the Misses McArthur. Although she refrained from saying so, she was far from happy at the prospect of presiding over the education of such elegant young ladies. Their father had made such a point of French that Connie concluded his "girls" were already proficient in that language and doubtless better prepared to teach her than she was to teach them. Nevertheless, because some further remark seemed called for, she said, in French, that it was a beautiful day and the garden scents ravishing. The blank expressions on all three fair faces restored her confidence somewhat, and she repeated the remark in English.

At this point the parents came in, and after a brief exchange of greetings the family sat down. By daylight, and in a simple calico morning gown, Mrs. McArthur looked older than in the dimly lit hall last night. There were threads of gray in the chestnut curls over her ears and in the *chignon* coiled high on her head and held with a huge tortoise-shell comb. Minus the matronly comb, Effie's bright curls and the paler ringlets of her sisters were arranged in similar fashion. Now that their gaze was on their plates, the governess could observe the trio more closely. They, too, wore calico in varied shades of blue and so simply made that Connie felt overdressed and uncomfortable. All the more because the master of the house wore a shabby old suit of homespun, heavy boots, and a pre-

226

occupied frown that discouraged conversation. The meal was served in silence broken only by the faint clink of silver on china. Then in silence Duncan McArthur rose and clomped out.

At once his wife said, "Girls, suppose you pick posies in the garden while I interview Miss Field in the library."

When Connie had followed the mistress of the house across the hall her gaze was caught by shelves of books reaching from floor to ceiling. There was no time to read any of the titles before the two women were seated facing each other across a large flat-topped desk.

"That is a very becoming gown you have on, Miss Field," remarked Nancy McArthur. "Made by yourself, no doubt."

Connie said no. A New Orleans dressmaker had made it for—— she was about to say, "for my sister-in-law" when interrupted.

"New Orleans!" exclaimed Mrs. McArthur. "If you came direct from that city, I hope you brought the latest designs in petit point. As you must have noticed, the dining room chairs are disgracefully shabby. My grandmother McDonald worked those seats and backs, and now I wish them replaced by my girls to hand down to *their* grandchildren. One of your chief duties here, Miss Field, will be superintending this project."

Connie hesitated, then confessed that, while she could patch and darn, fine needlework was not one of her talents.

At that Mrs. McArthur exclaimed, "But I distinctly impressed it upon my husband to engage a governess skilled in embroidery."

"So he told me," Connie replied. "But he seemed to think——" she stopped, reluctant to quote her employer's exact words.

Nancy McArthur said, "I know what my husband thinks. He wants our daughters taught to do sums and keep ledgers. But with three businessmen in the family, *I* see no reason my girls should puzzle their pretty heads over such matters. Besides, as you are doubtless aware, Miss Field, when a girl marries, her husband assumes complete control of her property. Margaret, our eldest daughter, is already wed to the editor of the local newspaper, the *Scioto Gazette,* and lives in town. Effie is engaged to a gentleman she met in Washington, where Eliza was also besieged with beaux.

"I mention these personal matters," the lady went on, "merely to prove my point—that the time and thoughts of young ladies are most profitably employed in making themselves charming. Learning to sing, for instance, and to play the harp or the pianoforte. Which instrument do you play, Miss Field?"

Connie, who had considered Stasie's warbling and tinkling a waste of time, was obliged to confess that she could not carry a tune and did not know one note from another.

"Dear me!" exclaimed the matron, aghast. "What *do* you know, Miss Field?"

The subjects in which she excelled were, obviously, not those calculated to impress this lady. But, recalling what the general had said of the value she placed upon French, Connie said that, before engaging her, the general had consulted the French professor at the Lancaster Seminary with regard to her qualifications. She could see that mention of this famous educational institution impressed the lady, and her fears of dismissal for incompetence lightened a little.

After a moment, Nancy McArthur said, "Well, you are here, so we shall have to make the best of it, for the present at least. Fortunately, a music master has recently come to town. Effie shall take lessons from him, if they can be arranged for the same afternoon as the other girls' dancing class and my own day at home. Other afternoons, I need the carriage to make calls." She paused and surveyed the new governess with fresh misgivings. "I must admit that your youth was another disappointment, since I must depend on you to act as duenna whenever my own social duties prevent my accompanying the girls from home."

Connie's heart sank anew. Clearly, her stay at Fruit Hill would be short unless she could fill the mistress' social requirements as well as the scholastic requirements of the master. A tall order! A very tall order indeed. Choosing her words with care, she said that, while young in years, she was old in experience and well able to protect her charges on afternoon excursions to town. "Mornings," she made haste to add, "I presume the general will expect me to hold classes here." She meant somewhere on the premises, but as she spoke Connie's gaze instinctively roamed over the crowded shelves.

"Here!" cried the general's wife, raising delicate eyebrows. "Oh, no! This is my husband's office. He is in and out at all hours."

After a moment, while the delicate brows were knit in thought, she said, "I do not use the parlor, mornings. You may teach the younger girls there while Effie does her practicing, provided you take care not to disturb her."

Connie ventured to protest that, while writing classes could be carried on in silence, it was scarcely possible to teach oral arithmetic and spelling without making some sound. Perhaps it would be better if oral instruction were carried on elsewhere, or on such afternoons as all three girls were at home and their mother absent. Whereupon their mother remarked that Chillicothe society was quite gay. There were many evening parties which made "a beauty sleep" on those afternoons imperative.

"I suppose you could teach Eliza and Mary in their chamber, mornings," she said. "That is, after the maid has made the bed and tidied up. I do not allow anything to upset the servants' routine."

It was becoming increasingly clear that social and domestic routines were considered more important than lessons, and Connie said humbly, "Whatever arrangement suits you, ma'am, I'll do my best."

When the mistress of the house had rustled out of the library, Connie longed to stay and browse among the books, but duty drove her out to seek her charges in the garden. She found the three girls chatting and giggling in a rose arbor. At sight of her, they ceased and sobered so that Connie was certain she had been under discussion. What did they think of her, she wondered, painfully conscious of her ignorance of social graces. Instinctively she put her best foot forward by suggesting that lessons begin here and now in *"le jardin des belles fleurs."*

This transferred the disadvantage to the girls whose blank stares proved that they knew less than Connie about that language. For what remained of the morning, the garden and its products provided subjects for French conversation. It was at least some satisfaction to have made a start along educational lines, although success in those approved by the girls' father did not look promising. He was master of the estate, but his wife was mistress of the mansion. The last thing Connie wanted to do was stir up discord between the parents of her charges—discord almost sure to end in her own dismissal.

That the general had already dismissed the new governess from his mind was apparent at lunch. He did ask Connie how she was "making out," but when her evasive reply evoked no further remark, she knew it had fallen on deaf ears. Even when his wife inquired whether she could count on him to accompany her and their daughters to a lecture in town that evening, Duncan McArthur made no answer, which apparently satisfied his family that his attendance could not be counted on.

Connie did not dine with the family that evening because, as Mrs. McArthur explained, "the boys" and their wives were coming to dine and go on to the lecture. "The boys," it seemed, were the McArthurs' two sons, older than any of the girls, and both engaged in their father's various enterprises. Miss Field would find family dinners dull, and anyway, there would not be room for so many at the table. Her dinner would be sent to her room on a tray. Whether or not the general did accompany his family to the lecture, Connie did not learn, but all the McArthurs left the house directly after dinner.

Connie decided to take advantage of the free evening to write some letters, and since she had brought neither pens, ink nor paper, she ventured into the library where materials for correspondence were laid out under the astral lamp.

The note enclosed in the volume of Shakespeare contained her present address, and until Ben acknowledged the gift, she did not feel inclined to write him again. She did feel duty-bound to acquaint Jed with her safe arrival, even though no reply could be expected. To Mal, she wrote at some length, sure of his joy in her good news. After that Connie debated whether or not to write her mother. Since that ultimatum of her father's which she had disregarded, no further word had come from Cleveland, and this prolonged silence decided Connie to leave the news of her present whereabouts to be passed on by Mal.

Mal's reply to that news came promptly. He expressed deep satisfaction in her progress toward the goal of her desire. Serena sent her love. Of Mercy he wrote only that she was well. About their son he wrote freely. Marvin was a truly remarkable child, sunny and sweet, yet with a mind of much promise. He was learning to speak Latin simultaneously with English, and already knew the names of the planets and some stars. Other news from Athens was not good. The college was experiencing difficulty in the collection of rents from its land grants, and in consequence salaries were in arrears.

That evening Connie wrote, offering to send all or part of her first month's stipend, and continue the practice so long as Mal needed money. The loan could be repaid at his convenience. He replied at once with strict orders to send nothing. She was to put aside every cent toward her college expenses.

Ben, on the contrary, wrote urging his "dearest girl" to give up the "crazy idea" of college once and for all. He wanted her to give up "this fancy job," too, and return to wed him at once, "and the devil take the consequences." Although Ben's penmanship was hard to decipher, his resentment of her "desertion" was clear.

Instead of even replying to his letter "at once," Connie resolved to wait until her own resentment subsided. Nothing was to be gained, and much might be lost by retaliating in kind—telling Ben that it was *he* who was "crazy" to press for marriage when he couldn't support a wife. She waited a fortnight and then wrote Ben begging him to try harder to understand her motives. In her absence, the gossip about her would die and if, after a year at Fruit Hill, she returned with a recommendation from General McArthur, she might be able to secure a position in one of the recently opened young ladies' seminaries in Cincinnati. Then, if Ben's father carried out his threat to turn Ben out of the business if he married Connie, they could live on her earnings until he found some other occupation. Meanwhile, she urged him to cultivate a taste for books. If he couldn't learn to like Shakespeare, he might try some other author. He must be eligible to borrow books from the new Apprentices' Library established for the intellectual and moral improvement of young mechanics and laborers. Many an older man who lacked early advantages had pulled himself up by his own bootstraps to a position of wealth and respect by spending his spare time in study. As a case in point, Connie added that General McArthur was a self-made man.

In the light of that fact she found the library at Fruit Hill all the more remarkable, for it was stocked with history, biography, philosophy and literature. Authors included Plato, Cervantes and

Shakespeare, and even such living authors as Sir Walter Scott and Mr. James Fenimore Cooper.

Whenever the family was out of an evening, the governess was free to browse among the books until the front door slammed and the general's bluff voice sounded in the hall. With his permission, she often carried up to her room the current volume and read on and on until her candle went out.

Connie had a guilty feeling that her own education was progressing faster than that of the girls she was hired to instruct. Although this was no fault of hers, she remained reluctant to tell the general that lessons given in off moments and in odd places were not conducive to rapid advancement. Complaint of Mrs. McArthur's regime seemed ungrateful and in poor taste.

One noon, at the end of her first month at Fruit Hill, the general looked up from his lunch directly into the eyes of the governess and told her curtly, "See you in the library directly."

The governess' appetite failed at the thought that Mrs. McArthur had complained that she was unsatisfactory. It was in breathless suspense that she faced her employer across his desk, watched him unlock a drawer, and take out a metal box. Then he unlocked the box and withdrew a package of bank notes, counted off ten one-dollar bills, and pushed them across the desk.

"Your first month's salary, Miss Field," he said. "If I forget to give you the same amount regularly, just remind me. I have a great deal on my mind these days and do not always remember trifles."

To Connie ten dollars was no trifle. It was a small fortune. She kept that little roll of paper currency under her pillow until her next trip to town with the girls. While they pursued the arts and graces, she visited the Bank of Chillicothe and deposited her entire stipend.

The bank occupied a mansion larger and more commodious than Fruit Hill or Adena, the neighboring Worthington estate, and other handsome town houses lined the broad shady streets where Connie wandered while the coachman took the team to the blacksmith's shop. The founders of Chillicothe had not destroyed all the ancient forest monarchs as had the founders of Cleveland and Cincinnati. Many enormous sycamores and oaks towered above pillared porticoes or wide verandahs overlooking sunny gardens gorgeous with bloom. There were mansions equally spacious and handsome in Cincinnati, but not adjacent to the business section as here. Compared with the teeming wharves and warehouses on the Ohio water front, Chillicothe's main street seemed almost rural. Even the former capitol, now serving as the Ross County Courthouse, looked insignificant to the girl who had watched the new Hamilton County Courthouse go up out beyond Northern Row. With so many rich and influential residents, Connie wondered why the metropolis of the Scioto Valley did not expand as rapidly as that of the Ohio Valley.

By now she knew that it was for "business reasons" that Duncan McArthur had declined to run again for the United States Congress. Besides large tracts of Ross County land and large herds of cattle, he was a partner in several of the saw, grist and paper mills turned by Paint and Salt Creeks, and with his brother, owner of the local iron works. Yet, for all these enterprises and others owned by Worthington and Massey, Chillicothe looked asleep on this warm summer afternoon. Connie strolled down the wide deserted thoroughfare to the river and there discovered the reason business was so slow. At this season the Scioto had shrunk to a mere brook between sandbanks. On these bars flatboats lay at crazy angles and other boats were tied up at the wharves, mute testimony that the Scioto, like the Cuyahoga, did not furnish year-round navigation. No wonder Cincinnati was stealing the cream of all trade. No wonder General McArthur's thoughts and energies were absorbed in the problem of circumventing nature and getting his products to market.

As the months passed, Connie's personal problems absorbed much of her thoughts. Ben wrote that, could he afford it, he would come to Chillicothe and insist on wedding her there. But stage fare and the cost of three meals each day and a bed each night, en route, would run into money. Money Ben did not have because all the profits of the hat shop, except for family living expenses, were being put back into the business. His father was aging and ailing, and Amos no help at all. For these reasons Ben was bound to the business "for better, for worse."

Connie wrote back that news of his father's poor health was disturbing, but she was thankful the family had a dependable prop like Ben to lean upon. If he needed financial support, he could count on her for a loan.

This offer Ben refused with more heat than gratitude. What did she take him for? If he needed a loan, he'd borrow from the bank and not from his girl. Beneath these curt statements Connie read bitter resentment of her earning capacity. Ben was jealous. And jealousy boded ill for their future happiness. How far, she asked herself, was she willing to accept Ben's point of view? Would she be willing to sacrifice her ambition and settle down to becoming a mere household drudge? That prospect grew less and less attractive. She told herself she was growing spoiled here in the mansion where she did not have to carry the wood for her own fire, or even water for the painted bowl in the adjoining washroom.

With the first frost, fires crackled on the hearths of every room in the house. And when the garden turned sere and brown, tutor and tutored came indoors, perforce. There was less room for lessons and less time for them now, for embroidery frames were set up in the big bedroom shared by Eliza and Mary. Not only did three frames take up all tthe space in front of the three windows, but more space was filled by three of the dining room chairs, brought up to serve as models. For, lacking new and original French ideas in petit point, Nancy McArthur decided that her grandmother's designs should be duplicated, stitch for stitch. Because of the incompetence of the governess, she herself started the work of copying her heirlooms.

Competition and competence among the girls grew as the worsted flowers began to bloom on the canvas and interest in book learning lagged. Connie racked her brain for fresh stimulus and hit upon the plan for making the needlework a French conversation piece. Eliza began to develop facility in that language which spurred Effie and Mary to greater efforts. Fingers and tongues flew in unison and when both grew tired, the governess produced a book and read passages aloud. The tragedies, *Macbeth* and *Hamlet,* wounded delicate female sensibilities. But *Midsummer Night's Dream* captured their fancy, and all three girls took to quoting favorite passages from it at dinner, greatly to the delight of their father. Nancy McArthur was equally delighted with the rapid progress of her pet project and began to view the "bluestocking" in a more favorable light. As a direct result, the governess shared the family dinners that winter while the general was in Columbus as a recently elected member of the General Assembly.

After the spring mud season was over and roads became passable again, the general frequently brought home fellow assemblymen over the Sabbath. In the absence of those three dining room chairs, the governess was also absent from the dining room when several guests were present. But after the legislature adjourned and guests were fewer, Connie was included at dinner where the man-talk was more to her taste than feminine chitchat. She was much interested to learn how, some years earlier, a commission headed by Thomas Worthington had been set up to study several routes possible for connecting the Great Lakes and the Ohio River by canal. Later, when the canal bill, authorizing work on one or more of these projects, came up in the General Assembly, its passage had been blocked by thirteen diehards.

Those same diehards had opposed the bill again during this year's session which, Connie gathered, had been exceedingly stormy. This time, however, the canal bill had passed, and with it a "rider"—something to do with the establishment of public schools. Connie pricked up her ears, eager to learn more of this project, but it was merely mentioned in passing. What General McArthur and his friends were interested in was the financing of two canals, the one to connect Dayton with Cincinnati, and the longer more ambitious project discussed years ago in Ashbel Field's office—the Ohio and Erie Canal.

Now she heard it discussed again with more detail. The "big ditch" actually was going to be dug up the Cuyahoga Valley to the height of land, descend from there along the course of the Muskingum tributaries to the vicinity of Circleville, and then down the Scioto Valley through Chillicothe to enter the Ohio River. To the girl who had covered much of this route on foot, it seemed incredible that men who had never so much as ridden a horse over it should be so sure a ditch could be dug all that distance, a ditch deep enough and wide enough to float flatboats loaded with corn, lumber and other heavy freight. As for financing the stupendous undertaking, despite her aptitude for figures, Connie was bewildered by the sum total discussed as though it were only grains of corn. Two and one-half million dollars! She had not dreamed there was so much money in the whole world.

From later fragments of dinner conversation, she learned that New York bigwigs had agreed to loan the State of Ohio four hundred thousand dollars at five per cent interest to be guaranteed by taxes. For further funds, the state was preparing to issue bonds. Local men, including McArthur and Worthington, were firm believers in the safety of this investment and pledged themselves to buy those bonds to the limit of their available resources. Duncan McArthur even urged his daughters' governess to follow that example.

Connie had, indeed, accumulated more than enough to buy a hundred-dollar canal bond by the end of her first year at Fruit Hill. But she had another sort of investment in mind and, instead of taking her employer's advice, she resolved to leave her money in the bank. This proved a wise decision, for the summer of 1825 brought a sudden and urgent need for cash.

One warm June evening when the girls were dining and spending the night with their married sister after a garden party in town, there were only four persons at the McArthur dinner table: the master and mistress of the house, their daughters' governess, and one guest. He was a slender wiry man in his middle thirties whose mouse-colored hair was already receding from a high forehead. He had seen Constitution Field many times when she was a child, but he did not recognize that child in the tall handsome young woman to whom he was introduced hurriedly in the hall just before dinner.

The conversation, interrupted at that time, was resumed by the general over the soup. "So De Witt Clinton has accepted the honor of turning the first spadeful of earth for our canal, you say, Kelley."

Alfred Kelley nodded. "Yes," he said, "the New York governor will come to Cleveland by steamer from Buffalo, and we are making great preparations for his reception and transportation to Licking Summit where the main ceremony will take place."

"Good lord!" exclaimed McArthur. "What made the committee hit on a spot so deep in the wilderness? It will be difficult to reach and once there, it will be impossible to extend proper hospitality. Surely there are many other places along the route where private homes would be open to visiting dignitaries. Here, for instance."

Mr. Kelley explained that one reason for the choice of Licking Summit for turning the first spadeful of earth was because it was located at the highest point on the route. "But we had other reasons," he went on. "Would you approve Cleveland as the place to celebrate this great event, General?"

"Certainly *not!*" retorted McArthur. "None of the Chillicothe backers would agree to that."

Suppressing a smile, Kelley said, "We suspected as much. Also Cleveland, where the canal will enter the lake, would never hear of having the first spadeful of earth turned anywhere in the Scioto Valley. Therefore this compromise. I trust you will not find the ride to Licking Summit too exhausting, General, or that you will object to sleeping in a tent."

With a snort, McArthur retorted, "What do you take me for, Kelley? An old man with one foot in the grave? Why, I'm only fifty-three and tough as rawhide. After riding a horse all over Northwest Territory and chasing the British Army into Canada, I'm not likely to shrink from a few days in the saddle, or a few nights under canvas."

Kelley said, "I am much relieved to hear that you will be present. Far too few of Ohio's early settlers have lived to see this day. Sam Huntington died nearly eight years ago and Return Jonathan Meigs more recently. Old General Putnam, too, has at last gone to his reward. A blessed release. We in Cleveland have come to hope that a similar release will not be denied Ashbel Field much longer. Ash had a stroke last November, and since then he has been unable to speak or rise from his bed."

Ash's daughter was paralyzed by this news. Why had she been left to learn of it in this way? Surely, Ash's sons must have been notified. Jed, she had never heard from since leaving his house, over a year ago. But she did hear from Mal now and then. Why had he failed to mention their father's condition? Was it because Mal was sure she would not care?

Connie did care, deeply, intensely. The idea of that strong vital body lying helpless in the blockhouse, that resonant voice stilled, was unbearable. For years she had believed that she hated her father. Now Connie knew that she had never hated him—had hated only his violent opposition to her heart's desire. Ash himself was suddenly dearer to her than that desire—dearer than anything else in the world. She must go to Cleveland and tell him so, if he could still hear that confession. If he could not—if Ashbel Field died believing his rowan hated him, Connie felt that she must die of remorse.

Some trace of these powerful emotions must have been reflected on her face, for Nancy McArthur exclaimed, "Dear me! You look positively ill. Is this neighbor of Mr. Kelley's a kinsman of yours, Miss Field?"

Before she could reply, Alfred Kelley repeated, "Miss Field! Forgive me, but I didn't catch the name before dinner. You can't be— yes, you *must* be that girl of Ash's who left home for school."

Connie nodded. Then, as soon as she could master her voice, she said, "Please General, I've got to go home. How can I get to Cleveland from here? Is there a stage direct, or——"

Mr. Kelley interposed, "I'm starting for home tomorrow, Connie. I didn't come by carriage because the roads are so vile. But if General McArthur will lend you a horse, I shall be only too glad to take you home."

"Horse?" said the general. "Of course I'll provide a nag and anything else needed. How about money?"

Unless Mr. Kelley proposed to start before the bank opened in the morning, Connie said, she could pay her own way. As for a horse, she hesitated about accepting the use of one when she had no idea how it might be returned. "It may be I can't come back at all," she told him. "Certainly not as long as my father lives. Nor after he's—he's gone, so long as my mother needs me."

At that Mrs. McArthur murmured "Of course."

Then Alfred Kelley said, "If you are still tied in Cleveland when I leave there for the ceremony at Licking Summit, I'll be only too glad to take the general's horse there. As for money——" He broke off an offer to defray her traveling expenses and stable bills, checked by the proud look on the girl's face. He might have known Ashbel Field's daughter would accept no such gift, even from a family friend. "As for money," he repeated, "Leonard Case can arrange later to have your funds transferred from this bank to his. Then you can reimburse me for the costs of your journey, for you see we shall have to start very early tomorrow in order to reach suitable lodgings by nightfall."

Somehow, Connie managed to express thanks for all these kind offers. "And now, ma'am," she added, looking at Nancy McArthur, "if you'll excuse me, I must go and pack." Somehow, she got out of her high-backed chair, and up the stairs to the room she had grown to love.

Now that she was leaving it behind, perhaps forever, Connie realized how much she had come to love Fruit Hill—the easy life, the warmth and comfort of the big house full of servants, the master she admired, and the mistress for whom she had increasing respect. She thought of the books in the library, the flowers in the garden, but most of all of the flower-like girls whose minds had begun to put forth fresh buds under her care. It was hard to go without a word of farewell, and the best she could do was write a note and leave it on Effie's bureau, begging them not to forget her, ever.

Then she went to bed, not to sleep, but to think of her father—the father whose love she had forfeited in pursuit of a dream. That she had also forfeited her rights in his estate as a direct result, was forgotten. She was abandoning her dream voluntarily now with no thought of regaining anything except the love and forgiveness of Ashbel Field before it was too late.

Chapter 20

THE THOUGHTS of Constitution Field on that journey back to Cleveland were very different from those which had tormented her when she left home. Then she had been an angry, ignorant girl bent on going her own way. Since that time she had learned a great deal, and not all of that knowledge had come from books. Dear experience had taught her that females who defied the rules laid down for them by men encountered dangers undreamed of by homekeeping girls. In the light of this experience Connie saw that it was awareness of these dangers, and desire to save her from them, which had moved Ashbel Field to deny his daughter the kind of education he had sacrificed so much to give his sons. Not all those sons had inherited his brains and tastes, and when he saw those qualities budding in his daughter, no wonder Ash was appalled. It had been to keep her from tilting at windmills, like the mad old hero of Cervantes' tale, that her father had used the sharp spear of parental authority. And when that failed to turn her from the flailing sails of convention, he had sought to interpose the shield of matrimony.

After all this time Connie shuddered afresh, remembering the widower's wolflike smile and avid eyes. At long last, she realized that her father's very eagerness to thrust her into Mr. Jones's arms was the measure of his anxiety. That anxiety had been well founded, Connie knew now. She had defied the windmill and escaped destruction only by good luck and the assistance of several men—her brothers, her cousin, Mr. Longworth and finally General McArthur. Nevertheless, she knew that, rearmed with a fresh weapon in the shape of cash, she would have returned to tilt at the same windmill again, had not duty intervened. That was one of the differences between men and women. Women had a keener sense of duty than men. Even Mal, whose conscience was tender as a woman's, would not resign his professorship, ill-paid as it was, to care for the father who had sent him to Yale. Yet Connie, whose ambition Ash had fought and frustrated, the daughter he had disinherited for disobedience, was turning her back on her first real success for the sake of easing his last days.

Connie had never before ridden a sidesaddle, or indeed any saddle at all except Mal's for one day. As a child she had ridden bareback, like her brothers. During the war there had been no horse to ride, and afterward no occasion for travel until she left home—afoot. The end of this first day of the return journey found her so stiff and sore that she could scarcely dismount with the help of her escort. Every bone in her body, every cramped muscle, rebelled at the prospect of more such days ahead.

Yet, after a night's rest, she mounted again in the gray dawn.

That second day and those following were all much the same. Where the road was wide enough for two horses abreast, Alfred Kelley rode beside her, hoping to distract and ease her mind. Everything possible was being done for Ashbel Field, he said. Dr. David Long was devoted to him and dropped around frequently. Neighbors came in to help Ash's wife turn him, or lift him bodily while she turned the feather bed. Faith Field was a wonderful woman, everybody agreed. Never a word of complaint, although all Cleveland knew her whole life was bound up in her husband.

Connie could only nod agreement. She could not tell Mr. Kelley how she felt—could not voice her regret that neighbors had been doing for Ash and Faith what should have been done by their children. Well, their daughter would soon be doing her share, doing her best to make up for her own neglect and that of her brothers. Although she expressed none of these thoughts in words, they must have been revealed on her face, for Alfred Kelley changed the subject to one near his own heart.

The previous March, he said, Congress had appropriated five thousand dollars to build a pier six hundred feet out into Lake Erie at the mouth of the Cuyahoga. It was hoped that this pier, or jetty, would keep the river free of sand at the point where the canal would enter the lake. The two projects would provide work for every able-bodied man in Cleveland and attract more settlers. Merchants would profit in consequence and land values would rise rapidly. "Your father," Kelley concluded, "was smart to hang onto his city lots all this time."

Connie inquired, "Does Pa realize that now? Does his mind remain clear?"

"It's hard to tell," replied Mr. Kelley. "Some think so. Some don't. Before long now you can judge for yourself."

Could she, indeed, Connie wondered? Would she even see her father alive? To be sure, paralyzed people often lingered for years, mute and helpless. Quite as frequently a second or third stroke took them off in a minute. Increasing fear that she might be too late gave Connie the feeling that the horses crawled when, as a matter of fact, both the Kelley gelding and the McArthur mare made good time in spite of adverse conditions.

The roads, which in the spring had been quagmires, were now

deep in dust. Dust stirred up by four pair of hooves rose in clouds to blind and to choke horses and riders. Other clouds of insects—black flies, gnats and mosquitoes—stung animals and humans alike in the vicinity of the many upland swamps and added to the discomfort of what seemed an endless journey.

At length, however, the tired horses and the equally tired and dirty riders emerged from the forest into Cleveland at dusk. After the mushroom city on the Ohio and the handsome former capital on the Scioto, the settlement on the east bank of the Cuyahoga looked shrunken to Connie, like a nut too long overlooked in some attic. If any new structures had been erected in her absence, Connie did not see them in the failing light.

When Alfred Kelley left her in front of the Field blockhouse, it looked deserted. All the front windows were dark. But when she rode around to the barn, a flicker of flames reddened the kitchen window. Connie had been brought up to consider domestic animals, and she suppressed her anxiety and eagerness until the mare had been unsaddled, rubbed down, watered and fed. Then she followed the familiar path in the dark to the back entrance, where she paused for a moment to gather courage, before pushing open the door to stand framed against the black velvet of the summer night.

At the sound of the latch, Faith, kneeling on the hearth, looked up. The smile, summoned to greet some kindly neighbor, faded to a look of wonder and unbelief. For a moment neither woman spoke. Then Faith whispered, "Darter! Darter, mine! 'Tis you and not your ghost!"

The heart of the returned wanderer swelled so that she could only gasp, "Ma! Oh, Ma!"

The dam broke then—the dam built up by generations of New Englanders to hold back emotions. Mother and daughter were in a close embrace, weeping on one another's shoulder.

Finally, Connie released herself, wiped her eyes, and asked, "You forgive me now, Ma?"

"Not now," Faith replied, "but long ago, just as I forgave your father for driving you away."

Connie repeated, "Father!" Then, in an urgent whisper, "Has he forgiven me, too?"

Slowly, reluctantly, Faith shook her head. "I can't tell you that,

Darter, for I don't know. When we was young, I used to think I could read Ash's mind, but I'm not so sure these days." Then, suddenly remembering that their daughter had never been notified of the family tragedy, she said, "I wrote all three boys as how their pa had had a stroke, but as he'd bid me never to write you——" she broke off to begin again, "I figured you'd see Jed's letter."

Connie said, "I've neither seen nor heard from Jed in over a year. Didn't Mal write you about——" she, in turn, broke off. What did anything matter except that she had come home, not in response to any communication or request, but of her own free will? She said, "Never mind all that now, Ma. Tell me! How *is* Pa? Will he know me?"

Again Faith shook her head. Again she said slowly, "I don't know. Sometimes there's a look in his eyes like maybe he sees and hears? Then again I'm not sure. But come, it's past time to feed him his supper. You light the candle, Darter, whilst I dish up."

It was Connie who carried the porringer behind Faith bearing the candlestick into the kitchen chamber. The night was warm. Yet in the big bed Ashbel Field lay, as though frozen, eyes closed in a thin blanched face. A moan escaped his daughter, but there was no evidence that the sound penetrated the cold that held him captive.

But when his wife laid a hand on the sheet, the eyes opened as black and as brilliant as ever, beneath bushy brows turned white like the hair that had once been raven.

Faith said very slowly and distinctly, "Ash! Look!" Standing aside, she lifted the candle high. "Look! Our darter's come home to help nurse you."

The black gaze followed the gesture. Yet whether he sensed his wife's meaning, or recognized the face illuminated by the candle there was no knowing.

Faith said, "You feed him, Darter. Maybe that'll help."

Awkwardly, because her hands trembled, Connie spooned the gruel between lips parted just enough to receive the pap. Pap! For Pa! Infant food for the man who had conquered a wilderness and forced it to feed a family. Tears blinded the girl and she could no longer see his face.

Faith said, "Here! Let me do it! You're spilling his supper all over him." The hand that took the spoon was so steady that Connie marveled.

How could Ma remain so calm, so competent, under such heartbreaking calamity? Searching her mother's face for the answer, she saw what emotion had blinded her to in the moments of meeting. Faith's face looked older—older, indeed, than the face on the pillow, although she was ten years Ash's junior. Faith Field's outward calm must stem from her husband's need. That's what marriage means, thought Connie—marriage of spirit as well as body. You bore a man's children, some in his image, some in your own, shared their upbringing, shared the grief of their loss or desertion. Neither the innocent victim of accident nor the victim of war could come back from the grave. But one of the living children had buried hope and ambition to pay her debt and share the care and final parting in which this death in life must end. Connie knew that she, like Faith, would find the courage to face that end when it came. But just now she couldn't endure the sight of the man in the bed and the woman bending over him so tenderly. Turning away, Connie went out hastily, leaving her parents alone together.

Soon Faith joined her at the hearth, more from habit than from need of warmth, for the summer night had grown stifling. When a moth flew in at the open window to flutter about the flame, Faith, in pity, blew out the candle. Outside a million other insects wove a soft symphony of sound with their wings, but the only sound in the blockhouse came from the dying fire.

Then, out of the night came the sound of approaching footsteps. A tall figure stood framed in the doorway, a figure Connie did not recognize in the firelight. Then he spoke and she knew the voice. Although it had deepened, lost much of its rich brogue, it was still the voice of the wild Irish lad her father had befriended. Seumas McSeumas! How she had hated him! The years had cooled that hatred to resentment which flared up afresh at the way he came in, without invitation, just as though he belonged here in the blockhouse.

Faith showed neither resentment nor surprise, but rose to relight the candle, saying, "Look, lad. We've got help now. My darter's come home."

Out of the shadowy ingle Connie faced the Irishman across the trestle table with the candle between them. This was no lad. This was a man, a big rawboned ox of a man—a red ox, for the stubble on his chin matched the curls that fell over his eyes. But those eyes were not the eyes of an ox. They were as blue as the inland sea, and twinkled like Erie under the summer sun.

Before she could formulate an appropriate greeting he said, "Welcome home, ma'am."

Resentment flared afresh that this outsider should presume to extend the welcome of her father's house. To put him in his place, she said stiffly, "I've just arrived, tired and dirty and hungry after a long hard journey." Surely, she thought, he'll take the hint and go.

It was Faith who took the hint. She said, "Forgive me, Darter! The lad must be starved, too. Supper'll be ready by the time the both of you have washed up."

"Don't bother about me, Ma," said Seumas. "The gang worked until dark. Then I had a bite with the boys after taking a dip in the lake. So I'll leave you and——" he hesitated a fraction of a second and then went on "—and the lass to your supper whilst I catch forty winks before the wag-on-the-wall rouses me to take my turn at the mister's bedside."

When he had vanished up the stairs, Faith said, "I don't know how I'd of made out without that lad. The neighbors were good, at first, but after a while—well, you can't expect too much of folks for the long pull." Faith sighed wearily and started for the buttery.

Connie commanded, "You sit down, Ma. I'll find something for us to eat."

Over bread and milk, she pressed for further account of the Irishman and how long he had been an inmate of the blockhouse.

"Only since Ash was took," Faith replied. "After you run off, your pa offered Seumas your room, but he wouldn't take it. I guess he figured he'd already took too much of what was yours by rights and maybe drove you to leaving."

In all fairness, Connie felt obliged to remind her mother that it was her father who had driven her away by insisting on a hateful marriage. "I expect Mr. Jones wed somebody else," she concluded.

Faith admitted that he had, indeed, consoled himself, "But not right off. It wasn't until you'd turned eighteen that he gave up hoping you'd come back. Then he started to look around again. A widder-woman took him, finally. Her own family was growed up and gone, and I guess she was lonesome and poor and needed a home and a provider." With a sympathetic sigh, Faith dismissed the Joneses. "Tell me about my grandbabies," she said. "Jed's young ones, I mean. Mal writes about Marvin, but Jed never writes at all. He's like my folks that way."

Connie recounted as much as she thought best about Jed and his family, without mentioning the fact that it was divided. By this time Jed's wife might have come back to him with Julie and the other twin. Then she said, "Speaking of your folks, Ma, I've news for you." She went on to relate how she had met the Benedicts. Faith asked so many eager questions about Hope and Hope's children that, before Connie got round to mention the fact that she was engaged to marry one of them, the wag-on-the-wall began to strike twelve.

On the last stroke the Irishman appeared, and Faith went with him into the sickroom. Connie rose to follow, thought better of it, and sat down again. Tomorrow was time enough to assert her rights and assume the duties of daughter of the house. Faith soon returned, and together the two women went upstairs to share the bed Connie had formerly occupied alone. Utter exhaustion—mental, emotional and physical—overwhelmed the returned wanderer, and she slept until awakened by the sun shining in her eyes, to find herself again alone.

Her mother was alone in the kitchen when Connie came down. McSeumas, it seemed, had breakfasted hours ago, taken his lunch pail, and gone for the day. Faith, however, had waited to breakfast with her daughter.

Over the frugal meal of hasty pudding and molasses, she said, "I don't know how he makes out with so little sleep. I made up a trundle for him in there," she nodded toward the sickroom, "but he never lies down—claims if he did, he might sleep so sound he'd not wake if needed."

"There'll be less need for him from now on," asserted Connie. "In fact, there'll be less work for us if he left. Feeding such a big fellow must take a lot of food and food costs money."

"It does so," Faith agreed. "At first folks brought in victuals, cooked and raw, but that's tapered off now and I can't seem to get what's owing Ash for——" she hesitated, at a loss for the proper words.

Connie supplied them. "Services rendered, I presume you mean, Ma. All the more reason to stop feeding that Irishman."

Quickly Faith said, "Oh, the lad more than pays for his keep."

Taking her mother to mean in personal service rendered the invalid, Connie persisted that such services were no longer needed enough to compensate for victuals devoured by a hearty man.

Faith retorted, "What that lad does for Ash isn't all he does around here, and I don't mean just the wood he chops and the water he brings from the town pump. McSeumas brings me every cent of the wages he gets for bossing the gang that's building the pier."

The lateness of the hour at which McSeumas had appeared last night led Connie to say, "You mean the bank is closed before he gets back, so he gives you his wages to deposit for him."

While Faith admitted to banking a bit for the lad, it was unknown to him. "It's not what he means me to do," she asserted. "He says as how every cent he earns isn't half enough to pay for— what did you call it—'services rendered.' He means the money Ash paid out for his schooling and books. And he doesn't just have schoolbooks, either. He's bought books for himself too, before Ash was took sick. He's got more books up there in his room than you can shake a stick at, and now and again he talks like a book and I can't made head nor tail of it."

In spite of herself Connie grew interested. At the same time her resentment grew that this fellow who was no kin should assume the prerogatives of a son of the house. Could it be that his purpose was not all exemplary? Did he have in mind making claims on the Field Estate for "services rendered?" Aloud, she said, "Pa isn't a poor man. A great deal of local real estate stands his name, according to Mr. Kelley."

Faith said, "I know. But not one single lot can be sold now Ash isn't able to sign the deed, they tell me at the courthouse. It's the law."

Connie remarked that a clever lawyer could find means to circumvent the law, under such circumstances. "I'll look into it," she added, "so you won't need to use this Irishman's money."

"You'll do no such thing, Darter," Faith retorted. "Ash may come out of this any day and tend to his own business."

"Indeed, I hope so, from the bottom of my heart," replied Connie, unwilling to shake her mother's trust in miracles. For it would certainly be a miracle if Ashbel Field emerged from this dreadful state in full possession of all his faculties. Whether he did or not, the present financial dilemma must be solved by his own family. "Ma," she inquired, "have any of the boys offered to help out with cash?"

"Mal did," Faith told her. "At least, he said he would as soon as he got paid what was owing him by the college. Zeke sent ten dollars, but he hasn't been heard from since." After a moment, she added, "Jed, I never heard from at all."

Furious at Jed's heartlessness and Zeke's meager response, Connie said, "Well, I've saved a hundred dollars. As long as that lasts, Ma, we'll take no charity from strangers. This McSeumas can take his books and his wages elsewhere."

Seumas McSeumas himself had something to say about that, however. He returned at suppertime, his stubbly beard gone, shaved off during the previous night, evidently, for the skin on his square denuded jaw was painfully blistered.

"Why did you do it, lad?" Faith exclaimed. "You know what the sun does to the light complected. But don't you fret. Henbane will ease the hurt. I'll go fix you a poultice."

When her mother had gone into the buttery in search of the healing herb, Connie took advantage of the moment to drop a hint. "Ma waits on everybody in the house no matter how worn out she may be."

That Seumas caught the implication was evident in the way his eyes darkened, but all he said was, "I never knew what it was to have a mother until your ma took me under her wing. She and your father have done more for me than any of my own folks ever did. I'll not leave their house so long as they need me."

Connie ceased beating about the bush and came straight out with it. "Now I'm home," she said, "you need feel no further obligation to stay here, Mr. McSeumas."

The blue-black eyes narrowed in the sunburned face. "So," he said softly, "You still 'feed fat the ancient grudge.'"

Recognizing the source of the quotation, Connie retorted with another from *The Merchant of Venice,* "'Must I hold a candle to my shames?'"

The cloud vanished from his face and once more his eyes danced like the lake under the summer sun as he said, "Nobody can hold a candle to you, my lady, either for wit or beauty."

The compliment, so neatly turned, was disarming. In spite of herself, Connie laughed.

Faith, emerging from the buttery with a bowl, said, "This yarb will ease the inflammation, and I got others in my chest for the shakes and for lung fever. But nothing eases a heavy heart like a good laugh. And there's nobody like Seumas for brewing a joke out of any common weed, as you might say. Many's the time he's made me smile when I never thought to smile again."

What could Connie say then but, "If that's how you feel, Ma, I hope Mr. McSeumas will stay on with us."

"Never fear, ma'am," he told her. "As your mother would say, 'wild horses couldn't drive me away.'" Nor you, either, my fine lady, his eyes added silently, as did the jut of his jaw.

Adages and literary allusions alike evaded her. But since, being a woman, she had to have the last word, Connie remarked, "Speaking of horses, I'd better go out and have a look after the borrowed mare."

This proved a futile evasion, for the Irishman asserted, "I'll see to the mare along with the gelding and the cow directly after supper."

It would be foolish to make an issue of barnyard chores and, as the meal was ready to dish up, the three of them ate in silence. Then, while the man went out to the livestock, the two women went into the sickroom.

Connie's second attempt to feed the invalid was more successful. She had schooled herself to face the situation and to make the best of it. While she spooned gruel slowly between the half-parted lips, she talked softly and slowly, but distinctly, hoping her father's ears might catch some of her words and the clouded brain grasp who she was and why she had come home. But although Ash gazed at her steadily during the awkward operation, Connie was not at all sure that he recognized her.

Anxious to do more for his comfort, she said, "Now, Pa, I'm going to lift you and give you fresh sheets."

Faith, coming in with an armful of linen, said, "You'll do no such thing. Bag o'bones that he is, your pa's dead weight, too heavy for females to handle. When the lad comes in from the barn, he'll lift Ash as easy as you would a cradle infant."

This was no exaggeration, Connie had to admit as she stood by while the Irishman bent over the bed, thrust both bare brawny arms under the wasted form, and held it with no evidence of strain or effort while the two women quickly remade the bed.

When Faith went out with the soiled linen, Connie lingered to watch the man whose strength and devotion eased life for the afflicted. Although it was no longer possible to resent his presence, she did resent his familiarity. The idea of the Irishman calling her mother "Ma"! Next thing he'd be calling her Sis!

As though he could read her thoughts, Seumas said, "Ma'am, your given name were better fitted for a judge than for a lass like the one in the old Irish song."

In spite of herself, Connie could not resist asking, "What song?"

"The one that goes like this," he replied, and whistled a few bars of wistful melody, then crooned the last line of "The Lass with the Delicate Air." Before she recovered from astonishment, he told her, "'Oft in the stilly night' I sing to your father. It seems to soothe him. Other times, I read to him out of the books he gave me."

Connie exclaimed, "But surely, you don't think he *hears!*"

"Who knows?" replied Seumas. "Sometimes I've a notion he rests easier when I read something from Shakespeare. Sure, and old Will was a wizard with words."

She said, "An inheritance from your grandsir, that taste, if my memory serves me."

Seumas' eyes brightened. "You remember about him?"

"Yes," she said. "I also remember that my father deprived me of the first book I ever owned and took it back to the store to exchange for *your* first book."

"I still have that book," said Seumas. "It is my most prized possession. But if you will accept it as a——"

Connie broke in, "I don't want it, whatever it is. The damage is done. It's too late for mending."

For a moment he was silent. Then he said softly, "'Let us not burden ourselves with a heaviness that is gone.' You must have forgiven your father, else you'd not have come back, at what sacrifice I can only guess. Can't you forgive me, too? Can't we be—friends?"

Connie hesitated. It was not in her nature to forgive and forget easily, and she was unwilling to admit, even to herself, how much she wanted the friendship of someone who spoke the language of books. But instead of replying directly, she told him, "You seem to have 'a mint of phrases' in your brain."

Not to be evaded, he said, "That's no answer to my question."

Something in the tone forced her gaze to meet his gaze that burned ice-blue in the candlelight. Then the black lashes veiled her eyes as she said, "I shall have to sleep on it—after midnight."

He took the hint and left her to keep vigil until that hour—to keep it alone, for when Faith returned, Connie urged her to go to bed. "There's nothing to do here but watch. In case of a change, I'll call you, Ma," she promised.

All day she had been busy with tasks spared her at Fruit Hill: with carrying water, with washing a vast pile of sheets and pillow slips, and then smoothing them with an iron heated in a fire that made the kitchen all but unbearable. Connie was tired. For a time it was good just to sit still and do nothing, not even think, and for economy's sake, she blew out the candle. Yet when an hour passed with neither sound nor movement in the bed, she grew alarmed. Fumbling in the dark, she found the tinderbox, the flint and the candle, and made a light. Her fears were groundless. Ash was not dead, only sleeping like a baby. Then she saw something not noticed before—the book on the candlestand. It was *"A Midsummer Night's Dream."*

The place where Seumas had evidently left off reading was marked with a slip of paper, and Connie read on from there.

Caught up in the fantasy, she was lost to the world of reality until recalled to it by the iron tongue of midnight.

When Seumas relieved her, Connie retired to lie for a time pondering his preferred friendship. Hers was a stubborn nature, however, and she fell asleep still resisting her own inclinations.

McSeumas himself was too stiff-necked or too wise to bring up the subject again, and so they remained as before—inmates of the same house, sharers of family responsibilities, yet strangers.

A week passed, a work-filled week before Connie had occasion to leave the blockhouse. Then, obliged to go to the general store for provisions, she became aware of changes which passed unnoticed in the dusk of arrival. Stumps still disfigured the public square, but around it and along some of the streets young trees had been set out at regular intervals. The town fathers, the very men who had denuded the entire area, now in their old age repented such reckless destruction and had labored to plant saplings they would not live to see shade the frame houses which had replaced pioneer cabins.

Aside from the Field blockhouse, none of the original dwellings seemed to have survived. But on closer observation Connie recognized some of them, added to and clapboarded over and given a coat of white paint. On St. Clair Street, however, almost opposite the site of her brief schooling, stood a structure quite obviously entirely new. It was a large two-story brick building topped by a central bell tower. It couldn't be a new county courthouse, or it would have been built on the public square. It might be a church, although it didn't look like any Connie had seen. Although she began to suspect the purpose of the fine new edifice, Connie accosted a passing child to make sure.

The boy eyed her with scorn. "That?" he said. "Why that's the academy, of course. Everybody knows that." Then, in response to another question, he replied, "No, ma'am. I ain't old enough. The Academy's for big fellers and girls."

Connie did not see her informant run on about his business. She was staring into the past with eyes as blind to the present as the windows of the new school, shuttered and closed for the summer. With the eyes of the mind she was seeing all to clearly the irony of things. Here in the town she had deserted to get an education, stood an institution which, if not housed in as imposing a shell as the Lancaster Seminary, doubtless offered just as good book learning to "big fellers and girls." Still, had she stayed at home, the doors of the Academy would scarcely have been open to a married woman with ten stepchildren! In spite of the humid summer day, Connie shivered.

The clerk at the store was one of the boys who had pulled her pigtail. She recognized him at once from his turned-up nose and two missing front teeth. But if he recognized his customer as the cause of those lost teeth, he gave no sign. Surely, Connie thought, I can't have changed so much. All Cleveland must know I've come home. While the clerk stowed her purchases in her basket, she scanned the other customers for a familiar face. All were strangers.

When she commented upon this, Faith explained that quite recently another boatload of emigrants from Ireland had come to work on the pier and on the canal. "They live down on the flats," she concluded.

Connie remarked that McSeumas must be glad to see some of his own kind.

"But they're not," Faith replied. "These Irish are different." Yet in what that difference lay, she could not say, and suggested that Seumas himself be asked to explain.

Connie had no intention of doing anything of the kind. Nor did she.

It was Faith who, over the supper table, said, "Lad, I disremember what you told me about where these bogtrotters came from. Tell me again."

Seumas replied, willingly enough. "They're from the southern counties. My grandsir, who was educated for the priesthood, was a Dubliner. But when he deserted the church to wed, he went to live with his bride's people in Ulster. Their children were born and brought up there—in her religion."

Connie understood then what her mother had been unable to grasp—the difference between McSeumas and the newcomers from the Emerald Isle. She herself was as free from religious prejudices as she was from prejudice against color, but living with the aristocratic Stasie had taught her many things besides French. She was not at all surprised, therefore, a few days later when McSeumas came home bearing the scars of battle. While Faith questioned him and bandaged him simultaneously, he admitted that the cuts and bruises had been inflicted by newly engaged workers on his gang. "I was obliged to prove who's boss," he said.

Connie could not forbear asking, "Well, did you?"

"I did," replied Seumas thickly, through swollen lips. "But it took some doing and——" he added with a grin that turned to a grimace of pain, "—like enough I'll have to prove it again."

In the light of that prophesy, Connie was undismayed when McSeumas came home several nights later bearing fresh marks of violence. This time Faith tended his wounds in silence. Nor did Connie ask any questions. Had she probed for the source of these latest injuries, McSeumas would have lied like a gentleman. For this second fight had not been to establish authority over his workmen. It had been with a gang of local bullies who cast aspersions on the name of a female recently returned from adventures which evil minds assumed to be evil.

Unknighted, and unarmed except with furious fists, McSeumas had fought ten men in defense of the honor of "the lass with the delicate air."

Chapter 21

THE LAST DAY of June was a heavenly day, not a cloud in the sky, the lake as calm as the Cuyahoga when the steamer *Superior* hove to off the river mouth and fired a signal gun. Small boats with flying flags put out from shore to take off the New York governor and his suite and bring them up the river to the landing.

The sound of cheers and gun salutes penetrated the blockhouse, and Faith urged her daughter to join the crowd and report on the festivities planned for the reception of the bigwigs. Before Connie reached the public square, it was packed with people, men, women and children, so that, but for her height she would not have caught so much as a glimpse of the procession bound for the Mansion House. Behind the local band, braying a tune inaudible above the deafening shouts, yells and whistles, came the Kelley carriage. The slender owner of the town's finest equipage was dwarfed by a broad-shouldered man wearing the tallest, blackest and shiniest of stovepipe hats which he kept removing to wave in response to the cheers of welcome. The day was warm and his florid face shone, not only with pleasure but with the streams of perspiration that ran down from his black hair to his costly cravat.

Other vehicles, less elegant, followed with lesser celebrities, including two New York financiers pledge to furnish funds—at six per cent—to build the canal. When all the dignitaries had entered the Mansion House the crowd streamed toward it, carrying Constitution Field along, as helpless as a leaf in a high wind. Because of the heat, the windows of the hostelry were open. Nevertheless, the address of welcome was lost in the stamping of boots, the curses of men trod upon, the shriller protests of females, and the screeching of children. Shouts of "Quiet!" only added to the din.

Finally, however, order was restored sufficiently so that De Witt Clinton's reply speech became audible. His voice matched his shoulders. It was broad and deep and carried his polished periods to the very edge of the crowd. Among the remarks Constitution Field stowed away in memory was his assertion that, even if the canal should cost five million dollars, "the money saved on transportation of goods" would equal that amount in twenty years, and that canal tolls would eventually "refund the entire cost, principal and interest."

It had been Connie's intention to waylay Mr. Kelley after the speechmaking and inquire what day and hour he and the rest of the party would leave for Licking Summit, but she could not get anywhere near the Mansion House nor the hitching-rail where the Kelley carriage waited.

At supper she declared her intention of walking out to the Kelley house. McSeumas made no comment, but when she set out he fell into step beside her.

255

Annoyed that he should assume that his escort was either needed or desired, she asked, "Hadn't you better be attending to the chores? It will be dark before I get back."

"It will," he agreed, "which is why you'd better not come back alone."

Connie laughed shortly, and reminded him that she had traveled alone in the dark streets of a town many times larger than this one.

"Yes, I know," replied Seumas. "I also have knowledge of a situation here you are ignorant of. For that reason I must insist that you put up with my company, even though you refuse my friendship." And when she denied having done that, he retorted, " 'Actions speak louder than words.' "

Connie turned the tables on him, rather neatly she thought, with a reminder that Plutarch had asserted " 'It is circumstance and proper measure that give action its character, and make it either good or bad.' " Contrary to her expectation, Seumas made no attempt to top that with some other wise saw.

All he said was, "Don't take refuge behind so old and leafless a bush, lass."

While she sought another figurative bush with thicker foliage, a catcall came from the underbrush bordering the road. The derisive sound was followed with words strange to Connie's ears, yet whose meaning was all too clearly scurrilous.

In a whisper that trembled with anger, she told her companion, "Had I come alone, I'd have escaped such insults."

"If so," he retorted quickly, "it might have been to encounter actions more offensive than words. I'd hoped to spare you the knowledge of what's the talk of the town."

Mistaking his meaning, she said, "You hoped to keep me, like my mother, ignorant of your bad reputation?"

Seumas exploded, "Good lord, no! My life is an open book in this town. It's *your* life since you left here, lass, that's a closed book and therefore suspect."

Connie gasped. Anger choked off speech. But the anger was not directed at him who made the statement. After a moment she said in a muffled voice, "Do *you* believe I'm—what that hoodlum called me?"

"I know you're not," he said quickly.

"How?" she prodded. "How could you know any better than that hoodlum what kind of a life I lived away from these parts?"

"I know," he repeated, "because—because——" he stopped, seeking how best to express what he felt. When he spoke again it was in the words of his favorite bard, "Because 'I hold you as a thing ensky'd and sainted.'"

Connie, who also reveled in the stately Elizabethan language, did not find the words high-flown or ridiculous. Moreover, Seumas' tone—like that of the hoodlum—conveyed more than any words in any language, lewd or lovely. And with the certainty of his faith in her integrity came certainty that he had not fought to defend the Prince of Orange a second time. Yet, she asked breathlessly, "Tell me! That last fight you had, was it on my account?"

He nodded. Then, realizing that she could not see his face in the dark, he said, "Yes."

For a moment the lump in her throat held her voice captive. Then, swallowing hard, she managed to say, "Thank you! Thank you from the bottom of my heart." After another pause, she added, "If you still want my friendship—for all you've done for me and mine—it's little enough to give."

"For me," he replied, "it is enough. Enough, at least, for now."

What did he mean, she wondered and might have asked him, had not they reached her destination.

The stiffness with which Mrs. Kelley received her, asking her errand but not asking her in, convinced Connie that the hoodlums were not alone in their suspicions. On learning that Mr. Kelley had not forgotten his promise, and would collect the McArthur mare in passing the blockhouse, two days later, Connie made her manners and rejoined Seumas. In silence they returned home, for he sensed that she did not wish to discuss his revelations further.

The more she thought about them, however, the worse her situation appeared, and at the same time the less surprising was the local opinion of her. From the day she had joined the arithmetic class, the only female, she had been eyed askance. And it was not difficult to imagine what was said of her when she ran away—in breeches. In so small a community, there were no secrets. Ashbel Field's will must be common knowledge. A disobedient daughter who defied her father's orders, refused to wed the man selected for her, and who had been disinherited in consequence, could scarcely expect to be welcomed back with open arms, like the Prodigal Son. She had wondered why the only callers at the blockhouse had been her parents' friends. Now she knew. Constitution Field was an outcast. The only friends she had were her mother and her mother's boarder.

Connie was beginning to wonder if, indeed, even Ben had turned against her when, as the weeks passed, there was no reply to the news she had sent him from Cleveland upon arrival. Shortly after Independence Day, however, came a letter from Ben explaining his long silence. Solomon Benedict had taken to his bed in May, and since then Ben had been doing double duty—long days in the hat shop and longer nights at his father's bedside. Now death had released Solomon from suffering, and the entire burden of the household rested on Ben. His letter concluded, "From what you write me, I don't see how your pa can last much longer. When he kicks the bucket, you come straight here and we'll wed. If Ma raises a row, she can just go live with Faith who got married since you left."

The tone of Ben's letter troubled Connie more than his bad spelling and grammar. She told herself that he wasn't really hard-hearted. It was his Marvin ineptitude with a pen which gave that impression—an impression Connie was loath to give her mother. And so, instead of handing over the letter to Faith, Connie simply announced the demise of Solomon Benedict.

Faith, who had never met her brother-in-law, was less concerned on his account than for her sister. She must write Hope. But what? It had been so long since they had seen each other—so long, in fact, since Faith had penned a word that tears came to her eyes and her hand trembled at the thought of composing a letter of condolence.

"Never mind, Ma," Connie told her. "Aunt Hope will understand. She's no letter writer herself, remember. I'll send her your love and sympathy with mine."

After suitable expressions of these sentiments, Connie wrote Ben that her own father's release did not appear imminent. "Anyway," she went on, "you seem to have forgotten that I, too, have a mother, but no sisters to share the care of her, now or later. And so, dear Ben, since I am not free to share your responsibilities, it seems to me no more than fair to release you from your promise, leave you free to seek happiness and a helpmate elsewhere." After a moment's hesitation, she signed herself, "Your devoted cousin, Connie." As she sanded the sheet, a tear fell on that word *cousin,* blotting it out as though hand and heart repented at the last moment. Indeed, breaking her word, breaking her plighted troth, made Connie very solemn and sad.

Her feelings on receipt of Ben's reply, which came promptly, were considerably more varied. Ben refused to accept his freedom, or grant hers. He was prepared to be patient until Ashbel Field followed Solomon Benedict to the grave. But after her father was gone, he saw no reason why his promised bride should not return to Cincinnati and bring her mother along. As he pointed out, quite unnecessarily, Faith and Hope were sisters—both born Marvin. And since they had been brought up by the same mother, Ben saw no reason why, as widows, they should not be able to live together in peace.

This solution of her problem and Ben's struck Connie as by no means ideal, particularly as the Marvin sisters might share the prejudice against the marriage of cousins. It had been partly for that reason that Connie had never confided to her mother that she was engaged to Ben. Nor did she mention it now that the marriage seemed more remote than ever.

In any case, an addition to the blockhouse family soon occupied Faith's attention. The stall vacated by the borrowed mare shortly was occupied by another horse—the old black gelding, Satan. Professor Field had left Athens after the college had closed for the summer, but because of Satan's advanced age the journey had been slow.

Mal himself looked old beyond his years to the mother who had not seen him for so long. Even to Connie, who had left Mal's home only five years ago, the change in him was a shock. Why, he was just thirty-seven, yet his balding dome and the crows' feet at the corners of his near-sighted eyes made him look like a man of fifty. While Faith lamented aloud over the premature aging of her eldest son, Connie silently attributed it to living with a woman who remained a child, a willful selfish child who refused to accept the cares of wifehood and motherhood.

Although both Field women tried to prepare Mal before taking him into the sickroom, he was visibly shaken at sight of his father. Ash, too, showed signs of emotion—the first Connie had witnessed since her arrival. From the light that burned in the sunken eyes, it seemed certain that Ash recognized his first-born—the one son who had inherited his ideals and ambition. Connie glanced toward her mother and with one accord the two of them went out, leaving father and son alone together.

Supper was on the table when Mal emerged from the sickroom to meet the man who had taken a son's place in the household. To Connie's surprise, Mal seemed to know more about McSeumas than she did.

After thanking Seumas for all he had done and was doing for "the home folks," Mal inquired how he was doing in school. "Or have you finished at the Academy since Pa last reported your progress?"

Seamus looked embarrassed, apologetic, as he said, "I'm afraid my progress has been pretty slow, Professor."

"That," replied Mal, "is inevitable. With schools open only three months in twelve, naturally more years are required to get an education than where sessions are longer. When the Academy opened, three years ago, Pa wrote me that you intended to enroll for the winter semester, even though all your classmates were sure to be considerably your juniors."

"They were that!" remarked Seumas with a short laugh. "In fact I was the only adult in any class. A marked man, as you might say, fair game for whippersnappers."

Mal nodded with understanding. "I know boys," he said. "Their wit can be barbed. I conclude you bore the pricks for the sake of the prize. I trust you won it, McSeumas."

"You're right about the pricks, Professor," said the Irishman. "What could I do but ignore them, seeing a man can't fight schoolboys? As for the prize, you mean a diploma, I presume. Yes, I got that, for what it's worth. At least I went as far as the academy could take me up to this year. Now I hear there's to be a new master, by name Harvey Rice, who proposes to add chemistry and natural and moral philosophy to the curriculum, so I plan to go back to school as soon as work on the pier stops for the winter."

For some moments the room was silent except for the faint

crackle of the dying supper fire. Neither of the women wished to intrude on this conversation between men. Finally Mal said, "Have you given a thought to entering college when you are ready, McSeumas?"

"Have I?" exclaimed the Irishman, eyes lighting. "Indeed, I've thought of little else for years and years. But now——" the glow in the blue eyes faded as he broke off speaking, rose and said in a flat voice, "You've made me forget the time, Professor. I must be off to bed."

When the outsider had gone up the stairs, leaving the Fields alone in the kitchen, Mal said, "Ma! Sister! He knew me! Pa knew me. He even spoke to me!"

Faith cried, "No! Oh, Sonny, what did he say? What did your pa say to you?"

Mal replied more slowly, "The words were few and thick, uttered with difficulty. One only came out clear and that——" he turned to look at Connie, "—that was your name, Sister. Only your name was clear, but from the look in his eyes, I'm sure Pa was trying to tell me that he regretted the way he treated you."

Tears came to the girl's eyes and her voice trembled as she whispered, "Oh, I'm so glad. Ever since I came home I've tried to get through to him, tried so hard to make Pa understand that I'm sorry, too. Sorry, I mean for—well——"

"Never mind, Darter," Faith interposed. "Mal and me, we understand how you feel. If Ash does, too, then the good Lord be praised. I never could bear to think of Ash going to heaven believing his only darter bore him a grudge. Now I pray the good Lord will take him soon, without any more sufferin'."

To the extent that the helpless man showed no signs of pain, his wife's prayer appeared to be answered. In fact, Ash's condition showed signs of slight improvement. Instead of lying motionless, he could turn his head toward whoever happened to be in the room.

Several times, feeling his gaze upon her, Connie bent over the bed and gently smoothed back the thick white hair. "What is it, Pa?" she asked softly. "What can I do for you? Try—try and tell me."

A spasm contracted the gaunt throat and the dry lips moved

with what was evidently almost superhuman effort. Ash said, "Get
—Mal."

Yet, by the time Mal had been brought in from the barn, the
invalid had relapsed into a state of inarticulate weakness that made
questioning him not only futile but dangerous.

Since his stay must, of necessity, be short, Mal spent the better
part of each day with his father, freeing his sister to do all
the household chores in order that their mother might get sorely
needed rest. Ash's hearing was the one faculty unimpaired, and at
the suggestion of the self-constituted night nurse, by day the son
read aloud passages marked in *Measure for Measure, Much Ado
about Nothing,* or *The Tempest.* This proved but poor comfort as
it grew more and more evident that something lay heavy on
Ash's mind.

What it was, Mal had begun to suspect, and one day when the
invalid seemed a bit brighter and stronger, he ventured to say,
"Now don't try to talk, Pa. Just shake your head in answer. That
day you sent Sister to find me, what was it you wanted to tell me?
Was it something about your will?"

A gleam of relief came into the cavernous black eyes and Ash
nodded. Whereupon Mal asked, quickly, "Do you want that will
destroyed?"

Again Ash nodded. But when Mal tried to find out the whereabouts of the document, each question brought the same negative
motion of the sick man's head, and increasing exhaustion. In alarm,
Mal said finally, "Pa, don't worry. Ma must know where you keep
it." And when the head moved once in negation, Mal repeated,
"Don't worry. Wherever it is, we'll find it, and when we do, I'll
bring it straight here where you can see me burn it."

To Mal's mind, the most promising place to search was the cabin
across the street which had been the Field law office. It had not
been opened since Ash himself closed the door and went home to
supper the night he had suffered his stroke. Mal found the single
room full of dust, mice, bats and insects that scurried and flew
about at his entrance. He began his search in the desk. One drawer
held an accumulation of old letters, several of which Mal recognized as his own. Another drawer held nothing except blank legal
forms. The bottom drawer was filled with a jumble of odds and
ends—buttons, fishhooks, rifle ammunition, a broken clay pipe

and a baby's shoe. The shoe was filled with finely shredded paper which, dislodged, brought with it a litter of newborn mice.

Mal saw no point in destroying the little family in a place already overrun with rodents, and he turned to examine the shelves. One by one, he took down the law books, dusted them off and shook them. A few loose leaves fluttered out, but no document of any kind. The only place remaining unsearched was the woodbox. Mal lifted a log to reveal nothing more than a hornets' nest—a delicate papery marvel from which a swarm emerged in fine frenzy to defend its peaceful home. Mal retreated in haste.

Outside, it occurred to him that, although hornets manufactured their own nesting material, rats, like mice, appropriated man-made paper. If the will had been left in the office, some remnant of it might very well lie under the puncheon floor. No attack on the floor, however, could be made unprotected from attack by those angry hornets, and Mal went back to the blockhouse for his father's bee-hat and gloves.

His mother, however, reminded him that although dislodging the hornets would be simple enough, dislodging the floor timbers was no work for a college professor, singlehanded. And in any case, it was a chore to be undertaken only as a last resort.

"Wait till your sister and I have searched the house," Faith begged. "Then, if that will don't come to light, Seumas'll help you take up that floor some Sunday. I do hope that won't be needful, though, on account of labor on Lord's Day is forbid by the Bible."

The Bible, indeed, seemed to Faith the most likely repository for any precious paper. To be sure, nightly Scripture reading had ceased when Connie ran away, and the Book had remained, covered with a green baize cloth, on the center table in the unused front room. Ash might very well have gone in without Faith's knowledge and thrust his will between the pages at the back where the births of their six children were recorded with the deaths of two.

Faith stayed so long in the front room that Connie grew anxious and was about to enter when her mother came out, wet-eyed. "It's not there," Faith said. "Wherever Ash put that paper, it wasn't in the Bible. Tomorrow, I'll start going through the chests in the attic."

Although she was as good as her word, the only result of long hours spent among the cobwebs and keepsakes of a lifetime was exhaustion, physical and emotional.

Connie cautioned, "Ma, if you go up there again in this hot weather, you'll be sick abed yourself. Either wait until fall, or let me clean out the attic."

The word *clean* was unfortunate—a reminder of what young-folks did to old folks' cherished treasures. Faith said, "You'll do no such thing, Darter. The first cool day, we'll go up there *together*. Meantime, we'll go through the second floor rooms."

There were several chambers abovestairs beside those occupied by mother and daughter and by the boarder. Faith was a neat housekeeper and the unused rooms held nothing but beds and bureaus, soon examined, even to making sure Ash had not ripped open a tick and entrusted his will to the feathers, as some folks did spare cash.

The boarder had no cash to secrete, Faith knew, because he gave her all his wages. Nevertheless, she gave him fair warning that his chamber must be invaded.

It was the first time Connie had entered that room since she came home, and she was not a little surprised to see how well filled was the bookcase Seumas had built into one corner. Ordinarily, she would never have touched another person's property, but under the circumstances she took down book after book and leafed through the pages, caught time after time by some marked passage. Some of the passages were her own favorites. Others, unfamiliar, she recognized as the source of the Irishman's colorful conversation. No wonder his ignorant companions regarded Seumas with suspicion. They had no idea what he was talking about, half the time! Here, in his private quarters Connie felt the force of his personality more keenly than ever she had been aware of it in his physical presence. And she read on and on, forgetting the purpose of her intrusion until recalled to it by a voice in the hall.

"Well, it isn't in this chamber, either," Faith said, coming to the door. "Unless it's hid under the eaves, or in some bag or trunk in the attic, it just isn't in this house."

That the missing will did not repose in any of these places, mother and daughter proved one day after an all-night downpour had cooled the roof and made the attic endurable.

Meanwhile Mal explored the barn, although it seemed the most unlikely of places for a man like Ashbel Field to choose as a repository for anything of value. It took Mal an entire day to make sure no tin box lay hidden under what remained of last year's hay, or at the bottom of the meal bin or corncrib. The only result of these labors was increased certainty that the only other place to look was under the office floor.

The following Sabbath, while Ash's daughter sat with him, and his wife went to meeting, his oldest son and the man who had been like a son to the old man veiled themselves in mosquito netting and invaded the hornets' stronghold. There, it was the boss of the pier gang who gave orders to the college professor. Being the smaller man of the two, Mal climbed up on the broad McSeumas shoulders and stuffed the last of the family buckskin breeches far up the chimney throat. Then, together they built a fire. Smoke soon filled the room, driving out invaders as well as invaded.

Following the cold Sunday dinner, Malachi and Seumas returned to the office, opened all the windows, and freed the chimney. Then the brawny Irishman pulled up several of the floor timbers beneath which the slender professor was able to crawl about on all fours. More odds and ends were dredged up from the ground under the cabin. There were the things lost or dragged through the cracks in the floor from time to time: more buttons and fishhooks, a broken knife blade, several coppers, one silver coin, and many pieces of paper.

A number of the larger fragments were charred around the edges as though some document had been torn up, thrown into the fire which had died down before the refuse was entirely consumed. Later, rats must have dragged these fragments under the floor for their own use. Here and there a word or a phrase written in Ashbel Field's bold hand was still visible. And when on one scrap Mal found a portion of his father's signature, he was convinced that Ash himself had destroyed the will disinheriting Constitution.

Seumas agreed with Mal, and together they went back to the blockhouse where both women accepted that opinion. Furthermore, Faith who knew Ash better than anyone else, believed that Connie's return had brought back to his mind the making of that will, the destruction of which, illness had erased from his memory. This would account for the disturbed state of the inarticulate invalid. Yet, if told all the facts, Ash would worry over his loss of memory.

Malachi, the conscientious one, considered the situation in silence for some time. Then he said, "All I promised Pa was to burn the will in his presence, if found. From the bed, he can't see the fire-place, so I'll just put these pieces on the coals and tell him there's the end of it."

When silence gave consent to this action, Mal went on to explain that if no will were produced after Ashbel Field's death, the law would declare him intestate. Ma would be entitled to her widow's dower, and the remainder of the estate would be divided equally among the Field children. Faith, who never tried to fathom any details of men's business, was content to leave all this to her learned son.

Constitution made no comment. She was struck speechless by the certainty that all Cleveland must be aware that Ashbel Field had made a will disinheriting her. How many of Ash's old friends and neighbors would believe she had come home with no thought be-yond seeking her father's forgiveness, and not in the hope of shar-ing his property? How many men would accept the story of his eldest son and the orphan he had befriended regarding what had happened to that will? How many women, piling rumor on rumor, would believe *she* had discovered the will and burned it in secret, and that Mal and Seumas "lied like gentlemen" to save the Field rowan from prosecution for her crime? So long as Ashbel Field lived, there could be no answer to any of these questions.

Chapter 22

SUMMER WAS soon gone and with it Malachi Field, called back to Athens for the college Commencement. The foliage on the saplings around the public square turned from green to gold and russet, and then fell covering the ground with a restless carpet. And still Ashbel Field clung to life, the last leaf, the last pioneer in Cleveland.

New faces appeared on the streets and in the taverns, and in the shops there was new and wonderful merchandise. For that autumn the opening of Governor Clinton's personal project, the Erie Canal across New York State, brought a quick drop in freight rates. Where a barrel of salt had cost more than a miller got for forty barrels of flour, now flour sold outside Ohio for ten times the cost of imported salt. This sudden reversal of prices, this sudden revival of hope in Cleveland's commercial future, encouraged merchants to stock unheard-of luxuries, such as red Morocco shoes, fine fabrics with foreign names: toinettes, valentias and Florentine silks, to tempt female customers, and even "elegant vestings" for men. Few men coveted such foppery, but beauty-starved wives and daughters were eager to replace drab homespun with a Sunday go-to-meetin' gown of satinette of lustring. For although Cleveland still lacked an edifice dedicated exclusively to worship, the recently organized First Presbyterian Society met in the academy every Sabbath Day.

Faith Field went to the "preachifying" in garments reserved "for best" the last twenty years. But she went alone, not because her daughter was ashamed of Faith's old-fashioned appearance, but because Connie knew her own appearance in Stasie's elegant castoffs would seem to confirm public opinion that the years of her absence had been spent in bad company. McSeumas, on the contrary, excused himself from church attendance on the grounds that his only clothes, the patched and faded blue jeans he wore to work, would disgrace the sanctuary.

When the river froze over and work on the pier and on the canal ceased for the winter, Seumas gave no reason for his failure to attend the Academy on weekdays, even though fewer adult males took advantage of the new classes in philosophy than bought brocaded weskits. He was never idle, however, for when not needed in the sickroom to free the women for household chores, he busied himself with chores outdoors. The corn he had grown had to be husked and cribbed, the stalks cut for fodder, and a huge pile of logs reduced to fireplace lengths.

Apples reddened in the orchard behind the barn, but the promised friendship between the two young people in the blockhouse failed to ripen. Perhaps this was because they were never alone. Only at meals was there time to talk, and then Faith's presence confined the conversation to homespun topics. Connie, who had overheard the conversation between her brother and the boarder on the subject of higher education, was sure his reason for spending all his free time about the place was because he lacked funds for schooling. This opinion she passed on to her mother one day when the sound of axe blows assured their privacy.

"Land sakes!" exclaimed Faith. "He has *so* money! I put some in the bank for him, like I told you."

"But did you tell *him?*" Connie inquired.

"Well, no. Come to think of it, I guess I didn't. I guess I was afraid of starting an argument, and I'm no match for that lad at words."

The girl, better equipped to match wits with the Irishman, decided the time had come to break down the reserve that had grown up between them.

Seumas did not hear her approach the woodpile, and for several moments she stood, watching the ease of his motions as he lifted the axe high with both hands, then brought it down squarely, splitting the logs in two.

Perhaps the intentness of her gaze drew his, for he turned. "Need more kindling?" he inquired. Then, seeing she carried no basket, "Well, what *can* I do for you?"

Connie replied, "You can stop work long enough to listen to what I've got to say because Ma can't screw herself up to it."

A cloud darkened the bright blue eyes as he turned away to bury the blade in the chopping block. "Well," he said, brusquely, "out with it! Does your mother want me to go? Or——" he turned to regard her narrowly, "Or—do you?"

"Good heavens!" she exclaimed. "I asked you to stay, didn't I? You must know by this time that I'm not one to change my mind with every shift in the wind."

Seumas said slowly, "I thought maybe the wind of gossip had reached your mother's ears at last, and that you'd both agreed the best way to scotch it would be for me to leave town."

268

The girl gasped, as though touched by icy fingers. He wants to go, she thought. He wants to go and won't say so. And lest he suspect how lost and lonely she would feel without him, Connie said stiffly, "I'm sure Ma is as ignorant of what's said about me as I have been that your name has been dragged into it. I don't blame you for wanting to escape involvement in what, after all, is no concern of yours, Mr. McSeumas. Pray, don't let any sense of knight-errantry keep you here."

Anger lighted his eyes with blue flame and exploded in his voice. "What do you take me for? A dunghill cock to be routed by a shrew's broom? Do you think I'm a poltroon, a craven, a lily-livered thing afraid of poisoned tongues?"

The extravagance of his denial, the white heat of his rage, warmed her, stilled her fear that he wanted to get out of an embarrassing situation. Eager now to placate the angry man, she cried, "No, no! You've taken the wrong trail entirely, and it's my fault for misleading you. Please, let me try to explain." With that, she broached the matter of money directly and without further meanderings.

The Irishman's anger gave way to shame at his quick offense— shame that he should so have misjudged the character to the two women who were his best, perhaps his only real friends. For once his glib tongue failed him and he muttered, "Sure, and I don't know how I'm to make it up to Ma—I mean to your mother. As for you, lass——" he turned away, his throat working.

Connie's throat, too, felt so tight that she could not speak. And because, somehow, she had to make him aware of her forgiveness, she laid a hand on the blue jean sleeve.

As though stung, Seumas flinched, flung off her fingers, and seizing the axe, muttered something about the need to get chores done before dark.

Affronted afresh, the girl returned to the house wondering at the man's mercurial behavior. Was it because he was Irish and red-headed? Or had she made still another mistake in thinking—well, what *had* she thought, anyway? Confusion regarding her own behavior as well as his, acted like a frost on the small green bud of friendship between them.

Seumas' thoughts on the subject of money were revealed to

Faith in the sickroom when her daughter was not present. Later, she confided to Connie that "the lad vowed he'd not touch a penny of the money in the bank unless our own children provided for us. I told them one of them had, which was no lie because you *did* offer, Darter."

Connie said sharply, "You didn't tell him that, Ma!"

"No," replied Faith. "I didn't tell him which one it was, and if he thinks 'twas Mal, I see no harm in that, either, seeing Mal *would* give me money, if he had any."

It was true, Connie knew, and under the circumstances Connie, like Faith, felt no more need be said. For if the McSeumas learned that it was *her* savings that paid for the food he ate that winter, nothing would have induced him to take from the bank enough cash to pay for a term's schooling.

Now every morning saw him leave the house to join the crowd of adolescents over which he towered like a tree among saplings. If he heard the snickers and sneers of his companions, Seumas ignored them as he ignored the jibes of his former fellow workers who now spent their freedom in taverns and their savings on beer instead of books.

Connie knew Seumas bought a new book because she found it on the candlestand one morning after the night watcher had gone. During the day, whenever she had a free moment, she dipped into the volume. Her quick mind grasped the rudiments of philosophy enough to question the student on the subject that night after supper. This resulted in a discussion so absorbing that they both forgot the courtesy due elders until recalled to it by a sonorous sigh.

"Dear knows what you two are talking about," Faith said, "for I can't make head nor tail of it."

Both students apologized and turned to topics Faith could understand. Seumas soon rose, saying he must get some sleep and went upstairs leaving the book on the table. Faith went in to sit with her husband. Connie reopened the book and read on and on, seeing nothing but the printed page, hearing nothing, not even the voice of the wag-on-the-wall, until Faith touched her shoulder.

"Twelve o'clock," Faith said. "Time the two of us went to bed."

When Connie came down next morning, the book was gone from the kitchen. But again she found it in the sickroom and wondered whether it had been left by mistake, or deliberately, to provoke further discussion. In either case, she found no time to read further during a day when the patient needed more attention than usual.

At the time, Malachi's ruse regarding the will had appeared to satisfy his father. But since Mal left, Ash's restlessness had returned. Connie could not help wondering whether Pa had suddenly recollected destroying the will himself and was troubled by Mal's curious behavior. Was Pa worrying lest overwork and worry had unhinged Mal's mind? Connie, of course, did not discuss this possibility with her mother.

Faith had her own and quite different theory regarding the cause of this new restlessness, but she too kept her thoughts to herself. And if McSeumas formed any opinion on the matter, he also kept his own counsel.

When the volume of moral philosophy disappeared from the candlestand and was replaced by one of the old favorites, Connie concluded that the student required the textbook in class. A splinter inserted between the leaves of the replacement suggested that the night watcher had resumed his habit of reading aloud when the patient could not sleep.

As soon as she had made her father as comfortable as was possible, Connie sat beside him and opened *Macbeth* where the splinter was inserted. On the margin beside a marked line were the initials A. F.

Curious as to whether the line had aroused some response in the sick man, Connie read it aloud: " 'More is thy due than more than all can pay.' " Glancing up, she caught a gleam in the sunken eyes and inquired, "What is it, Pa? Ma wants no pay. Nor do I. Do you think we ought to pay your protégé? Do you want him to have some of your property?"

The questions seemed to confuse the sick man, for he nodded and then shook his head, which left Connie wondering whether his mental powers were failing at last, as his power of speech and movement had failed long since. Reluctant to trouble him further, she sat on in the deepening twilight. When, at length, she rose to light a candle and replenish the fire, Ash's quiet breathing told her he had fallen asleep. Rather than disturb him, she sat down again,

271

beside the dying fire, seeing in its fading glow a symbol of the life that was nearing its end.

It had been a long life, well spent, Connie comforted herself. Surely, if any man had "fought the good fight and kept the faith," it was Ashbel Field. He had done more than his share in freeing the young nation from tyranny, and keeping it free for the generations to come after him—for his children's children, and their children's children. From this reverie Connie was startled by a low rich voice.

"'A penny for your thoughts,'" said Seumas.

A year ago she would have replied with some quip or quotation calculated to conceal her thoughts rather than reveal them to the Irishman. Now, perhaps, because in the deepening twilight he seemed more like a mirror than a man, she told him her thoughts about her father and the miracle which had come to pass in his lifetime.

Silence fell when she had finished. Then, after a moment, Seumas said, "Being a student of history, lass, you should know that children content to rest on the laurels won by their fathers never grow to full stature. The battle of life goes on. Each generation must fight its own fight, one way or another, to keep what has been won, or to gain fresh freedoms." Then, as though a little ashamed of pontificating, Seumas added, "'Lest too light winning made the prize light.'"

This won no smile from the girl. Indeed, perhaps she did not hear what he said, for her mind was still intent on his remark about fresh freedoms. Slowly, she said, "No woman is free. I used to think men were wholly to blame for keeping us females in the bondage of ignorance. But I've come to believe women themselves are partly to blame because they don't make a fight for what the French call *'liberté, égalité et fraternité.'* I beg your pardon," she added quickly, "I forgot you're not studying French at the academy."

"But I *am* studying Latin," he reminded, "and anyway those words mean the same in any tongue. They were what drove me out a country where there is neither liberty, equality nor brotherhood, and landed me on these shores with nothing in me pockets except holes." As always, when deeply moved, the tongue of

McSeumas was tinged with brogue. "What would that first winter have been but for your fayther, I shiver to think of."

The gravity in the tone, the gratitude sent a shiver along Connie's spine. Suddenly she seemed to see again the ragged, half-frozen, half-starved boy on the doorstep holding out the only gift he had to give his benefactor—that string of fish caught through the ice. Tears of shame stung her eyes at the memory of how heartless she had been at the time, how cruel. And to keep from giving way to emotion, she rose, saying, "No wonder I'm shivering. The fire's almost out. Put a log on, Seumas, while I go put the kettle on for Pa's porridge."

As the days of the new year began to lengthen, the cold strengthened, and with it the certainty that something lay heavy on Ashbel Field's mind.

"It can't be the property," Faith said. "For Mal made him easy about that. Still, I've got a feeling it's something to do with you, Darter."

Connie had reached the same conclusion, but she did not want to go into her reasons for it and alarm her mother needlessly about something which might never come to pass. She said, "If so, what do you think it is, Ma?"

Instead of a direct reply, Faith said, "I think you've been looking in the wrong books for the answer. Why don't you try the Bible?"

"But Pa was never a great Scripture reader," Connie protested.

Faith said, "I know. Just the same, I wish you'd try it. Sometimes, when folks nears their ends, they get a sort of second sight —clearer than natural—and see things other folks are blind to." To this cryptic remark, she added a repetition of the plea. "Try Scripture. Skip the begats, though. It's not likely Ash has them in mind. Besides, they're pretty slow going, and I've a feeling there ain't too much time."

More to please her mother than with any hope it would solve the mystery, Connie fetched the Bible from the front room. Once before—how long ago it seemed now—she had opened to the first page and read, " 'In the beginning, God——' " Slowly and distinctly, she read on and on, aloud, pausing to glance at the bed at the end of each verse.

With Genesis 19.14, her glance encountered Ash's eyes, lighted with eagerness, and she repeated, "'And Lot went out and spoke unto his sons-in-law which had married his daughters.'" Connie stopped reading to look at the man who had no sons-in-law. "Is it something about your daughters-in-law, Pa?" she asked. "About Stasie, or about Mercy?"

The light faded from Ash's eyes and his head made a slight negative movement. Connie read on until, when she looked up again, the brilliant sunken eyes were closed. Ashbel Field was asleep. Belatedly, the thought occurred to Connie, only to be discarded. Pa couldn't have meant a *future* son-in-law because he didn't know about Ben.

The next morning, as Faith set a plate of flapjacks before the boarder, she asked if *his* reading of the Book had brought any new ideas.

Connie, watching McSeumas, saw a closed look come over his face as he replied, "None worth passing on, ma'am."

If he had any surmise at all, why keep it to himself? Connie wondered impatiently. Why not share it with Ashbel Field's womenfolk and let *them* judge it's value?

After Seumas had gone, after routine duties in the sickroom were completed and Faith busied herself in the kitchen, Connie sat down, took the Book on her knees and opened it where the splinter had been left—at the twenty-fourth chapter of Deuteronomy. There was nothing to indicate where last night's reading had ended and, anxious to miss no clue, Connie began to read aloud at verse one and read on without pause through verse five: "'When a man hath taken a new wife, he shall not go out to war, neither shall he be charged with any business; but shall be free at home for one year and shall cheer up his wife which he has taken.'"

An inarticulate sound from the bed caused Connie to look up, startled. Pa hadn't spoken a word since those few words to Mal. Now he was trying desperately to speak again. Connie rose and bent over him to catch the faintest whisper. But the effort had been too great. Ashbel Field's breath became so labored and his face so pale that Connie, alarmed, called her mother.

Faith came, looking almost as white as her husband. "What gave him such a turn?" she demanded.

Connie, reluctant to answer in his hearing, pointed to the verse she had been reading. Faith bent over the page. After a moment she looked up into her daughter's anxious eyes and, finger on lip, pointed to the door. Obediently, Connie went and Faith followed. When they were out of earshot, Faith said, "I know now I've not lost the knack of reading his mind after all. Some time back, I begun to suspicion what hatcheled him, but I want sure. Now I am."

"Was I right in thinking it was something to do with me?" Connie asked. And when Faith nodded, she begged, "Tell me. What does Pa want me to do?"

Even then she had no inkling of what was in Faith's mind, what Faith was now sure troubled the mind of her husband. "Not now," Faith said. "Wait till the lad comes home and I'll tell you both at the same time."

For the rest of the day the girl pondered her mother's odd behavior, pondered what Ma had said about the uncanny sense of the dying. Could Pa have surmised, somehow, that she had found the man she wanted to wed and wished her to know the marriage had his blessing? Several times during the day, Connie was on the point of telling her mother about Ben and decided against it. A confidence of that kind, so long delayed, would need considerable explaining. Ma had enough problems without adding another until it could no longer be avoided.

After supper, as was their nightly custom, all three housemates entered the sickroom together. While Seumas lifted the invalid, the two women worked swiftly, plumping up the pillows and the feather bed and providing fresh linen.

When Ash was back in the bed, Faith said, "Ash! Listen! I've figured out what you want done. You want to see our darter married. Am I right?" The old light came into the black eyes and he nodded. "Praise be!" cried his wife. "I felt it in my bones you and me were of one mind, like always. It's this lad here you want she should wed without delay. Am I right—again?"

When again the head on the pillow indicated agreement, Connie turned white and speechless. McSeumas, equally at a loss for words—for once—turned scarlet. They were standing side by side at the foot of the bed. Connie forced herself to look at him, beg him silently with her eyes to forgive these dear sentimental old fools for putting him in such an awkward position.

The expression in the lake-blue eyes that met hers squarely took the girl's breath away. Her head whirled and her heart seemed to turn over. Then, without knowing how it came about, she found herself in strong arms, her ear pressed down over a heart beating faster, more furiously than her own. Neither of them spoke, nor had they need for words. For several moments the crackling of the fire was the only sound in the room.

Then Faith broke the spell. "Well, I must say, for book-larned folks, you two took an awful long time to larn your own minds. But now you know, the sooner you are made man and wife, the better."

Those words woke Connie to reality—the dreadful reality of her promise to wed another man, a man she had loved, but never as she loved this man whose arms held her as though they would never let her go. The horror of her situation gave Connie strength to release herself from Seumas' embrace. But how she was to release herself from this awful dilemma she could not think. She only knew that no explanations must be made under Ashbel Field's eyes, or within his hearing. Yet how was she to escape from that urgent black gaze without agreeing to a marriage she was not free to contract?

Faith came to the rescue, saying, "You two hanker to be alone to talk it over, I presume to say. Go on out, and God bless you. I'll stay with Ash."

In the kitchen, Connie took care to put the trestle table between them. And when Seumas moved to come around to her side, she said, "Please! Wait! There's something I've got to tell you."

The gravity of her tone held him where he was. "Out with it, then," he said. "Tell me quickly. If you were playing a game with me in there to hearten your father——"

Connie interrupted with a shake of her head, but when he started again in her direction, she said again, "Wait! Please! Don't —don't touch me."

"Why ever not," Seumas demanded. "What stands between us?"

Somehow, she found it impossible to tell him what she had never told her mother. To be sure, she had told Ben that he was free, but Ben had refused to accept his freedom, and until she was "off with the old love," she could not, with clear conscience, be "on with the new."

The new love was fast losing patience and, lest refusal to answer his questions lose her his love, Connie told him, "What stands between us is something I did in Cincinnati. Oh, it was nothing—sinful, but wrong, as I see it now. I must set matters straight before I can tell you any more."

Seumas was puzzled. It occurred to him that so handsome a young woman could scarcely have failed to excite desire in other men. But what was "wrong" about that? Nothing! Unless, indeed, those rumors afloat regarding the Field rowan were not, as he had repeatedly asserted, mere malicious lies. What was that old saying about there being "no fire without some smoke"? For the first time a flicker of doubt sprang to life in the Irishman's mind. It was the measure of his love for this maid that he was ready to forgive any "wrong" she might have committed, if only she confessed it frankly and asked his forgiveness.

But it was not forgiveness Connie asked when she spoke again. It was patience. She said, "Don't press me for my reasons, now, Seumas. I'll explain everything after I've tried to set matters right. Until then, please trust me, Seumas, because—because——" She could not bring herself to say *because I love you* while her love was still promised to another man. Instead, she finished, "—because there's nothing I want more than to see my father die happy."

Chapter 23

THE PROBLEM of how to keep her father happy without immediate fulfillment of his wish Connie was not forced to solve. That night Ashbel Field died in his sleep with a smile on his lips.

Since his sons lived so far away, there was no question of delaying the funeral for their arrival. Faith and Constitution were the only members of the family to see the mortal remains of Ashbel Field laid to rest in the new burying ground far out on Erie Street beyond the limits of the little settlement he had helped to survey. Every prominent citizen of Cleveland was present to do honor to the last of the pioneers. But the alien who honored Ash most was absent. Seumas McSeumas felt that, under the circumstances, his presence would be an embarrassment rather than a solace.

Faith, feeling utterly unequal to the task of notifying her sons, begged Connie to take on that duty. And the girl, after writing to each of her brothers, also wrote to Ben. She did not find it too hard to acquaint him with the news of what was, for all concerned, a blessed release. It *was* hard to break her other news—that she had learned to love another man. She did not ask to be released from her promise to Ben, feeling sure that he would not hold her to it after he knew the truth.

When that letter, and the other three had been posted, Connie felt somewhat relieved, but until Ben replied she was anxious not to meet Seumas alone. She did not find him difficult to avoid, for when he was not at the academy, he seemed to find a great deal to do in the woodshed or in the barn.

Barn chores were increased a fortnight later when Mal stabled Satan. He brought his mother the sympathy of her old friend, Serena Pomeroy, and apology for not bringing more practical assistance than a sack of oats for his horse and a sack of meal for the family larder. The following day brought Zeke's four-horse team and the Conestoga wagon, empty except for the driver and a single passenger.

By sheer good luck, Zeke said, his sister's letter, addressed in care of the Zanesville tavern, had found him there, westbound with a load of goods. In Columbus, by another coincidence, Zeke had run into Jed, headed for Cleveland by the first means available.

"So," Jed took up the story, "just as soon as Zeke unloaded his wagon I put my portmanteau aboard, and—— That reminds me, Sis, I've got something for you in that bag."

While Jed rummaged through his baggage, Connie had a fleeting hope that what he had brought her was all, or part of the money he still owed her. What Jed handed his sister, however, was a letter.

"From Ben," he said. "He asked me to bring it along, to save postage."

Connie was about to take that letter somewhere to read in privacy when Jed went on to say that he had dropped everything to come, in order to speed the reading of the will. At the word *will*, the girl sat down again, suddenly.

Malachi regarded Jedediah severely through horn-rimmed spectacles. "Pa left no will," he said.

"What?" Jed ejaculated. "Pa, a lawyer, died intestate? I don't believe it. Matter of fact, I happen to know Pa made a will some years back when Sis was living with me. Pa wrote her he was cutting her off unless she came straight home and married some feller he'd picked out for her. She never did. So, except for Ma's mite, us boys gets the whole caboodle. I need my share soon's I can lay hands on it." Jed explained that his haste was the result of a contract to buy a whole block of city lots out beyond Northern Row in Cincinnati, a contract he'd made immediately on learning of his father's death. "The feller agreed to hold those lots for me only till I'd made the round trip to Cleveland and back with enough cash to bind the bargain."

"Land here is what Ash left, mostly," Faith said in a tired voice. "He never had much cash. We've been living on your sister's savings this winter. As for a will, like Mal says, Ash left none. We did make search last summer when we felt sure Ash had changed his mind about our darter, but all we found——" Faith turned to appeal to her oldest, most trusted son, "You explain Mal, what you found."

Malachi took his time in telling about the discovery under the office floor of the charred remnants of a legal document bearing part of Ashbel Field's signature, the logical conclusion being that Ash himself had burned his will before becoming incapacitated.

"Burned!" shouted Jed. "More like Sis burned it. Like enough 'twas what she came home for." He stared accusingly at Connie. "Don't you know destroying other folks' wills is a crime?"

Long pent-up resentment toward Jed oerflowed, and she cried, "How dare you accuse me of such a crime? Because it's the kind of thing you'd do yourself, if you stood to gain by it. I've known for a long time that you're a mean man, miserly and self-seeking, but I never dreamed you'd be as mean as this."

"Children! Children!" cried Faith. *"I never dreamed you'd be* quarreling over your pa's property soon's he was cold in his grave. I—I can't bear it." Her voice broke and she turned to petition her eldest, "Mal, stop them. For heaven's sake stop them!"

There was no need for Mal to intervene. Faith's distress silenced recriminations for the time being. But it was clear to all the younger Fields that the subject of their father's will had merely been deferred, not abandoned.

Connie made excuse of meal-getting to escape to the buttery where she broke the seal on Ben's letter. He wasted no words in hypocritical grief over her father's release. The subject of his brief and labored scrawl was Connie's confession which he refused to take seriously. Trouble was, they'd been too long apart. If only he could leave home, he'd come to Cleveland and claim her promise. But since it was impossible for him to leave the hat shop, Ben ordered his "girl" to return to Cincinnati with her brother and keep her promise without further delay. Once she was his wife, Ben felt confident that he could make Connie forget her "passing fancy for another feller."

Just as confident that he couldn't—that nothing could make her forget Seumas McSeumas, Connie felt bound to Ben, nevertheless. Somehow, she had failed to convince him that theirs had been the "passing fancy," and her new love the love of a lifetime. How, then, was she to convince Seumas of this and still refuse to marry him? If she told him the whole story now could she make him understand why it had been withheld so long? Would not the impetuous, hot-tempered Irishman believe that she had been playing both ends against the middle?

Before Connie could decide what course to pursue, the whole matter was taken out of her hands. The midday dinner had scarcely been cleared away when a knock was heard at the front door. It was a portentous sound, for friends and neighbors always came around to the back and entered without ceremony.

When Connie rose to answer the summons, Faith said, "No, Darter, I'll go."

On the doorstep she found Alfred Kelley. Behind him, the lame banker Leonard Case was getting out of the Kelley carriage. Awed and alarmed by such important visitors, Faith ushered them into the cold front room and left them with half-coherent apology—something about "the makings" of a fire.

Almost at once Mal came in, staggering under a load of logs, followed by Zeke with kindling, and Connie carrying a basket of pine cones. Jed brought up the rear of the procession, supporting the thoroughly flustered Faith.

The family Bible had been restored to its usual place on the center table, and when all the family was assembled, Mr. Kelley laid upon the Book a document sealed with red wax. He then proceeded to relate at some length how he had been called into Ashbel Field's office to witness a will, and having done so, had accompanied the testator to the bank where Mr. Case had signed as the necessary second witness and then deposited the document in his new iron safe.

"So many log houses have gone up in flames with all their contents," Mr. Kelley went on, "that the custom of keeping valuable papers in feather beds or old boots is no longer followed by responsible people. However, many other old customs remain unchanged, and one of them is the custom of deferring the ceremony of reading wills until they can be read in the presence of all concerned. Therefore, Leonard and I waited until today when he saw Jedediah and Ezekiel arrive by goods-wagon. Now——" Mr. Kelley paused to clear his throat while he broke the wax wafer and opened parchment on the Bible.

Then, slowly and distinctly, he began to read, " 'I, Ashbel Field, being of sound mind and in full possession of all my faculties, do hereby declare this to be my last will and testament.' " More legal phrases followed, bequeathing and devising as to how the estate should be apportioned among the heirs. " 'Firstly, to my beloved wife, Faith, one half of all my property, real and personal.' " This occasioned no surprise since all the young Fields knew the devotion existing between their parents.

After clearing his throat again, Mr. Kelley continued, " 'The remaining half of my estate is to be divided into four equal parts.' " A snort from Jed interrupted, but the lawyer gave him an angry glance and went on, " 'Of these four portions, one is to be given to each of my three sons, Malachi, Jedediah and Ezekiel. The fourth portion, which in the usual course of events would fall to my daughter, Constitution, I hereby designate shall be divided into two equal parts: one of these parts to be divided between the twin sons of my son Jedediah: the other half of this subdivided fourth portion is to be held in trust for the education of my grandson, Marvin Field.' "

Of all the Fields, only the disinherited daughter knew the origin of the last bequest. It was in accordance with her own suggestion after the birth of Mal's son. Mal himself was speechless with surprise, Faith no less so. Jed and Zeke both began talking at once, but Connie did not hear a word they said. Although many fresh problems might well arise from this unexpected development, for the moment Connie was concerned with only one thing. And that was the certainty that Ashbel Field's mind had *not* wandered toward the end. He had *not* forgotten having destroyed his first will. What he had tried so hard—and so vainly—to communicate was the whereabouts of this *last* will. Connie was sure that her father had forgiven her, and she was equally certain that he regretted this will, too, and wished it destroyed. Well, he must have died convinced that this had been done.

Somehow, the loss of her share in the estate was insignificant beside the certainty that Ashbel Field had died happy—happy in the belief that he had righted the wrong done his daughter, doubly happy in the assurance of her future happiness with the man of his choice and hers. Seumas! The problem of how to tell him she could never marry him, and why, returned to hatchel her heart. Then her heart seemed to stand still as Jed's harsh voice cut through her reverie.

"By the date of this will," Jed was saying, "there's no doubt it was Pa's last. But was he, like it claims, 'in his right mind and in full possession of' his faculties? Sounds crazy to me—all this dividin' and dividin', and then givin' Mal's boy as much as both my boys together. I, for one, question the validity of this will."

The lawyer, who had been listening with growing impatience, now said, "As to Ash being of sound mind when he made this will, I will testify as will also any number of other men in this town. As to the fairness of any will, it is not a lawyer's province to pass judgment. But let me point out, Jedediah, that if by any chance you should succeed in getting this will set aside, the court would declare your father intestate and divide his estate according to law, that is, your mother would receive only the regular widow's dower and your boys would get nothing, while your sister would share the remainder equally with you and your brothers."

"But if Sis destroyed the first will, thinking——" Jed began.

Alfred Kelley interrupted, "I can prove that she didn't, for I my-self saw Ash tear up that will and toss it into the fire just as we were going out of the office to put his new will in the bank. So, if you had in mind claiming——"

"—the pound of flesh," interposed a voice from behind the company.

All heads turned toward the kitchen door. Seumas, coming in the back way, must have heard voices in the front room, never used, and come to investigate just in time to hear Jed's remark about Connie.

Jaw jetting belligerently, Jed demanded, "Who are you, you Mick, to come shoving your oar into what's none of your business?"

For the first time since the reading of the will, Faith spoke. "It is so his business, Jed, because Seumas is going to be one of the family. He's going to marry your sister."

Before Connie could gather her wits to meet this new situation, Jed laughed in derision. "You mean, Ma, this feller figured on get-ting a rich wife. Well, you figured wrong, Mick. Sis don't get a cent, and anyway, she's been promised for years to another feller—feller name of Benedict in Cincinnati."

Seumas ignored the insult. He was looking at Connie. She, un-able to deny Jed's revelation and equally unable to bear the accusa-tion in the blue Irish eyes, looked down at her own tightly clasped hands. For a moment the only sound in the room was Faith's smothered gasp of surprise and consternation.

Then Seumas, still looking at the girl as though no one else were present, asked very low, "Why have you kept this secret?"

Connie drew a long breath and forced herself to meet his gaze. "I can explain," she said, "but not now." Involuntarily he looked around at the company. And the lawyer and the banker having completed their business, rose hastily. Mal saw them to the door. Then returning to the front room, reminded his brothers of the livestock in the barn where chores were more easily done before dark.

After all her sons had departed, Faith repeated Seumas' ques-tion, "Why have you kept this secret?"

There was nothing Connie could do but tell the whole story in detail. And now her reason for withholding it from her mother became her one hope of escape from the bondage of a mistaken marriage. If Faith Field shared Hope Benedict's prejudice against the marriage of cousins, perhaps Ben would bow to the combined disapproval of both mothers. When Connie had finished her confession, she looked not at Seumas, but at her mother, and when Faith remained silent, she prompted, "Well, Ma?"

Faith said slowly, "I see now why you didn't tell me before, Darter. You were afraid I'd forbid the match."

Connie nodded, and when her mother made no further remark, she cried again, "Well, now you know, what about it, Ma? What about it?"

There was no hesitation in Faith's reply. It was prompt and assured. "I dare say, if you'd asked me before you come of age, I'd have forbid you to wed my sister's boy, and counseled you agin it after. But since you're a woman growed and pledged your word to Ben long ago, I can't see my way to counsel you breakin' your vow to Ben, even though it breaks my heart to think——" Faith broke off to look at Seumas.

He was standing against the wall as though in need of support. Standing very straight, very stiff, with arms crossed as though to keep a tight grip on himself. Tight, too, were his sensitive lips, and the lake-blue eyes were as hard as ice, staring at nothing.

Faith caught her breath, then said in a faint voice, "I'm fair beat out, and can't stand any more. I guess I'd better go to bed."

"Do, Ma," urged Connie. "I'll bring up a hot bottle."

The business of filling the narrow-necked stone crock with boiling water from the kettle on the crane, wrapping the bottle in flannel to retain the warmth, and carrying it up to comfort her mother, kept Connie occupied for some time.

When she came down again, Seumas was staring into the kitchen fire. Connie knew she faced the hardest moment of her life. How could she make him understand that she had not deliberately deceived him for the sake of pacifying her dying father, that the emotion which had driven her into his arms had not been feigned, that love for him was so sudden, so strong, so overpowering as to make her forget for a moment—for a long wonderful moment—that there was any other man in the world? How could she make

Seumas understand all this, and then make him understand that, like her mother, she still felt that a promise was binding.

Her troubled eyes, darkly circled with grief, must have communicated something of what she found too hard to put into words. For, after gazing deep into those black depths, Seumas said gently, "I think I see—at least 'as through a glass, darkly.' Don't tear out your heart, acushla, trying to explain—everything. One thing though, you've got to tell me. I know you must have loved this Benedict, or thought you did at the time. But do you love him now?"

Connie hesitated. Then, scarcely above a whisper, she said, "Yes, as much as I ever did. Too much to hurt him." She could not meet those lake-blue eyes from which all the ice had melted. But she heard the sound—the sound of his strangled agony, and her own heart was twisted in sympathy.

"You'd rather hurt me!" he said sharply.

As sharply, she cried, "I would, because—oh, don't you see. It's because I love you more, oh so much more deeply. It's all so complicated, so hard to explain. Please, my dear, my very very dear, try to understand why I plighted my troth to Ben, and why I can't break my word to him now."

Seumas made no move to touch her as she feared he might do, fearing that if he took her in his arms she could never hold out against him. All Seumas did was to look at her with an expression she could not endure. Under the blinding light of his eyes, hers closed. She heard the sharp intake of his breath, then the rich Celtic voice saying softly.

"Sure, and I do understand, acushla, although I believe you are wrong. You are wrong to give yourself to any man who does not have your whole heart. If Benedict is the kind of man who could win your love in the first place, you could scarcely keep him from sensing, after your marriage, that he hadn't got what counts most. Do you get my meaning, acushla? Have I made myself clear?"

"Quite clear," she replied. "But you don't know Ben. He's a simple soul, really. I'm sure I can make him—happy."

"How about yourself?" Seumas demanded sharply. "Could you be happy in the arms of a man so simple that he'd never know all he had was your *body?*"

A hot flush dyed the girl's pale cheeks. But she managed to say steadily, "If I broke my pledged word to Ben, I'd never be happy anywhere, even with you, Seumas."

He was silent a moment. Then he said softly, "No, mavourneen, you wouldn't, you being you. And because I love you just as you are, I wouldn't have you different." When, unconsciously, she took a step toward him, he raised a hand. And again his voice was sharp as he said, "Don't. I'm only human. I can't stand—everything. Go, please! Go—go see to your mother."

Aware that she, too, was "only human," that if she stayed, tried to comfort this man she loved so deeply, she could never resist the powerful emotion they shared, Constitution Field fled up the stairs.

Faith was asleep. Quietly Connie prepared for the night. Quietly she crept under the coverlet beside her mother, and lay wide-eyed and wakeful, staring into the dark.

After a time she heard Mal's voice below in the kitchen and the murmur of a deeper voice, although the conversation was inaudible. Then one pair of boots clomped up the stairs and along the hall to the room shared by the brothers. The other brothers came in much later, evidently from the tavern, for Jed's voice boomed thickly in the upper hall despite Zeke's whispered caution.

The Academy clock had struck one when Connie heard the stairs creak again under bootless feet, then the same muted footfalls in the room across the landing, padding back and forth, back and forth, restlessly. Once the girl put her own feet out of bed to go to him—to tell him—— But what could she tell McSeumas that would not make a bad matter worse? Withdrawing under the coverlet again, Connie shivered with cold against the warm body of her sleeping mother who, for once, was no comfort. At last, worn out by warring emotions, she fell into uneasy slumber.

When Connie awakened, the sun was streaming into the room and she was alone in the bed. She dressed slowly, dreading to meet the day and the new problems which must be faced. When, finally, she descended the stairs it was to face her mother, alone in the kitchen.

Faith said, "He's gone."

None of her brothers was meant, Connie knew, for she could see all three of them through the window—Mal at the woodpile, Zeke carrying a bucket of water into the barn, and Jed standing idle, hands in his pockets. Her glance came back to three soiled plates on the table and she said, "You mean Seumas went to school without any breakfast?"

"Without a bite," Faith replied, "but not to the Academy, although he took all his books with him. All he left was this——" she held out a scrap of paper.

Connie sensed the contents of that note even before she read the words, "God bless you, Ma Field, for all you have done for me. Now the best thing I can do for all concerned is take myself off."

Chapter 24

Soon all three Field brothers, too, had gone their separate ways. The first to go was Jed, disgruntled over refusal of the executors to advance him any cash on account. His sister's refusal to accompany him was a matter of indifference. Indeed, had she asked for his escort, Jed would have refused to assume the added expense.

Nothing would have induced Connie to ask any favors of Jed. Nothing remained of her savings, either, but that was not her reason for refusing Ben's plea for immediate marriage. Now, of all times, she could not leave her mother, nor could the Widow Field leave Cleveland until the estate was settled, Connie wrote her betrothed. To prove this was her real reason for delaying their nuptials, Connie added that "the other man" had accepted her refusal to break her promise to Ben and had gone away.

Zeke delayed departure for another day in order to cut and carry enough firewood to fill the kitchen woodbox. Then he went, as he said, before his nags ate their heads off in idleness.

Last to go was Mal, reluctant to leave, yet more reluctant to stay after the oats and meal he had brought were gone. Ever since leaving home, Mal's conscience had troubled him about leaving his little family. Now he was returning to home duties, he worried over leaving his mother and sister alone.

Two lonely women with time on their hands! The duties of the reduced household were not enough to keep those hands occupied all day and leave them tired enough at night to sleep soundly. Mother and daughter continued to occupy the same bed even after all the other beds in the blockhouse were empty. The thoughts occupying their sleepless nights were the same, to some extent, for both Faith and Connie found the future hard to face. Without Seumas, the girl saw her future stretch ahead like a long rocky road leading nowhere. What future there was for Faith now, lay in her daughter. Sympathy for the girl's suffering helped to ease a little the pain of her own irreparable loss.

Although the mother had never sympathized with the daughter's longing for book learning she herself lacked, Faith had acquired much wisdom in the school of experience. She knew that the best balm for heartache was work for mind or hands.

And the evening after Mal left, Faith said, "All the chores here are scarce enough now to keep me busy, and the barn chores will keep you busy only night and morning. No reason you can't go to school here till the academy lets out for the summer and again, come fall. For you don't aim to wed during the mourning year, I presume to say."

To Connie the words were a reprieve. "Bless you, Ma," she said. "The custom had slipped my mind. I expect it has slipped Ben's mind, too. I must write and remind him, so he won't urge me again until the year is up. But about school——" she added, then stopped. It must have slipped Ma's mind that cash would be scarce as hen's teeth until the estate was settled.

Faith said, "If you're thinking there's no money, there's that I put in the bank for the lad. Unless he took it with him."

The girl's breath caught sharply. "If he didn't, I couldn't, I mean——"

Faith interrupted, "Mr. Case called it a 'joint account.' 'Twas his idea it should stand in both our names, mine and the lad's, so either of us could draw it out in—'in an emergency,' was the way Mr. Case put it."

"That wasn't what I meant, Ma," Connie said. "He went in the night, the very same night he learned about—about Ben, so he must have gone without a cent, except what he had in his pockets, if anything. But I couldn't. Oh, Ma, don't you see? How could I use his money after sending him away?"

"But you didn't," Faith reminded. "He went of his own accord——"

"Because of me," the girl interposed. "It comes to the same thing. Nobody knows where he went. But I know that he'll never come back."

Faith, equally certain, seized upon that certainty to say, "All the lad ever used of that money was for his schooling. What's left, he'd want you to use the same way, I make no doubt."

There was no doubt about it in Connie's mind, either. But profiting at Seumas' expense after what she had done to him was so repugnant that she changed the subject. "It seems strange that you should urge me to go to school, Ma, after all Pa said, and *did*, to keep me from getting any education."

"Folks," said Faith, "have been known to change their minds. Oh, I don't mean I've come to see things your way, instead of your pa's, exactly. I still can't understand why any female should crave book larnin', but it 'twill ease your heart, Darter——"

Tears came to Connie's eyes and a lump filled her throat so that she could not speak. She, too, had experienced a change of mind, and of heart, toward her mother. Once she had believed that books were the source of all knowledge. She had learned, the hard way, that there were many many kinds of knowledge. Faith Field, who had never read any book except the Bible, had learned to read human hearts.

"Ma," she said softly, "if you think he would want me to go on to school with what little he left in the bank, then that's what I want to do."

While Faith went to the bank next day, Connie went to the Academy. The master, Mr. Rice, questioned her at some length about her studies and standing at the Lancaster Seminary, and then remarked that she had already advanced beyond any classes open to females here. And when Connie inquired about the new classes in natural and moral philosophy, Mr. Rice shook his head. Perhaps it was her obvious disappointment, and a kindly desire to mitigate it, that led him to remind Miss Field that she already had more education than was deemed needful, or even desirable, for members of her sex.

Instead of comfort, this reiteration of the prevailing opinion had the opposite effect. Connie went back to the blockhouse thoroughly discouraged and downhearted. Must this year of freedom—her last, as she saw it—be wasted?

If Faith could not actually read her daughter's mind, frustration was plain to read on the girl's face. Asked the cause of her dejection, Connie explained that it was too late for her to profit by the academy. She was ready for college.

"College!" Faith repeated. "But only menfolks go to college."

"Don't remind me of that, Ma," Connie cried sharply. "It's only too true, everywhere except in Cincinnati."

Faith looked skeptical. "Do you mean to say there's a college in Cincy as takes *gals?*" And when Connie nodded, the widow's shoulders sagged as though fresh weight had been laid upon them. After a moment, she drew herself erect, saying, "If so be you want to go back to Jed's, don't let me keep you. Take the lad's money and go. *I* can make out, somehow, till I get my dower."

"I don't doubt it, Ma," said the girl. "You always *could* make out, somehow, but——" she hesitated. Any expression of reluctance to leave her mother so soon after their bereavement would suggest personal sacrifice which Connie knew Faith would refuse to accept.

Faith said, "If you're thinking how Jed acted about the will, I don't wonder you don't want to be beholden to him. Maybe, was I to write to Hope how I feel about your marriage, she'll see it the same way and take you in during the mourning year."

Although Connie was skeptical about that, nevertheless there was a chance that the elder sister's opinion would prevail with the younger. There was nothing Connie wanted less than to share the Benedict roof under the circumstances. Ben, who did not share her thirst for book learning, was sure to object to further expenditure of time and money on the education of the girl shortly to become his wife. It did occur to Connie that a serious quarrel over the matter might well end in Ben's breaking off the engagement. She had no wish to regain her freedom by any such means. And anyway, what good would come of a break now that Seumas had disappeared? So involved were her feelings that she knew she could never make them all clear to her mother. Yet some reply must be made to Faith's suggestion.

"You're right, Ma," she said. "I don't want any favors from Jed. If his children needed me, I might feel differently about going to his house, but they love Delphine and she loves them devotedly. Aunt Hope doesn't need me either. And if you don't, Ma, I'd better get back to breadwinning. That is, if I'm still needed at Fruit Hill."

A letter of inquiry, addressed to General McArthur, brought a reply from Chillicothe within a fortnight, but not in the general's bold hand. His wife wrote explaining that, after waiting a reasonable length of time for Miss Field's return, she had been replaced by an older female skilled in the art of embroidery. Half of the dining room chairs had already been recovered with exact replicas of Grandmother McDonald's needlework, and covers for the remainder were well under way. She remained, "With kind regards, Nancy McArthur."

Mere polite convention, Connie knew. Mrs. McArthur did not regard her kindly enough to speak in her behalf to other well-to-do Chillicothe families with young daughters. Connie considered writing the general again to request a recommendation, then discarded the idea. The busy man, burdened with public duties, so many and so varied private affairs, and the added demands of the great new transportation project, now well under way, would have neither time nor thought to spare a penniless girl he had once befriended.

For with spring, work was being pushed hard all along the route of the Ohio and Erie Canal. Manual labor, however, was beneath the dignity of the native male redskins who formerly had brought peltry into Cleveland to exchange for brass kettles, axes and firewater. These sons of the soil—what was left of them—fled further west before the advance of civilization. The taverns formerly frequented by Indians were now full of farmers' sons who trooped into Cleveland as soon as spring planting was done, eager to work on the canal from sunup to sundown "twenty-six dry days a month" for eight dollars, plus food and lodging. Huddles of huts sprang up all along the route of the canal. And to these shantytowns flocked other seekers after employment. Foreigners, landed at the port of New York, came up the Hudson River, through the Erie Canal, to embark on lake steamers bound for Cleveland. These immigrants, in passing, crowded the taverns to slake their thirst for what they called "the critter," and roamed the streets in search of shelter for a night or two.

Seumas' old room in the blockhouse need never have lacked a temporary tenant. But these Irish were a different breed: belligerent, bold-eyed braggarts who regarded any passing female with a hunger equal to their thirst for hard liquor. Hitherto, the Field latchstring had, literally, never been pulled in. Now it never hung out, even during the day. As added protection by night, Connie fitted a stout crossbar into a pair of brackets nailed fast, one on each side of the doorframe. Faith had never returned to the kitchen chamber she and Ash had shared for so many happy years. She and Connie continued to sleep together upstairs. And under these new conditions, the girl would not have left her mother alone in the blockhouse, even had any other place been open to her.

Reduced indoor chores, as Faith had said, required only one pair of hands. That summer Connie kept busy growing grain for the livestock (reduced to one cow) and growing garden "sass" for the table. She was on her knees weeding the onion bed one morning when a shadow fell across the row, and she looked up into the face of the banker.

Leonard Case said, "Glad to find you alone, Constitution. I've a customer for this property, and I don't know how best to broach the business to your mother."

"Sell this property!" Connie exclaimed. "Oh, I know it's part of Pa's estate, but somehow it never occurred to me it would be sold over our—over Ma's head. I took it for granted, as I'm sure she did, that this house and lot would fall to her as part of her dower."

"Your father," Mr. Case replied, "owned lots all over town. This one, however, is by far the most valuable. The others may, in fact I am sure, will grow in value, but at the moment it is for this lot I have a customer willing to pay more than the market price. Therefore—"

Connie surmised what made the banker hesitate and she said quickly, "I'm sure Mal would never turn Ma out of her home, and I don't believe Zeke would, either. But Jed—well, you are probably thinking of Jed's remarks about money."

The banker nodded. "Correct," he said. "It was for that reason I wanted to talk the situation over with you before approaching your mother. I suggested to Kelley that we put the matter before the heirs, but he thinks it could be done to better advantage by Mrs. Field herself. If she begged her sons to leave her in peace, they could scarcely refuse. What is your opinion, Constitution?"

Privately, the girl did not believe Faith would consent to ask favors of her sons. But what she said was, "It's my opinion, Mr. Case, that you'd better ask Ma. You'll find her in the kitchen. I'll stay here."

The result of this conference, in which Connie took no part, ended as she had anticipated, with the widow's refusal to stand in the way of settling the Field estate as quickly and as profitably as possible. If Faith suffered in secret at the thought of breaking up her home, there was no sign of regret in the calm and practical way she discussed the matter with her daughter after the banker had gone.

"This place is too big for you and me, anyway," she said. "And after you get married, I can live with less work in your pa's old office. So, why don't we move over there now?"

Connie's only objection to the move was the growing demand for Superior Street property. There was no telling how long before the office, like the blockhouse, would have to go, she pointed out.

Faith Field's comment reflected her Marvin upbringing. "We won't start 'crossing bridges' until we get to them," she said. " 'Sufficient unto the day is the evil thereof.' "

The transfer of their scanty personal property and necessities for setting up housekeeping on a smaller scale was accomplished within a few days. The cow could be left in the barn for the present, and the grain and garden "sass" gathered as it ripened.

Demolition of the blockhouse—the last of its kind—began at once and foundations laid on the site for a large three-story hostelry, the first of that size to be erected in all Western Reserve. Work on the new Franklin House was hurried to meet rapidly increasing calls for hotel accommodations. In April a new stage line had begun to operate twice a week to Pittsburgh. There was a daily mail stage to Presque Isle, renamed Erie, which advertised to take passengers there for three dollars. For a like sum another stage line would transport them from Erie to Buffalo, the combined journies—two hundred miles—to be accomplished in the fast time of forty-one hours.

The Franklin House became the headquarters for these and numerous other stage lines, and was also popular with travelers by water. For now the lake steamers docked at the end of the new pier where passengers could hire a hack to take them the two miles into town, or they could walk, followed by their goods in horse- or hand-drawn carts. Eastern lawyers, sent west to straighten out long tangled land claims, put up at the Franklin House, as did monied men who saw in the lake terminus of the new canal opportunity for large future profits. Prospective merchants came, too, and all sorts of other men, honest or otherwise, with a taste for a gamble. But none of the men who did the actual digging of the big ditch for less than forty cents a day, could afford the luxuries of the Franklin House beds, or its bar, and the old taverns continued to resound with a babble of tongues.

Whenever Constitution Field went to the post office, she caught herself straining her ears at the sound of a bit of brogue, and her eyes searched the crowd for a curly redhead. Irishmen there were in growing numbers, but never any sign of Seumas. Nor did any word of him come by mail. Letters from Ben arrived from time to time, letters that grew shorter along with the days of the dying year. After Connie had harvested her little crop, and piled firewood high on either side of the office door, she was at a loss how to fill her days.

The idea of opening a dame school in the office came to her and was discarded immediately. There were free classes at the academy for poor folks' small children, and those of the well-to-do would never be sent to a female teacher long the subject of gossip. The fact that Connie remained unwed at twenty-four was, in the opinion of her mother's old friends, proof that town talk was well founded. The Widow Field, to be sure, gave out that her daughter was betrothed, and only waiting out the mourning year to get married. But if the gal had, indeed, captured a beau during her wanderings, it was unthinkable that she hadn't made sure of him before returning to Cleveland. Faith was reluctant to explain this laggardness clearly, and the reason she gave failed to convince the gossips. Mourning did, indeed, forbid the Fields' attendance at quilting bees that winter, and over the frames rumor was circulated that the gal had been jilted, and her ma was trying to cover up the disgrace.

By the time this tale reached Faith's ears, she was in no position to give it the lie. In January a letter had come from Ben after being weeks on the way because of a succession of storms that tied up mail stages. More storms followed, as the cold strengthened, and the days lengthened slowly so that failure to receive any further word from Ben caused Connie no concern.

It was well into the March mud-season before another letter came from Cincinnati, a letter addressed, not to the Field rowan, but to the "Widder Field." Hope Benedict had overcome the Marvin hatred of letter writing because Ben couldn't bring himself to break the news, and Rooshy refused to do it. Hope's cramped characters were hard to decipher, her sentences misspelled and unpunctuated. Nevertheless, it was clear that Ben had broken his promise to his cousin. He and a friend of Rooshy's had run off to Kentucky and gotten married. Hope tried to excuse her son on the grounds that long engagements were always a mistake and this one had been a mistake from the beginning, not only because Ben and Con were too "close related," but because they "want close enough in sperit." Hope, on Ben's behalf, begged the forgiveness of the girl he had jilted. The Widow Benedict then closed with expressions of sympathy for her widowed sister and the certainty that all husbands and wives would be reunited in heaven.

Because of Hope's difficult penmanship, and Faith's difficulty in reading "writing" of any kind, it took her a long time to read the letter aloud. When finally, she laid it down, Faith drew a deep breath and looked at her daughter.

Connie did not see that look; she was staring into the fire. Nor did she see the dancing flames. What she saw was the flaming head of the man who had gone away because she felt honor-bound to keep her word to Ben Benedict. Now it was too late, Ben had broken *his* word. She was free, free to wed Seumas, if he could be found. Locating one Irishman among the hundreds of new immigrants from the Emerald Isle and the Isle of Man who had passed through Cleveland to seek work all along the two hundred mile stretch of the canal during the last six or eight months, would be like searching for the proverbial needle in the proverbial haystack.

Similar thoughts must have occupied Faith's mind, for after a few moments' silence, she said, "Well, if that don't beat all! I never did hold with folks' breaking promises like they was bread or biscuits, but I'm not minded to cry over Ben breaking his word to you, Darter. Nor——" she added, after a slight hesitation, "—will you, I presume to say."

"No," replied the girl, looking up from the fire to meet her mother's gaze squarely. "In fact, I'm grateful to Ben for setting me free, even though it is too late——" Her breath caught and she cried, "Oh, Ma, I—I——" and could say no more. Tears dimmed the brilliance of the black Field eyes and ran down cheeks grown pale and thin with grief.

Faith comforted, "There! There! Don't take on so. I know what it's cost you, deary, but it's all over now. All you got to do is write the lad a letter, and he'll come a-running."

It was by no means as simple as that, Connie pointed out, since they had no idea where Seumas had gone.

"But surely the post office folks will know where to send him a letter!" Faith exclaimed.

At this childlike trust in the omnipotence of the United States mail, Connie smiled through her tears. "Ma, dear," she said, "the government can't keep track of every citizen in the nation. A letter has to be addressed to a place as well as a person. I can write Ben in Cincinnati telling him he's forgiven. But I can't write Seumas in care of the wide wide world."

The literal-minded mother remarked that, without money, a body couldn't get a very "far piece" in the world. The sum she had deposited for "the lad" had been intact when Faith went to the bank to withdraw a little for Connie's schooling, and she had returned it later.

It occurred to Connie that, since then, Seumas might have made arrangements to transfer his funds to another bank elsewhere, as Mr. Kelley had had her savings transferred from Chillicothe. In this case the bank would have an address. On the chance, Connie called on Mr. Leonard Case.

The banker reported the account intact, but Seumas was still unheard from. The only suggestion he had to offer was that Mr. Kelley, as one of the canal commissioners, might have some idea. But Alfred Kelley was also a member of the General Assembly, presently in session in Columbus. If she could wait until he came home——

It was a long wait. The 1827 session of the Ohio Legislature sat much longer than usual for several reasons. One reason was that members who, like old Ephraim Cutler, had worked for free schooling in vain, and only got the school bill passed as a rider to the canal bill two years earlier, now pushed their advantage. The infringement of the state in school matters provoked the enmity of many local diehards and the argument as to how, and to what extent public education was to be financed, provoked a fight which kept the lawmakers in Columbus until June.

Meanwhile work on the canal had been resumed as soon as the frost was out of the ground and the spring freshets subsided. Eagerness to get the project into operation, and goods flowing to market on the artificial waterway, mounted to madness. Farmers neglected their plowing and hired out with their sons and ox teams. By the lake steamers came an ever-increasing stream of immigrants from seaboard cities and from overseas. Cleveland's floating population could not be counted, so many strangers came to work in the neighborhood, and so many more passed through and pushed up the Cuyahoga Valley to the new settlement called Akron on the height of land. Even the shantytown erected there could not house all this influx of labor, and it flowed on south, a human river, to swell the earlier wilderness settlements, or form new towns.

This surge of humanity brought increasing optimism to Cleveland and a sharp rise in the price of central property. The likelihood that the Field estate would turn out to be richer than Ash's wildest dreams, was no consolation to Connie whose lover was lost in the rising flood of prosperity. By the time Kelley came home, the girl had no hope that he could aid in her quest. Nevertheless, since her father's old friend was her last resort, Connie forced herself to visit the commissioner.

Although she had thought herself prepared for disappointment, her spirits took another drop as she watched Alfred Kelley's face. He pointed out that she had no basis for assuming that McSeumas had found work on the canal and that, in any case, locating one laborer would be almost as impossible as finding one individual ant in a series of anthills.

"However," he said, "I do have a list of contractors." He went on to explain the system by which some local man, frequently a farmer, contracted to dig a section of canal, sometimes only a mile, often through his own township. Each contractor engaged his own gang, paid his men, paid for their housing and feeding, and collected from the commission the sum agreed upon. "I can give you my list of these contractors," Kelley repeated, "but I must warn you, Constitution, that some of these men can barely read and write and that none of them are what you'd call ready writers. It is for you to decide whether the slim chance of locating McSeumas by this means is worth the postage.

Plenty of pens, ink and paper remained in Ashbel Field's office. Money in the bank had dwindled, however, and what little remained was all the two women had to live on until the widow came into her dower. Nevertheless, Connie wrote reams of letters that summer, and not only prepaid the postage on every one, but promised to pay the Cleveland postmaster for each and every reply. Fortunately, or unfortunately, only a few replies came back and none of them brought news of one Seumas McSeumas.

Seven years earlier, the Field rowan had set out alone, penniless and afoot through the sparsely inhabited back-of-beyond to seek her fortune. She was no less courageous now, but she was older, wiser, and the face of the land had changed. To be sure, she could cut her hair again and in her father's old clothes might pass for a young man so long as she kept her mouth shut. But she was too mature now to pass as an adolescent boy whose voice was changing. Questions would have to be asked in every shantytown—questions certain to reveal her sex and lead to the belief that she was "in trouble" and seeking the man accountable. Even worse, she might be taken for a female of easy virtue, looking for no man in particular—just any man ready to pay for her favors.

Nor would shantytowns be the only places of danger. In these teeming times, a night in a tree would offer no refuge from woods where all the night prowlers were not animals. As for taking refuge in some wayside inn, if her disguise fooled the host, he would assign her a bed in the men's chamber where her sex could not be concealed from fellow travelers. If they were respectable citizens, they could have her arrested for masquerading in male garments. If they were not respectable—Connie shuddered, recalling her experience in the Cincinnati waterside tavern. She had escaped with her virtue only through Jed's timely intervention.

Connie thought of other men under whose protection she had traveled in safety—Zeke, in his Conestoga wagon, the captain of the steamer *Washington,* General McArthur and Canal Commissioner Kelley. For a moment she considered making another appeal to the commissioner, asking him to take her along on one of his tours of inspection. Then she recalled the expression on Mrs. Kelley's face. No, she could not ask Alfred Kelley's escort on her search for the man who, all Cleveland believed, had seduced and deserted the Field rowan. That would be asking too much of her father's friend and executor.

Constitution resigned herself to the fact that Seumas McSeumas was lost to her forever. She knew that she would never forget him, never cease to love him, never wed any other man. A long life of spinsterhood stretched before her. It would be a lonely life, indeed, after her mother passed on, a life that could only be filled by the fulfillment of her old ambition. If she could go on and acquire a college education, and use it to inspire younger generations of females with the courage and desire to break free from tradition and superstition, to demand and get an education equal to that given their brothers, then at least she would not have lived in vain.

For the present, however, even that consolation was denied her. The unselfish mother might insist that she could "make out alone," and even offer to help finance her daughter's college course, after the estate was settled. But Connie knew she would not accept the sacrifice. For a month or so, while she searched for her lost lover, Connie might have been content to leave Faith with some local friend. Going away to college was another matter. A course would take years, and Faith's remaining years must not be passed in solitude.

They two, the widow and the unwed daughter of Ashbel Field were bound together, for better, for worse, by a tie that had grown stronger with mutual bereavement, mutual respect and love.

Chapter 25

WHAT DIEHARDS called "canal madness," drove its "crazy" enthusiasts into performing a feat little short of miraculous. Except for the last two of the forty-one locks designed to raise or lower craft the thirty-eight miles between the upland lake region and the great lake, the big ditch was completed from Akron to Cleveland by the end of June, 1827.

Clevelanders had planned to celebrate the opening of the canal on Independence Day. And celebrate it they did, even though the barge bringing down the guests of honor stopped short at the unfinished locks, six miles above the town. Up to this point a double span of stout mules hauled another barge, the *Pioneer*, gay with flags a welcoming party, and a brass band. When the Governor of Ohio and other bigwigs had transferred themselves to the *Pioneer*, the mule team headed back to Cleveland to the strains of *The Star-Spangled Banner*.

Every citizen in the county seat who could walk, creep or hobble down to the landing place, greeted the guests with cheers, whistles and catcalls that drowned out the band and were, in turn, drowned out by a salvo fired from the old cannon on the public square.

Their "mourning year" being over, the Field women joined the gay crowd. Connie searched the sea of faces for one face she had never ceased to see in her dreams. As Faith's gaze wandered over the multitude, her thoughts went back to the time when Ash and a few other "madmen" had dreamed of what this day had actually brought to pass. Memory did not bring sadness, for Faith was certain that her husband could look down from on high and see that his dream had come true.

Alfred Kelley's carriage carried Governor Allen Trimble from the waterside up the slope of Superior Street to the public square where oratory, interspersed with cheers and band music, flowed freely for hours. Late in the afternoon, when the speakers had grown hoarse and their hearers hungry, the crowd broke up. Local bigwigs escorted the guests of honor to the Franklin House, and plain folks from Newburg and other hamlets in the eastern hills opened lunch baskets on the trampled square, among other folks who had brought baskets from across the river. Common Clevelanders went home to cold suppers, for on holidays, like Sundays, no woman labored over a hot kettle.

In Ashbel Field's old office, his widow and spinster daughter ate bread and cheese and listened to the sounds of celebration continuing across the street. The orators and hosts, stomachs filled at the banquet board, and parched throats lubricated with local liquor, proposed toast after toast in rhetoric that soared to fresh heights as the sun dropped lower and lower and finally disappeared in a blaze of glory, reddening both the Indians' river and the white man's canal. It was a great day.

During the days that followed, Cleveland gradually came down to earth. But the enthusiasm generated by the formal opening of the canal made local earth look more precious and sent land prices soaring. At the peak of this boom, the Field executors came to call on the widow. Alfred Kelley explained that as soon as the last parcel of land was sold, the estate could be settled and the proceeds divided according to Ash's last will and testament. Kelley paused, cleared his throat, and looked at the banker.

Leonard Case hemmed and hawed and then remarked that the last lot referred to was the one on which the widow's present residence stood. "We don't want to hurry you, ma'am," he went on, "but neither do we want to miss a good sale. It never was your intention to spend the rest of your days in this old log cabin, I presume to say. Why, it's little better than a pigsty, no fit home for a well-to-do widow."

If Faith flinched inwardly at the slur on the shelter Ash had built before bringing his family to Cleveland, there was no sign of resentment or regret on her placid face. She said, "I saw this coming and made my plans."

Connie, to whom this was news, wondered if Ma might be planning to build a cottage outside of town where land was cheaper, perhaps way out on Erie Street in the neighborhood of the cemetery. The lawyer and the banker looked relieved. Evidently, they had feared the widow might take it hard, so hard that it would be difficult to dislodge her and wind up their duties as executors. With cordial offers of help in the investment of her dower, the two men made their manners and departed.

The two women did not immediately break into speech. Faith seemed lost in thoughts her daughter was loath to disturb. Finally, anxious to offer some small crumb of comfort, Connie voiced her thought about a cottage convenient to her father's last resting place.

Slowly Faith shook her head. "Your pa's not there," she said. "No matter where I go, Ash will always be with me, in spirit. Like I said, I foresaw we'd have to move again, you and me. Just as soon as I get my dower, I aim to move to Cincinnati."

For a moment Connie's heart leaped, then fell. "I could never live under Jed's roof again," she said.

Faith said, "I wouldn't ask you to, Darter. But, remembering as how Jed rents the little house he lives in, thinks I we could hire one like it just for ourselves, not too near by. You wouldn't have to see Jed. But when all is said and done, he's my son and I want to see my grandbabies. Besides," she added, after a moment, "I long to see my sister, too. Hope and me was close in the old days before either of us wed, and 'twill be good to talk over those days with her whilst you're busy at that college."

There was no doubt in the girl's mind what motivated this decision. "Ma, dear," she expostulated, "I can't let you pull yourself up by the roots and part with friends of a lifetime just on my account. That's too great a sacrifice."

"It's no such thing!" Faith retorted. "Nothing and nobody on earth means as much to me as you and your happiness, Darter. Now the lad's gone, heaven knows where, you're not apt to wed just for the sake of having *Mrs.* carved on your tombstone. Now you don't have to wed for a home, either. We're simple folks, you and me. We can make out on my dower. What's left of it, I aim to make sure goes to you, after I go to Ash. He'd want it that way, I know, for he died happy believing you'd share with the boys."

This was a very long speech for Faith. It left Connie, who was more articulate by nature, too full of gratitude for words. Here was Ma, who had never understood her longing for learning, ready to aid in its attainment, nevertheless. Connie longed to beg Faith's forgiveness for past neglect, past blindness, past failure to recognize that all the wells of wisdom did not lie in the mind. Acknowledgment of this belated discovery found expression through an agency older than any language. Connie threw both arms around her mother. Taken aback, Faith stiffened instinctively. Then the warmth of the girl's spontaneous action melted the lifelong habit of repression. The mother's arms went around the daughter and so they stood, silent, wrapped in a close embrace.

It was Faith who broke the silence finally. "Well," she said, in a matter-of-fact tone, "now it's settled about where to move, what shall we take along? Too bad the gelding was sold. What he brought won't buy another horse, let alone a stout wagon for our chests, kettles and feather beds, and the cherry four-poster your great-grandsir made and the two spinning wheels your pa——"

Connie felt forced to interrupt before Faith went further. "Ma, you've no idea what a long way Cincinnati is from here. It's much too long a journey for you to make in a wagon."

"Who said I aimed to ride in a wagon?" Faith cried. "I got no idea of *riding*. Didn't I walk most of the way out here from Connecticut before you were born? That's not so long ago but what I can still walk quite a piece, days on end."

Connie did not contradict this assertion, knowing how old folks resented any reminder of failing faculties. Instead, she reminded her mother that, while the canal was designed primarily as a goods-carrier, it would also transport passengers. Faith agreed then, to travel by water, if they could get ready to go before the canal was closed for the winter.

As it turned out, winter came and went, and another summer and fall as well, before the Field estate was settled. The prospective buyer for the old office plot could not raise the cash to bind the bargain. And it was nearly a year later before another buyer was found with sufficient capital to buy—at a higher figure.

When, finally, they were ready to go, Alfred Kelley drove the Fields down to the landing place and put them aboard the packet in which their household goods had already been deposited. Compared with the Ohio River steamers, the *Pioneer* was a little craft, but it was just as comfortable. There was a separate cabin for each sex and a main salon where both sexes ate at a single table, or sat around the wood stove in inclement weather. When it was fine, passengers preferred the deck overhead from which they could watch the mules detached at the approach to each lock, and the process by which the packet was raised to the next level.

Passage through the locks was slow, and Constitution was able to ask the lock-master at every one of the forty-one locks if, by chance, he knew or had encountered an Irishman by the name of McSeumas. Months ago, she had given up hope of finding him— told herself that the canal was not the sole source of employment. Seumas could just as well have boarded a lake steamer and worked his way west, or east. Still, she could not resist the impulse to ask for him all the way to Akron, and beyond.

Beyond the height of land the process in the locks was reversed. Instead of rising with rising water, the packet sank lower and lower as the water ran out, and when the gates were raised, floated out on the new level where fresh mules were attached. South of the height of land the canal was fed by the Licking, the Tuscarawas, and the Scioto in turn, although it did not follow these meandering streams, but cut across them to shorten the work of digging the ditch and the time of travel through what, so little time before, had been deep wilderness. Now raw new towns were springing up like mushrooms on or near the canal. One of these mushrooms was Massillon, born as a result of Canton diehards' refusal to have the canal cut through their town. This, and many other bits of information, Connie picked up from table talk, or while walking the deck to ease limbs cramped from so much unaccustomed leisure. Between the time spent in locks and time spent tied up at docks while firkins of butter, cheese, maple sugar and other local products were put aboard, and imports from the outer world discharged, the progress of the packet was slower than Connie's progress on foot through this same country had been nine years ago.

At length, however, the *Pioneer* reached the end of the voyage at Dresden, some twelve miles north of Zanesville. With spring, the canal proper would be pushed on toward the Scioto, and a branch dug from Dresden to Zanesville. Locks were in the course of construction on the Muskingum River so that, eventually, small steamers would run between Zanesville and Marietta on the Ohio River.

At the close of the year 1828, however, Dresden was the southern terminus of the Ohio and Erie Canal. And here a surprise awaited Faith Field. The widow, after making the momentous decision to move, left transportation arrangements to her daughter and Commissioner Kelley, taking for granted one of her sons would meet her at the end of the voyage.

When Faith stepped off the *Pioneer,* therefore, she looked about expectantly. But the man who came toward her was not a young man. He was a stooped, gray-headed old man she recognized only because he had the Marvin eyes.

"Si!" exclaimed Faith, seizing both her brother's gnarled hands. "What lucky chance brought you here?"

Silas Marvin explained that it was not chance at all, but a letter from his niece. "Tell you all about it as we go," he said. "My team is hitched over yonder and we'd better git started or we won't git to my place before dark."

As the wagon bumped along the narrow road, all the driver's attention was needed to keep the vehicle from overturning. And it was Connie who supplied the information as to how this meeting had come about. Well in advance of the start, she had written Zeke about the move and asked if he could meet them in Dresden with his wagon and in it take his mother, sister and their goods as far as Columbus, at least, and if no further, then make arrangements for their transportation to Cincinnati.

Zeke had replied that he couldn't be sure of being any given place at a given date, especially in winter. A better plan was for Sis to get in touch with Uncle Si, whose land in the old Military Tract lay in the present Dresden Township. At this season of the year time hung heavy on farmers' hands. No doubt Silas Marvin would be glad to meet Ma and Sis, put them up at his place for a night, or longer, then put them aboard the weekly mail stage between Zanesville and Dayton, and dicker with some regular goods-wagon on the route, to transport their goods later. The Miami Canal, which had been in process of construction simultaneously with the Ohio and Erie, was scheduled to open in January, and would furnish the shortest and most comfortable route south.

Scarcely had Connie completed this explanation than the road emerged from the forest into a large clearing where smoke rose from a cabin chimney. Hundreds of great trees had been felled to expand the clearing since the Fields had stopped here on the way from Marietta to Cleveland, but none of the timber sacrificed had gone to enlarge the domicile.

When Connie remarked that the cabin looked just the same, Silas said he'd no call to add an ell or raise the roof, seeing all the family he had was a wife and one gal. The inference was that with sons to help clear and cultivate the land, the "old man" would have had more time and incentive to improve his domicile. "You and Ash had four sons," he reminded his sister.

Faith might have reminded Silas that none of her sons had remained at home, but all she said was, "You and Tildy are lucky to have a darter. I'm eager to see her and Sereny again."

Matilda Marvin was many years younger than she who had been Faith Marvin, yet she looked much older. The ripe apple-red was gone from Penn-Dutch cheeks no longer round, and what hair was left on her head was less like corn silk than the sere and faded leaf of the corn. In the vernacular she had never lost, Tildy blamed "der shakes" for her vanished youth and prettiness. Sereny, too, suffered from the prevailing malady. She was a pale and colorless creature except for wistful eyes, larger and bluer than those of most Marvins. Overcome by shyness, the girl looked away from her handsome cousin and could not voice the awe and admiration that stirred her lonely heart. The plain and faded face of the widow, and her insistance on helping with supper, won the wilderness wife, and the two older women were soon exchanging recipes over pots and pans.

Over the meal, Si's curiosity overcame his lifelong habit of minding his own business, and he wanted to know what "possessed" his sister to pull up stakes and move again, at *her* age. And when Faith replied frankly that it was to enable her daughter to attend the only college open to females, Silas disbelieved his ears.

"Must be I'm goin' deef," he remarked. "I thought you said *college.*" And when Faith assured him that he was not losing his hearing, he told her, "Then ye must be losin' yer mind. Schoolin' fer females is a sinful waste of time and money. What's more, it's agin nature."

Faith was about to change the subject, before her daughter forgot good manners and clashed with their host, when Si's daughter spoke for the first time since the Fields' arrival.

"Ever since I was knee-high to a duck," Sereny said, "I've hankered after book larnin'. But there ain't never been no school hereabouts."

"If there's no school in Dresden," Connie comforted, "there will be soon." She went on to explain what little she knew about the school bill, passed with the canal bill.

Evidently both subjects were equally sore with Silas, for he interrupted his niece with a bitter tirade against the rise in taxes sure to come as a result of "both them newfangled notions."

Connie pointed out that the canal would raise land values. To prove this she gave Silas the figures of the fortune her mother had lately acquired from the Field estate. Undoubtedly, within a few years Uncle Si could sell his farm for a figure which would enable him to move to any town he or his womenfolks fancied, and live in luxury and idleness for the rest of his days.

The opinion of a female on this, or any other subject, did not impress Silas Marvin. He did grant that the canal might make marketing his produce easier and more profitable, but land—land had been too long a drug on the market to skyrocket overnight. It was clear that he discredited, not his niece's honesty, but her knowledge of finance. Females, who never handled money, considered one dollar a fortune. Silas Marvin, who had never handled more than two silver coins at a time, did not look forward to selling his section, or any part of it, for a large sum, or for that matter, for any figure at all.

Since Silas was not given to revealing his thoughts to females, he must have been thinking out loud when he said, "I cleared this whole quarter section with my own hands, and I don't aim to leave it as long as I'm above ground."

He left home, temporarily, next day to drive his sister and niece down to Zanesville. As the westbound mail stage came through sometime between midnight and dawn, Silas left Faith and Connie at the inn and left their household goods at a warehouse to be forwarded when possible. Brother and sister had been separated so many years that this parting, although probably final, occasioned no visible regret. Connie's chief regret was her helplessness to help Sereny. Since Uncle Si was determined to die on the farm, Sereny was bound to stay with the old folks and "see them through."

It was in the cold dark hour of four, next morning, that Constitution helped Faith into the mail stage and climbed in after her mother. Their pigskin trunks, the one which had come from New Orleans with Stasie, and the one which had come from Connecticut with Faith, were behind in the boot. The only piece of baggage taken inside was Connie's reticule, clutched tightly because it held all the cash for the journey. Further funds, in amply supply, had already been transferred to Mr. Piett's bank in Cincinnati for the Widow Field.

Like the night before in the inn, the journey was Faith's first experience of the kind, and although she did not complain as the coach bounced and bounded along the Trace, privately she preferred the slow pace of a springless wagon. When a cold rain began to fall, however, she was quite ready to concede that a closed coach was more comfortable. And since Connie had seen to it that her mother's foot stove was filled with live coals before starting, Faith was as cosy under the fur robe as ever she had been by her own fireside.

A rousing blaze lighted as well as warmed the inn at Lancaster where mother and daughter dismounted to spend the night. From the conversation in the taproom where they had supper, the girl heard the National Road mentioned and pricked up her ears. The paved highway over the mountains, under construction for years, had progressed as far west as Zanesville. Now, it seemed, bids had recently been "let" for the fifty-two miles from Zanesville to Columbus. And until that stretch of the National Road was completed, the best route was that used by the mail stages, as Alfred Kelley well knew when he planned this journey for the Field women.

Faith was astonished to find another fire in the ladies' chamber which, owing to the season of light travel, she and Connie did not have to share with strangers. The next night at Circleville, however, they had not only a pair of roommates but a bedfellow—the wife of a Dayton man, homeward bound. It was the same inn where Connie had stopped on the way to Chillicothe, and from here on to Dayton the route would be the same, too, except that it would be in the opposite direction, and the opposite season of the year.

Where dust had smothered summer travelers, winter travelers suffered from cold and delay caused by the weather. All the way to Circleville rain had fallen heavily so that the mail stage was late in arriving. Next morning it left early with the mail, but took no passengers. During the night rain continued to fall, and with it the temperature dropped to a point below freezing. All too often horses foundered on icy roads, sometimes overturning the vehicle behind them with dire consequences. Passengers went on at their own risk, or waited at the stagehouses for better weather.

The Fields were in no particular hurry. When the rains ceased and the icy roads thawed, they proceeded by a coach that floundered through the mud to Dayton. Although there was a nip in the air there, compared with the windy city on the shore of Lake Erie, the city between the Great and the Little Miami seemed almost balmy. There was no apparent reason why the Miami Canal should not open on schedule.

For this great event public accommodations in Dayton were crowded with visitors. But as Canal Commissioner Kelley had written the proprietor of the best hotel to expect the Field ladies, they were given a bed in a room overlooking the main thoroughfare. The celebration held in the hotel was much like that conducted in the Franklin House in Cleveland some eighteen months earlier. Upon the arrival of the packet *Governor Brown,* the last Sunday in January, the banquet hall resounded with toasts and oratory. Although none of this flowery rhetoric was audible through windows, hermetically sealed for the winter, people outside could see through the glass and cheer each speaker to the echo.

From the window in the ladies' chamber, Constitution Field looked down on the crowd and caught herself searching it for a high-held redhead, just as she had searched the crowds at each lock or landing between Cleveland and Dresden, just as she had looked over the passengers in every stagecoach and the occupants of every taproom, and just as vainly. She was forced to remind herself that, even had Seumas come this way, there were steamers on the Ohio River as well as on Lake Erie. By now, in all probability, the address of Seumas McSeumas was, indeed, "the wide wide world." He was gone out of her life for good. Thanks to her mother, she could fill that life with the old love—the love of study. Constitution turned away from the window, determined to stop wasting time and thought on a love that was lost forever.

Following the celebration, the Miami Canal was open for traffic. The *Governor Brown* was advertised to carry passengers twice each week between Dayton and Howell's Basin, four miles west of Cincinnati. Determined to outdo the rival canal, the Miami management had lavished money on the appointments of the *Brown*. All three of the cabins were covered with thick carpet, and to preserve these in the main salon and in the "Gentlemen's Cabin," huge brass cuspidors were provided. In the "Ladies' Cabin" no such precautions were needed. That retreat, however, was provided with china pitchers, washbasins and slop jars painted with every known flower, wild or cultivated, and many which bloomed only in the artist's imagination. No means for preserving modesty was provided, and females in every stage of undress had to wait their turn in the washroom, the only refuge from public gaze being behind the heavy hangings which also shut out every current of air from the berths they covered.

Connie, tossing sleepless in the upper berth was conscious of her mother's restless turning in the berth below. But if Faith found breathing difficult in such close quarters, she breathed no word of complaint, but only praise for such lavish luxuries as she had never enjoyed before. The Field ladies neither enjoyed those luxuries long, nor did they suffer a second night's suffocation, for the *Brown's* tow team brought the packet to the landing in Howell's Basin early on the second morning.

Breakfast was served aboard the boat, and then passengers went ashore to hire hacks for the last leg of the journey into the Ohio River metropolis. As the Fields were in no hurry, they were the last to disembark, Faith on the arm of the packet captain. Connie scorned assistance for so short a gangplank. Yet she came very near falling into the canal between ship and shore. She had taken only a step or two when her gaze was caught by a sight that turned her giddy, unsure of her footing as she was unsure of her eyes. That tall fellow in the coonskin cap could not be the man she had abandoned hope of ever seeing again. This was just a trick of the imagination—a mirage, an illusion.

The man in the coonskin cap was flesh and blood, however, and at sight of a female tottering on the gangplank Irish gallantry made him leap forward and lead her safely to shore. Hooded and shawled as she was against the cold, he did not recognize her until she tilted up her face to thank her rescuer.

Then Connie could not utter a word. For below the coonskin that hid his red curls as completely as her calash hid her hair, her grateful gaze plunged into the lake-blue eyes of Seumas McSeumas. For a moment surprise held them both speechless.

Then she gasped, "You! Here! What brought you here, of all places?"

"The Miami Canal," he replied. "Digging it offered the same pay as the other ditch, and this one was a lot further from Cleveland. Besides, it led to the place I aimed to go to college." When the girl gasped again, he reassured her, "Oh, don't be afraid of running into me after your wedding." His voice faltered, and in a desperate effort to sound casual, he said, "You see, Cincinnati College got so deep it had to shut up shop a couple of years back." He was staring over the girl's head now to avoid the eyes that haunted him day and night, and so he was unaware that she turned white and sick at this blow to her hopes and plans.

"When the endowment accumulates enough to pay off those debts," he went on, still staring at nothing, "the college may re-open again. But I can't afford to wait on that chance. I've saved up a sum that will see me through my first year at Miami University. That's at Oxford, some twenty-five miles northwest of here. So," Seumas repeated, "you won't be running into me after you're Mrs. Benjamin Benedict. Of course, that's what brought you here— your wedding."

By then Connie had recovered herself and she told him, "No, I didn't come here to wed Ben, because he's already married to another girl. I came because—"

Seumas cut her off. In a voice husky with eagerness, he said, "Acushla! Did you come looking for me—to tell me you're free? Free to wed *me?*"

In all truth she could not tell him that this was the case. Nor did she dare tell him that in his arms she might be able to recover from the blow his first piece of news had dealt her. She dared not because his second piece of news sealed her lips against that confession. When she could trust herself to speak, she told him, "No, I came, like you, to go to college. Now I can't, but you can if you stay single. At least you'll have to, if this college at Oxford is like Yale. Yale doesn't admit married men and never did. I'll not stand in the way of your getting a college degree."

His Irish temper flared quick and hot. "The devil you won't!" he cried. "I'll decide about that." Then, belatedly realizing what his news must have done to her, he forgot everything else. "Take heart," he said. "There's another college about to open in Oxford, a college just for females. Think of it, lass, a female college!"

Faith, completely forgotten and glad of it, interposed at this point. "Now isn't that nice! *I* came here to hire a house in Cincinnati so my darter could go to college. I expect I could find a house in this other place just as well. If you two could give each other up, forever, because my girl was honor-bound to her cousin, I should think you could manage to wait two or three years to get married. Why, you've had no proper courtin' time at all!"

For a moment the lake-blue eyes turned black with rebellion. Then, after a deep look into the girl's eyes, McSeumas said softly, "If that's the way you want it, acushla, then it's a bargain and 'there's my hand on it.'"

And she, quick to recognize the words of their favorite bard, laid her fingers lightly on the outstretched horny palm. Smiling up at him, she gave him back Miranda's reply to Ferdinand, "'And here's mine, with my heart in it.'"